"PHILIPPA."
HE MADE HER NAME
A PLEA, HIS VOICE
HOARSE AND DEEP.

Stunned by his familiar address and his intimate tone, she looked up. His face was soft with masculine need for her, his eyes golden with desire. A cool breeze surrounded them. It ruffled the neat strands of his dark hair. He reached for her, but she was frozen with fear. His arms encircled her in a light embrace, drawing her close. "May God have mercy on my soul," he barely breathed as he lowered his head and brushed his mouth against hers.

He was gentle, and the taste of him was surprisingly pleasant. Philippa's eyes opened wide and she caught her breath waiting for more kisses. And when he touched her lips again, she shivered. This was better than a dream. . . .

ANNOUNCING THE

TOPAZ FREQUENT READERS CLUB
COMMEMORATING TOPAZ'S
1 YEAR ANNIVERSARY!

THE MORE YOU BUY, THE MORE YOU GET

Redeem coupons found here and in the back of all new Topaz titles for FREE Topaz gifts:

Send in:

 2 coupons for a free TOPAZ novel (choose from the list below);
- ☐ THE KISSING BANDIT, Margaret Brownley
- ☐ BY LOVE UNVEILED, Deborah Martin
- ☐ TOUCH THE DAWN, Chelley Kitzmiller
- ☐ WILD EMBRACE, Cassie Edwards

 4 coupons for an "I Love the Topaz Man" on-board sign

 6 coupons for a TOPAZ compact mirror

 8 coupons for a Topaz Man T-shirt

Just fill out this certificate and send with original sales receipts to:

TOPAZ FREQUENT READERS CLUB-IST ANNIVERSARY
Penguin USA • Mass Market Promotion; Dept. H.U.G.
375 Hudson St., NY, NY 10014

Name_____

Address_____

City_____State_____Zip_____

Offer expires 1/31 1995

This certificate must accompany your request. No duplicates accepted. Void where prohibited, taxed or restricted. Allow 4-6 weeks for receipt of merchandise. Offer good only in U.S., its territories, and Canada.

Summer's
Storm

~

by

Denise Domning

A TOPAZ BOOK

TOPAZ
Published by the Penguin Group
Penguin Books USA Inc., 375 Hudson Street,
New York, New York 10014, U.S.A.
Penguin Books Ltd, 27 Wrights Lane,
London W8 5TZ, England
Penguin Books Australia Ltd, Ringwood,
Victoria, Australia
Penguin Books Canada Ltd, 10 Alcorn Avenue,
Toronto, Ontario, Canada M4V 3B2
Penguin Books (N.Z.) Ltd, 182–190 Wairau Road,
Auckland 10, New Zealand

Penguin Books Ltd, Registered Offices:
Harmondsworth, Middlesex, England

First published by Topaz,
an imprint of Dutton Signet,
a division of Penguin Books USA Inc.

First Printing, August, 1994
10 9 8 7 6 5 4 3 2 1

 Topaz is a trademark of Dutton Signet,
a division of Penguin Books USA Inc.

Printed in the United States of America

To my other family who dare see no more than a surface resemblance. I only borrowed the situation, not the people.

And to Adam: Was my life not worth more than six months?

Chapter One

"Ungrateful wretch," hissed the old noble-woman. Her fist landed with bruising impact between Lady Philippa's shoulder blades. "I give you a morning spent outside the walls and how do you thank me? You drag your feet apurpose to steal from me more than I would concede. When my son returns, he will hear how you have misused me this day." Lord Lindhurst's mother limped irately past her son's wife on the grassy track.

Philippa of Lindhurst made no comment, only hunched her back to ease the pain. Better an ancient fist for a morning spent outside the walls than Roger's oppressive attentions. She offered a swift prayer that it might be days and days before her husband returned from wherever it was he'd gone.

Sighing against the weight of wet linen in her basket, Philippa walked slowly after her mother-by-marriage. The walls of their home now stood no more than a furlong distant. For the past twelve years that homely gate in those mossy walls had been the door to her prison.

If only there were some way to prolong her freedom

just a little longer. She shut her eyes. Lark and thrush sang, their voices twined in summer's harmony, against an insect chorus, droning in sleepy plainsong. In the distance oxen bellowed and men called as they worked in the fields. Air, quickened by a midday sun in a cloudless sky, danced against her skin. This June's rare warmth had awakened spicy scents from the fertile earth and her lungs filled with the richness of it.

"Hie, hie, you stupid cow. Come quickly or you'll pay my penalty," chided Margaret, unwilling to give her any opportunity to linger.

Philippa glanced at the old woman, who glared back, watery blue eyes narrowed in irritation. When her husband's dam spun on her walking stick, it was to waddle ponderously toward the walls. A tiny flare of defiance flickered within Philippa. Cow, was it? Who of the two of them looked more bovine?

With Roger away, it was safe to indulge in a bit of mockery. Where Margaret was usually content with screams and curses against the little games Philippa played, Roger was not so easily placated. He always made her pay for her small acts of rebellion with bruises and spilled blood. Philippa twisted her face into an idiot's expression and shambled after her husband's mother, exactly mimicking the old woman's painful gait.

When Margaret glanced over her shoulder, she gasped. "Do you dare?" Hatred cut deep creases in her sagging face and flared in the knife-thin line of her nose. Even the gray spikes of hair escaping from her head covering seemed to quiver with insulted pride.

"What is it?" Philippa sobbed in feigned distress. Oh, but Lindhurst's serving women would have been proud to see this performance. Her mummery finished with a pitiful catch in her voice as she stared at her coarse wooden shoes. "I beg you, tell me what I have done!"

"Barren imbecile." Roger's dam made the words a curse. "Why did my precious lad insist upon Benfield's spawn, an idiot bitch with golden hair and airs too fine for her station? Neither you nor those paltry fields are worth the coins I paid for you. Mark me now, I'll find a way to keep your dowry while ridding my son of you," she finished, her voice low and hard.

When no blow followed Margaret's tirade, triumph coursed through Philippa; she'd won! "Aye, Mother, you are right. One as valueless as I am to you should not be allowed to live."

Margaret said nothing. After a moment of silence passed, Philippa peered cautiously up from her demure pose. The old woman stared out at the wooded, rolling hills surrounding Roger's simple manor.

Philippa followed her gaze, but there was nothing to see. Then, from just beyond the closest trees came the indistinct sound of a man's voice, the creaking groan of a wagon, and the muffled thud of hooves against hard-packed earthen track.

"Who dares to come trespassing here?" the elder noblewoman demanded of no one in particular.

Roger guarded his cloying privacy and his few possessions, of which his wife was one, with an iron fist. Visitors, even itinerant merchants usually welcome everywhere, were sent sternly from this gate with a warning never to return. The need to see who came rushed through her, but Philippa hesitated. Nothing drove her husband into greater viciousness than a man looking upon her or she upon any man save Roger.

That Margaret would tell him these strangers had come was beyond doubt.

Then again, if the old woman forgot to instruct her daughter-by-marriage to go within the walls, Philippa could be excused for remaining. Ever so cautiously, she eased her basket to the ground, then slipped with tiny, noiseless steps to stand directly behind Mother Margaret. Praying she remained concealed from both the old woman's thoughts and her line of sight, she gaped in awe at the first visitors in all her dozen years here.

They exited the forest not twenty yards distant. Astride a spirited palfrey, trappings and saddlecloth shot with gleaming metal threads, came a young, black-haired man. His vibrant blue riding gown and stockings of bright scarlet spoke clearly of his consequence. A deep green cap and a cloak the color of an autumn oak clasped with a golden pin completed his attire.

Harnesses jangling, four men-at-arms followed this coxcomb, each sporting a vest of boiled leather sewn with steel links and a metal cap upon his head. They wore their swords fast buckled to their sides, while crossbows and bolts were strapped to their backs. If their mounts weren't the quality of their master's steed, the beasts were still better than any in Lindhurst's stables.

Lurching and skittering along behind them came a silly little cart drawn by sturdy ponies. Too small for hauling crops or any other goods Philippa could imagine, it bore a brightly painted frame raised above the bed with rolls of sheeting at the ready to shade the wagon's load.

Lastly came a single knight atop a massive steed.

His knitted steel shirt and chausses clung to a powerful frame, yet the sleeveless surcoat atop his armor
was unembellished. Likewise was his shield bare of
any design, but there was something in his solitary air
that warned of his prowess with the long sword belted
at his hip.

Once they were all clear of the woodlands, the
leader lifted his hand and the troop halted. He and
the knight dismounted, the warrior pausing to wrench
off his helmet and set it atop his saddle. Philippa
watched as he pushed back his coif to reveal brown
hair dampened with sweat and a jawline covered by a
carefully trimmed beard. Then he led his steed forward to halt alongside the rich man.

There he waited patiently as the well-dressed one
fought his nervous mount into obedience. Where
Roger would have long since been frothing in rage,
this quiet soldier gave no hint of irritation. With the
spirited horse now calm, the two men started toward
her and Margaret.

The smaller man was by far the grander, but 'twas
the knight who kept her interest. Against Roger's fine
and golden beauty, this warrior's face was plainer,
rawboned with a bold jaw beneath his short beard.
His nose was strong with a slight crook, the little flaw
adding character. Dark, expressive brows curved gently above eyes . . . Philippa caught her breath in shock.

Brown eyes alive with golden lights watched her
with equal interest. Even as his lips began the upward
quirk of a smile, she snapped her attention to her
toes. *Idiot!* she chastised herself. What if Margaret had
noticed? The old woman would take the whip to her.
Her need to stare at the travelers sated to the limits of
her courage, Philippa studied her shoes and listened.

*   *   *

Temric FitzHenry, bastard of Graistan, permitted himself the warm breath of amusement that passed as laughter for him. The little minx had stared boldly enough when she'd thought he hadn't noticed. Then again, with such an evil-looking hag for a mistress, he could understand her shyness. Too bad, for the glimpse he'd caught of her suggested she was a pretty thing despite her homespun gown and rough headcloth.

He frowned slightly, struck by a vague sense of recognition, then dismissed it when nothing came to mind. Perhaps it was that at eight and thirty, he was flattered to think one so young might find him interesting.

When Oswald stopped a few feet from the women, Temric did the same. "Speak for me, Temric. My English will not suffice," his cousin said to him, unaware his request was insulting to one of mingled Norman and English blood. "Ask after their lord and lady." Oswald of Hereford added a sound of derision to his request and jerked his head toward Lindhurst's simple walls. "Mayhap, they'll let something useful slip about those who rule here. Bah, so rustic a place hardly justifies the man's strutting arrogance. I'll wager the manor house within yon gate uses the same thatch for roofing and mud and manure walls as do his peasants."

Temric made him no reply, only stepped forward and said in his mother's native tongue, "A fine day to you, goodwives. We've come seeking Lady Lindhurst. Do you know of her?"

The elder woman stared sourly at him for the briefest instant, then turned her formidable gaze on the smaller Norman cleric. She made no attempt to straighten her patched gown or to push straggling hairs back beneath a worn headcloth. When she spoke, it was in the Norman French of England's ruling class. "I am Margaret of Lindhurst, lady of this place. By whose leave do you come trespassing on my lands?"

"Well met, indeed, my lady," Oswald replied, smoothly ignoring the fact that he'd just insulted the woman's son in her hearing. He offered her a courtly bow as if meeting noblewomen dressed in ragged homespun and wandering unescorted about fields was an everyday occurrence for him.

Temric snorted in sudden realization. Like Oswald's fine clothing and his constant prattle, the young man's manners made innocent mockery of his idol, the powerful churchman Oswald served.

"I am Oswald, administrator to Bishop William of Hereford. My lord sends us here at Lord Lindhurst's request to fetch his wife, Lady Philippa. Her attendance is required in the legal matter your son brought before my lord."

Temric watched as the maid behind the old woman jerked up her head. Her gaze skimmed over Oswald, then flew across himself as well, her look one of confusion mingled with fear. As swiftly as he'd been aware of her reaction, it was gone and she'd regained her servile posture.

"How unfortunate for you that you've ridden so far only to turn around and ride back," replied Lady Margaret. "My daughter-by-marriage goes nowhere save in my son's company."

"Do you refuse us?" Oswald stiffened, his dark brows drawn down over snapping black eyes. "Do not. Bishop William, your overlord," he enunciated for effect, "was very displeased when your son appeared alone against his specific command to bring Lady Philippa. I'm not to leave this place save with the lady at my side."

The old woman shrugged in complete disinterest. "I care naught for your problems. Be gone with you. And do not take anything as you leave. Those who steal the fruits of my holdings pay dearly for it." She lifted her walking stick and touched the working end of it midpoint of the young man's chest. At her gentle shove torn grass and chalky dirt stained his expensive gown.

Oswald slapped the crutch aside and thrust out his hand. Sunlight caught against the bishop's heavy ring that he wore atop his glove. "Madam, see this and know I have the right to insist upon your compliance. This ring is also your assurance that the Lady Philippa will be safely delivered into my lord's presence. For your son's sake, do not defy your overlord's command. Now release her to me."

The dowager lifted her brows and sneered, "Fine clothing, pretty glass, and a nimble tongue are all that stands before me. You show me not even a scrap of parchment or a bit of wax to prove your claims. If Bishop William truly wishes to speak with her, he should come here as my son requests instead of allowing Lord Graistan to curry his favor with hunting and riches."

She pivoted on her walking stick only to come face-to-face with the young woman behind her. "I forgot you. Stupid bitch, you've no more brains than a fly. Have you not yet learned anything of proper behavior? No modest woman lets foreigners look upon her," she snapped. "Go!"

When the girl did not move, the dowager waved furiously toward the walls as if gesture alone would spur her to action. "Go, be off with you," she snarled.

"Nay." A single word, barely given sound enough to be heard.

"What? What did you say?" Lady Margaret's noisy shock died away into a soundless gaping.

Sudden respect rose in Temric; it would appear that this day pigs flew in Lindhurst.

The lass spoke, her voice growing in strength. "I would know what a bishop wants from one so insignificant as I." At the end of that incredible statement, she fell silent having never lifted her gaze from her toes.

Temric stared, unable to reconcile the meek creature standing before him with the bitter image who had haunted his dreams for the past year. He and Philippa of Lindhurst were kindred spirits; raised to noble expectations, only to lose all because of their bastard births. Nay, this must be some imposter. This woman was not capable of the raging missive that had scorned her sister's right to inherit as crass thievery. Yet, his heart demanded proof. Two steps took him to her side.

"Hey, your man is too close to her," Lady Margaret cried out in sudden anxiety. "Call him back." She tottered forward as if she meant to physically thrust the knight away from her son's wife. Temric ignored the old woman.

"He'll do her no harm," Oswald snapped. "Is it she?" he demanded of Temric as Lady Margaret made a frantic noise deep within her chest.

Deferring to the maid's shyness, Temric kept his voice low. "Are you Philippa, wife to Lord Roger?"

"Aye, that I am."

Only then did she look up and Temric caught his breath in shock. Dear God, but she was nearly her mother's twin despite the difference in their years. Where Edith of Benfield's eyes were a clear green, Lady Philippa's were both green and blue in one glorious instant. They shimmered like jewels against her creamy skin. Golden hair, a shade or two lighter than Lady Benfield's, escaped the rough wimple to straggle charmingly along soft cheeks. All else was exactly the same: the lilt of the brows, the wide cheekbones, and the gentle curve of jaw and mouth. How had a virago like Lady Edith produced a daughter so like her, yet as meek as this woman seemed to be?

He turned to Oswald. "We have found Lord Roger's wife."

"Nay," Margaret cried, her voice rising in desperation, "you are mistaken. This is not she, just the village whore who pants after my son. Would any lord dress his wife thusly? She is nothing but a lying slut." She glared at Temric, as if she thought her look might intimidate him.

"There is no error," Temric replied mildly. "Do not waste your breath in further protest, my lady, for I am acquainted with her mother. For your sake, Oswald, I shall give you further proof." He returned his attention to the shy woman. She tilted her head a little, anticipating a question. "Lady Lindhurst, can you tell to me your sister's Christian name?"

Philippa of Lindhurst's eyes glowed bright as joy touched her lips and flushed in her cheeks. "Rowena. My sister's name is Rowena. Tell me," she then pleaded gently, "what do you know of my sister?" In her tone he heard the longing for a beloved sibling.

It proved that she knew nothing of the legal battle being waged in her name.

With that came a gut-deep relief. It had seemed vaguely dishonorable to let his thoughts linger on one who was attempting to ruin his brother's wife. He'd tried to stop, especially after his dreams had become inappropriate. His efforts had failed, for a part of him held to the belief she was the only woman capable of understanding him.

He hadn't realized he'd grinned until she smiled in return. If so open a display of emotion on his part had startled him, Temric was even more shocked by the sudden stirrings in his heart. His dream image of Lady Philippa had been only a poor counterfeit of her sister's fire and spirit. Instead of disappointment at realizing her actual character, she touched his emotions more deeply than he'd ever imagined possible.

He forced himself to look away from her as he struggled to regain control of his wayward heart. "I think you can have no further doubt," he said to his cousin. "We were right to suspect Lady Philippa had no hand in this."

"I am content with the proofs you've given me," the cleric replied. "Lady Lindhurst, will you come with us?"

Margaret shrieked in frustration. "Damn you, I'll not let you have her!" She turned on the girl, her mouth twisted in a vicious snarl. Before either man understood her intent, she'd wielded her stick like a club and struck her daughter-by-marriage a mighty blow across the back.

"Nay!" Temric roared as he watched Philippa fall to the ground without a noise and make no move to rise. He tore the weapon from the old woman's gnarled grasp and hurled it away from her. It landed yards distant.

"Aaiye!" the dowager screamed. "He attacks me! Come, come," she yelled toward the walls of her home, "I am attacked!"

"Oswald, mount up," Temric ordered, "and, Will, you stay here. Protect our cart and driver as best you can. You three are with me." He nodded to the rest, sharply regretting he rode with so few. But the bishop had expected the lady to come willingly and under the protection of her husband's men.

Temric bent and lifted Lady Lindhurst into his arms, cradling her close. Her bulky, ill-fitting garments disguised a form as tiny as her sister's. The need to protect her was so strong, every fiber in his being demanded the old woman's head for misusing her.

"Lecher! Defiler," Margaret trumpeted in shock when she saw how intimately he held Lord Roger's wife. "You soil her with your touch!"

The woman in his arms gasped. He glanced down to find she watched him in both surprise and trepidation. No tears filled her eyes at what must have been a bruising blow. His arms on her tightened as he suddenly understood how his dreams had made his heart vulnerable. He was holding her as if she belonged to him. Let God damn him for it, but he'd not leave her here to be abused.

"You are taking me?" she breathed.

"Aye, but fear not," he said over Lady Margaret's continued complaint, "I vow you are safer with me than you are here."

"Commoner! You dare to touch her when you have no right! I will have you skinned alive for this."

Temric shot the old woman a scathing glance. "If

you wish to complain, come and tell Bishop William that Temric, Henry of Graistan's bastard, has obeyed his command and fetched Lady Lindhurst for him."

"Graistan! That thief!" Margaret hobbled away, her arms pumping up and down in agitation as she went. "To me, to me. I am attacked and Graistan's men kidnap your lord's wife. To arms!"

Temric turned. From atop his palfrey Oswald extended his arm, indicating he meant to take Lady Philippa up with him. Instead, Temric set another man's wife sideways on his own saddle, her back to his shield, and mounted behind her. With the old woman throwing curses at him, he pulled his half sister-by-marriage close into the protection of his body and spurred his horse into a gallop.

The need to keep her forever in his arms was strong. Mary, Mother of God, forgive him, but he'd allowed himself to fall hopelessly in love with the one woman on earth more unattainable to him than any other.

Chapter Two

Philippa leaned her head against the knight's broad shoulder and reveled in the strength of his arm holding her tightly against him. His care and kindness enveloped her. She was safer with him than in her husband's home.

The horse beneath her broke into a gallop. She was free! Air rushed past her, filled with the scent of places she'd never seen and things she'd never done. It tore at her wimple and curled sweetly around her neck.

Rather than return to the forest, the five horsemen headed south through fields of rye and wheat. Peasants screamed against the destruction they wrought, throwing rocks and rakes at them as they passed.

It was only as the fields began their gentle rise into rolling hills that Philippa's euphoria died away. What a fool she was! This knight was taking her to the bishop where her husband also awaited. After the churchman was quit of her, she must needs accompany Roger back to Lindhurst. She stiffened in sudden fear. Oh, dear God, but she'd played her game of defiance too far this time.

Why, oh, why, had she dared to identify herself? Not only would Margaret never forgive her for it, she'd make certain Roger learned his wife had left Lindhurst in another man's arms. He would be wracked by jealousy. Such an outrage demanded relief. In repayment for defiance, Margaret would happily raise no hand to stop him. Without his mother's control would he kill her? Nay, surely not. Philippa struggled to convince herself. Roger never meant to hurt her. Each time he did, he wept in shame afterward and begged her forgiveness. This time he would stop himself.

False hope! The day would come when he beat her until she was no more, swearing as he did so that it was for love's sake. She shut her eyes and turned her face against her shoulder as fear ate up every other emotion. Four and twenty was too young to die. She had done this to herself; she had said her name and this knight had touched her. Acceptance, dull and dark, crept over her. Not even God Himself could spare her from her husband's fists.

The churchman's shout broke through her mournful thoughts. "Hold tight to her, Temric. They are after us."

"Then we shall play fox to their hounds," the man behind her replied, his mellow voice grim. "You two go more slowly and toward Benfield. Here." A swift yank tore Philippa's headcloth from her head before she had a chance to gasp or resist. "Drop this as you ride and do what you can to convince them you have her. Return to Graistan when you can. Robin, you are with us."

When he reined his mount into a sharp turn, Philippa gasped and instinctively wound an arm around his waist to steady her sideways seat on the saddle.

He responded to her clutch with a quick sound of

amusement. "Good. I've no wish to lose you now. Hold me tight and I will keep you safe."

Would that it were true. Philippa wanted to cry, but she shook it away. Nay, she'd not waste in sorrow what little life was left her. From this instant until she faced Roger, all that mattered was the moment. She vowed to live each one to its very fullest, savoring every experience. With her eyes closed, Philippa opened her mouth to taste the wind.

They stopped to rest in a glade. Lindhurst's men had been left behind hours ago as had the other soldier whose horse was lame. It was peaceful here, the air tangy with the scent of thick woodlands. Philippa looked up. Sycamores towered high above her, filtering the midafternoon sun until everything below was dappled and gilded. Temric's massive brown steed wore patches of light and dark, some sweat, some shade. It snorted and shivered as it rested, mouthing the saplings and spindly grass that coated the woodland floor. The churchman's smaller beast answered with a frustrated toss of its head at the bit between its teeth.

Oswald had been the last to excuse himself. While they awaited his return, Temric was speaking to her about the bishop's call. She let his words eddy unheeded around her. Far more important was every breath of breeze, every flicker of light, even the smell of the damp vegetation beneath her feet. It all flowed through her in rich waves of sensation.

"—reach Graistan by early evening if you can bear—"

Must she confront Roger so soon? Why must this happen to her? Bitterness flowed through her. She'd been told often enough by both Margaret and Lind-hurst's priest the reason her life was pain. It was God's rightful penance on womankind for Eve's tempting of Adam. How unfair. What right had God to punish her for something some other woman had done? On the heels of that came the memory of Roger's last rage. The blows, then the aching bruises lingering for weeks.

Desperately unwilling to think on her husband any longer, Philippa focused her attention on the knight in front of her. He was removing his steel-sewn gloves, carefully freeing each finger, one by one. When his hands were bare, he tucked the gloves into the belly of his surcoat. Temric; that was what he'd told her to call him, allowing her to set no title before his name. She rolled the odd name against her tongue a few times and decided it suited him despite its strangeness. How old was he? Surely no more than two score.

She liked his mouth. His lips were finely molded and curved ever so slightly upward at the corners. The carefully trimmed beard he wore only set off its beauty. While he continued speaking, he shifted into a patch of light. The sun lay a shadow along the crooked line of his nose and streaked gold into his deep brown hair. How could she ever have thought so bold a face ordinary?

"My lady," he said suddenly, leaning toward her to trap her attention.

His sharp tone and aggressive motion were too rem-iniscent of Roger; years of habit folded her hands and turned her gaze to the moldy carpet beneath her stockinged feet. Her wooden shoes had slipped from her toes and been lost hours ago.

"My lady," he spoke more softly this time, as if in recognition of her fear, "why do you not listen?

Would you rather that it was Oswald who explained this to you?" His gentle voice bore a hurt tone as if her inattention had somehow slighted him.

Philippa dared a sly glance and found evidence of her accidental insult in the dark cast of his eyes. "Forgive me, you have been kind and deserve better from me. I think your stealing of me has so addled my thoughts that I am incapable of concentration."

At the reminder of her leave-taking, Philippa instantly saw herself helplessly awaiting Roger's first blow. She tried to ignore it, but fear was stronger. Anxious words tumbled unbidden from her lips. "Oh, why did I let you take me? I should be safe behind Lindhurst's walls instead of here. Would that this were but a dream and I could awaken to find you have been naught but a shadow in my mind." She clapped a hand to her mouth, but was too late to still her words.

His face softened in pity. "Poor lass, are you so frightened? Do not believe what your lord's dam said of my brother, Lord Graistan. Rannulf has not stolen you. Oswald truly is commanded to take you to his master, Bishop William. Or do you fret because now only I ride with you as protector? Know you, I am well seasoned in the ways of battle having been for nigh on twenty years my brother's master-at-arms. Here, touch me and be assured when you feel my strength." He extended his hand so she might do as he suggested.

Startled by his complete misunderstanding of her fear, Philippa could only stare mutely at his hand. His fingers were beautiful. Strong and supple, they tapered gracefully to their tips, better suited to a saint than a warrior. She looked shyly up at him. He offered her a brief smile, the motion waking fiery lights in his brown eyes.

From the recesses of her mind came the echo of Margaret's voice, screaming of indecency. Philippa silenced it in growing curiosity. Was one man's touch the same as another? In an act of daring far beyond any she'd ever contemplated, she laid her fingers into the rough cradle of his palm.

It was different! Where Roger's hands were always moist, this man's skin was warm and dry. His palm was hard with calluses, yet as her hand slid against his, it was a surprisingly silky sensation. His fingers closed around hers. Her pulse leapt. A rush of heat flushed against her throat and burnt in her cheeks. Very different, indeed, she thought breathlessly. How could so large and powerful a man touch her so gently? She turned her hand in his to align their palms.

He laced his fingers between hers. This simple joining woke an alien warmth within her, both disturbing and oddly welcome at the same time. She stared at their hands as this new feeling flooded her with unnerving sensation. Her toes buried into the seeping coolness of the earth beneath her feet. It did nothing to stem her reaction. Panicked, she tore free of him and sighed in relief as her whirling senses steadied.

"Philippa." He made her name a plea, his voice hoarse and deep.

Stunned by his familiar address and his intimate tone, she looked up. His face was soft with masculine need for her, his eyes golden with desire. She drew a quick, fearful breath. Margaret was right, all men were the same. They used any woman they could to satisfy their base needs. Although Temric had disguised his carnal nature with gentle behavior, he would now take her just as Roger did. Trapped between sharp disappointment and terror at what would surely follow, she could only stare helplessly up at him.

A cool breeze circled them. It ruffled the neat strands of his dark hair. He reached for her. The horses snorted and stamped. She was frozen by her fear. His arms encircled her in a light embrace. A crow cawed in the distance. He splayed his hands against her back to draw her close. His lips parted. "May God have mercy on my soul." He barely breathed the words, then lowered his head until his mouth brushed hers.

The rasp of his beard against her jaw was rough-soft. His mouth was gentle against her, a quiet caress, the taste of him surprisingly pleasant. Philippa's eyes opened wide and her breath caught when there was no hurt. Ever so slightly his lips moved on hers. A shiver wracked her. This was better than touching his hand.

And wrong, terribly, terribly wrong.

Oh, Lord, what if Oswald saw and told Roger? What little hope she cherished that her husband might forgive her for this day would be destroyed. Fear of Roger's fists overwhelmed her and Philippa dared to take a small step back from him. Temric only sighed, making no attempt to grab her back. His hands came to rest on her hips. Confused and unsure of what next to do, she watched silently as he opened his eyes. Their fiery depths were now dull and dead.

"Forgive me," he pleaded in a whisper. "I had no right."

In that instant Philippa knew Margaret was wrong. This man was not like Roger in any way. Suddenly his touch was welcome and his nearness awoke a need within her to come closer still. She ran her tongue over her lips and savored the taste of his kiss. To think there had been no pain! Could this be why some of Lindhurst's serving women spoke with fondness of their men?

Temric watched her, the longing in his gaze so intense it hurt her. "You should have been mine," he finally said, his voice filled with despair. "How I wish I had known of your existence. Had I, I would never have let another wed you. To see how his dam mistreats you tears my heart in two."

Philippa gasped softly, then closed her eyes at the new ache within her. What pain she could have been spared had she been given to this knight instead of the one who had bought her. It was as if she glimpsed heaven, only to be denied entry.

When he raised his hands from her hips to once again embrace her, she knew no fear. His arms tightened, begging her to again come close to him. Philippa leaned willingly into the circle of his arms, raising her mouth so he might touch it with his. Their lips met, hers softening beneath his at the pleasure of his caress.

"By the curly hairs on Christ's holy ass, what is this?" Oswald's cry rang through the glade, sending birds screeching from the trees and his palfrey into a nervous, whinnying dance.

Philippa stiffened in terror at what the cleric had witnessed. Temric only shook his head. "Nay, *ma petite,* you must not fear. I will not allow you to bear any blame for this." He dropped his arms from about her and stepped back.

Her release from his embrace sent a rending loss through her. It was all she could do to stop herself from grabbing him back to her. Instead, she forced herself to face Oswald.

The cleric yet stood where shock had halted him, his blue gown hitched high above his scarlet-stockinged knees. When he realized she watched him, he swiftly tied the drawstring of his chausses and shoved his gown back into place. "Temric, I cannot believe what my eyes have seen," he protested.

"Would that you had not seen it," Temric retorted with no sign of either shame or embarrassment. "However, if you choose to relate to her husband how I so cruelly forced my attentions upon his wife, then I will accept the responsibility and he may have my head."

Philippa stared in horror at him. Holy Jesus, but Roger would kill not just her, but him as well for this. Fear for herself disappeared beneath a desperate need to save him from her husband. "Nay," she cried out, "my lord, you must not believe him. Temric seeks only to protect me from my sin when it was I who tempted him. Mother Margaret knows that I am Eve incarnate and now you have seen how right she is." She folded her hands in supplication as she lied.

"My lady, you must not abase yourself on my behalf," Temric said hoarsely. "Oswald, this would never have happened had I not ignored Father Edwin's warnings and spent this past year in conversation with Lady Lindhurst."

Philippa whirled on him, astounded. He made it seem that they were lovers. "What sort of explanation is this? I have never seen you before this very day," she vowed, glancing between the cleric and the knight to watch their reactions. "I swear it, my lord."

Temric's mouth twisted in wry amusement. "He already knows that, little one. The conversations in which I have indulged were all of my imagining. If my thoughts were inappropriate, well then, I never believed I would meet you." He shrugged. The gesture, meant to be nonchalant, failed.

She rubbed anxious hands over her throbbing temples. "Why would anyone wish to imagine me? I am nothing to no one."

"We are equals, you and I," he replied tersely.

Equals? She blinked in surprise, then remembered his parting words to Margaret. He was bastard born and somehow knew that she was, too. That was why she should have belonged to him. They were equals. She stared up at him, only to be awed by the look he bent on her. In his eyes she found far more than his words revealed. 'Twas his heart he offered her. If he had begun his caring for her because of their births, he now wanted her solely for who she was and nothing else. In his gentleness she might have found her own value—

—But never would. All she would ever know of him were these past moments. As if he shared this terrible realization, Temric's eyes darkened and he returned his attention to Oswald. "I will say that you are not the only one who would be astounded to learn that I had behaved with such abandon."

The churchman made a sarcastic noise. "What you have done cannot be so easily waved away. Mayhap, with prayer and penance there is yet hope for your soul, but your case would be better served with at least a pretense of shame."

"Shame?" Temric snorted. "I am not ashamed to bear some feeling for her. Who could not after witnessing how she is abused by those who should care for her."

"I'll not have you make less of what has happened with excuses," Oswald bellowed in frustration. He grabbed Philippa by the arm and drew her away from the knight. "Do you speak this way presuming our blood ties will keep me silent?"

"I care not what you say or to whom you say it," Temric snarled back. "God forbid I should be spared anything for the sake of my sire's filthy blood."

"Churl," Oswald threw back. "Your words do my uncle a great disservice. He loved you."

"If my sire had loved me, he'd not have forgotten me in his will," Temric roared back. "If I die and am condemned to hell for this day's events, I shall do it alone and unsupported just as my father willed it."

The ancient hurt in his voice cut Philippa so deeply she cried out. She knew his pain. His father had betrayed him where her mother had blithely wed her to a monster. Equals. She tore from Oswald's grasp to kneel before the knight. "No more, I pray you. I cannot bear that you might die because of me." Her words crumpled into a sob.

The tenseness melted from him as his eyes came back to life, but it was life tainted with hopeless sadness. He rubbed his knuckles against her cheek. "I was a fool to dream. I should never have journeyed to Lindhurst, for now I have hurt you as I never intended. Come, stand, *ma petite,* you must never kneel before me. It is not meet." He lifted her to her feet.

Oswald swiftly grabbed Philippa's hand and dragged her out of Temric's reach. "Nay, you must not touch her. I beg you for your soul's sake, Temric, vow you'll not touch Lady Lindhurst during the whole of her stay at Graistan. Swear, too, that you will seek out Graistan's priest and make your confession."

Temric set his hand atop his sword's hilt. "You have my vow. I will not touch her while she resides in my brother's house and will speak with Father Edwin upon my return." The words were bitter and harsh.

"I am satisfied with that," the cleric sighed. When he spoke on, the relief in his voice was almost palpable. "I think it is in my master's best interest if we all forget what has happened in this glade. Come, my lady, it is time to go. You ride with me." He tried to draw her toward his steed, but Philippa resisted to look back at the knight.

Temric glanced briefly at her, then his expression closed, wiping away all evidence of his care for her as well as his bitterness. Like hers, his pain lay buried deep within him. She watched him mount his big gelding with the economical motion of a man long familiar with the saddle. Only when he was seated did she allow Oswald to lead her to his palfrey.

If the cleric prattled to her as they rode out of the glade, she was too deep in thought to notice what he said. That Temric knew of her parentage was certain, but how? Her stepfather had told her he was sworn to secrecy over the true nature of her birth, while her mother had refused to acknowledge her sin, even to the child she'd stained by it. How was it Temric knew?

Chapter Three

It was nigh on Vespers when they reached Graistan. With Midsummer just around the corner, the keep tower atop a sharp rise of land above a river was yet bathed in the full light of day. Gnawing worry over her husband's reaction to her arrival gave way to awe. The great square castle shielded beneath it more houses than she could ever have imagined existed. In testimony to Lord Graistan's might, a peaceful patchwork of village and field found safety in its shadow. How had her husband ever come into disagreement with the owner of such a place as this?

They entered the town gate and Philippa drew back against the cleric in claustrophobic reaction. Crowds of people, dressed in everything from homespun to bright gowns rivaling Oswald's own, rushed up and down the narrow streets. Tall houses, slate roofs gleaming like tarnished silver, were crammed one against the other. The air reeked of tanning and butchering, while tendrils of cooking smoke snaked into alleys and down lanes. She suddenly longed for Lindhurst's simpler surrounds, no matter if it cost her blood to return.

Terror rose within her as they passed through the keep's outer defense, a curtain wall so thick it made a tunnel of its gateway. What if Roger lurked just inside, waiting to fall upon her? She breathed a silly sigh of relief for they entered the bailey without incident. Aye, this grassy expanse of land caught between inner and outer walls teemed with life, but nowhere did she see Roger.

Every conceivable fowl, from peacocks to finches, screeched, quacked, or chittered in their cages. Hobbled horses grazed, penned cattle lowed, while sheep and pigs contributed their own voices to the evening cacophony. In the armory, the smith's hammer rang against steel, then his bellows sighed in great gusts. Other byres and houses, flimsy wooden pens topped with reed roofs, leaned against the walls. She recognized the potter and the carpenter, but God knew what other craftsmen lived here. Their children laughed and chased each other a goodly distance apart from where the castle guard drilled, their swords clashing, at the field's far end.

Then they entered the second gateway and she could only gawk, wonder overwhelming any other emotion. The huge keep tower soared high above her. Its door lay a full story above the courtyard, accessible by stairs clinging to the building's steep side. At the stable, an old man with hair as white as winter appeared and raised a leathery hand in greeting to Temric. He called out in the commoner's tongue, "What, home so soon? Where's my cart and ponies?"

Philippa listened, understanding the guttural language of England's peasantry with ease. It had been Margaret's distrust of her serfs that had started her lessons, but Philippa's love for those same commoners had made her fluent.

"We've brought the lady with us and left the cart

behind," was Temric's short reply in that same language. "Where is everyone?"

Philippa's brows rose. Everyone? How could there possibly be more people living here than there were now?

"Gone hunting. Won't be back for three days." At the stable master's signal two boys came forward to take the reins of their mounts. "Arnult will be glad to see you. He doesn't much like playing at castellan beneath our fine lady."

"Rannulf left him behind?" It was a surprised question.

"Aye, and took instead that arrogant Lord Lindhurst. I cannot see how they tolerate him and his strutting."

Philippa choked back startled laughter at his words as Oswald dismounted around her. Then she sighed in pleased understanding. Not only was Roger not here, but he would not be back for days. How wondrous! Days of freedom. Surely, that would be time enough in which to concoct some palatable excuse to win his forgiveness.

Oswald reached up to lift her off his tired palfrey. "Come," he said, his tone brusque, "my lord will be pleased that we have so swiftly returned."

"Your lord is away," Temric said, now using the Norman tongue of his noble father. "Gareth, here, tells me that Bishop William has gone hunting with Lord Rannulf."

"Without me?" Oswald's cry was petulant.

Temric gave a brief shrug. "So, ride out and join them if you wish. You know well enough where Rannulf's hunting lodge lies."

Philippa stiffened against his words. If Oswald arrived, would the bishop not hurry home and cheat her of her freedom? "Nay," she cried out, wracking her brain for some excuse to keep him here.

That brought Oswald's attention back onto her. "I cannot leave her unchaperoned with you," he said, misunderstanding her concern.

Temric drew a harsh, shocked breath. "Oswald, you took from me my vow with regard to Lady Lindhurst. My word has always sufficed in the past or has this one incident erased all my years of honorable behavior?"

Oswald gave a start, then said more gently, "I beg pardon, cousin. You are right. I have no cause to doubt your word. Why do you not come with me to join the huntsmen?"

"I cannot and you know it," Temric retorted with yet a touch of irritation in his words. "Bishop William has no tolerance for servants such as I in his presence."

Oswald grimaced. "I forgot me. Sometimes your dual roles are confusing. It would be much easier if you accepted what your father meant for you to have. Be knighted, join us as a full member of our family."

"Do not tread on what is my private life." Temric's words were cold and hard. "When my father failed to write down what he had promised me, he gave me the right to make that decision my own. I will not be pushed in this, not by anyone."

Philippa looked up at him. Once again, Temric had made his expression bland to hide the pain residing within him. Now, why would a man who already lived the life refuse the honor and title of knighthood when it had been offered to him?

Oswald shrugged. "I think you are a fool, but more fool I who stands here arguing with a blockhead instead of racing for the hunting lodge. My lady." He gave her a brief nod and dashed across the courtyard, then up the stairs and into the hall.

"Nay," Philippa called out after him, "they'll come when you tell them I am here. Do not go!"

"Not likely," Temric said dryly. "Bishop William came tapping at our door because he hungers for the creatures residing in my brother's chase. If the prelate says he'll not return for three days, then save that heaven and earth move, he'll not return."

"Are you certain?" she demanded of him, hope spiraling again within her.

"Absolutely. Come, my lady, come into Graistan hall and take your ease with your sister." Temric offered her a brief smile in invitation, if he could not extend his hand.

Philippa only stared at him as she comprehended what he'd said. "What?"

He sighed. "Your sister is married to my half brother, Lord Graistan."

Excitement exploded within her at the thought of seeing her beloved sister again after so many years, then crashed into devastating awareness. She drew a long, agonized breath. "Nay. The marriage of our siblings makes of us brother and sister. What we have done is worse than adultery. It is incest."

"Thus does Oswald command me to seek out Graistan's priest and beg for penance," he replied, working to keep all emotion from his voice.

She stared up at him. His eyes were dark and sad. She let her gaze trace the crooked line of his nose, then the fine upward tilt of his mouth. That mouth had touched hers with such incredible gentleness, giving her pleasure where before there had been only pain. Nay, she would not let their glorious sharing be such a sin.

Within her awoke a tiny voice. Half-related, it whispered. Philippa smiled, then repeated in a low voice what rang within her. "We are but half-related. 'Twas the unrelated halves of us that kissed." She had never realized how capable a sinner she was.

Temric's eyes widened at her suggestion, then their depths glowed golden and his expression mellowed in pleasure. "For shame, my lady," he said with a breath of laughter. "I do not think Oswald would agree that such a thing is possible, but I thank you for your forgiveness toward me."

"And I would thank you for your kindness," she said, keeping her voice low in sudden shyness. "You have stolen me from Margaret and brought me here in safety. So, too, have you given me three full days of freedom in my sister's company when I thought never to see her again. There are not words enough to express what lies in my heart for you."

He jerked as if her words had physically touched him. "Say no more," he breathed harshly, "I cannot bear it." With that, he turned and strode across the courtyard for the keep stairs.

Philippa followed him up and into the tower, but when they entered the hall, she had to stop and stare like the bumpkin she was. The room seemed to stretch endlessly out before her, its floor carpeted in a thick layer of rushes. The walls were covered in painted linen panels and two hearths spewed their warmth into the chilly atmosphere. Massive painted beams held aloft the ceiling, each tree a different color: red, yellow, or green. A second story extended halfway into the hall.

"What lies up there?" she asked, rushing to catch Temric by his elbow.

He yanked his arm out of her reach. "You must not touch me," he warned. "I am sworn."

Philippa was too awed to hear him. "Up there"— she pointed—"what is up there?"

"That is where my brother has his bedchamber. Lady Rowena's solar and the women's quarters are there as well." He called out to someone.

"Oh, Mary," Philippa breathed. Private rooms? At Lindhurst they all lived in one room half the size of this one. Roger's bed was pushed back against the far wall. Everyone else, herself included, found their rest on the hard-packed earthen floor with Margaret hoarding the spot nearest the firepit.

"Lady Lindhurst," he said, drawing her attention back to him. Next to Temric now stood a round, dark-eyed serving woman. "This is Anne, maid to Lady Graistan. She will escort you upstairs to the women's quarters."

"My lady," Anne bobbed in greeting. "We did not expect you for days." Although the woman's words were appropriately respectful, she stared in open disbelief. Finally, she turned on Temric and said in English, "Are you certain this is Lady Lindhurst?"

Philippa was suddenly aware of the ragged image she presented, with no headdress to cover her hair and no shoes upon her feet. Her gown had once been Margaret's and was too big, with only a thick bit of yarn to serve as her belt. She stared in envy at Anne's neat white undergown revealed beneath a plain green overgown.

If this maid was repulsed, what scorn would Rowena have for her beggarly relation? The lady of such a place as this would want nothing to do with her and Philippa's few days of freedom would pass in lonely isolation. Oh, Lord, but if Temric had been raised amid such wealth, he, too, must scorn the rustic wench she portrayed. Her cheeks flushed in humiliation and she stared helplessly at him, praying it could not be true.

"Little one," Temric said softly, "go upstairs into your sister's protection. Tell Lady Rowena I am returned and will stay to support the castellan until Lord Graistan's return."

Philippa straightened and smiled at him in thanks as her heart steadied. He'd seen and understood her reaction. By using the endearment, he reminded her of how he valued her as his equal in birth.

He watched her for a brief moment longer, his mouth lifting into a smile. "Enjoy your stay at Graistan, my lady." Then he turned and strode away.

Philippa watched him until he reached the far side of the room. When she moved to join the maid beside her, she found the woman also staring after the knight. Anne's mouth was ajar and her eyes wide until she realized she was being observed. She snapped her mouth shut and turned with a brusque "This way, my lady."

They climbed the stairs, then walked along the balcony that fronted the rooms. Anne led her to the final door, threw it open, and walked in, expecting the noblewoman to follow. Philippa hung back in nervous worry.

Narrow windows were hewn from the big chamber's west and south walls, letting ribbons of daylight reveal

its many occupants. With the door open, a breeze
flowed through the room, ruffling plain wimples and
neat gowns, dyed in bright, clear colors. Four women
sat on stools, distaffs tucked beneath their arms, spin-
dles whirling at their feet, turning wool into yarn as
they chatted. One woman wove on a loom in the far
corner. Three others sewed finished cloth into the garments used to pay those who labored for Lord Graistan. On a narrow cot at the far end of the room sat
a small boy whose hair glowed coppery in the light.
Beside him sat a woman in a pretty blue gown touched
with golden embroidery. One braid lay over her shoulder, as glossy and dark as a raven's wing.

"Rowena?" she asked quietly.

The woman looked up. In fourteen years much had
changed, but then much had stayed the same. There
was no mistaking Lord Benfield's stamp upon his
daughter for Rowena bore his blue eyes and ebony
hair. But the slender jawline, the upward tilt of her
eyes, and the short, straight nose, those features they
shared in common with their mother.

All her worries dropped away. Who cared that her
gown was ragged and her feet bare? This was her
sister! Joy bubbled up within her, making her grin
with its pressure. Memories, cherished for all these
years, washed over her, each one feeding the love in
her heart.

"Rowena," Philippa cried, this time more loudly,
"I cannot credit the miracle that brings me here
to you!"

Her sister stared at her, then replied in worry, not
disgust, "Who are you?" All activity in the room
ceased at her words and the women stared at the
intruder.

"Oh, say you have not forgotten me when the years did not dim my memory." Philippa's chastisement lost its effectiveness when laughter spilled from her. "Truly, I shall not be content until you tell me how it is you are here, lady of this glorious place, when you should be in some convent, veiled and serene."

Then her happiness ebbed enough to let her see the dark circles beneath her sister's eyes and pallor that touched her cheeks. "Are you ill? Pray assure me it is not serious."

"She is not going to die," called the boy who sat with her. "Papa told me so. She was to have a baby, but now it is gone. That makes her cry and be tired and I am not to pester her."

"Jordan," her sister uttered the child's name in protest at his bluntness. Her voice was suddenly choked with tears, then she sighed. "Nay, no more. Crying is self-indulgent. The babe is gone and I must go on." Weak as Rowena's voice was Philippa still heard the trace of her sister's forceful nature.

"Take comfort in knowing your womb is not lifeless as mine is," she offered her sister in quiet consolation. Her barrenness cut deeply. An heir for Lindhurst was what Roger'd wanted most of her and the only thing she would have gladly given.

"Are you going to play with me or no?" demanded the boy of the noblewoman who sat beside him.

"Lady Lindhurst has come and we must speak," Rowena said to him. "Why do you not run to the stables and tell Gareth to saddle Scherewind for you?"

He screamed in glee and tore past Philippa as he aimed for the door. Then he caught himself, and in an entirely too proper attitude for a lad of his years, he returned to Rowena. "Thank you, Lady Wren," he said and kissed her on the cheek, only to bound out of the room.

At his departure, Rowena glanced around the room. "And the rest of you need not use Lady Lindhurst's arrival as a reason for laziness." Instantly the women returned their attention to their chores.

"Wren?" Philippa asked with a laugh as she came to sit beside her sister on the cot. The narrow bed was comfortable, its blankets smooth and soft. It was set close enough to the windows to catch the echoes of the folk below them. "What is that name? Is he your son?"

"Nay, my stepson. He calls me Wren because his tongue snarls when he tries to say 'Rowena.'" Her affection for the boy glowed in every word. Then she paused to stare in bewilderment at her sister. "How can you be here laughing and speaking fondly to me when you seek to steal from me my inheritance? And do not pretend otherwise. The bishop received a petition from you as well as my mother requesting that he circumvent my father's will."

"John of Benfield is dead?" The shocked cry tore from Philippa. Her family was all that she could call her own and she had cherished her stepfather as much as she did Rowena. A fist placed against her chest helped to ease her heartache. "When? Why did Maman not send word? Oh, that I could have seen him one last time."

Then she started in surprise. "I sent no petition. What sort of inheritance is there save Benfield's manor house? Nay, there must be more than that if it buys you a place as grand as Graistan. What goes afoot here?" Philippa startled herself with her forcefulness.

Rowena stared at her in astonishment. "You truly know nothing of this, do you?" Then she hesitated as if afraid to say more.

"Tell me. If someone has spoken in my name, it is my right to know who and why," Philippa insisted, already suspecting the who and deeply troubled by the why.

Her sister's voice was low as she began her tale. "Last year our grandsire died after outliving all his sons and leaving no heir but our mother. By the dictates of his will, his rich holdings pass through her to her legitimate children.

"Our father—" Rowena paused, then said slowly, "my father wrote a will before I was wed in which he named you our mother's bastard, making me his only heir. Now, your husband and our mother protest your disinheritance, claiming that you are legitimately born of my father, just as I am. They seek to take all or part of what should be mine."

Philippa drew a swift breath. So, this was how Temric had known of her birth. Her grandsire's death had freed Rowena's father from his vow of secrecy. It also explained why Margaret had so raged over Temric's taking of her. Only under their control could they be certain what she might say.

A smile flitted across her lips. By God, but they quaked in their boots over what she might hold within her! If she spewed the truth, Roger would be revealed as a liar and a thief. For doing so, he would surely kill her. Ah, but if she held what she knew close, he would grant her his forgiveness for what had happened this day.

Would Rowena then lose what was rightfully hers? For want of the promised dowry, Lord Graistan would set aside his wife to have another, richer bride. Sweet Mary, but what if he killed her instead? Rowena's death would lay directly upon her shoulders. Philippa grimaced in confusion, then sighed in the knowledge that she had three days to ponder over what to do. "I suppose this is why you are not overjoyed to see me. Who would happily greet a thief?"

"Say you will not support our mother in this," Rowena begged, then, before Philippa had a chance to respond, contradicted herself. "Nay, say nothing. It is not fair of me to beg your aid when you have no knowledge of what goes forward. Let me be pleased that you come to me without hauteur or scorn. I expected to see your hate and your envy for what I own."

"Me? Scorn and envy?" Philippa's laugh was wry that her sister would fear just as she had. "What reason have I to hate you? I am only happy at this chance to be with you." Then she paused. "Oh, well, I did envy you once, but that was long ago."

A sharp shake of her sister's dark head negated the possibility. "Now I know you lie for you had no cause. It was you who had our mother to yourself, the pretty gowns, the lessons, and even a cot of your own. I had nothing, save scraps of my father's love."

"But you were free," Philippa exclaimed, "while I was forever trapped inside. No one stood over you saying that if you were not obedient or did not make perfect stitches, sing on key or eat just so at the table, no man would have you to wife. I wanted so badly to run with you, but I never dared Maman's ire. She did not like it much when I spoke of you." She took Rowena's hand into her own in gentle apology for her cowardice.

Pain marred her sister's beautiful eyes. "Do you know where I went when I ran? Into the woods where I could pretend that the birds were my father and the flowers, my mother. I often lingered past dark to see if I was missed, but I never was."

Philippa stroked her arm, the fine linen of Rowena's sleeve smooth to her touch. "How could you have suffered such loneliness when you had so many companions? Whenever I could, I pushed Maman's trunk under that tiny window in her room. From there I could watch you and the other children.

"I remember"—Philippa's smile widened as she delighted in her unfolding recall—"I remember a time when that big boy was taunting you, saying you were not truly the lord's daughter, just another serving wench's brat. You were so angry you knocked him down. You were atop him, pummeling, biting, and scratching while he screamed for help. It took three of the others to pull you off him. I was very proud of you."

"Dickon," Rowena murmured, her eyes half-closed as she slipped back into her own memories. "He was the miller's son and always thought himself better than the rest of us for it. How he hated being reminded that I was a nobleman's daughter. I had forgotten both him and how much I enjoyed beating him," she said in satisfaction.

"Oh, Rowena," Philippa cried out, throwing her arms around her sister and hugging her close.

But her sister bit back a sob and pushed away. "How I dreaded your arrival. Instead, here you are with cherished memories of me. Of me!" she repeated, as if such a thing were incomprehensible.

"And why should I not? You are my only sister." Philippa's voice quivered with emotion.

Rowena hugged her this time, releasing her after a moment to study her face, then the rest of her. "Sweet Jesú, look at you. Why are you dressed in rags? Where are your shoes and head covering?"

Philippa hesitated. To reveal how she'd left Lindhurst might throw disparagement onto Roger when she desperately needed his forgiveness. "I was working out-of-doors, with only a headcloth over my hair and sabots on my toes. We left so suddenly there was no time to change into a better gown and the wind took my headcloth as we rode." She finished with what she hoped would distract her sister. "Oh, I almost forgot. I am to tell you that Temric says he will stay to support the castellan until your lord's return."

"Good," Rowena said with a firm nod. "Unlike my husband, I put no great confidence in the abilities of a knight only a year older than myself. Anne, make for my sister a bath and, Ilsa, you and Emma search our coffers for something suitable for her to wear." The maid who had led her here hurried out of the room to call for hot water, while the other two started throwing open trunks. Rowena stretched out her leg. "Let me see your foot."

Philippa laughed and extended her leg. "Do we match?"

"Aye," Rowena said in subtle pleasure. "Ilsa, she can use my footwear. Did you know no one expects your arrival for another week? We were all told that you were quite ill."

"Me?" Philippa's brows shot up in surprise. "I am never ill. Who told you this?"

As she spoke, Anne reentered the chamber at a trot, then grabbed up a roll of greased cloth to spread on the floor in front of them. Philippa gave a sudden smile. Of course, to put beneath the tub so water did not stain the wooden floor. Since everyone at Lindhurst bathed outside, there was never any need of this sort of protection.

"Lord Roger did so," Rowena was saying, "but only after the bishop raged at him for appearing here three days ago without you." She paused. "Perhaps Bishop William's sharp tongue caused him to fabricate an explanation for his failure to do as commanded."

Philippa only shrugged, unwilling to let any thought of Roger steal an instant of her time with Rowena. There was a tap at the door and a big wooden tub was rolled into the room. "Look at that!" she cried. "It must take an entire well's worth of water to fill it. Why, I could sink beneath its rim and drown!"

"Lord Graistan is tall and needs the extra room," Rowena said, then she smiled and leaned near to whisper into Philippa's ear. "If it is filled almost to the rim, the water covers me to the neck. I swear there is no finer sensation."

Servants entered, one after the other, with yoke and buckets. Philippa sighed in happy expectation. There was no Margaret here to chastise her against laziness; she could soak for as long as she wanted. She started, remembering Rowena chiding her servants a few moments ago. "You do not mind if I linger in the water, do you?"

"Mind! You may stay until your whole body creases. Never let it be said that Graistan is stingy toward its visitors," Rowena added with a smile.

"My lady," said an ancient serving woman, "look

what I have found for your sister." She and a second woman displayed between them an overgown of aqua, its surface figured with woven pattern. At its neckline and sleeves lay intricate embroidery studded with tiny, glittering stones. The undergown was of a darker green silk. "If the cut is out-of-date, the color will suit Lady Lindhurst well. I think her eyes are just this shade," the woman pointed to the overgown.

"For me to wear?" Philippa breathed in shock. "Nay, I dare not. I'd not bear the responsibility for such fine garments."

"My lady, it has sat in yon chest for over twenty years. I think it is a joy to have a use for it again," the maid said.

"Rowena, are you certain your lord will allow this?" Philippa protested, even as she yearned to wear such a beautiful gown. "Oh"—she reached out to finger a tiny stone—"but it is so lovely."

"*I* allow this," Rowena said with a quick smile. "Rannulf has no say in my women's quarters. Why do you not rid yourself of those filthy rags? Here comes the hot water. You'll want to be into the tub as quickly as you can. The water cools rapidly up here."

"Thank you, thank you." Philippa laughed and leapt to her feet, her fingers ripping at her cord belt. A moment later and the laces were loose. She yanked the gown off over her head, then her rough undergown and chemise. Margaret would have bellowed at the way she tossed the garments aside without care or concern for the material.

She turned to step into the tub. Anne's eyes widened in shock. "Mary, Mother of God," she cried.

Philippa glanced down at her torso and the knife-point scars that crisscrossed her midsection. "They do not hurt," she said, unashamed at the marks she bore. "Roger paid dearly for laying them." For every day of the weeks she'd spent recovering, Margaret had beaten her. Roger was no longer allowed to damage her so badly that she could not work the next day.

"Why did he do such a thing?" Rowena breathed in horror.

Philippa glanced at her sister. The shock on Lady Graistan's face was mirrored on those of her maids. "Because he owns me. Because his mother makes him do things to her that shame him. He hurts me rather than hurt himself."

She stepped into the tub and sank into the water. As Rowena had promised, she was covered to the neck. Ah, but it was deliciously warm. Rose petals drifted on the surface. Philippa let her arms rise buoyantly, the pretty bits of flowers drifting sweetly away from the gentle motion of her hands.

"My God," Rowena said in a shaken voice, "we cannot let him do such things to you."

Rowena's attempt at protection eased Philippa's nagging sense of abandonment. Still, she sent her sister a disbelieving look. "Who is to stop him?"

"I will," her sister retorted. "I will protest to the bishop. Philippa! While the bishop is here, we can request a dissolution of your marriage."

"On what grounds?" Philippa asked as Anne worked to free her braids. When the heavy mass of her hair was loosened, Philippa sank beneath the water's surface to wet it. She rose, sputtering happily as she wiped the moisture from her eyes.

Rowena brought a stool and sat at the tub's side. "What if there were some degree of kinship between you and Lord Lindhurst? Might there be anyone in your histories, a godparent or a previous marriage joining your two houses prior to this one? If we could prove your marriage incestuous—"

"You grasp at straws in the wind," Philippa interrupted. "Margaret would never have been so careless with my dowry. What Lindhurst owns, it holds forever. Anyway, it would make no difference," Philippa added as Anne began to massage soap into her hair. How strange and wonderful it felt to have someone else do this task for her. "Roger will not let me go. Despite what you see, he loves me."

"Love?" Rowena made a rude sound of disbelief. "It is not love when he hurts you."

Philippa raised her brows in consideration, then nodded in agreement. Until today, and the experience of Temric's gentleness, she had wondered if it was she who wronged her husband by not returning his "affection" for her. "So we might say, but Roger sees it differently. I think he may be mad."

"Oh, sweet Mary," Rowena said quietly, "let me ponder this a moment."

In the ensuing quiet, Philippa leaned her head forward to let Anne work at her nape. The taste of Temric's gentle kiss re-awoke in her and the pleasure his caress had caused flooded through her. Would that there were an honest order to life. Bastards, equals, like herself and Temric should be wed.

Rowena gave a cry as an idea occurred to her. "What of your father? Is there any heritage there we can use?"

"Benfield?" Philippa asked in surprise. "Nay, Margaret researched him as well as our mother."

"Nay, Philippa," Rowena said slowly, "your true father. Is there any possibility of relationship there?"

Philippa caught back her answer. She had no idea who her true father was, but to reveal to Rowena she knew she was a bastard would cheat her of Roger's forgiveness. If Rowena knew, she would surely tell the bishop. Nay, Philippa was not ready to give up the only bit of power over her husband that she had ever owned. At last, she said, "Leave it go, Rowena. Only a husband can petition and Roger will never do so. He holds me very dear."

"I hate feeling helpless," Rowena cried harshly. "How could our mother have given her favorite to such a monster?"

Philippa straightened, her sudden motion causing Anne to step back. Had she not wondered the same thing for the past twelve years? "I cling to the belief that she does not know what he is," she said, then sighed. "It cannot explain why she did not once send a missive or try to visit even though there are but a few leagues between Benfield and Lindhurst." Philippa consoled herself in knowing Roger would surely have refused to let her mother contact her. But Maman should have tried harder and found some way.

Rowena lay a soothing hand on her arm. "Then again, even if she'd come, what could she have done? You are right to say he owns you. I think she cannot know, for she speaks of you with great love."

"My thanks for that," Philippa replied softly, the image of her caring mother once again restored. "I only wish I knew why she chose him and not any of the others who offered to wed me."

Rowena waited for Anne to dump several bucketsful of water over Philippa's hair to rinse away the soap before answering. "I think our mother knows too many tales of love. I have seen your husband and by all appearances he is the perfect knight. He is tall, but not too broad, with golden hair and long, straight limbs."

"Aye, and a face like an angel, eh?" Philippa managed a small laugh. Roger's features were exceedingly fine, with a perfectly shaped nose and jaw. "In Maman's stories, the handsome knights are always kind and honorable. Mayhap our mother forgot that tales are only tales," she finished tiredly. Once, long ago, she had believed in them as well. Now she knew better. She thought of Temric, whose plainer face hid a good, kind man, while Roger's fairness disguised cruelty.

Rowena sighed. "With no cause for dissolution, the bishop will have no interest in you. The nuns at the convent who had been wives first said that ofttimes priests dismiss the most severe beating of a woman by her husband as rightful discipline."

"Of course they do. 'Tis our cross to bear in life," she said, then frowned in curiosity. "Rowena, does your husband not use his fists to discipline you when you err?"

Rowena gave her head a small shake, the corners of her mouth lifting slightly. When she spoke her words were very quiet, as if she were unaccustomed to discussing her marriage. "Nay, Rannulf loves me, and how well I know my fortune in that."

Philippa's momentary jealousy passed away into pleasure for her sister. Of course Rowena was not beaten. Temric's brother would be no less gentle than Temric for it was a father who taught his son about a wife's care. "I am glad for you. I pray that you and your lord lead a long and happy life."

"Do not tell our mother this," Rowena said with a harsh laugh, "for she is praying against you."

"What do you mean?" Philippa asked in surprise.

"She despises me." Rowena offered her a wry smile, but it was touched with just enough hurt to belie her casual attitude. "Thus was I not overjoyed to meet you. I thought you would be like her, because she raised you at her knee."

"What reason could she have to hate you?" Philippa took soap and cloth from the maid and washed as she spoke. The water was, indeed, cooling quickly. "Surely, you are mistaken."

"Nay, she is very vocal in her dislike. She hated my father and the emotion carries over onto me who so resembles him. I think, also, that she'd not wanted to give him any heir, thus forcing my sire to grant you what he has now willed to me. She cannot forgive me for the simple fact of my existence and sees me as a threat to you, the child she loves."

Rowena tried to smile, but it trembled badly. "Philippa, I suddenly find I have a precious bit of family where I believed none existed. How can I let him hurt you? Tell me how to help you."

Lady Lindhurst only shrugged in response. "I expect nothing from you save the happiness of our time together. You cannot know the comfort I draw from being near you. Hmm, but I am tired," she said, her limbs now fully loosened from the long day's travel.

"Then you shall find your rest on a soft cot and in the days to come I will fill your hours with pleasant activity. Let me hold you safe from your husband until the last minute." Her sister frowned in determination.

"Emma, fetch my sister something to eat and wine to drink so she might rest in contentment."

"My lady, what shall I do with her clothing?" Anne stood tubside, holding Philippa's gowns by forefinger and thumb alone.

"Burn them. I think they are useless even as cleaning rags," Lady Graistan replied.

Philippa smiled softly and uttered not one word to stop the destruction of Margaret's precious garments.

Chapter Four

Temric walked swiftly away from Lady Lindhurst, willing his heart to heal itself. He could not bear to look another instant upon the woman who should have been his lady. Not only was she another man's wife, but in the eyes of the Christian world, she was also his sister. Even if Philippa forgave him his trespass, no one else could. His love for her was worse than hopeless.

A sudden loneliness snapped at him. The onset of Lady Rowena's rule had forced right and proper changes into life at Graistan. If Temric begrudged him none of it, as Rannulf had achieved the closeness with a woman he'd always desired, their relationship as brothers had altered. Never before had Temric seen how empty this life he'd made for himself was. Without Rannulf, there would be no one left for him.

He strode to the hall's end and down a short flight of stairs. Here lay Graistan's chapel and at its far end was the door to his garrison. Temric hesitated. Damn, but he did not want to speak with Edwin just now. He needed time to prepare, else the old man would take him to pieces over what had happened. With good reason.

The chapel was dim, lit only by three narrow, east-facing windows behind an altar draped with heavily embroidered cloths. Ornate candle branches hung beneath each stone arch, empty and lifeless like the room's atmosphere. Gloomy shadows skulked at the feet of the columns and wrapped around their capitals, carved to look like oak leaves studded with acorns. So, too, were the plastered and painted walls behind them disguised.

He sighed with relief when he saw no one and started quietly toward his garrison door. There was only one hurdle left to pass. Although Father Edwin had been stone-deaf for years, Temric found himself taking careful steps as he neared the altar. He prayed the priest was not in his alcove, but in town visiting the abbey as he often did this time of day.

"Temric!" Edwin's voice rang with astonishing power against the stone walls and arches to echo into the chapel's corners. Graistan's master-at-arms grimaced, then turned to face the altar's south end. There, hewn from the very thickness of the keep's walls, was Edwin's tiny room.

The ancient priest who had baptized both Rannulf and himself rose from his cot, then shuffled toward him, his back bowed with age. Only wisps of pale hair yet covered the old man's freckled pate and his smile had long ago become gap-toothed. Where time had robbed Edwin of his vigor and his ears, it had not touched either his intelligence or the power of his beautiful voice.

When the priest was close enough to read the words upon his lips, Temric spoke, "Edwin, I did not see you."

"Is that so? Odd, I thought me you were tiptoeing by my door. I had the strangest visit from Oswald.

It kept me here, instead of going to the abbey as I usually do."

Temric managed a halfhearted shrug. "So, here I am."

"Come in." Edwin inserted a gnarled hand into the bend of Temric's arm. "Sit across from me so we can talk."

"Father, I am tired to death and yet in my armor. Can this not wait an hour so I might bathe and change?"

Edwin focused his sharp blue gaze on him. "Can it?"

"Nay, I suppose not." He sighed and let the old man lead him into the tiny alcove. It was barely wide enough for the two of them to sit, knee to knee, but it made up in length what it lost in width. At the far end sat Father Edwin's prayer station, the wall behind it painted with a biblical scene, revealed in flickering lamplight. Both long walls had been carved full of niches. In these little holes sat all the bits and pieces the priest used for services, as well as lamps, candles, wax, writing implements, and ink for his other duties.

"Find a stool and light these lamps from that one so I can see you more clearly," the old man commanded, handing him two small tallow lamps and pointing to the prayer station.

Temric did as he was told, then reluctantly faced the priest. "We have returned with Lady Lindhurst."

"Ah, and did you find she matched your dreams of her?"

"Nay, she is much different than I expected. I thought she would be like Lady Graistan. Instead, she is gentle and fearful, and innocent of all that has been done in her name." And even dressed in rags, her precious beauty glowed like a gem against pebbles, he added to himself. How was it he could have come to love so completely in such a short space of time?

"Then you were disappointed?" Edwin raised a shaggy brow.

Temric let his mouth twist into a brief, wry grin. "I was not."

"Would you like to tell me why Oswald thinks your soul is in jeopardy?"

He fought to present a shamed expression, but found he could not. "I kissed Lady Lindhurst and he came upon us whilst I was at it." His words were defiant.

"Boy, I will admit that when you choose to sin, you do it with great flair." Edwin sighed and shook his head. "Did I not warn you that your dreams would make your heart vulnerable? Now, you have not only broken God's law by coveting another man's wife, 'tis adultery you court."

"If this were a just world, she would belong to me. I would have met her before she was wed to her husband or my brother had married her sister," Temric retorted, leaning back on his stool, fists on his knees.

"What life could you have offered her?" Edwin snapped back. "You have made of yourself nothing but a servant, while she is a noblewoman."

"Are we not equals?" he said, hoarding the emotion now living in his heart for another man's wife. "Both of us are bastard born and each betrayed by a father's will."

"Temric, your father did not—"

His eyes narrowed at this complaint. "Nay, Edwin, do not waste your breath on that again. If I have not changed my mind in seventeen years, I will not change it now."

"As you wish," the old priest said, his expression souring. "Go ahead, you've got more to say. I see it lingering on your mouth."

"For all my life I have known what limits being baseborn laid on me."

"Or the limits you've laid upon yourself."

"You do not live the life, you cannot know," Temric flared back. "I thought you were going to listen, not interrupt and argue."

"Aye, there's no point in arguing with you. You hear less than I do." Edwin's blue eyes were hard with impatience, but when Temric struggled to speak aloud the words festering within him, the old man's face softened. "I beg your pardon for snapping. You so seldom have need of my counsel, I've forgotten how to treat you as a penitent." He reached out and lay his twisted fingers atop one of Temric's fists.

At the priest's touch, words poured from Temric in aching complaint. "Jesu, Edwin, when I met Philippa, 'twas as if all my control and discipline shattered. Even the threat of heavenly wrath could not stop me from tasting of the forbidden fruit. Now I know that God will not be mocked, for all I want is the one woman on this earth I cannot have. Father, my heart is broken. She should have been mine."

"But she cannot be. I grieve for you, son. You cannot entertain any hope toward her."

Temric threw himself up off the stool. "I know it," he bellowed, then whirled on his heel. "Is it not enough for you that my heart is breaking?"

"Wait, I have not given you your penance," Edwin

called after him. "You should at least stay away from her while she resides at Graistan."

"Nay, I will not accept your penance. I have no contrition in my soul," he shouted back, knowing full well the priest could not hear him.

He had not changed his mind before the midday meal the following day. Then again, neither had he caught any glimpse of Philippa. Now, Temric straightened his long brown tunic over chausses equally as dark. His best garment brushed the tops of his soft shoes as he strode into the hall along with the rest of Graistan's folk.

As always, the dual hearths were alive with fire, for even in the depths of summer this room remained cool and damp. The tables, their benches set along only one side, stood ready. Cloths were draped atop their surfaces, spoons and cups sat beside plates made from thick slices of yesterday's breads. The few dogs left behind, mostly whelping bitches, snarled and growled as they staked their territories for scraps.

From the pantlery came the rich aroma of fish stew, it being the day for it. Shellfish as well. His nose also caught the scent of a vegetable porray made from spring greens. Above it all rose the yeasty aroma of freshly baked breads. Good, he was hungry. He started toward his usual place, at the top of the second table.

"Temric," Lady Rowena called out from the high table where Graistan's noble family sat. At her right, as befitted a castellan however titular the position, sat young Arnult. To her left sat a richly dressed woman, braids as bright as newly polished gold hanging over either shoulder.

Philippa.

He could not stop himself; he stared openly. Good God, but he'd thought her lovely in her rags, never realizing how truly beautiful she was. Gowns of aqua and green accentuated her creamy skin and made the mingled blue-green shade of her eyes more noticeable. The wisp of her wimple did little to hide the soft line of her cheeks or the gentle curve of her jaw.

"Temric, are you listening? I said you must sit with us today," Lady Rowena's voice was brusque against his apparent inattention. "My sister needs a partner for the meal."

Philippa glanced at him, a shy smile touching her lips. This simple motion conjured up the sensation of brushing his mouth on hers. Would that she had rejected him. She should have for she was wed already. Instead, she'd raised her lips to his in invitation. However tentative her movement, it showed her marriage was not of the heart. Dear God, but could he sit next to her for an hour's time and not touch her? Impossible.

"Nay, my lady, I cannot. I do not belong at your table."

"Temric," his brother's wife commanded, "you belong at this table as much as Rannulf does and I will not accept your ridiculous posturing when I have a need."

Temric was already bracing himself to flare back in refusal, when Philippa said quietly, "Nay, Rowena, if he does not wish to sit with me, he need not." Her attention was now focused on the table in front of her and there was just a hint of pain in her tone.

Temric responded to her hurt. "I bow to your command, my lady." To think Philippa believed he might reject her, the very idea struck him to the core. He came to sit on the bench beside her, only to realize his grave mistake. They were close enough that her scent flowed to him in fragrant waves. He glanced down. The tightly laced gown displayed the full curves of her breasts, the narrow turn of her waist and well-formed hips. Lord, not only was she her sister's rival in beauty, but she was every bit as well made.

"I will excuse you, if Rowena will not," Philippa murmured, not lifting her gaze from the table. "I know you are sworn not to touch me."

"Would you rather I not sit with you?" he asked softly. Had he read rejection where she actually fretted for her soul's safety despite her flippant words of last even?

"Nay," she gasped, quickly raising her head to stare directly into his eyes. "Please stay, but do not be disappointed in me. We are not so formal at Lindhurst and I fear I've forgotten all my mother taught me of etiquette."

Temric grinned in relief, enormously glad that she wanted him to stay. Lord, but she was lovely. He let his gaze touch the slight length of her nose, the upward tilt of her eyes, and the outline of her lips.

"My lady," he managed, "if you need a tutor in manners, I may not be the right one to ask. I sit with my men who are a rough and surly bunch. Worries over etiquette bother them not in the slightest."

"Then I will be safe with you," she said with a quiet smile. His soul screamed that she was not at all safe with him, while his heart leapt with joy at her trust.

"Look what my sister has lent me," she said, laying happy fingers against the sleeve of her overgown. "Is it not beautiful?"

"Aye," he retorted bluntly, breathing deeply in his

struggle to control his need for her. So the hour would pass, him tortured by her nearness, while her closeness fed his desires.

"I think me so," she sighed, then laughed again, this time the sound wry. "But so do I think me a sparrow pretending to be a peacock."

"Nay," he breathed harshly, his arms aching to hold her just once more, "it suits you well."

"My thanks," she murmured shyly.

Temric could think of a multitude of things he wanted to ask her, but none were appropriate. Instead, the quiet between them grew thick, a bubble of silence in the rising noise level of the room. The hall filled as every servant Graistan claimed came to eat their meal.

He breathed in her scent, let her warmth reach out to him. Her sleeve brushed his as she moved. The shiny plait that crossed her shoulder gleamed in the light, hinting that it would be silky soft if he dared touch it.

"Why are you not knighted?" she asked suddenly, looking up from her hands to study his face with a careful gaze.

"Pardon?" he replied, unable to believe she'd asked so personal a question.

"Rowena says you have been offered lands and title, but will not accept them. She says you are foolish, but I think there must be some great purpose in you to refuse such a gift."

Temric felt his expression stiffen. "My father promised me knighthood and lands. When he died, his will bore not even the mention of my name. I will accept from no one else what my father denied me. It is no different than what your stepfather has done to you, by revealing your birth and denying you an inheritance."

"Therefore do you see us as equals," Philippa replied softly. "I understand you better now."

A tiny smile lifted one corner of his mouth. "Do you?" he said in quiet disbelief.

She shrugged, the movement shy. "When you are alone and unsupported, you clutch tightly to what is special within you, letting no one force you to be what you are not."

He drew a sharp breath. Without effort or thought, she lay his soul out before him to see.

"So is it with me. We are equals, you and I," she said quietly, "when I had always believed myself alone."

Temric had to turn away, fearing she would see the pain in him. He should have swallowed his pride and taken the inheritance his father denied him when Rannulf offered it seventeen years ago. Might he not have been wed to Philippa now? Then he sighed. It was pointless to torture himself with hindsight. What was done could not be changed.

He marshaled his heart and turned back to her. "So, my lady, how have you enjoyed your stay at Graistan thus far?" It was an incredibly bland statement.

Philippa stared at him for a moment and Temric drew the impression that he had not managed to hide his hurt from her. Then she smiled, letting a natural enthusiasm fill her tone. "Oh, Temric, it is so wonderful here. Everyone is kind and gentle. 'Tis as if I were only dreaming, save I could never have imagined so grand a place as Graistan. Do you know my sister even has her own private garden?"

Temric laughed quietly, amused and gratified by her obvious joy. "Aye, my lady, I did."

"Of course you did," she said in mock dismay at

herself. "Oh, but it is lovely in there, all flowers and
fruit. I refused to leave it until it was time to eat.
Actually"—now she leaned closer as if to share a private confidence—"Rowena's maid and I have plotted
ways to keep my sister off her feet. She exerts herself
too much and too soon after losing a babe."

Temric's senses all came violently to life at her nearness. Jesus God Almighty. Every inch of him screamed
to touch her. His hand remembered the incredible sensation of her fingers between his. Her mouth had been
so soft beneath his, yet her innocent response to his
caress hinted at lurking passion. He need only stretch
out his arm behind her to draw her close. All of her
would be pressed to him, this time without his mail
between them. That thought sent his pulse to stuttering and his blood became fire in his veins.

Then the ewerer stepped between them, offering
water basin and towel so they might wash their hands.
Temric breathed a swift sigh of relief, mingled with
disappointment. After Father Edwin said his prayer,
table service commenced.

As always, Graistan's cook fed them well. Although
it was only fish, there were three sorts, each drenched
in thick sauces, along with the green porray and fresh
breads. In his temporary role of a gentle knight, it was
his duty to find for Philippa the best bits from every
dish. Her reaction to what she tasted made him laugh.

"Are the dishes so plain at Lindhurst?" he finally
asked when she fairly moaned at a bit of trout flavored
with ginger and cloves.

"Aye, save for what herbs our garden supplies us.
Please, I know the meal is almost over, but might I
have more from that one?"

He dug a thick piece from the tray with the spoon

and set it onto her trencher. She lifted it to her mouth and he watched her lips close over it, then damned himself for looking. To distract himself, he offered her the cup they shared. A sudden warmth rushed through him when she set her mouth to the same spot he drank from, the way lovers did.

Color stained her cheeks as she realized what she'd done. "Pardon," she gasped, fumbling the cup in embarrassment as she attempted to set it down. He reached out to steady it, his fingers accidentally closing over hers at the silver container's base. She jerked her hand away even as he released his grasp. The cup fell to the table, toppling onto its side as wine poured from it, a red stain on the white cloth.

"Oh, Rowena, I am so sorry," Philippa cried out in true distress.

Temric laughed aloud. He was worse than some lovesick youth! He was so nervous around her it made his actions stupid. "Aye, my lady, see what you wrought when you put me where I do not belong?" he called across Philippa to her sister. Amusement still lightened his voice. When his words died away, he realized that the room was suddenly deathly still. Temric looked out into a sea of familiar faces and found nearly every eye on him.

"What are you all looking at," he asked them, "or did you think me incapable of such clumsiness?" The room echoed with their laughter and the noise level reverted to its usual din.

"Nay, 'twas my fault," Philippa cried out, her voice reed-thin. "Do not blame him, Rowena."

Lady Graistan shot him a single surprised glance, then looked to her sister. "Blame? For a spilled cup? Right it and fill it again," she commanded the butler, "unless they feel they've had too much." She narrowly eyed Temric.

"This is what comes of trying to make a noble out of a commoner," he retorted without rancor. "We all know the English like ale better than wine." Lady Graistan only made a sound of annoyance while the butler returned the cup to its proper position and refilled it with fine, rich wine.

"She did not care," Philippa breathed as if in shock, turning to look at him. Her face was white, her eyes wide.

"And why should she?" He studied her carefully for her behavior puzzled him. "We did no wrong, only fumbled a cup."

"We stained the cloth and wasted the wine," she protested quietly as she stared at the red blotch on the cloth. Then a moment later she raised her eyes to gaze carefully around the room. Temric watched her study every face. He looked, too, wondering what it was she thought to find in them. These were just ordinary folk, enjoying a meal before hurrying back to their daily chores.

Then Philippa looked at her sister, at Arnult who carefully and cautiously served his lady from the dishes in front of them. Temric's gaze moved beyond them to where Jordan and his nurse sat at the table's other end. His nephew bobbed on the bench as he swung his feet in a busy rhythm. Somehow, the lad had managed to smear sauce down the whole front of his gown while his nurse had been distracted with her own meal.

Temric rolled his eyes and leaned a little closer to Philippa to direct her gaze. "Look to the table's opposite end. That is Jordan, my brother's natural son. The hellion."

"Lord, but he's ruined his gown," Philippa breathed, her voice harsh with worry.

"Nay, not ruined, only made hard work for some laundress. Rannulf thinks his son will be ready for fostering in two more years. I think not, if the boy cannot even learn how to put food into his mouth without missing." He chuckled in fondness, for as much as he pretended to be dismayed by the lad's behavior, he loved his nephew.

Philippa shifted suddenly on the bench, turning to look at him. Their faces were so close he could feel her breath against his cheek. His arms tensed to embrace her; his lips parted to touch hers. Desire raged through him and he drew a sharp breath against his need for her.

"It does not matter," she whispered as if in wonder. "Here, it does not matter."

If he could make no sense of her words, at least they restored his control. Jesus God, but he'd nearly made a mockery of his vow to Oswald. Had he lost all his honor to his heart? Thank God, Arnult was raising his cup in the signal that the meal was at an end. He reared back, sliding away from her on the bench.

"My lady, thank you for your fine company over this hour," Temric managed through gritted teeth, then rose swiftly to flee the hall. Edwin was right, he should leave Graistan for the duration of Philippa's stay. One more meal like this one and he feared for his sanity.

Chapter Five

Temric brought his big steed clattering back into the courtyard just before sunset, both of them heaving and panting in exertion. Damn, but he could concoct no reason strong enough to rescind his offer of support to Arnult. Without one, he was trapped here until Rannulf's return. He swung out of the saddle and threw his reins to Gareth.

"So, laddie, did abusing this poor creature help to purge her out of your system?" The old man's husky voice was thick with amusement.

"You babble, old man, and I can make no sense of your words," Temric replied, gracing the stable master with a look of irritation.

The burly ancient set a fist on his hip and raised his shaggy brows in disbelief. "Huh. If you cannot understand me 'tis because lustful thoughts cloud your brain. 'Twas quite a spectacle you made of yourself at the meal. The lady's husband would have taken much amiss if he'd seen you look at his wife the way you did."

Temric straightened in shock. "Now you imagine, man. There has been nothing in either my face or my behavior worth noting."

"Do I?" Gareth's face, deeply creased from years

of exposure to the elements, cracked into a broad grin. "I'm not so blind yet that I cannot read a boy I've known all my life. Well, now, I'll warrant she's a beauty like her sister. Too bad she's married to that arrogant lordling. Do you know he came in here spouting and spewing that we'd offered his mounts moldy hay? Insulted Lord Rannulf in our presence, he did. He cannot leave soon enough to suit poor Harold whose eye was blackened during that complaint."

"You're serious," Temric said, ignoring the diatribe to focus on the old man's first comments. "What gives you cause to think me capable of dishonoring another man's wife?"

"Dishonor? Nay, no dishonor, but a man can't help where his interest lies. At the meal, you watched her the way a penned stallion eyes a mare in heat. Ah, laddie, you've long thought you could escape the trap that's eaten every man at one time or another. We all end up dancing to the tune of our hearts at least once, wondering all the while what became of our common sense." He squinted up at Lord Graistan's elder brother. "Thanks be to God for that, else we'd live a dull life indeed."

Temric could only stare at him in dismay. Jesú Christus, if Gareth could see it, and him half-blind, they all had seen.

"Do not take it so hard, laddie." Gareth laughed and patted his cheek. "Love's a good thing to feel on a fine summer's eve like this one. Rain on the morrow, or so my bones tell me. Now, hie yourself to the kitchen. Your mother's youngest son—Peter, is it?— arrived whilst you were out torturing this beastie. It seems there's been some crisis in Stanrudde. Humph.

If Alwyna had any sense, she'd return to Graistan rather than staying among those foreigners."

Temric's whole body relaxed in relief. If Alwyna had sent one of her precious sons, his mother's need was urgent, indeed. He could leave! Temric fought back a grin.

"I'll tell my mother you send your regards," he said, "but guarantee you she'll give up neither the trade nor that rich house that she and my stepfather worked so hard to build. And my thanks for your concern over my heart, Gareth."

"Coward," the old man chided in fond amusement, "you are running!"

"Aye, with great thanks to my mother for whatever crisis is at hand," Temric called back as he strode for the kitchen.

Relief quickly ebbed, bringing pain in its wake. He would never see Philippa again. It was just as well, he consoled himself. His desire for her was a terrible sin and he should banish her completely from his thoughts. Not possible! Rather that he died than lose a single precious memory of their short time together. As Gareth said, his heart would stay firmly fixed where it was without care for what havoc it wreaked. Oddly, in ceasing to resist there came the stirrings of peace. What would be, would be, and there was naught he could do to change it.

The cooking shed was a wooden building at the keep's back. Built against stone footings and directly below the pantlery, trays and platters were raised by an ingenious system of ropes and pulleys from the shed's doorway to hall level. This meant that meals at Graistan had the singular distinction of being warmer than those served in most other keeps.

At this late hour the ropes hung slack and the upper portal was shut for the night. The cook, his aides and assistants, all lingered around their great table. Once the sun had set, they would lay out their pallets and sleep, but for now they basked in the glow of one day's work completed and another's begun. Bowls, spits, spoons, ladles, and sieves were once again clean and organized, knives honed and stored. One scullery lad was sand-scouring a final caldron.

In the room's far corner the cooking fire still burned, but its usual broad blaze had been banked to a smaller area. As always a great pot of simmering water hung over its coals. Two smaller pots, fitted with tiny feet, stood among the ashes, their contents sending up a fragrant steam.

Temric nodded in greeting to the cook. "You have a new admirer in Lady Lindhurst. She was quite taken with your trout this afternoon."

"And I understand she has one in you," said the big man with a laugh, his oily face shining in the low light, "but my thanks for the compliment. I think I've improved myself some since our fine visitor arrived. His rich tastes are a never-ending challenge." Not a little pride touched his words.

"I can imagine," Temric retorted, hiding his dismay. Had he truly been that obvious? "Is Peter here?"

"Alwyna's son? Aye, your little brother is back in that corner against the hearth"—a jerk of the cook's balding head indicated the gaping maw of the fireplace—"playing with charcoal. Ever since he heard we had a bishop here, we've barely been able to pry him free of that corner. You needn't roust him out. He's been no trouble and can stay if he likes."

"My thanks," Temric said, then wended his way through their ranks to the corner indicated.

His mother's youngest son had squeezed his lanky, sixteen-year-old frame onto a tiny stool. Fine, dark hair straggled down into his face as Peter leaned intently over a plank balanced on his knees. Long fingers worked in tiny motions as he drew onto his scrap of parchment.

"The light grows too dim for scribbling," Temric whispered into his ear.

Peter shot straight up, board flying one way, charcoal the other, while his hands clasped over his chest in surprise. "Sweet Mary," he panted, "I did not see you coming."

Temric freed a quick breath of amusement. "So it would seem. What is it that brings you here?"

"Jehan," Peter replied. "He fell while working in the warehouse and cannot walk although nothing is broken."

Temric raised his brows in reaction. At twenty-five, his middle brother by his mother was an angry man. He could not imagine Jehan enduring a life without the use of his legs. "And so?" he offered, prodding Peter to continue his tale.

The boy sighed knowingly, then said in the peculiar tone common to half-grown children speaking of their elders, "Jehan is not hurt so badly as to be bedridden, but he will not even try to walk with the crutches Mama had made for him. Instead, he sits the day long spewing insults and rancor at everyone. Mama already aches so from Papa's death, she can bear no more. She seeks both one to protect her and to take up Jehan's tasks for a time. She claims to want you as you calm her while the rest of us drive her into insanity." The boy made a face, then leaned down to gather up his bits and pieces.

Temric gave a tiny snort. "Do not believe it. It has not been so many years since she vowed insanity caused by Lord Graistan and myself." A yawn caught him unaware and he stretched in its wake. He wanted no more than to rinse clean, then crawl onto his cot and find peace in exhausted sleep. "Best hie yourself to bed, boy. We'll be off at first light."

"The morrow?" The boy's newly deepened voice cracked in disappointment.

Temric quirked up a brow. "Mama sent you here to fetch me because her need is urgent. I would do her a disservice if I lingered."

"But the bishop is not expected to return for another day," Peter cried softly, his hand closing so tightly over his bit of charcoal it flaked. The parchment in his other hand crackled.

"What of it?" Temric gave the lad a calculating look. "You do not mean—I thought you told Mama you were finished with dreams of the monastery and scribbling."

Peter started to hang his head, then jerked into a defiant pose. "I never said so, those were her words. After Papa's death I thought she'd give me what I needed to buy my entrance to a monastery, but she refused. She says I must do her counting because Jehan cannot, but I know she only means to keep from me what I want!" Peter's voice broke, but it was emotion not his age that did it this time. "Why can she not understand how important this is to me?"

Temric shook his head. Alwyna loved the Church as well as anyone, but she could not understand Peter's desire to turn his back on an established trade and the possibility of wife and family. He laid a hand on the lad's bony shoulder. "You know your mother. Her affection for her sons ofttimes blinds her. Take consolation in the knowledge that she struggles mightily to comprehend me as well. Here now, why not show me what you've done. Do you know I've never before seen any of your scribblings?"

"Promise you will not laugh," the lad begged, clutching his scrap close.

"I never laugh," Temric replied and took the parchment from him. Peter had sketched out Graistan in full detail, then bordered it with summer's richness. Grapes and apples, pears and pomegranates, clung together in improbable bounty on the same twining vine. "This is very good," he said and meant it.

"Do you think so?" Then the boy grinned, knowing full well it was. Pride disappeared into an anxious hopefulness. "Do you think a bishop might have interest in my work?"

In the boy's dark eyes Temric saw his own fire and pain. But where everything conspired to forbid Temric Philippa, Peter need only wait for his majority to gain what he wanted. If this bit of sheep's skin represented his talent, some monastery would have him, coins or no. Temric paused. Why should Peter be forced to wait?

"Lad, did you know my noble cousin Oswald is one of Bishop William's administrators? I think he would look at this for you, especially if it is Rannulf who delivers it to him."

The boy grew so pale that Temric feared he might faint. "You would ask Lord Graistan to do that for me?" he begged breathlessly, then his hopes crashed with despair. "But he is also gone with the bishop."

"Graistan's chaplain will hold it until their return. Now, does that make the morrow's leave-taking easier for you?"

"Aye," Peter said, "it does. When the bishop has found a place for me, he will send word to Stanrudde."

Temric held up a warning hand. "Take heed, this is but a door opening. It could just as easily slam shut in your face."

"It shan't," the boy cried, "I know it shan't. But you are right, I should not hope too high and I am not." Not one shred of reservation colored his disclaimer. The cook and all his assistants laughed and Peter had the grace to grin along with them.

Temric cuffed him gently. "Go find a bed, you silly pup," he said with true affection. "I'll deliver this to Father Edwin before I seek my rest."

"Thank you, Temric, thank you. God will bless you for this, I know it, aye. Your noble cousin, as well." When Temric made a scornful sound, Peter insisted, "Nay, 'tis true, I feel it."

"I doubt it," his elder brother replied. "Neither God nor Oswald are particularily fond of me just now." With that, Temric turned and strode from the kitchen shed, his brother's precious fragment cradled carefully in his hands.

As he made his way up the steep stairs along the keep's side, the sun sank beneath the horizon. Twilight lay long shadows on house and tree, keep and wall, cloaking what it touched in shades of gray. Against the softness of nightfall, the raucous noise within the hall was a startling contrast.

Graistan presently housed a troupe of acrobats and entertainers meant to prevent their auspicious guest from suffering a moment's boredom. While musicians played a merry tune, a juggler stood in the center of the hall tossing his pretty balls. Philippa sat next to her sister at the high table, her face alight with pleasure.

He watched her for a moment. It seemed as though she saw everything through innocent eyes, as if she'd never before experienced even the most ordinary of life's pleasures. Her wonder reminded him of what he'd come to take for granted, like a fine gown or a rich meal, or a tumbler walking across the floor on his hands. Temric saw her gape with awe as the same acrobat flipped himself over and over again between the hearths.

This night would be his last chance to see her glow with joy, to hear her sweet voice and look upon her face. If he could not touch her, at least he would have the memory of their nearness to take from Graistan with him. Aye, Rowena would not complain if he sat with them.

He took a step, then froze in disbelief at where his heart had almost led him. Had he not already made fool enough of himself? Nay, he'd risk no further incidents. Temric turned swiftly away from the hall to descend the chapel stairs. He swore he left his heart atop its highest step.

Save for a single candle burning on the altar, the chapel lay in full darkness. Edwin was most likely in the hall watching the performers. Well, Temric needed only the priest's quill and ink, not personal conversation, to do this task. Aye, he'd leave this drawing with a note of explanation for Edwin, and another note as a message of farewell for Rannulf. He turned toward the narrow alcove. It lay deep in shadow. He'd have to light a lamp to find the writing tools he needed.

Leaving Peter's sketch atop the altar, habit alone

led Temric through the darkened chamber to its end
and the lamp that sat on Father Edwin's prayer station. Once he returned to the chapel, he leaned the
candle toward the tallow-filled bowl, touching wick
to wick.

The bit of lint sputtered and caught in smoky flame.
Someone tapped him on the shoulder. He jerked in
response, hot oil and wax splashing onto his hand.
Setting the lamp down to rub his stinging hand against
the body of his gown, he glanced behind him.

There was no one there. Temric rolled his eyes in
disbelief. Aye, if he stayed another day, he'd be mad
for certain. The air stirred violently within the room
as the last of day's light died in a rasping breath of
wind. Both the candle and the lamp snuffed out, leaving the chapel air dark and reeking of wick.

"Jesu," Temric muttered in irritation. Now he had
to relight the candle. To do that he had to take the
lamp into either the hall or garrison. He closed his
hand around where the lamp should be and felt fingers, instead. He yanked back his hand with a sharp
cry and stared in horror at the altar's surface.

Where the bowl had sat, there was now a pale and
ghostly hand. It lay atop the altar without arm or body
to accompany it, fingers outstretched, the middle one
bearing a heavy silver ring. "Nay!" he breathed in
panic as bone-deep fear roared over him.

"Richard." The simple, sad word seemed to echo
all around him.

"Nay!" Staring at the apparition, his terror deepened as he recognized whose hand it was. "This is not
possible," he said, his voice rising steadily. He refused
to believe either his ears or his eyes.

Caught in horror, he only managed a small, trembling

step back. Misty and thin, the hand persisted where it could not be. "Nay," he said more loudly, his heart hammering in his chest. "This is not happening to me."

"Now who has gone and left my chapel dark?"

The eerie vision flickered instantly into nothingness. Temric cried out in relief, "Edwin, come light the candle!"

"I will have to light the candle once again," the deaf cleric muttered. He stopped at the altar and found his flint and tinder. The scrape of the stone into a twist of straw was as wondrously familiar as the old man's bent and fragile frame revealed in the newly reborn candlelight.

The lamp sat just where Temric had set it.

The priest looked up and started in surprise to discover he was not alone. "Temric, you must not do an old man so. Why do you stand here in the dark?"

Graistan's master-at-arms grabbed for Edwin's thick and twisted hand. As hard as he worked to convince himself these were the fingers he'd seen the moment before, he could not. He knew Edwin's hand as well as he knew that other one, and they were not the same.

"Nay, I will not do this to myself," he said hoarsely, releasing Edwin from his shaking grasp. "I am tired, too tired, and overwrought from the day. Here."

Temric scrabbled at the edges of Peter's drawing on the altar and was unable to gain purchase with his trembling fingers. "Here, this is from Alwyna's youngest. You—"

He stopped, knowing he'd spoken faster than the priest could follow. After a deep, calming breath, Temric carefully faced Edwin and gently lifted the parchment. "Do you recall my mother, Alwyna?"

"Of course. What do you think I am, a doddering ancient?" Edwin snorted.

"There has been an accident at her house and I must leave early on the morrow to attend her."

"Good," the cleric said. "That will prevent what I see happening before my aged and all-too-innocent eyes."

"I am going, am I not?" Temric retorted harshly, then sighed. "Beg pardon, Father. Here, this drawing comes from the hand of Alwyna's youngest son, Peter. Will you give it to Rannulf so he might show it to Oswald? Peter seeks to take his vows at any monastery with a well-staffed scriptorium."

"He has a calling?" Edwin asked.

"He does and has expressed it from an early age."

The chaplain smiled, a gap-toothed grin. "It is reassuring to hear there is one who craves with his heart the passion of God's love. Then, again, I would expect no less from Alwyna's spawn."

"My thanks, Father," Temric said swiftly, desperate to escape the room.

"Stay, we have things yet to discuss," the priest began.

"Nay, forgive me, Edwin, not tonight. This day has so exhausted me that I see things that cannot be." And felt them, as well. He turned without another word and fled the chapel along with both the souls it held within it.

Philippa glanced across the room at Temric. The knight stood before the chapel stairs as if deciding whether or not to join them in the hall. She sighed in disappointment when he turned and hurried down into the chapel. What had she done during the meal to cause him to spurn her company?

"Are you tired, my lady?" It was Anne. Rowena had commanded the dark-haired maid to be her own personal servant for the duration of her visit. A quirk of wonder shot through her depression. Imagine, someone to wait on her when she was accustomed to waiting on others.

"Nay," Philippa replied quietly, "only wondering what I have done to insult Temric. He left so quickly after the meal and his words were so strained."

"You did nothing, my lady," the maid replied, then added to herself in English, " 'tis himself he seeks to escape."

"Are you certain?" Philippa asked, then chewed on her lip in worry. "He has been naught but kind and gentle toward me and I would not wish to do him harm."

"My lady, pay him no heed. Temric is one who lives life to the strictures of his own rules. 'Tis a great compliment that he chose to join you for the meal. Not even Lord Rannulf has been able to sit him at that table." Anne laughed at her own words, a feathery cobweb of lines appearing at the corners of her dark eyes.

"Truly?" Philippa asked, her spirits raising some.

"Aye, and do not mistake him for a servant. He is never commanded, only accedes to those tasks he deems fit for him. When we heard Lady Rowena order him to sit beside you, we thought for sure the battle would be joined. Then, with but a few quiet words from you, there he was." She laughed again, the sound merry and gay.

Philippa knew a sudden rush of pleasure at the

maid's words. She'd feared his strange behavior meant she'd disgusted him somehow. That would have destroyed her. She needed him to value her not because he owned her or she was dowered, but simply because she was like him. Not only that, but his touch was gentle and painless.

In her mind she gathered together every instant they had spent together. She polished each incident to a shiny brightness, then stored them into her memory like the precious jewels they were. If nothing else, she could carry these back with her to her hell at Lindhurst.

Chapter Six

"**L**ady Lindhurst, awaken, you must awaken. My lady, please, please, rise!"

The cry brought Philippa instantly alert. She sat straight up on her cot, tossing soft blankets to one side as she threw her hair out of her face. "What is it?"

Anne was poised above her holding a tangle of clothing, her kind eyes wide in fright. "You must dress. Lady Rowena says you must go immediately to hide in the north tower chamber. Someone comes searching for you."

"Aye, hurry," said another of the maids crowding around her here at the back of the women's quarters.

"My husband?" Philippa leapt to her feet and shrugged into a thin chemise Anne handed her, pulling the loose garment over her head. She shoved her hands through the narrow sleeves of her green undergown. Her fingers snarled in the laces at the wrist opening.

"I know not," the maid replied, holding at the ready her beaded overgown. Philippa lifted her arms and Anne pulled it over her head.

Another woman thrust shoes and belt into Philippa's hands. A comb was pushed into one shoe and the pile in her arms topped with a damp cloth for washing. "Take her, Anne," someone cried when men's voices, roaring in rage, echoed up to them from the courtyard.

"But her hair's undone," Anne protested as she tied the lacings on one side of Lady Lindhurst's outer gown.

"Never mind it," Philippa said shortly, now desperate to reach this place of safety before being found. She threw her free-flowing hair over her shoulders. "Take me to where my sister wills."

Anne made a hasty gesture of compliance, leaving the other side of Lady Lindhurst's gown undone. "This way."

The maid led her through the hall to a stairway at its far side. With her fear came nausea, and her stomach protested against the smell of freshly baked bread and bubbling pottage that filled the room. Philippa followed Anne up the tight, spiraling turns. They climbed steadily, their only light a misty dimness that shot in through the occasional arrow slits.

From these same openings came the indistinct sound of angry voices in the courtyard, but these defensive apertures were aimed toward the outer bailey and an enemy yet to breach the inner gate. None of what happened below their very noses could be seen. Shouting gave way to the clash of steel against steel.

"What is it, Anne?" she cried.

"I know not," the maid replied, her voice threaded with fear. "Thank the Lord that Temric had yet to leave this morn. He will hold us as safe. In here."

The woman pulled open the thick wooden door at the stairs' top and stepped inside with Philippa close on her heels. The small chamber was barely big enough for three men to lie in, side by side. Each of the two exterior walls had been cut with a single arrow slit. A solitary stool sat in the room's center.

Anne rushed to stare out one opening, but Philippa sank onto the tiny seat, her heart in tatters. She cradled her face in her hands, elbows braced on her knees. "Temric leaves?" she asked quietly.

Although Philippa had known they must surely part, she hadn't felt the truth of it. Never again would she speak with him or touch his hand. Regrets tumbled over themselves in her mind. Would that she could lace her fingers between his once more and experience again the strange joy of his mouth touching hers. "Where is it that Temric goes?"

Anne continued speaking from the narrow window. "His mother has called for him. She's a new widow and now one of her sons has been crippled. To top that, her husband's trade lays heavily on her shoulders just now. . . . I can see naught from here!" she cried in frustration, then turned back into the room with a quick smile. "I would bring better than that cloth for your washing as well as something to break your fast. You look so worried. Shall I send someone to bear you company in my absence?"

Philippa gave her head a small shake. It was privacy she needed above all else just now. When she tried to smile, the corners of her mouth refused to lift.

"Ah, you poor chick, you must not fear," Anne said soothingly, mistaking sadness for fright. "Temric's no simple soldier for all his pretending. He is Lord Rannulf's equal here, although no one would dare say so to his face. He will hold you safe." Anne hurried from the room, unaware that her attempt at comfort had gone horribly awry.

Philippa blinked away tears as the pain grew in waves. Not only did Temric care for her, but he was the equal of Lord Graistan who loved her sister so dearly he did not mistreat her.

Philippa dropped her shoes and belt, then pressed her face into the damp washing cloth, her throat tight against her loss. No bit of linen could ease the almost intolerable emptiness within her. She wiped away her tears at the same time she cleaned face and teeth.

Suddenly the stairwell beyond the closed door echoed with noises. A man shouted. His voice rose into the sound of pleading, then lowered into a depth given only to threats. Philippa leapt up, backing steadily away from the door as the scuffing of feet grew nearer.

"I'll not be treated so," the man demanded. "Unhand me, Guy. I'm no puling infant to be banished at another's will. God's blood, Walter, this is my home and my fight, no one else's." His voice grew deep with outrage.

"Temric—" Philippa breathed.

The door swung open and a single man was shoved inside. Although he fell to one knee against the violence of their push, he was back onto his feet and at the thick wooden panel before they could slam the door shut behind him. The men outside were hard-pressed to keep it closed against his attack.

She stared at him. He hardly looked like a knight dressed as he was, in a commoner's short brown tunic over dark chausses and knee-high boots bound to his calves with cross garters. For a cloak he wore only a capuchin the same deep color of his stockings, hood thrown back to reveal his bare head. The only difference between him and any other servant lay in the empty sword belt at his waist, for it was intricately worked and chased in brass.

"Damn you, free me," he raged. "You have no right to do me thusly."

"Temric," she said faintly, cautiously, for his boiling anger frightened her.

He did not hear her as he again threw himself at the door. It gave not an inch, being held closed by the two men on its other side. Through the thick oak came a meek call. "Master, do not resist so. My lady has commanded that you be held safe until Lord Rannulf and the bishop can be called home. I must do her bidding. Please"—there was no mistaking this poor servant's anxiety—"I pray you do not try to escape. It would force me to do what would break my heart, but bind you I will if you fight us."

Temric slammed a fist against the door. "Damn her," he bellowed. "This is none of hers to meddle with." He turned and leaned against the door, eyes shut and his head thrown back in frustration. "What right has she to treat a son of Graistan this way?" he muttered to himself. His clenched fist pounded a tattoo of futility against the door.

Philippa gasped in shock. The side of his face oozed blood from brow to chin. His capuchin was stained with it all the way to the garment's short hem that crossed him midchest. "Temric, you are injured," she cried out, fear banished by her concern for him.

"Philippa?" He jerked in surprise, filling the syllables of her name with both terror and joy. "Dear God, she does not know what she's done. Guy, you must hold me elsewhere," he shouted, making no attempt to open the door. There was no response from the other side.

She came to his side, her washcloth in her hand. "Be easy, we'll not be alone for long." The cut on his face was the mark of a whip, and not as deep as the amount of bleeding had led her to believe. It would heal thin and white, leaving a stripe through his beard.

As she tried to lay her cloth to his brow, he stepped away from the door to the adjoining wall. When she came again to stand beside him, her bit of material at the ready, he turned his head as if her nearness hurt him worse than his wound. "Nay, you must not. We have sinned enough as it is." His voice was flat and dead.

She gave him a quick, wry grin. "I am only going to clean your wound. I think that cannot be a sin."

Despite his obvious worry over her touch, he smiled, his eyes glowing golden brown in response. " 'Tis silly of me, eh?" Yet, when she again raised her cloth to his brow, he still turned his head aside. "Leave it for another to treat. I have given my word that I will not touch you."

Philippa made a soft sound of irritation. "Your vow is safe. It is I who touches you." She caught his chin in her hand and lay her cloth against his face. When he raised a hand to stop her, he caught it back, then loosed a ragged sigh in defeat.

Her mouth quirked up in sudden amusement. Was he so honor-bound? If so, did he realize how he freed her to touch him without concern for his reaction? There was a powerful temptation in that.

For now she concentrated on gently wiping away the blood from the slash on his face. In some places it barely split the skin. Along the cheek and brow it was deeper. He must have taken only the finest tip of the lash.

"Temric, who has done this to you?" she asked. "Why does Rowena hold us here?"

He yet stood stiff and tense, pressed hard against the wall. "Your lord's mother has come here in Graistan's own cart. She caught me in the courtyard preparing to leave. It's the skin off my back she wants for my supposed attack as well as my taking of you."

Philippa's hand fell away from his face. One day of freedom was all she would have. Now, her husband's mother would wrest her away from her sister and her real life would begin again. Then she gasped at what Temric had said. "Why does she have the right to hurt you? You were only completing the task the bishop gave you. Surely Lord Graistan will protect you."

Temric's response was bitter. "If my brother's wife tears from me my own men and makes them bow to her wishes when I command otherwise, why should that old hag not have my flesh?" Then his mouth twisted in irony. "I should not have touched you. I am my father's unacknowledged bastard, therefore common. It is death for a commoner to attack a Norman. Aye, she has the right."

"Nay," Philippa breathed. "I'll not let her hurt you simply because I dared to tell you my name. Rowena must give me to Margaret. For control of me, she will relinquish her complaints against you."

"You would dishonor me so?" he hissed. "I will take her blows for I earned them with the kiss I pressed on you. Nay, you dare not defy me. I have seen how much this stay at Graistan has pleased you. If my life can buy you even one more day of happiness, let me die." He reached for her, as if to embrace her, then his hands fell, empty, to his sides. A low cry of pain escaped him and he looked away.

Philippa cherished the harsh lines of his face. He ached to hold her, she could see it in his expression. "That you should care so for me you would sacrifice yourself," she said in wonder. "It would only be wasted. If it's me she wants, she'll take you and demand me despite you." When he turned his gaze to her, she found his dark eyes filled with the ferocious need to keep her safe. It was no less than what she felt for him. When she spoke, her words were quiet but firm. "If you try to do this, I will only stop you. You have already given me far more than you can ever know and left me no way to repay you."

His smile was crooked and sad. "I would be content if I might yet dream of you."

Philippa shook her head sharply. "I think you are not the sort of man to indulge in such useless pinings. Would you make me your lady love and foolishly sigh for the barest sight of me? That is what the knights in my mother's stories do, spending their hearts on what they cannot have. Nay, you may not dream of me. Go to your mother's home and forget me, for ours is a hopeless cause."

He stared down at her, the light in his eyes dying away. "Do you spurn my love for you?" His voice was so low she had to strain to hear him. In his taut expression she saw hints of the pain her seeming rejection caused him.

Astonishment tore through her. She could never refuse him. She belonged to him. Her voice quivered when she spoke, "Would that I had my life to begin again and the freedom to live it as I would. You would be the choice of my heart. I break beneath the knowledge of what might have been and what I can never have."

His cry was no more than a strangled sound of joy and pain. She lay gentle fingers against his lips. Although he tensed, he did not move his head away from her touch. "You must not hurt for me," she begged softly.

"You cannot deny me that," he whispered, "my heart is breaking." The slight movement of his mouth against her fingers felt soft and warm, his beard tickling her skin. When she did not remove her hand, he tried to free his face from her touch with a turn of his head. "I am sworn," he started.

"Then do not touch me," Philippa interrupted, equally as quietly.

He was leaving, Margaret had come, and Roger would soon be here. So, too, would Anne, bringing with her the bonds of propriety that had dictated all of Philippa's life. Her only chance to know this wonderful man was slipping away. She brushed the ruffled hairs of his beard back into place. From there her fingers stroked a light caress up his jaw, along the curve of his whole cheek, across the rise of his brow, then down the crooked line of his nose. His eyes closed and he drew a slow breath, leaning his head back against the wall.

Within her rose a warm, soft feeling, encouraged by his sigh. She once again brushed her fingertips across his lips. Trailing her fingers down the strong line of his neck, she followed the breadth of his shoulder and the hard curve of his upper arm. The warmth increased. Never before had she felt so alive or aware. Her hand came to a rest against the powerful swell of his chest. Where his mail had made any human contact impossible, the soft material of his shirt and tunic provided no such barrier. His body's warmth flowed unhindered through her fingers and into her own flesh. Instead of inspiring caution, the aggressive heat of him urged her into leaning nearer. Her blood tingled. It was a heady feeling, like the strong wine she'd tasted yesterday.

Beneath her palm she felt the steady beat of his heart. The regular thrumming seemed to grow in intensity until the coursing of her own life's blood met and matched it. Her roaring pulse demanded movement. Bracing both hands against his chest, she rose to her toes. Ever so gently, she lay her mouth atop his. He drew a short, sharp gasp against her caress, but made no other motion. Her eyes shut against the rush of sensation. His lips were soft beneath hers, his beard rasped against her jaw. The taste of him was pleasant. When she leaned more heavily against him, her mouth shifted on his. The pressure intensified in this new position, sending the most incredible tingle through her from her head to her toes.

A responding quiver shot through him, startling her. She retreated, but only a little way, until their lips met in a light grazing of flesh against flesh. The new heat within her cried out against the loss of physical contact. Her eyes opened.

His brow was furrowed almost as if in pain, his eyes still shut. His shoulders were tensed, his hands splayed against the wall. She sighed and started to ease back down onto her heels. From deep in his throat came a sound of such loss, she gasped against it. "Nay," he breathed in plea. His eyes opened slowly to watch her, again their dark depths alight with the knowledge that what he wanted he could not have. "Philippa, how am I to continue without you now that I know you? You are mine."

Crying out in her longing for him, she leaned against

him, twining her arms around his neck in a desperate need to be as close as possible. She gasped against a sudden quickening in her most female of places. He shifted slightly and that shivery life reoccurred. She pressed her lips to his neck. He murmured in pleasure and she trembled. She raised her mouth to his again, but this time his lips caught hers, his kiss deepening until he devoured her in his need. His passion overwhelmed her until she tore her mouth free of his and drank in air with tearing gasps.

When their gazes met, she laughed in sheer joy at the blaze of wanting in his eyes. Oh, to be cherished so, to be so deeply loved. Mary, but it was agony not to feel his mouth on hers. She threw herself against him, her lips taking his with a burning need of her own. He groaned deeply. Every second of contact fed her starving heart.

Crockery clattered against the floor. *"Mon Dieu,"* Anne cried out. "Temric, what are you doing? Have you gone mad?" she finished in English.

"Too soon," Philippa cried out softly against his mouth. She slipped down, heels returning to the floor, then rested her head against his neck.

"Not soon enough," Temric breathed, leaning his cheek against her head. "You must release me, *ma petite*."

"But I am so empty without you," she murmured, her words broken by the slightest sob as she turned just a little to face the maid.

Anne was not alone. Behind her stood a slim youth with dark hair spilling into his face. Although he gawked at her, Philippa kept her attention on the maidservant. "It is not his fault, Anne," she began in explanation.

"Hie," the servant interrupted, gesturing that Philippa should step away. "Your sister comes. Temric, sit on that stool and do not move."

Too late. Lady Rowena pushed past the boy to enter the now crowded chamber. Her swift glance took in her sister's loosened gown, bare feet, and uncovered hair, then noted her intimate nearness to Graistan's master-at-arms. "Philippa, what is this?" Her voice was hard and cold.

Temric stepped around her to stand before his lady. "How dare you imprison me," he said harshly. "You have no right to treat me in this way."

"Do I not?" Lady Graistan's tone was icy with the power she owned. She was not in the least intimidated by the man towering over her, despite his clenched fists and threatening stance. Philippa stared at her in awe.

"That old hag drove our ponies so hard that Gareth says they must be destroyed. Does she think I will give her free rein to abuse one of my servants, as well? Over my dead body and do not dare to open your mouth to tell me you are no man's servant. You cannot have it both ways. Either you are common or you accept what Rannulf has tried to give you."

"I am a son of Graistan," Temric roared. "You have stripped me of all honor. Let the bitch of Lindhurst have the rest of me."

Rowena pressed her fingertips into his chest. "I am sick of all this prattle over honor. It was Rannulf's filthy honor that nearly cost us both our lives and caused me to miscarry. Now hold your tongue and sit down. Anne, come look at his face." There was no brooking the command in her voice.

Philippa stared openmouthed as the warrior let himself be forced into sitting down on the tiny stool. Rowena was not finished. She whirled to face her sister. "Shame on you for such improper behavior. You look like a harlot."

Philippa's mouth tightened. What right had her sister to judge her? Like Margaret, she would steal what little joy could be wrung from life. Rage rushed through her, the anger so surprising, Philippa gulped it back in shock. It simmered within her, barely under her control.

Anne stepped between the two noblewomen. "My lady," she said to Rowena, "mayhap I misunderstood your command for I thought only to bring Lady Lindhurst here as swiftly as possible. I would not let her finish dressing. Then I left her without help or companion, not realizing you meant to bring Temric here as well. Which should I do first, your sister's hair and gown or the sewing of Temric's face?"

"Well, that is at least half an explanation," Rowena replied, her tone still angry. "Go, get your healing things. I can help my sister." As Anne left, Lady Graistan turned her attention to the youth. "Who is this boy?"

"My half brother, Peter," Temric retorted. "My mother's youngest son."

Rowena made a sound of extreme irritation. "Jesu, this place has more brothers than rats have fleas. Make yourself useful, Peter. Pick up those bits of pottery so my sister does not cut her feet."

Her French was too fluid for a boy still being tutored in the language. "She spoke too quickly, Temric, what did she say?" At Temric's swift translation, Peter complied without complaint.

Rowena handed Philippa her shoes, then came to

tie her gown's laces. Every motion, even the sound of her breathing, was harsh and hostile. Philippa fought back her resentment. Sisters should understand and shield each other, not betray happiness with anger.

She shoved a foot into one shoe, snarled, tore it off, and pried the comb from its toe. Once it was empty, she stomped it and its mate on, then pulled their bindings tight. She dragged the comb through her tangles, then plaited the heavy mass with quick fingers. With no tie for the braid's end, the thing reopened halfway when she threw it over her shoulder. All the while, anger spiraled steadily upward and almost out of her control. She gulped it back where it belonged.

"Well, do not stand there, put on your head covering," Rowena said shortly.

Philippa grabbed up the wisp of material meant to guarantee modesty and untangled it to find it was not the simple square she knew. Yesterday, Anne had helped her with it, wrapping it around her throat and pinning it in place. "I do not know how." She threw it away from her, but it was so thin it only drifted lightly to the ground.

"Leave her be, Rowena," Temric said. "If you wish to spill your ire on someone, use me. My shoulders are broad enough to bear the consequences for both of us."

Rowena turned on him all too swiftly. "So you should! Dear God, what am I to think? First, you are attacked in our courtyard by that old woman who claims you kidnapped my sister. When I intervene to save you from a beating, you turn and attack Graistan's men. I send you to keep my sister safe from those bent on using her to their own ends only to find you embracing her."

Philippa shrieked in impotent fury. "Why do you assume I can be so easily used? It was me who held him in my arms and forced on him my attentions, even against his warning that I should not." She gasped, stunned by her anger. Never in twelve years of marriage had she expressed such rage. Now, here, after two days of freedom, it seemed she'd lost all control.

"I did not do enough to stop her for I did not wish her to do so," Temric added softly.

Rowena stared at them in growing horror. "Temric, you are brother to my husband and she is my married sister." In her voice lay the God-fearing tones of one raised by the Church.

"I do not care," Philippa retorted. "If I hurt you with my attitude, then I am sorry. It is my soul and if I choose to damn myself, let me."

"You must not speak so!" her sister breathed, glancing over her shoulder as if preparing for the devil's imminent arrival.

"Let it be, Rowena." Temric's voice was sad. "I am off to live with my mother for a goodly time to come, and Philippa returns to Lindhurst when the bishop is done with her. What lies in our hearts will ever be just that, the dreams and wishes of our hearts. At least you now understand my reason for haste in departing this morn."

Philippa caught her breath at the finality of it. He would never pursue her. If she chose to support Roger, she would be condemned to a life of unbearable loneliness. To have seen and been denied love was a sort of death in itself.

The thought of death reminded her of Margaret. "Rowena, now that you know he intended no wrong, tell me he is safe from Margaret and Roger. Truly, he did no more than stop my lord's mother from beating me into unconsciousness so Oswald would not bring me before the bishop. You cannot let her have him."

Rowena threw up her hands in disbelief. "Dear God, you make it sound as if I allow any passing stranger to murder Graistan's folk. Believe that I will do all I can to hold him safe, but it is not solely up to me. Margaret can and will present her complaint to the bishop. Since my husband's half brother so foolishly insists on maintaining his common status, she has the right to demand his punishment."

"I *am* common," he said irritably.

"And noble as well," Rowena snapped back. "When I see the life to which you condemn yourself, my heart quakes for Jordan. I pray he has more sense than his uncle."

Anne reentered, her healing wares on her tray. She glanced swiftly at each of the room's occupants as if to gauge the atmosphere before she knelt beside Temric. After wiping away the remains of his spilled blood, she gently pried and prodded at his face.

"It only needs stitching along the cheek," Philippa offered, then knelt beside her to search Anne's bits and pieces for a length of very fine thread. "If you use this I think it will make a thinner scar for him."

Temric grunted. "You can leave it as it is for all I care. Let me bear the mark as a reminder of what it cost me to lose control."

From behind them, Rowena made a quiet sound followed by Peter's yelp of dismay. Temric leapt from his stool as Philippa shot up from her heels. Rowena hung limply in the boy's arms.

"I did nothing," he protested squeakily in his native tongue. "Truly, Temric."

"Do not worry over it, Peter," Anne reassured the boy in the same language as she came more slowly to her feet. "Our lady is as fine a one as Graistan's ever known, but she cares not much for blood or the repairing of wounds."

Philippa laughed. "Rowena, squeamish? That is hard to believe for all the cuts and scrapes of her younger years." Her own English was almost accentless.

All three of them stared at her in stark surprise.

"What is it?" she asked with not a little pride. "Have you never heard one such as I speak English? Margaret made me learn. She thinks I am united with her against the commoners and tell her what they say about her, but as she cannot understand it, I tell her what I want." Her smile was smug.

Lady Graistan groaned and Peter gratefully shifted his burden to his elder sibling.

"Anne, where did Lady Rowena send Lord Lindhurst's dam?" Temric asked.

"To her son's tent out near the river."

"Good, then you may take both your lady and Lady Lindhurst back to the women's quarters. When she awakens, tell Rowena, Lady Rowena," Temric corrected himself, "that I will stay quietly here until the bishop calls. Once you've seen them safe, you may have at my face so long as you bring me a bite to eat. Peter, you can stay with me, but I warn you I will be precious poor company."

"I would lie down for a few moments," Rowena moaned, deathly pale as she leaned back against her brother-by-marriage.

"Come, sister." Philippa put her arm around her shoulders as Anne did the same from the other side. "We will take you to your cot."

As Peter moved out of the way, they led their charge to the door. There Philippa stopped, bringing Anne to a sudden halt as well. She looked at Temric and he met her gaze. His love for her was like a physical thing, enveloping her with his warmth, enfolding her with caring, as it encircled her heart with unfamiliar sweetness.

Breathing against the intensity of it, she willed he might see in her expression a taste of what she bore for him in her heart. An instant later, his eyes closed slightly and his mouth lifted in sad acknowledgment. Somehow, even his sadness comforted her in ways she'd not thought possible.

Chapter Seven

With Rowena between them Philippa and Anne left the room only to pause on the landing. Rowena sighed. "My stomach yet wrenches, but my head steadies. You can let me go."

Philippa stared down the twisting wedge-shaped steps. Passage was easy enough for one person, but it was doubtful that even two slender women might descend side by side. How had they ever forced Temric up here while he fought them? "Well, we cannot help you down these."

"I need no help," Rowena retorted, her voice yet quivering.

"She is so stubborn," Anne whispered in English to Philippa.

Philippa grinned in pleasure at this sharing of a confidence. "As you wish, sister," she said to Rowena. "One of us will walk ahead of you, the other behind in case you fall."

It was a long, slow process, but Rowena did not even slip. By the time they'd reached the hall, Lady Graistan was herself again. The noblewoman strode to the high table, intent on breaking her fast, but Philippa lingered with Anne. "I would thank you for stepping between my sister and I," she said swiftly and in

English. "There was more than a little risk in protecting me."

"No thanks are needed. I saw no point in there being trouble between you when there was no cause for it. You'd made enough for yourself already. It was no great risk on my part, although I think the same cannot be said were this Lindhurst's domain," Anne said.

"You would be right." Philippa nodded. "This place is a marvel of kindness."

Anne shook her head in agreement. "Aye, this place is a good one, but others are not so different. No lord should do to his wife as has been done to you. And if he treats his wife so, I would not much care to be a servant there."

Philippa murmured in agreement, then she frowned. "Truly, Graistan is not so different from other places?"

"There are servants here from a number of households. Ask them. Ilsa, Lady Rowena's maid, is one. Now, I must fetch my cousin a bite to eat and get back to him." She gave Lady Lindhurst a friendly wink.

"He is your cousin?" Philippa cried out, the need to know all she could about the man who loved her lending urgency to her words. "Will you speak to me of him?"

Anne reverted to the language of her masters. "My lady, I cannot. He is a very private man and I would not wish to hurt him."

The sense of companionship Philippa had so briefly cherished ebbed. At Lindhurst, she and its humble folk were bound together in a common hate. Here, her sister passed judgment on her happiness and the servants were much too formal, leaving her trapped between them in loneliness. Her feelings must have shown on her face, for the servant made a soothing noise and brushed gentle fingers against her cheek.

"Poor chick, 'tis no life at all you've had and here I am denying you even a wee bit of joy. I will see what Temric allows although you must not be surprised if he refuses." With a final, brief smile, the maid flew to the table and grabbed up rolls and cheese, then hurried back to the stairs.

Philippa crossed the hall more slowly, studying the bounty laid out on the tables. There were several sorts of fresh rolls beside the usual round manchet breads. Wheels of cheeses, both sheep and cow, lay ready for slicing. A great caldron of grain pottage bubbled on one hearth. Now, her stomach groaned in anticipation. 'Twas a far cry from Margaret's gruel and bread.

When she came to a halt beside Rowena at the high table, she again fought the anger lingering within her. How dare her sister try to make Temric's love for her something shameful. "Might I sit with you to eat, even if my head is yet uncovered?" She had not mastered her emotions, for there was irritation in her tone.

Rowena patted a space on the bench beside her. "Aye, and forgive me," she said, her usually forceful voice lowered to a gentle level. "I should not have chided you. My tongue is ofttimes swifter into motion than my thoughts can follow. You are a woman full grown and make your own decisions. Even still, you should not—ah, what does it matter? I would rather pass our time in happiness than in argument."

Philippa smiled and her spirits lifted. "So would I."

Rowena sighed. "We haven't much time left, you know."

"Nay? I thought they would not return until the

morrow." The roll in Philippa's hand crumbled under the pressure of her fingers.

"Your mother-by-marriage insists that the bishop be called back to hear her complaint against Temric. I've sent for them even though I think the bishop will not be much pleased."

Philippa's heart fell. As always, Margaret cheated her of what she held precious. "I see."

"Nor am I pleased. I do not want you to go," Rowena said quietly.

Philippa tore her roll in bits, the crumbs dropping to the table. "I would stay forever if I could. Rowena, you spent years at your convent. Were folk often beaten?"

Her sister eyed her speculatively. "I think you should not ask this question. It is better not to know what is different, if you cannot leave Lindhurst."

"Aye," Philippa breathed, "it is far easier to live in ignorance for with knowledge comes the need for something new."

From beyond the tall screens that guarded the hall against the door's draught came the porter. "The Lady Edith of Benfield arrives, my lady." He stepped back to his post at Graistan's massive doors.

Philippa leaned back in shock. "You did not tell me you expected Maman," she said.

Rowena gave a pained grin and shrugged. "She went hunting with the bishop and I thought I would have you to myself until their return. I do not know why she is come early. Our messenger has only just left and we cannot expect them until Vespers."

A slight woman dressed in mudstained gowns of green and gray raced the hall, her form yet girlishly slim despite her years. "Philippa! Philippa, my darling, where are you?" she called out. Then she caught sight of the one she sought.

"Philippa," she cried, her face the mirror image of her daughter's, beautiful with joy. Edith launched herself across the room to kneel beside the bench and embrace her child. "Philippa, my love, my darling," she crooned, "I could not believe it when that young cleric told me you were already at Graistan. We did not expect you for days. If I had been told I'd have been here to greet you."

Philippa held herself stiff beneath her mother's caresses. Had her mother known the sort of man Lindhurst was? Pain warred mightily with the part of her that cried out desperately for love. Unable to bear the conflict, she pulled free of her mother's grasp. "Stop," she said when her mother would have grabbed her back. "Stop it."

Edith was too caught up in her own emotions to notice her joy was not returned. "Oh, sweetling, how I have dreamed of this moment. Let me just look at you," she cried as she leaned back to arm's length.

Philippa turned her face to one side. "Maman, control yourself."

The older woman caught her breath in a torn hiccough. "You hate me, it is true! I see it in your face. Nay, it cannot be!" Without warning, Edith twisted to stare at her other child. "You have done this! What foul lies have you been telling her that has destroyed her love for me?"

"Maman," Philippa cried in shock at hatred so openly displayed as hurt flickered across Rowena's face to disappear behind a cold expression.

"Madam, restrain yourself. This is my home and I'll not tolerate your abuse here."

"Ha!" Edith's voice rose in spite as she continued. "Do you yet seek to hear 'yes, my lady' spill from my lips for you? How I will gloat when you must creep back to that convent of yours after tasting this." She waved a hand at the room around her.

"Think what you will, madam," her youngest daughter said with a tiny shrug, "but guard your tongue or be locked outside yon gates until the bishop calls for you. Now, be gone from me."

"Nay!" Edith's word was a protest of desperation as she grabbed Philippa's hands. "Nay, do not let her separate us. I cannot believe that my sweet child despises me. Deny it or I will surely die."

As much as Philippa wished to hate, happy memories welled within her, reminding her of her mother's love and care. "Maman, why did you never come to see me?" she pleaded, letting her mother draw her into an embrace. "You cannot know how I cried for you, but you never came or even sent a message."

"But I do send you missives. Your husband returns them, saying you hate me and despise our life-style at Benfield. How hard I have struggled to believe it cannot be true. When Benfield died and I was free to come, I begged your lord to let me see you, but he said you wanted nothing to do with me," Edith caught herself. Her eyes narrowed and her voice deepened in confusion. "What is this? Why do you know nothing of this?"

"Roger never gave me your messages and I would not have refused you if you'd come." Philippa's voice was quiet, belying her joy at her mother's words. "He would not have you see how I am treated at Lindhurst, I think. Rowena says he refuses Graistan's hospitality, residing instead in his tent down near their river. If he knew I was already here, he would insist I stay in that tent and refuse you access to me. He wants no interference in his ownership of me."

Edith's eyes flew wide at her words. "Do you say he hurts you and tries to hide that by keeping me away from you?"

"Hurts her?" Rowena said with a breath of scorn. "You should see the pretty belt of scars he's laid on her midsection. How could you have wed her to such a monster?"

Their mother paled in shock at her words, then shock disappeared into denial. "Nay, you lie," Edith said to her younger child. "Roger is a handsome knight, noble and true, who values my baby for her delicacy and cherishes her for the refinement and the civility she brings to his hall. You say these things because you are jealous of her."

"Nay. Maman. 'Tis I who am jealous of Rowena," Philippa said, her joy dying into disappointment. "Her husband is gentle and kind and loves her dearly."

"How can you defend her when she insults your husband?" Edith cried, persisting in her refusal to believe. The facade cracked ever so slightly. "He swore to me he would care gently for you and he is too fine a knight to be forsworn."

"Is he? How do you know this, Maman?" Philippa asked, depression swirling through her as her mother refused to admit her mistake. "What questions did you ask of him? What proofs did you take against his vows of caring? Maman, 'tis you who would make lies of the truth. Why did you give me to him? I was but twelve and could have lingered at your hearth a year or two longer." The ache in her heart made her voice break as she spoke.

Philippa watched her mother struggle with the truth, but her need to believe her child had been safe all these years was the victor. "Benfield forced my hand. He meant to pollute the fineness I'd given you with base things. I could not let him. You were no farm wife, but a true lady."

Philippa stared at her mother in shock. "But, Maman, I am a farm wife. What do you think Lindhurst is, save a tiny manor with fields and stock, just like Benfield."

"Well, I knew that," Edith snapped in irritation. "I had only a little dowry left to give you since Benfield would not let me offer our manor as your inheritance. Some of your suitors expected you to do manual labor, as Benfield would have taught you. That's why I chose Roger. He vowed himself pleased with your needle-work and songs, wanting no more than that from you. He said there were others to do the work at Lindhurst."

"Then he lied," Philippa said flatly, unable to believe her mother could be so blind. Every manorial lady worked alongside her servants; it was necessary for survival. "Maman, I am Lindhurst's most noble house servant."

Edith gasped and bent at her words. Then she reared back and grabbed her daughter's hands. "Oh, but they are ruined!"

Startled by her mother's odd reaction, Philippa looked at her hands and found she liked them. "Maman, I do not think them ruined. They are capable and strong. With the help of Lindhurst's midwife, I have even learned to heal with them."

Edith's eyes narrowed and her mouth became a ragged line. " 'Tis his mother who's done this to you. She is naught but an ale wife, always scrabbling in the dust for her next coin. How that woman produced so fine a son, I will never know. But to let you foul your hands with the blood of commoners?" Her final cry was one of outraged despair. By the smoky light of the fires and torches her mother's beautiful face became an ugly mask.

The new anger now residing within Philippa burst back into life. "Nay, I sought the lessons of my own volition."

Lady Benfield leapt to her feet, her voice rising with her. "Then you have betrayed all I tried to teach you."

Rowena gave a sharp laugh. "Madam, this haughtiness of yours stinks on one whose position as Lady Benfield places her barely above those who serve her."

"I was not always so," Edith snapped, ancient anger in her face. "I was intended for an earl."

"But for her, eh, madam?" Rowena pointed to Philippa.

"Is this the reason for my odd upbringing, Maman?" Philippa asked, her voice now strained and harsh as she came slowly to her feet. "Did you dream that I might claim what you had been denied? That some earl would ride by and see what you'd made of me, then beg to wed me?" She threw her hands up in disgust. "Ach, if marrying a powerful lord demands I treat those beneath me with cruelty and callousness, I spit on your teachings."

"Nay." Edith vehemently shook her head. "Nay, you twist my intentions. Is it wrong to want a fine home for a beloved daughter? Or that she should be insulated from the crudities of life?"

"It is when that daughter has no chance of achieving such a home." Philippa pressed clenched fists to her forehead. Her mother's professed love was tainted by motivations far less noble. If Temric had offered for her all those years ago, her mother would have refused him, regardless of the fact that he would have provided her with a much kinder life than she'd endured as Lady Lindhurst. Marrying her precious child to a bastard would never have suited Maman's grandiose pretensions.

"I cannot bear it," Philippa cried. Within her grew a need to weep until she could feel no more. She hurried away from the table, paying no heed to where she went. A moment later she leaned against the wall at the hall's far side, near the chapel stairs. Yet, her tears remained caught inside her. They choked her, made her work for breath. Edith came to stand beside her.

Philippa gasped against the pain and glared at her mother. "Sweet Mary, Maman, you made of me nothing but a silly plaything, of no value to anyone in the life I've had to live. How dare you despise the things about me that I have come to prize? You are no kinder than my husband if you rail against ruined hands when I tell you that you wed me to a monster." She shook her head in disbelief.

Edith's brow creased in despair and all trace of her youthfulness departed. "Forgive me. I could not bear to hear you say so when I thought he loved you. Look what my arrogance has done to you." Tears etched trails of hopelessness into her still smooth cheeks. "I cannot save you, not even with my inheritance. If I give it to him, he will yet keep you to abuse. If I take it from him, will he not abuse you all the more because of my betrayal? What am I to do?"

Philippa sighed. How carefully Margaret and Roger

had woven their tangle of lies around those they wished to use. Had Temric not stolen her from Lindhurst, they might well have succeeded in their plot before a single misdeed had been revealed. "Rowena thought to find some grounds for dissolution."

"Nay"—Edith sadly shook her head—"that cursed mother of his made certain that nothing would keep them from holding the fields you brought Lindhurst."

"What of my father? Is there any degree of relationship there?" She let the question slip quietly from her.

Edith frowned in confusion. "Benfield?"

"Nay, Maman," Philippa said slowly, "my true father."

Edith's eyes dulled until they were dark and empty. The arrogance was gone, leaving only festering hurt as ancient as her pride. "I would give you anything, even my life if you asked for it, but not that. To speak aloud what you desire would let them name me whore by calling you bastard. Your creation is the one precious thing left to me. I would die without that memory."

With that, she shut her eyes as if to block out her daughter's image, then turned and walked away. Philippa watched her go, her loneliness weighing all the more heavily upon her. If she admitted to the bishop what she knew of her birth, she would destroy her mother along with herself. Ignorance had been so easy. The tears trapped in her chest clamored for release.

"Lady Lindhurst?" The voice was rich and deep.

Philippa turned toward the short, downward stairs. From the shadows at their base appeared a small man, fragile with age, his freckled pate covered with only wispy clouds of pale hair. When he extended his hand, his blue eyes warm and inviting, her heart calmed. Without further consideration, she descended the few stairs to let his gnarled fingers close about hers.

"Come, take a moment to compose yourself." Hints of great power and beauty lurked in his voice.

"Father," she breathed, suddenly realizing who he was, "I should not be here. My hair is undone and uncovered."

"Child, I am deaf. You must speak directly at me so I might read your words upon your lips," he said, his tone easy and unhurried. "But if the concern I see on your face is due to your state of dress, be at ease. Your heart's need overwhelms all else."

He led her into the holy chamber. A few candles had been set into the ornate branches to drive away the day's dimness. Their meager light did little to lift the heavy atmosphere. Outside the narrow windows behind the altar, Philippa saw the steady drip of rain.

Here, too, she saw the painted wall, portraying the miracle of loaves and fishes. If her ill-thought words to Temric upon her arrival at Graistan had insulted God, she'd openly defied His law by her lust for Temric this day. "Father, I should not—" Her breath caught at the loneliness filling her.

"Sit, child," he said and urged her down to sit upon the altar step. Philippa freed her hand from his and accepted his arm around her shoulders. With her face buried into her palms, she cried until the pain emptied from her heart. Through it all, he crooned to her like a mother to her babe, his voice deep and soothing as he rocked her against his shoulder.

When she was at last hollow and gasping, she wiped her face with the hem of her overgown and looked up. There was evidence of her tears on the breast of his tunic. "I am sorry," she said brokenly, "I have stained your clothing."

He shook his head. "It is only water, the water of angels, but water nonetheless. Now, tell me why it is you mourn as if for the dead." Taking her chin, he gently held her face toward him so he could watch her lips.

"Oh, Father, I am so afraid," she said, her words breaking with dry sobs. "Do you know any of this business my lord has brought before the bishop?"

"I know that your husband claims you should take all from your sister Lady Rowena as you are the eldest, and denies the will which calls you illegitimate."

"Well," she said, trying desperately to keep her mouth from trembling, "I am not legitimate."

"You are certain?" He raised shaggy brows in question.

"Aye, my father—Lord Benfield explained it to me after he caught a maid taunting me for it."

"Do you believe your husband is aware of your bastardy?"

She nodded, the movement restrained by his continuing hold on her chin.

"Ah, then his claims are knowingly false. And is he aware also that you know you are not legitimate?"

"Aye, I believe so. For this reason my husband came alone when the bishop called for both of us. When the bishop's man, Oswald, asked for me, my lord's mother sought to convince them I was not myself."

"Ah," he said slowly, his eyes mellowing as he studied her. "I am understanding all much better now."

"What am I to do?" A single tear slipped from the corner of her eye and trailed down her cheek. "I cannot lie to a bishop if he asks me of my parentage, but my husband is a cruel man and I fear his reaction if I speak truthfully. Yet, if I allow my fear to keep me silent, he might well steal my sister's inheritance."

"Child, you make yourself more powerful than you are. Only our Lord can allow or disallow. You need only trust in your faith to show you the right path."

She shivered at his certainty, for she lacked what he believed would guide her. "Father, I think God wants no more of me for I have grievously sinned. I love a man who is not my husband and who is brother-by-marriage to my sister." Her eyes closed as she awaited his shock. Alone, in the warm darkness of her mind, the silence between them was painful.

When he finally spoke, his words were gentle, not accusing. "I know I am not your confessor, but for a man who cannot hear, I am a good listener."

She sighed and opened her eyes. "Aye, I think I need to spill what lies in my heart or else it may well drown me. On the day before yesterday, while on the road to Graistan, Temric and I were briefly alone. In that time he kissed me and said I should have belonged to him.

"Today, although I knew full well how wrong it was, I have kissed him. I cannot show you shame for what I've done. Instead, I am glad for every instant of my sin, even though my heart will be torn asunder when I must leave Temric and be gone from here. If you say I should love my husband, know that I did try, but he drove from me all feeling with his brutality."

She fell silent, braced to hear the priest's shocked contempt. He only regarded her with a bland interest.

His quiet drove her to ask, "Have I not committed both adultery and incest?"

"I would say you have contemplated adultery, but it has not yet happened. As for the incest," he paused here and pursed his lips for a moment, then continued. "What I am about to say must stay between just we two."

"Aye, as you wish, Father," she said, startled that he should trust her with a confidence.

"I think I have lived too many years to recite with any belief those bits of dogma that were created by man for man's sake." Her surprise teased from him a smile. "Have I startled you? I suppose it would, to hear a priest say such a thing. When any man, be he king or commoner, can so easily cry 'incest' to rid himself of an unwanted wife, the concept becomes suspect in my mind. That is especially so since the couple wed in full knowledge that they breached their degree of relationship."

His blue eyes glowed with wry amusement. "Now that you have confessed, shall I give you your penance?"

"Father, I will humbly perform all you lay upon me. Oh, were it all I would have to bear. I am so afraid to die." The words tore from her and she shuddered.

"What is it you mean by this?"

His calm tone coaxed from her what she could not spill to anyone else. Philippa looked steadily at him. "My husband is easily driven to violence by perceived insults. When Temric took me from Lindhurst, he did so in his arms. By this act alone am I irreparably tainted in my lord's eyes. Should this inheritance be denied him, I know he will want me no more. I think I will have to die so he might remarry."

"God's Church does not allow a man to murder his wife," the priest's voice rose in warning.

Again she shook her head against the constraints of his hand on her chin. "If his passions drive him to it, he will cry and mourn, truly grieving for the wrong he's done. If he means murder, well, my husband is no fool nor is his dam. Accidents happen," she added with a weary shrug. "You can protest all you wish, but I will be just as dead."

"I suppose it is no good to ask him to swear to hold you safe. The word of a man who so cravenly seeks to steal another's inheritance cannot be trusted."

"Accidents happen," she repeated quietly.

"You are certain, then?"

"I am." There was something soothing about stating it so directly, as if she spoke about another and not herself.

The old man's gaze clouded as he sat deep in thought. "Child," he said a moment later, "I think I will be beside you as Bishop William resolves this issue. After he is quit of it, I will tell him you spoke with me about your desire to enter a convent and serve God. In that way, you may be freed from your marriage and your husband freed of you so he can in time wed again."

Convent life would be better than Lindhurst, but it would still be life without the love she craved. "My heartfelt thanks for your offer, Father. I would gladly enter a nunnery rather than remain married to Lindhurst. Would you give me my penance now?"

He studied her a long moment, then nodded. "Aye, but you will not care much for what I say. I command you to stand before your husband and Bishop William and say nothing until you feel our Lord commanding from you some response."

"How will I recognize what is mine own response and what is coming from another source?" she protested.

"You will have no doubt when you feel it," he assured her, then released her chin to speak the required words of forgiveness and blessing over her. Before he would let her rise, he placed a swift kiss on her forehead. "What I lay upon you is a harder task than most folk can tolerate, but you are equal to it. Go with God."

"Thank you, Father," she said quietly, struggling with this strange penance and confused by his confidence in her. She was nothing but a pawn surrounded by rooks, knights, bishops, and one woman who believed herself a countess, if not a queen.

She turned to leave and found Anne standing in the chapel's doorway as if she'd been waiting for a goodly time. Philippa briefly wondered what the servant might have overheard, then dismissed it. No one eavesdropped on what was said between a priest and his penitent.

When she drew close enough, she asked in breathless question, "What of Temric?"

The serving woman shook her head briefly, her look filled with pity. "He says you are right and it is better if neither of you thinks any more of the other. It pained him terribly to say so. Know you, we all wagered that when he finally lost his heart it would be completely, and we were right. You own it now."

Philippa glanced away. Aye, and he owned hers, but for how long? If she lived through this ordeal, it would most surely be without him. Temric's care for her, and hers for him, would be no more than hidden memories, like those her mother cherished for the man who'd sired her child. Could she bear such emptiness?

"Have you had enough to eat?" Anne asked gently.

"I think I am not hungry," Philippa replied, so lost and lonely. She shoved her pain down deep inside and followed Anne back into the women's quarters.

Chapter Eight

The women had slowly drifted from their earlier
excitement back to everyday chores. Spinners
spun, sewers sewed, and those making baskets worked
with swift and flexible fingers. Her sadness sent Philippa to the narrow windows. She leaned into one,
stretching nearly her whole length along its depth.

The heavens wept fine tears as if in tune with her
heart. Clouds, gray and thin, slid past her airy perch,
borne by a dreary wind. She pressed her cheek against
the cool stones and prayed the mournful day might
ease her heart.

Rowena came to stand behind her, her hand stroking her back in a quiet caress. "If I had known her
reaction, I would have forbidden our mother to speak
with you. I fear you are hurt worse by her than by
your husband's behavior."

Philippa sighed as she straightened and turned
toward her sister. "I am so confused I no longer know
what to think, save that her love for me is hopelessly
tangled in her enormous pride." She managed a halfhearted laugh. "I think I might have been better
served if she'd split this ambition of hers between us
rather than giving it all to me."

Rowena made a quiet sound. "I think I will let you

keep it. No longer do I harbor any jealousy toward you for her twisted affections."

Somehow, their banter made Philippa's emotions steady and right themselves within her. When she smiled, it was genuine. "My thanks."

Her sister laid an arm around her waist. "Ilsa is dancing about back there because she wishes I would sit and rest. Will you join me? Anne has made a posset for you." She led her to a pair of well-cushioned chairs with backs like half barrels. "While you sip it, we can play a game. Do you like chess?"

"I did once, but I have not played since leaving Benfield," Philippa said, feeling the safety and peace of Graistan close around her. She did not have much longer. "If you do not mind that you must tell me the rules again, I would play with you."

"I do not mind at all." Rowena waited as her maids set the gaming table between them, then began to put the pieces into place. Philippa sipped from the cup Anne handed her, enjoying the rich flavors of warmed wine and herbs with a hint of honey for sweetness. The drink was potent, its effect spreading throughout her to ease her tenseness.

Rowena glanced at her, a pawn in hand. "How is it you continue to survive?"

Philippa smiled. "For you it would be impossible. My fiery lion of a sister would not long endure before exploding. I do not know who would be destroyed in what followed, you or them. But then, Roger would never have wanted you for he sought the quiet dove in me, believing I had not the strength to resist him. Still, I am not as helpless as they believe me. Or as unsupported as Roger wishes I were."

She drank the posset to its dregs, then handed Anne

the cup. "Things are different here. You are lady and they serve you, the line between you and them is clearly marked. At Lindhurst, those who serve have made me one of their own, while I have made them mine. Abuse is shared, one taking the beating for another who cannot tolerate it just then.

"It helps that I've convinced Margaret I am an idiot. She thinks I cannot cook or clean and am a dimwit when it comes to counting. Crockery slips from my fingers as if it were buttered. Do you have any idea how difficult it is to accidentally spill a jar of milk on purpose?" Philippa raised her brows at her own rhetorical question.

"You do not!" Rowena straightened in surprise.

"I do, then I take the punishment which follows with great pride in my achievement." Philippa laughed in satisfaction.

Pride and pain mingled in her sister's eyes. "I think now that I have complained over events in my own life without just cause."

With a mild sound of acknowledgment, Philippa leaned over the table. "Well, enough of that. I would rather forget everything in my past and future to enjoy each instant of my present. Is this piece not the rook? It moves straight ahead, does it not?"

"Aye," Rowena said and began to explain in earnest each piece and its function. With Father Edwin's promise and her sister's love, Philippa immersed herself in her last hours of freedom.

The midday meal came and went, far less elaborate than that of the previous day. Rowena said it was because the bishop was expected back and she wished to offer him a fine dinner rather than the usual cold tray. For all her insistence that she was well enough,

Rowena found her cot and dropped to sleep while Jordan was at his lessons. When none of the maids would allow her to assist in their chores, Philippa wandered around the room at a loss for something to do.

"My lady," Anne asked after a brief, whispered conversation with Ilsa. "It is yet hours before we expect the bishop to arrive and there's time to waste. Would you care to bathe again?"

"Bathe?" she replied in shock. "Again? So soon?"

"I only thought you might enjoy it," Anne replied. "It will be a pleasant way for you to pass your time," she offered.

"You will spoil me," Philippa protested weakly, remembering how the warm water had lapped at her chin and Anne's careful massage. "My sister would not mind?"

Ilsa waved away her comment. "Hardly. Anne, make for Lady Lindhurst a bath."

Philippa soaked in the water until she was nigh on blue with cold and Anne insisted she step out. Later, when she'd again donned her borrowed finery, she returned to her chair to let Anne tend her hair. The morning's mist had cooled into a thick fog. Clouds descended to swathe Graistan in their heavy folds, muffling all sound, even that which echoed up from the courtyard directly below the windows. Tallow lamps had been set out and a brazier was filled with hot coals to ward off the chill. In this hazy, lazy atmosphere, the long smooth draw of the comb through her hair lulled Philippa into a peaceful state. She listened with a smile as Anne and another maid argued amiably over the properties of certain herbal concoctions.

Suddenly the door burst open to slam against the wall behind it. Leather hinges groaned in agony, shattering all peace. Women screamed; Philippa leapt up, her hair spilling around her in a cloak of gold.

Her husband, still dressed in a coarse and filthy hunting gown beneath a sleeveless leather vest, stood in the doorway. His wide brow and high cheekbones were spattered with mud, his blond hair touseled from traveling, the smooth line of his jaw covered by several days' worth of beard. Perfectly arched brows were drawn over his long, thin nose as his savage blue gaze sought her in a sea of female faces.

She stood frozen, incapable of breathing. Father Edwin was wrong, she had no courage. Roger's full lips twisted into a cold snarl when he found her. In dull acceptance she sank into the chair and awaited his coming brutality.

"What lies have you been telling that your mother comes attacking me in the hall calling me wife beater?" His words were clipped and cold, all the more dangerous for their calmness.

Philippa hung her head in silence, knowing he sought no reply. She withered in the shadow of his hate, her soul racing for safety deep within her. What a fool she'd been to think her sister could hold her safe from her husband. Mud spewed from his boots as the tall, lean man stepped into the room. Now he would come claim what he owned.

"Stop him," Rowena said in quiet command as she rose from her cot. Instantly Graistan's women formed a solid wall between them, separating Lindhurst from his wife. With Ilsa at her side, Rowena took her place in front of her women. "How dare you enter into this private chamber." Her tone reflected all the power and influence of her position.

Philippa straightened a little. Aye, Rowena had not

a man's physical strength, but her sister's icy wrath had tamed Temric's rage. But her hope crashed at Roger's reply.

"Pampered bitch, you stand between me and what is mine." Lord Lindhurst turned his vicious gaze on his hostess. Philippa hunched her shoulders against his tone, protectively crossing her arms over her breasts.

"If I am a pampered bitch, then you are an arrogant, insolent piece of horse dung," Rowena replied as if stating fact rather than throwing an insult. Roger's fair complexion warmed to bright red.

"Rowena, you mustn't," Philippa gasped out. Not even Margaret dared cross Roger when he was like this. "I will do as he commands."

"You most certainly will not," Rowena snapped over her shoulder to her sister. "Anne, you keep her behind me if you have to knock her senseless to do it."

"Aye, my lady," the maid replied, her tone indicating she'd happily comply.

"Give me my wife." Roger took a step forward.

Philippa listened in shock. His voice had lost its ferocity. He was backing down!

"I will not. She does not leave this chamber until the bishop calls for her." For all her slight height, Rowena seemed to tower over him.

"She is mine," he growled, fists still clenched with rage. "You have no right to step between a man and his wife."

Rowena's shrug was as cool as her voice. "Go, then. Complain to the bishop that I keep her from you. If he insists upon her return, I will do so. But I warn you"—her voice grew more forceful—"I have already burned the rags in which she arrived and I will take back all I have given her. Will you parade a naked woman through a hall filled with churchmen? Even one as rude and ill-mannered as you or that ass who claims to have spawned you are not so addlepated. Now, immediately remove your stinking hide from my room."

Philippa watched in awe when her husband, his face now mottled in fury, hesitated in indecision. It was obvious he wanted her, but it was equally clear he had no idea how to take her now that intimidation had not worked. He stepped back.

Philippa blinked and in that instant Roger became Dickon, the child Rowena had once attacked. The two of them were no different, both of them all bluff and arrogance with only their size and the power of their rages to support their bloated estimations of themselves.

Roger raised a fist. "Sharp-tongued shrew, why does your husband tolerate you? If you were my wife, I would swiftly teach you to properly respect men."

These words echoed through Philippa and something deep inside her surged free, refusing to be controlled or denied. Her fingers shook and her knees trembled. The power of it rushing through her forced her to her feet. Was this what the priest had meant?

She stared over the women's heads at Roger without the slightest fear. He glared back, his look forceful and threatening. When her gaze did not falter, she saw surprise flicker across his expression. "Roger, it would be a wasted effort," she said quietly. "In all the times you have beaten me, I have never gained any respect for you. I think it is because there is nothing in you to respect."

Roger near screamed in outrage and threw himself

toward her, his arms outstretched to grab her. Several spinsters thrust the sharpened ends of their distaffs against his chest. He rebounded off them, moaning in frustration.

"You have infected her with your perverted ways, bitch," he roared at Rowena. "You have destroyed her affection for me!"

It was Philippa who responded. "Roger, how could you dream I might have some affection for you? If it is perverted to expect kind and gentle treatment from lord and home, then you are right to think me infected. Hie yourself back to your tent; I am not ready to leave my sister." If her voice trembled, it was with another wave of righteous anger. No more, her soul demanded, no more.

Rowena added, "Aye, go before we drive you out. Your pride will ache mightily if word were to circle that you were chased, cut and bruised, from Graistan's women's quarters."

"Damn you," he bellowed. His gaze was now frantic, his eyes so wide Philippa could see a ring of white around his irises. "I am your husband, you cannot deny me."

Rage roared through her, consuming not only her fear, but all sensible caution as well. Words tumbled from her lips in a soft and goading whisper. "Come, then," she urged, "come, beloved, tear what you own from their grasp, but what will you have when you are finished? I think I would rather be dead than be your wife."

He caught his breath in shock at her challenge, then released it in what was almost a sob. Hate, confusion, then even hurt flowed one after the other across the handsome planes of his face. Without another word, he turned and stormed out. A serving woman leapt to slam the door behind him.

Rowena whirled on Philippa. "Why did you dare him to kill you?" she cried out. "I've told you I cannot protect you once the bishop has ruled."

Philippa only shook her head. " 'Twas my anger at every bruise or scar he laid on me that demanded I speak. Mother of God, but this journey has shattered all my ignorance. How could I have expected myself to willingly return to hell after this?" She raised a hand to indicate not this rich home, but the folk who gathered around her in loving concern.

"How, indeed," Rowena sighed. "I do not think your husband is pleased at the difference in you." Love mingled with sadness in Rowena's face, but the sadness was tempered with growing respect.

Philippa nodded in agreement, holding tightly to Father Edwin's promise of the convent and peace. It would happen and she would never again return to Lindhurst. There was a touch on her arm and she turned to face Anne.

"Your husband's pride does not care much for what you've done. It will take a miracle to save you," the servant whispered in English. Respect mingled with pain in the maid's dark gaze. "I've come to be fond of you. Might I pray for you?"

"Aye, that would please me well," Philippa replied in the same language. The reality of what she'd done now settled heavily on her shoulders, but beneath its weight was a new liking for herself.

"If Lord Lindhurst is here, Rannulf is also come," Rowena said. "I think I will go greet him."

"You'll not either. Save your strength, my lady, else

this day's liable to lengthen beyond your tolerance," Ilsa warned. "He'll be here to see you soon enough."

It seemed Rowena returned almost gratefully to her chair. "I suppose you are right. I can wait as I have much to answer for. He'll not like it that I've put Temric under guard."

Philippa stared at her sister. "I thought you said he bore a fondness for you."

"So he does," Ilsa snorted, "but their fondness for each other can ofttimes be quite loud." Several women laughed at this, while Rowena made a face.

By the time Philippa's hair was braided with ribbons and properly covered with her wimple, there came a knock at the door. It opened to reveal a tall man dressed in mud-spattered leather garments similar to Roger's. His hair was dark and the planes of his face were harsh, giving him a dour appearance.

"Welcome home, Rannulf," Rowena said, a smile touching her lips, "how was your hunting?"

"I will give you credit for the attempt, but I am not diverted. Once again, you've set Graistan on its ear." Lord Graistan casually braced a shoulder against the door frame. Philippa stared at him, finding that he and Temric shared only their high cheekbones and the bend of their mouths.

When he continued, he seemed neither upset nor angry. "Gareth complains of dead ponies, your mother cries of abuse and protection, while Temric sits in the tower wearing a hair shirt for his loss of honor. Truly, you had no right to step between him and Lindhurst's mother."

"Nay," Philippa cried out, unable to still her complaint. "Nay, you cannot permit him to take that beating. His sacrifice would be wasted."

Lord Graistan's gaze swung around the room until he found her. "Do I assume you are Lady Lindhurst?" he asked. "Come forward, for I would like to see the woman who makes my brother determined to endure a whipping."

When Philippa hesitated, Anne leaned toward her and whispered, "His look is far harsher than he. You need not fear him."

She glanced gratefully at the maid, then threaded her way through the women. When she was as near as she dared, she managed only the faintest gesture of greeting and did not look directly up at him.

He drew her closer still, then raised her head with a hand beneath her chin. With eyes as gray as this day's clouds, he studied her. Then he laughed, his amusement tempering his face with kindness. "Wren, the two of you are as alike as peas, save for your coloring."

In that relaxed minute Philippa dared a plea. "My lord, I beg you, do not let Margaret hurt your brother. Never did he attack my lord's mother, he only took her stick to prevent her from doing me further harm."

He stared at her, his amusement dying. "I think your husband should not see your face when you speak of my brother," he said softly. "Nor my brother's when he speaks of you."

Philippa stepped back a few paces and turned her gaze to the floor. She would not apologize for what she held in her heart, so she said nothing.

It was Rowena who broke the silence. "Will the bishop soon call for her? A late meal awaits him, complete with all his requisite courses. I dared hope to prolong the time my sister spends with me."

Lord Graistan hesitated, then stretched out an arm

in invitation. Rowena rose from her chair to come stand next to him. He caressed her cheek with a gentle hand. "I think he will do nothing until after he bathes and eats, but who is to say for certain? Wren, you've done too well feeding him for he asked again about taking our cook when he leaves."

"What is it he offers us in return?" was her sister's swift reply as she stared up at her lord, the expression on her face suddenly calculating.

"Naught but his goodwill, near as I can tell."

"Hmph, then he cannot have him. Goodwill we gain through Oswald. Now, if he offers something we have use for, and he agrees to take Anne as well for she'll not be separated from her love, only then can we part from our cook."

Philippa glanced at a suddenly blushing Anne while Lord Rannulf laughed. "I missed you these past days and was grateful for your message, despite the crisis you precipitated. I would speak privately with you. Send your women to drive Temric from the tower room; he's martyred himself there long enough. Have them lay my bath in there first, then, afterward, our bedding. The tower chamber is too fine for those knights of William's. They can sleep in the garrison with our own men."

"As you wish, Rannulf," Lady Graistan said quietly.

Philippa watched as Anne gathered up the rolls of oiled cloth used beneath the bathing tub. The maid looked at her and Philippa found in her gaze a sad farewell. It seemed possible they would see no more of each other. She offered Anne a grateful smile and watched her depart the room.

Then her eyes were drawn back to her sister and Lord Graistan as he touched his lips to his wife's mouth. Philippa's heart clutched. Whether she lived or died, she would never again feel Temric's mouth against hers or know his sweet affection for her. Unable to face what she was to be denied, she returned to the window to shield her pain.

Chapter Nine

Temric resettled himself on the stool and stared up at the dark wood of the ceiling. He was tired of sitting here with nothing to occupy his hands. Yet, when Rannulf had told him to go, he'd let pride overrule boredom and refused. If Lady Graistan deemed it necessary to confine him, confined he would stay until the bishop called.

The door opened. He glanced up, then made an irritated sound. "Anne, tell my brother I will not leave. If he wants his bath, let him take it in the bathhouse."

His cousin's response was such an odd whimper, he sat forward to peer at her through the grayed dimness. Her face was a twist of sorrow. "Annette, what is it?"

"She is going to die," she cried softly. "Temric, she is going to die just like my Petrona."

"What do you mean?" he asked harshly, but he already knew of whom she spoke and the answer to his question. It drove him to his feet. Petrona, Anne's daughter, had perished at her husband's hands. Why had he not seen the obvious? No mother battered where a son did not allow it.

"I have seen Lord Lindhurst," Anne cried softly. "Once he owns her again, he will beat her until she

is no more. Lord, but I cannot watch it happen."
There was a terrible catch in her voice.

"Nay," Temric managed to choke out against the
rage that ate his heart.

"Aye," Anne sighed, "but it is worse for that poor
lady. She knows what my child did not. Oh, Temric,
she told Father Edwin that if she denies her husband
his part of this inheritance, he will be finished with
her. She will have to die so he can remarry."

Her words goaded him beyond all control. "I will
kill him," he breathed in a ferocious whisper and
pushed past the maid to run down the stairs.

"Temric, wait," Anne screamed after him. "Nay,
you cannot, you cannot interfere, not you! They will
kill you for it!"

He hurtled down the stairway, then through the
chapel to his garrison door at its opposite end. His
men scattered before him as he stormed into the
room. At his cot, he threw open his chest and ripped
into his neatly packed gear.

"Master," the bravest man finally called, "we meant
you no harm this morn. Please forgive us."

"Forgiven," he barked, now tearing through what
he'd just strewn across the cot. "Jesú Christus, where
is my sword?" There was a flurry of activity until the
weapon was produced.

"What is it, master?" Walter cried out as Temric
refitted the weapon into his belt. "Are we attacked?"

"Nay, we are not." He laughed, the sound evil even
to his own ears. "I would have your word, all of you.
No matter what occurs with me in the coming hours,
you will not move to stop me. When you've sworn,
get the oaths of those who presently guard our walls."
Men who'd previously sat or squatted about the room

rose and lifted their voices in agreement to his request. Their loyalty to their master-at-arms rivalled their loyalty to Lord Graistan.

"Good lads," he said with a nod. "I'll see blood flow before this night's done or die in the trying."

With a salute, he left his domain for the hall, intent on exiting to the courtyard. At the tall screens standing before the massive doors, a woman flew at him.

"Help me," Lady Benfield pleaded, clutching his arm in a desperate grip as she made herself a dead weight to halt him.

"Help you, madam? I think not." He angrily tried to free his arm.

"There is no one else," she cried, still clinging to him. "You are my only hope."

He pulled back on her fingers. She yelped shrilly in pain and released him. A shove sent her sprawling. She rolled to her feet, then wound her hands into his belt. "Nay, you cannot deny me, servant. Help me!"

Her arrogance penetrated his rage like nothing else could. Temric growled in irritation, grabbed her by the arm, and dragged her toward a panel of painted linen on the wall. Yanking the curtain aside, he forced her into a window alcove as deep and as wide as a man was tall. When the cloth fell back into place, they were private.

"Now, my lady, you will tell me why I should aid one who has lied, forged, and most likely murdered to steal from Lady Graistan what belongs to her." It was no request.

"Murder!" Edith shook her wimpled head, the face he'd thought so like her daughter's now swollen and ragged from crying. "Would that I could kill, for it is Lindhurst who would feel the bite of my hate." Her words were harsh and honed to a razor's edge. "There are those here who say you have a care for my daughter Philippa. Help me free her from him."

"My lady!" However softly spoken, his words were no less a shocked cry as he realized how public his affection for Philippa had become. Worse, he had nearly made the most public statement of all when he thought to attack Lindhurst for Philippa's sake. God's blood, it was suicide he'd contemplated. Temric bowed his head in defeat. Not even his own death would free Philippa from her husband.

"You will not help either. How much must I suffer for tying her to him?" She threw back her head and drew a bitter breath. "Now he and his mother hold me in their foul grasp, knowing I dare not spill the truth of her birth in fear of what they will do to her."

They both started when Margaret of Lindhurst's voice came from just outside their alcove. "Bishop William of Hereford, where are you?" Her age-deepened voice rang off the rafters. "That thief Graistan keeps what is my son's from him. Come, do as you are sworn and protect my son's wife from those who would turn her against her husband."

"Bitch!" Edith shrieked. She launched herself from the alcove before Temric could catch her. By the time he'd shoved the curtain aside, she was on Lindhurst's dam, her fingers grasping for the old woman's throat.

A wild swing of Margaret's stick landed a glancing blow on Edith. It was enough to loosen Lady Benfield's grasp. Temric caught the fair woman's arms from behind and lifted her off Margaret.

Edith strained against him, kicking and fighting. His lips close to her ear, Temric whispered, "My lady, do not. This will only make it worse for Philippa." She relaxed instantly and hung from his hold, sobbing with frustration.

"You idiot," Margaret coughed out, struggling up onto her feet as she shoved at her crooked wimple. She had not changed either it or her gown since he'd first seen her at Lindhurst and both were now badly stained. "Why do you attack me? Ho, so it is you again," she said, recognizing Temric.

Her eyes narrowed in satisfaction at his bruised and torn cheek. "Good, you already bear your first mark. You'll take the rest soon enough. I shall lay my complaint before the bishop at the same time I retrieve that dimwit who belongs to my son."

Edith's cry was ferocious. She leapt for the dowager, dragging Temric forward with her fury. "You swore to care for her as if she were your own! You said you would retire to a convent and give to her Lindhurst's keys. Instead, you have abused her and used her as no more than a servant."

Lady Lindhurst's strident voice overrode Edith's. "Abused her? Hardly. Carefully disciplined, surely and rightly so. It is you who abused us by passing off damaged goods as a whole woman. As for being lady of our manor," the woman sneered, "never. Thank the Lord she is barren or we'd have another one as deficient as she to worry over. At least we'll have this inheritance in compensation for all she's cost us."

"Who is it that calls for Bishop William?" Oswald stood on the overhanging balcony, two of the bishop's knights behind him.

"Oswald, Lady Lindhurst has a complaint against me and wishes also that your lord would command Lady Graistan to release Lord Roger's wife to him," Temric called up to him.

"I will not speak with you, little man," Margaret snapped out. "Only the bishop will serve me now."

Oswald's voice was brutal and cold in response. "As you will, my lady." The cleric moved suddenly aside as Rannulf exited Graistan's solar.

"Brother," Lord Graistan called down to him, his face a hard mask, "who enters my hall and names me 'thief'?"

"So here at last is Lord Graistan." Margaret's words were rife with derisive scorn. "Do you believe I might be swayed from punishing this commoner by your claim of relationship? You mistake me for I know well my right in this. Now I add another complaint to my list, this one against your lady for she has refused to give my son his wife."

"Your son violated my lady's private chambers. Be glad I do not peel that boy skin from bone for his audacity." If Margaret did not realize how dangerously she now tread, Temric did. His brother was not one to make idle threats.

The old woman snorted. "My son sought to prevent nonsense and lies from being poured into his wife's wee brain. Too late! You have already turned her against us. You will use her to steal away her inheritance from those who should rightly hold it."

"So, now I am more than just a thief, am I? Cousin," Lord Graistan said to Oswald, "do you hear the poison this snake spews in my hall?"

"Cousin?" Margaret cried in shock, turning her watery gaze on Edith. "Oswald of Hereford is Graistan's cousin? He is the churchman to whom your husband gave his will? Damn you, why did you not warn me before we put our claims before the bishop?"

"I said from the first I did not know who had my

lord's will. Now I am glad I did not know to tell you," Edith hissed in triumphant answer. "But do not let this sudden revelation stop you from dealing another blow to your crippled cause."

Margaret straightened in surprise, then frowned. "What do you mean," she demanded.

Edith gave a harsh laugh. "Shall I count them for you?" She ticked them off as she spoke. "You have disparaged Lord Graistan, insulted his wife, his brother, and his cousin. In demanding that the bishop return at your will, you have annoyed a powerful man, then struck again at him by dismissing his servant as unworthy of your attention. By your own efforts you are closing every ear once willing to listen to your case."

Margaret's thin lips pursed as she understood how she might well have done exactly that. Lady Benfield laughed in cold amusement. "Aye, look closely and see that you are nothing save an arrogant pest who has dared much beyond her station. Do go on," she goaded. "I would not dream of stopping you."

The old woman turned abruptly and tottered for the nearest hearth. There was a sudden franticness to her motions. Temric raised a brow, wondering if it had never occurred to her that the power she held so tightly at Lindhurst would not be the same beyond her own boundaries.

"Tom," Lord Graistan called down to a servant, "see to it that Lindhurst's dam has a bench to sit upon while she awaits the bishop. You may inform her that this matter which so troubles her will be resolved within the next quarter hour. Once William is finished, mayhap she can be induced into swiftly finding her way back whence she came so we might dine in peace."

Edith looked over her shoulder at Temric. "You heard," she said in a low voice. "They will be finished with her."

"Aye," he said bitterly, dropping his hands from her arms, "I heard. Anne, what is it with you?" He motioned for his English cousin to join them.

The maidservant held her tongue until she was near enough to speak without being overheard. "Father Edwin said," she started, then gasped and swiftly blessed herself, "forgive me, Lord, I should not have heard this, much less repeat."

If she battled with her conscience, it was a short war. "Father Edwin said that if he felt Lady Philippa's husband meant to take her life, he would ask the bishop to dissolve their marriage so she might join a convent. There could she live in peace and her husband would be free to remarry after a time."

"Thank God!" Edith cried while Temric grimaced against the thought. Philippa would yet be beyond his reach, but at least she would be safe. Anne's next words shattered his hopes.

"But I have seen her husband's hate for her. I fear no matter how swiftly the bishop moves, Lord Lindhurst will be the quicker. She will be destroyed before the churchman can save her."

"Nay!" Edith gasped out.

Temric smiled grimly. "Then we must be the faster. We will have to purchase the time needed for the bishop to offer her sanctuary."

"You will help," Edith breathed. Her knees weakened in relief and she sank to sit on the hall's rush-covered floor.

"Do not sit there, my lady," Anne said swiftly. She shot Temric a grateful look as she helped the noblewoman to rise. "Come to the farther hearth, away from that—awful person."

He returned to the alcove and let the cloth panel drop back into place. Here, surrounded by the warm closeness, he leaned against the stone and reminded himself he would never know more of Philippa than he did now.

The door opened and Philippa saw it was Lord Graistan once again. She came slowly to her feet, for the look on his face said he was to have no time for bathing. "Am I called for?" she asked quietly. He nodded.

"Rannulf, I would come with her," Rowena cried to her husband.

"Nay, you are too ill." When he saw the argument form on her lips, he warned, "I will brook no discussion on this, Wren."

Rowena turned in her chair to stare at Philippa, her eyes filled with sudden tears. "My heart aches in worry for you."

Philippa went to kneel at her sister's side. "You must not, sweetling. I spoke with your priest earlier. He will plead with the bishop to allow me to take my vows. This I will gladly do to be free of my husband. Does that ease your worry some? Now, dry your eyes and swear you'll bear me always in your heart as I have you in mine. It will be enough." She touched her sister's hand that lay, palm up, in her lap.

Rowena threw her arms around her and held her tightly. After a moment Philippa freed herself from her sister's embrace to wander around the room in farewell. Her hand closed around a distaff. She lifted it as if it were a spear, testing its familiar, balanced weight. "You truly had no fear of Roger, not even in the first instant?" Philippa glanced over her shoulder for Rowena's reaction to her question.

Her sister shook her head. "Why should I have? This is my home and he was grossly in the wrong when he opened that door. He knew that."

Philippa responded with a quiet nod, an inner coldness growing with each passing moment. She clung to Father Edwin's promise, using it as a shield against her fear. Like Temric and Rowena, like all of Graistan, he would keep her safe from harm. Remembering that, she breathed a sigh and said to her sister's husband, "I am ready."

Lord Rannulf offered her his arm and she took it without hesitation. Once past the door, they walked along the balcony toward the stairway. Philippa glanced over the edge at the hall below them.

With the bishop's return, the number of folk within the hall had doubled. Now, hunters, knights, and soldiers gamed at odd corners around the room, the winners' shouts mingling with the losers' moans. Dozens of dogs snapped and growled at each other while a hooded hawk atop a perch freed a single shrill cry, the bells on its hood delicately chiming. Philippa hung back, forcing Lord Graistan to a halt. "So many people," she murmured uneasily in explanation.

Her sister's husband lay a reassuring hand over hers. "They are not all mine. William travels with more folk than he needs so we who are not so powerful can be properly awed. How your sister complained over what their stay will cost us!" Lord Graistan shot her a quick, wry grin.

"It would be no burden if she receives the whole inheritance," Philippa swiftly replied.

Lord Graistan's responding look was quizzical, as if he could not believe she'd meant what she had said. "That is true enough. Come, the bishop would have us wait for him in the hall. He does not wish to appear as if he favors me by descending at my side."

It was a request, not a command. If she'd asked him to linger a moment longer, he would have acquiesced to her need. Temric's brother was as kind as he. It pleased her to know that her sister was wed to such a man. "Aye, my lord," she said, and stepped once again to his side.

Chapter Ten

Temric pushed aside the linen that curtained his alcove to watch his brother lead Philippa down the stairs to the hall. Dear God, but she shimmered, from her long golden braid to the warm apricot of her skin. As he watched his brother's gentle care for her, his rage roared up again, almost out of his control. Lindhurst would die if he hurt her, let the consequences be damned. Force of will alone reined in his blood lust. He needed his head clear until the time came to swing his blade.

She scanned the room and he knew she was looking for him. Pushing aside the drapery, he stepped out of the alcove to lean against the wall and watch her descend. When her gaze found him, she smiled slightly, a tiny private smile that filled him with joy. He returned hers with his own, hoping she would see in it his promise to hold her safe.

Color flushed suddenly into her cheeks, her expression softening. What trick of their births worked here that had left them so hopelessly intertwined in so short a time? He shrugged against the complexity of it all.

The moment Philippa and Rannulf reached the hall floor, the solar door above them opened and Bishop William emerged. A short man grown portly with age

and his position, the churchman strode briskly down
the stairs, his dark robe so heavily woven with golden
threads it flashed with every step. Atop his head sat
the cap of his rank and he held in his hand the staff
that represented his earthly might.

If there was no mistaking his station, there was also
no doubting his irritation. With Oswald at his heels,
he claimed Rannulf's massive wooden chair. Servants
removed the table from in front of him, giving all a
clear view of the powerful prelate. At the snap of his
fingers, another man brought the hawk, perch and all,
and set it beside the chair.

"Let's be done with it, then," Bishop William said,
his deep voice resonating without effort around the
hall. The normal noise level dropped into an instant
silence.

"Margaret of Lindhurst, come forward," Oswald
called out. "My lord bishop, this woman has a complaint to lay before you."

Lindhurst's dam hobbled into the churchman's field
of vision. Temric, expecting to be called upon, left the
back of the room to wind his way through folk he'd
known all his life. As they moved out of his path, he
accepted their hopeful signs of success and support-
ive glances.

"Well, old woman, spill it." Bishop William's dark
eyes were coolly focused on the one whose rude manner had stolen from him first a day of pleasure, then
a leisurely bath and meal.

"My lord, I would wait until my son is at my side,"
she replied with newfound humility.

"Where is Lord Lindhurst?" The bishop looked
around the room.

"I sent a man to fetch him from his tent, my lord bishop," Margaret said, "but he is not yet come."

"Then we must needs send another to speed him on his way." Even as the churchman nodded his command to Lord Graistan, Temric tapped a man's shoulder. The servant dashed away in obedient response. Rannulf turned and Temric met his brother's gaze. It took no more than the slightest bend of his head to tell his sibling, younger by only four months, that the matter was in hand.

Temric then glanced at Anne. His cousin hurried to the chapel. A moment later she and Father Edwin returned up that short stairway. The old priest joined Lord Graistan and Philippa.

Minutes passed, the bishop impatiently tapping his foot on the floor as he waited. At last Lindhurst appeared, still caked in the day's mud, his pretty face flushed with drink. Temric watched him push through the crowd, assessing him against the possibility of combat.

Lean and long, Roger of Lindhurst was almost half a head taller than himself. Temric dismissed the advantage height gave in reach, having lived his life with taller brothers. He also knew better than to assume leanness indicated weakness any more than bulk guaranteed slowness.

"Do not drag your spurs, man, you've made me wait long enough," the bishop snapped, his words carrying clearly about the room. "Come forward."

Lord Lindhurst stiffened, bristling at being publicly scolded. Temric smiled grimly. Now, a short temper, there was something he could exploit. The movement of his mouth made his cheek ache and he idly scratched at the wound. Content with what he'd learned, Graistan's master-at-arms drew a deep breath and cleared his mind of all emotion. He let himself drift down into the deep calm he always sought prior to entering battle. When his opportunity came, he would be ready.

Philippa watched Roger approach the bishop. She tensed, expecting to be suffused by either fear or anger, but there was nothing left within her save a desire to be done with him. Tonight, the priest would free her to begin a new life.

Her husband shot her only the briefest glance as he halted next to his mother. Philippa's brows lifted in surprise. She'd half expected him to rip her from Lord Graistan's side.

Her gaze shifted back to the prelate. Dark eyes, a thick beard, and a round face lent him a false air of kindliness. His true nature was better found in the power he wore like a cloak. It emanated from him, more awe-inspiring than his magnificent gown, the gold leaf on his crook, and the smooth pearls studding his cap.

"Now," the bishop said, not so very loudly, but the noise in the room once again stilled. "Lady Margaret, I understand you bring a complaint against one of Graistan's men."

"Aye, my lord, Temric by name." Margaret leaned heavily on her stick, as if feeble and ill-used. "He did me hurt when he took from Lindhurst my daughter-by-marriage. I would have him punished for his affront."

"He harmed this lady?" The bishop craned his neck to look behind him for Oswald.

Oswald shook his head. "Nay, my lord, he did not.

Temric did indeed take this woman's crutch from her. However, he did so only when he saw she intended to strike for a second time in our presence Lord Roger's wife. I believe he feared the girl would be hurt beyond any ability to speak for herself as you had commanded, my lord."

Margaret extended her hands in innocent explanation. "I had no missive from you and no true assurance it was you who sent for her. This man I knew not at all"—she pointed to Oswald—"and I feared that for the fortune involved others would deal less than honestly with me."

"Again you cast slurs upon my honor, implying I am a thief," Lord Graistan said, his arm beneath Philippa's hand tensing against the insult. "What cause have you for such an accusation?"

"I need point no further than your lady's refusal to release to my son his wife," Margaret snapped back, shedding her earlier helplessness in anger. "If you were not trying to convince her to betray us for your own benefit, why else would you hold her?"

To Philippa's utter astonishment, Roger turned on his mother and snarled, "Bite your tongue, woman. Can you not see you do us no good by this harangue? If Graistan's man put no mark on you, leave go."

"Roger, he is common born and he dared to touch me," Margaret sputtered out against her son's unexpected behavior. "Aye, and he also dared to lift your lady in his arms when he took her."

"He touched her?" Roger breathed, his eyes wide and his fair complexion darkening. He turned sharply to stare at Philippa. In his eyes she found the promise of her future pain. A litany of prayers rose within her as she begged God to allow Father Edwin's success.

"What reason had he for doing this?" the bishop asked of Oswald.

"Lord Lindhurst's dam would not allow Lindhurst's lady wife to depart. I think it may have been their intent to draw you to his house to resolve this issue, where Lady Lindhurst would not have the support and protection of her kin."

"Nay, you mistake me. I feared for her as I knew this man not at all," Margaret protested, again pointing at Oswald. "It is the insult of a commoner touching his betters that we need discuss and no more."

"My lord bishop," Lord Graistan called out, "Temric FitzHenry is no commoner. He is my brother, the acknowledged natural son of our father, raised in this hall and fostered with me. If he remains only my master-at-arms while refusing knighthood and those lands my father would have given him, he does so for reasons of his own."

"This is true, my lord," Oswald confirmed. "All in our family knows of my late uncle's fondness for his natural son as well as Lord Henry's spoken desire to see Temric knighted and enfeoffed."

Bishop William raised a brow in consideration, then looked at Margaret. "By all I have heard, I deem Temric innocent of the charge against him. I think he has only done me a favor with his actions."

"But he touched me! The commoner dared to touch me," Margaret cried out, shocked that her complaint against one baseborn could be ignored.

This time Roger grabbed his dam by the arm and gave her a furious shake. "Now you think to argue with your betters?" he hissed. "You stupid old woman, hold your tongue or I will beat you into silence."

Margaret gave a shrill cry and the hawk echoed her with its own. She stumbled away from her son, then silently stared at him, more in surprise than anger.

Bishop William turned his hooded gaze on Philippa's husband. "I would now be on to the matter of the wills so we can eat 'ere the wondrous dishes Graistan's cook has concocted grow cold and stale. Lindhurst." The bishop indicated that Roger should step nearer to his chair. When the young nobleman had complied, the prelate braced a thick hand against his thigh and leaned toward him.

"First, as your overlord I would have you know I find the manner in which you present your claim to this inheritance less than honest. Why was news of Benfield's death kept secret save for your single message to me? Had it not been for Oswald and his connection to Lord Graistan, I might have been duped into granting you the inheritance without knowledge of other claims. I look forward to seeing what proofs you offer me this day, but I warn you"—at this he paused to lower his voice to the level of a threat—"if what I hear and see in the next moments does not convince me that you are in the right, your actions will have won only my scorn."

Then he asked of Oswald, "Where is the widow?"

"Here, my lord," Edith said, rising from her seat at the far hearth. Although she yet wore her worn gowns, as Edith walked gracefully toward them they flowed around her like the finest silk. Gone was the despairing woman; the noblewoman for whom the servants parted was the churchman's equal, the proud daughter of a wealthy peer.

At his master's nod, Oswald took his place at the bishop's side and began speaking. "The first matter is the right of the Lady Edith of Benfield to inherit against the strictures of her father's will."

Oswald read aloud all the pertinent portions of that document. As the churchman listened he signaled for the butler to pour him a cup of wine, then handed it to his taster. Only after that servant had sipped and showed no sign of illness did he take the silver cup.

When his administrator was finished, William looked at Edith, a single brow raised. "So, Lady Benfield, we have now heard that your father passes over your right to hold these properties. In all fairness and in keeping with the law, they move through you to your legitimate heirs. 'Tis true so rich a dowry might likely win you an eager husband, but at your age it is doubtful you will bear more children. Therefore, the outcome remains the same—the lands pass to those legitimate children you have already borne. I see no reason to ignore his prohibitions."

Edith released a single quiet gasp and bowed her head.

"My lord bishop," said Lord Rannulf, "I would offer to become warden of this widow. Graistan will gladly feed and clothe her for the remainder of her life."

"You may have her," replied Margaret. "She's no different from her daughter, another useless mouth to fill and helpless back to cover."

"So be it," the churchman said, giving the parsimonious noblewoman a hard glance. "There are some among us who understand Christian charity. Now, the second matter. Where is Lady Graistan?" he asked of Graistan's lord.

"She remains too ill to descend. At your command, I will have her carried down."

"Not necessary," the bishop said with a sharp shake of his head. "You may stand on her behalf."

"My lord," Roger protested, "why should my wife be called when his is not?"

"Because her claim is not suspect," Bishop William said coldly. "His lady's right to inherit is stated clearly in her father's will. Yours is not."

Although Philippa saw resentment form on Roger's face, he had the sense to say no more. When she looked back at the bishop, she found the prelate had turned his stern gaze on her. He brusquely motioned her forward. She reluctantly released Lord Graistan's arm and took a single step nearer to him.

"My lord bishop," she said softly, her words barely audible as she bent in greeting.

"Well met, my lady," said the bishop. "I am glad to see you recovered so quickly from your illness." It was a blatantly sarcastic comment.

Philippa's hammering heart leapt into her throat. What should she say? The truth damned Roger, a lie damned her. Edith was suddenly at her side, bracing her with an arm. She glanced thankfully at her mother and leaned against her.

"Refresh my memory," Bishop William said to Oswald, apparently expecting no response from her.

"My lord bishop, in January, year of Our Lord 1194, delivered to me by Lord Benfield were his will and a contract for marriage between Rannulf FitzHenry, Lord of Graistan, and the daughter of his house, Rowena. I have held them in safekeeping at his request, for Lord Benfield feared an unexpected death and just such a challenge against his will."

"Hold a moment." William held up his hand. Oswald looked at him in curiosity. "Do you say the man feared he would be murdered?"

"No, my lord, he did not use that word," Oswald responded carefully. "He said just that he feared an unexpected death. He wished to protect his only daughter, Rowena, knowing full well that the husband of his wife's bastard would dispute the inheritance."

"Philippa is no bastard!" Edith cried out in protest. William stilled her with a sharp glance and nodded for his clerk to continue.

"In an attempt to avoid dispute, Lord Benfield gathered these witnessed accounts from his overlord's servants"—he held aloft several parchments, displaying the round wax circles that hung by threads from their edges—"with regard to Lady Lindhurst's birth. He also caused to be dictated this letter." He indicated yet another sealed parchment. "In it, he states that Philippa of Lindhurst, presumed to be elder daughter of his house, is not his spawn but a bastard born of his wife prior to their marriage. She was neither accepted nor acknowledged by him when they did wed. My lord, both wills specifically deny inheritance to any child born to the Lady Benfield outside of wedlock."

Edith's voice lifted against the sudden hum of excitement at this declaration, her tone now smooth and confident. "My husband has lied, my lord, and the accounts are crass forgery. We were wed before she was born, ask Lady Lindhurst for she attended our wedding feast."

"Aye, so I did," Margaret agreed, furiously nodding her head to her words. "I saw them wedded and bedded."

"What would drive a man to lie so against his own

daughter where there is more than enough inheritance here for both children?" It was a mild question.

"Hate, my lord bishop," Edith answered with just the right touch of shame in her voice. "My husband made no secret of his feelings for me. Also, he despised the love I bore our eldest. Look, too"—she leaned her head close to Philippa's—"we are as alike as twins. His hate for me spilled over onto the daughter who so resembles me.

"My lord, study the document I gave your servant to hold. It was dictated by Lord Benfield and bears his seal and mark as well as the mark of Benfield's priest. This was done as my lord husband lay upon his deathbed. In it, he rescinds his charge of bastardy and acknowledges Philippa as his own."

The bishop's gaze was speculative. "This he did to clear his conscience before his death, eh?"

"Aye, my lord."

"So, where is this priest of yours? Why is he not here to bear witness to the events of that day?"

"My lord, he is dead," she replied in a clear, firm voice. "The same illness that felled my husband felled him as well."

"How convenient." The bishop's wry comment encouraged the servants into a round of muttered asides and muted laughter.

"It is all there," Edith insisted. "All properly signed and sealed as well."

"Aye, and so that leaves us with but one question left to ask." Bishop William turned his hard gaze onto Philippa. "Lady Lindhurst, what say you? Are you your mother's bastard or Benfield's daughter?"

Philippa glanced at Father Edwin. The priest smiled at her. She prayed he could, indeed, hold her safe.

The need to speak the truth had risen so strongly in her, words tumbled past her lips before she even knew what she might say.

"My lord, I am not legitimate. My stepfather Lord Benfield was sworn to secrecy by my grandsire with regards my birth. This was not to protect my mother or me from any stain. Rather, it was because he could not bear to hear anyone else speak of his daughter's shame even while he heaped more of it upon us. My stepfather told me he had offered to take me as his own, but my grandsire refused. As willed, I remain a bastard always to remind my mother of her sin."

"Shut up, you addlepated bitch," Roger roared at her, but his tone was tempered by sadness. "Why could you not have held your tongue or said you did not know?"

"Nay, no longer," Philippa said quietly. "My life has been a tangle of other people's lies and pretense. I am not ashamed of what I am." Aye, Temric had made her priceless because of her birth. She looked at her mother. Edith's expression was horrified.

"Nor will I allow you, Maman, to stain Lord Benfield's name or his memory with your falsehoods. He was a good man whose care for me was not affected by our lack of kinship. If you'd had less pride, you might have seen that in him and made your life an easier one."

"It seems your wife would name you liar," Bishop William said with surprising gentleness to Lord Lindhurst.

"Nay," Margaret screeched, her hands grasping futilely in the air as if chasing the coins she felt escaping her. "Lord Graistan and his wife have made her say these things, my lord. They took her by force from our home. They brought her here and kept her from us in their hall. Look again, look at that paper. A man does not lie in his last confession."

"Have you been asked to say these things?" It was a quiet question to Philippa, yet the bishop's tone suggested it was the most important inquiry of the night. "Has Graistan or his lady had any influence over you?"

Philippa looked up at William of Hereford, her gaze steadily meeting his. The rightness of what she did flowed through her. If this was the holy guidance Father Edwin had promised her, she was content to do as it urged. "Nay, my lord. Until your servant, Oswald, brought me here to Graistan, I knew nothing of this inheritance or even that Lord Benfield had died. When my sister mentioned it, believing that I knew all, I forced her to explain. Once she was done, she said in the presence of her servants that I should say no more to her. She preferred not to know how I might speak."

"You would swear to this? Bring the relic box," he said to Oswald. His young cleric produced a small casket, rich with golden filigree and tiny rubies. "Understand that if you speak falsely with your hand on these holy bones, God will strike you down and damn your soul to hell for all eternity. Now, place your hand upon it and swear that you've not been told to say these things."

Without hesitation she touched the tiny box. "As God is my witness I do so swear that Lord Benfield confessed to me he was not my father and did not take me as his own when he wed my mother. All I have said is true and I have not been asked by anyone to say what I have said."

The smallest of smiles touched her mouth as she withdrew her hand. It was over. Her conscience was clear and her soul clean.

William leaned back in his chair. "Then, I have no choice but to honor the will of Lord Benfield. Lady Graistan, as his only legitimate child, is sole heir of all those lands and holdings described in the wills. Begone with you, Lindhurst. Hie yourself back to your home and keep close to your own borders whilst I think on what has happened here this day."

"Nay!" Edith screamed.

"Three hides of land and not even that wreck, Benfield," Margaret cried out. "All this cost and what do we have? Less than we started with. Well, we will keep her dress to replace what your lady destroyed," she snarled at Lord Graistan. "At least that is some compensation."

With his mother at his heels, Roger elbowed his way through the sudden crowd of Graistan's servants who had rushed forward to congratulate their lord on his success. As he took vicious possession of her arm, Philippa let loose a single cry of protest. Her complaint was lost in their laughs and screams of victory. Roger forced his way through their ranks toward the door, his hand on her arm demanding that she keep up with his swift pace.

Philippa glanced frantically behind her at Father Edwin, waiting for him to make the bishop stop her husband. The priest stood peering in confusion at the crowd around him. Only then did she realize that her prayers had been in vain. This decision had altered nothing; she was still Roger's wife and no one, not even the Church, had the right to intervene between them.

Philippa's heart plummeted. She freed a single, helpless cry, then fell silent as they exited the keep. Despite all of Graistan's power, it could not keep her safe from her husband.

"Why," Roger now cried, his eyes wet with tears as if her revelation had hurt him more than angered him. The coldness within her grew colder still, eating up all hope and life. With Margaret at their heels, Roger forced her down the outer stairs and across the courtyard toward the keep's inner gate. She saw the old stable master stare at them as they passed that building.

"Why," Roger repeated once they'd entered the bailey, "why have you rejected me? I am your husband, you owe me your loyalty." She heard the beginnings of rage in his voice.

Too deep in her depression to speak, she let him pull her past the pens of cattle to the postern gate. There was no one to save her now. She lost her footing against the rain-slick grass and fell. Roger dragged her along, refusing to stop even when his mother begged him to wait so Philippa's dress would not be ruined. At the postern, he yanked her back onto her feet, then shoved her through the tiny portal. Now, she was beyond Graistan's reach. His tent lay near the river's bend.

"By God, I loved you and you have turned against me!" His palm met her cheek with stinging impact. Philippa stumbled back and would have fallen again but for his grip on her elbow. She straightened slowly, her ears ringing. Again, he lifted his hand, this time clenched into a fist.

"Nay, Roger," Margaret cried, throwing herself between her son and his wife. "Let us remove these expensive gowns so they will not be fouled with blood."

Roger dropped onto his dam the blow he'd meant for his wife. Margaret screamed as she toppled to the ground, blood trickling from her mouth. "Roger," she moaned, too stunned by his attack to rise.

"I am done with you, you old hag. You will quit yourself from my life."

"My precious boy," she cried in heartbreak. "Do not let this paltry bitch destroy your love for me! Help me, Roger, I cannot rise."

Roger ignored her as he stared at his wife. "Answer me. Why have you betrayed me?" His command had more the flavor of tears than the bark of command.

Philippa stared at him, beyond all feeling. "I am not turned against you, for you have never had me. It is I who should ask the question for 'twas you who abandoned me. Were not the marks you laid on me a sign of that? How could you have done such a thing? I was so young and frightened. I could have loved you. I could have forgiven much had you been but a little kind," she finished, her tone weary.

He jerked back as if she'd struck him, his teeth gritted in pain. "I could not help myself," he breathed. "You were mine to do with, mine alone. Afterward, I took my beatings and prayed for forgiveness, then vowed never to do so again. I honored that vow. Your wounds healed," he pleaded, begging for the understanding she could never grant him.

His blue eyes clouded with unbearable shame, then cleared in the predictable flare of rage, for only behind the shield of his anger could Roger hide from what he was. "Whore! What good did it do me to mark you? You've let another man touch you, now I want you no longer."

With that, Philippa's soul found its way to that tiny spot within her where the pain could not reach. Her thoughts diminished until there was nothing left but blankness.

Edith whirled to search the crowd for Temric's face as Roger pulled his wife from the hall. "Help me, she has killed herself!" she keened.

Temric was already pushing through the crowd for Father Edwin. The old man was staring blankly around the room waiting for an explanation. "Now, my friend," he said to the priest. "It is time to fulfill your promise to her." If Edwin was surprised by what Henry of Graistan's eldest son knew, he showed no sign of it. Instead, he nodded gratefully and stepped forward to speak with the bishop. Temric turned, already loosening his sword in its scabbard.

"Temric, what are you about?" Rannulf asked swiftly, grabbing for his brother's arms.

Temric sidled out of his reach. "Leave me be, Rannulf," he said, his voice without inflection or emotion. Blindly focused on the task at hand, he turned and loped toward the hall door.

"Stop him," Lord Graistan commanded. Graistan's soldiers sifted themselves from the crowd to follow after their master-at-arms in twos and threes, but not one of them made any attempt to halt him. Edith lifted her skirts to her knees and ran after him.

By the time Temric had entered the bailey, Roger and his wife were at the postern, with Margaret waddling close behind. They disappeared from his view. Temric's mouth pulled into a fierce grimace, tearing

Anne's fine stitching. Power roared through him. It would feel good to swing his sword, to feel it bite into flesh and bone.

He reached the postern gate. Through its narrow opening he saw Lindhurst's tent. The man stood before his wife, his mother's stick lifted like a club. As he raced forward, Temric watched the knobby end of it slam against the woman he loved. She reeled, then fell. Blood flowed from the side of her head to stain her gown.

His hand on his hilt, he heard the satisfying hiss of steel blade against leather sheath as he freed his weapon. The familiar grip fit perfectly into the cup of his hand. Only yards away, Lindhurst again raised his dam's stick to deliver a second blow.

Temric's mouth opened against the terrible emotion within him. He raised his sword above his head. The muscles of his shoulders bunched, then released. His sword cleaved empty air as he brought it down toward Lindhurst's back.

It rebounded against another blade and Roger's men were upon him.

Chapter Eleven

Even as Temric lost his footing and fell, expecting that his life had ended, men shouted from behind him. His attackers were attacked and steel rang against steel. Deep within him he knew a flicker of gratitude toward Graistan's men. He heaved himself to his feet as Lindhurst grabbed his sword from just inside the tent's opening.

Temric's spirits soared as he swung. His foe's ill-begotten blade crashed against his own. The leather-wrapped grip vibrated in his ungloved hands, tearing at his palm. He stepped out of the blow, his blood lust dimming enough to show him that he and Lindhurst fought at the center of a circle formed by his own men. So, it would be only the two of them, knight to knight. Grinning madly, he surged toward the nobleman.

"You godforsaken whoresons," Lindhurst cried to his men, raising his sword against Temric's ferocious attack. "Break free! Cowards! Earn your keep by killing this foul commoner."

"Help, help, we are attacked!" cried Margaret. Then she grabbed the unconscious Philippa by the arm and dragged her into the tent.

Lindhurst arrogantly slashed out, underestimating

his opponent. Temric knew a brutal pleasure when his sword's tip probed the front of the nobleman's vest, scoring the younger man's chest. Blood seeped into Lindhurst's shirt, but it was no more than a scratch and slowed the man not a whit.

"Damn you," Lord Lindhurst screamed, throwing himself at Graistan's bastard. Their blades met in well-matched strokes, again and again.

"Stop, I say," Bishop William's voice boomed.

Startled, Roger fell back. It was the opportunity Temric needed, but it came almost too late. He threw himself at his momentarily vulnerable opponent, desperate to destroy the man before he, himself, was destroyed.

"Hold your master," the prelate demanded of Graistan's soldiery. Not a man moved. Lindhurst hastily threw his sword up to block Temric's blow.

"Hold him!" the bishop bellowed to his own knights who stood behind him.

An instant later they had Temric's arms and he made his first sound since speaking to Rannulf. It was a quiet, short moan of despair. He had failed. Now he would die, never knowing if he'd saved Philippa.

"Your lordship," Lindhurst's mother screeched, "this dog attacked my son."

"I want his head," Roger screamed, his face near purple with rage.

"Murderer!" Temric surged against those who restrained him, his eyes wide with hatred. Then Rannulf was beside him.

Temric looked from his brother's grim face to the all-too-familiar sword, still encased in belt and scabbard, which lay across his sibling's hands. Shock stunned him, making his voice rise in frantic complaint. "What do you think you're doing?"

"There is no help for it now," Rannulf said. "Your actions have forced it on me." He held the blade toward Bishop William. The prelate made a quick sign over the sheathed weapon, then nodded to Lord Graistan.

"Nay," Temric bellowed in pain and rage. "You will not do me so."

"He has no choice, commoner. Die like the insolent pig you are," Lindhurst sneered. His words revealed that he'd not yet recognized Lord Graistan's intentions.

As Rannulf wrapped the sword belt around his brother's waist, Temric strained hopelessly against the men who held him. Against his writhing efforts, Rannulf could barely close the clasp. "Make him kneel," Lord Graistan commanded the bishop's men.

"Nay," Temric hissed in agony as they forced him down. Two men, then three, set themselves to the task. His knees touched the stony soil. "Damn you, Rannulf," he raged, nearly lifting himself despite the men who pinned him down. "You have no right to do me thusly."

"I will enjoy watching your blood stain the ground," Lindhurst gloated in anticipation, then his voice broke. "What are you doing?" he sputtered in horror, finally understanding what was happening.

Lord Graistan raised his fist and struck his brother a hard blow upon the shoulder. "Richard of Graistan, I dub you knight."

Temric choked back his cry, his heart stopping as he heard his brother utter for the first time in nineteen years both the name and title he had refused. "Damn you to hell, Rannulf," he sobbed quietly.

"False knight," Lindhurst screeched in protest. He exploded from those who held him.

Temric did not need to look up to know Lindhurst stood above him, sword drawn back to behead him. He willed him to succeed. Better to die than live with what his brother had just forced upon him.

"Halt, you fool," the bishop commanded. With his own blade and well-honed skill, he stopped the man's blow. Again, Graistan's men imprisoned Lindhurst with their arms.

"Put your hands between mine," Rannulf demanded.

"Nay," Temric cried out raggedly. "Let him finish me."

"I will not. Put your hands between mine and swear. Swear for the lands our father meant as your own."

Temric slowly lifted his hands and placed them between his brother's. The words he'd eagerly anticipated saying as a young squire now fell, wooden and cold, from his lips. "I am your loyal man." Then he sagged in heartbreak. "Better that I'd died," he whispered to himself.

The churchman laughed in grim amusement. "Well done, Rannulf. Very efficient and without any cost. I will have to remember this the next time I must do it."

"Nay!" Lindhurst writhed and twisted against those who held him, his fury driving him beyond all sense. "You think to deny me my rightful revenge with your posturing? This man is baseborn and he has attacked me. I want his life in return for his outrage."

"He was no knight when he did it," his mother chimed in. "Aye, he committed the offense while commoner still—what are you doing in there," she barked out, suddenly noticing Lady Edith had crept inside their tent. "Trespasser! Get her out." Lindhurst's men went happily to drag the woman out.

Blood stained the front of Edith's gown. She scrambled to her feet. "They've battered my poor Philippa senseless," she cried out for all to hear, "but she lives still."

"Of course she does," Lady Lindhurst retorted. "She's barely bruised. We're not murderers."

Temric eased back from his knees to sit upon the ground as Edith turned on the old woman. "Liar," she hissed. "You would have her dead so your son can remarry."

"Be at ease, Lady Benfield," the bishop's powerful voice rang out, "Graistan's priest has told me she wishes to take her vows as she has had a call."

"Nay," Margaret gasped in protest. "My lord bishop, please do not allow this. It might well be years before she takes her final vows. Roger will remain tied to her all that while, forced to support her when he has no use of her."

Lindhurst shook his head violently. "Nay, I'll not let her go. She is mine, I keep her until I am done with her," he roared, spittle flying from his lips. "Die, bastard," he screamed, nearly winning free of those who held him. His pale eyes were filled with insane fire. "Nay, I'll not be frustrated in this. His life is mine."

"If you want it, come and take it from me, boy." Temric leapt to his feet, his need to kill this man returning full force. "It is not I who am the false knight. For these past years I have carried in my heart a knight's honor without bearing that title. You, you

have urged your men to attack me while I fairly engaged you."

"Foul commoner, do you question me when I am
true born to mine own rank? Meet me on the field,
one to one, so I might cleanse the stain of your words
from my soul with your life's blood."

Temric narrowed his eyes. "Ah, but you have
named me craven commoner. When you do so, you
leave me free to refuse your challenge. Come, boy,"
he goaded, "offer me something to persuade me to
meet you. What could be as precious to you as my
life is to me?"

Lord Lindhurst's eyes flashed with savage intelligence. "If you prevail, I will set my wife in a convent.
Either way, I will win. You die and I keep her. You
live and you cannot have her. She is useless to me
now, anyway."

"Nay, Roger, do not swear so," his mother cried in
rotest. "It will cost too much."

"Be still, old hag," her son growled.

Temric's breath hissed from him in outrage. "Do
you dare to name me adulterer atop false knight? On
what evidence do you base your accusation?"

"Aye, Lindhurst," Bishop William interrupted
coldly, "prove your charge and you may take his life
right here. If you've no evidence, then retract the
charge."

"Proof? What more do I need save that he has held
my wife within his arms and now steps between us
when I chose to chastise her for her defiance of me.
Who but her lover would do so?"

"If ever there were a lady in need of a protector,
it would be your wife," Bishop William said, his voice
hard. "Sir Richard," he said, turning to Temric,

"swear to me that you have not committed adultery with this man's wife."

"On my honor and my brother's life I swear I have not, my lord," Temric responded, his eyes half closing. Had there been more time and opportunity, would he have been able to speak these words?

Lindhurst's face was a mask of hate. "I withdraw the charge."

Bishop William gave a terse nod. "Then, at my command you meet on the morrow, two hours before midday. If Sir Richard prevails, Lady Lindhurst retires to a convent. If you are the stronger, Lindhurst, you may take his life on the field as you so desire," he said.

Only then did a wicked smile touch Lindhurst's face. "So I shall. You will die and my wife remains mine to do with as I please."

In the nobleman's expression Temric found his error. The man would not wait for the morrow's result. His wife would die this evening, while their combat would still go forward on the morrow.

Temric whirled on the bishop. "My lord bishop, as Lady Lindhurst's safety has become part of this challenge, I ask you to once again afford her your protection. She should be held safe until the issue is decided. Let her wounds be treated by one of Graistan's healers."

William's gaze flickered from him to Lindhurst. A hint of disgust touched his stony features. "You will complain over this, no doubt."

The younger man's face went hard, devoid of all emotion. "Nay. Send whom you want to treat her wounds, but they'll do so without the help of her mother or any of Lord Graistan's kin. I'll have no further foreign interference with her."

"If our kin cannot see her, then you and yours should be banned as well," Temric retorted.

"As long as she stays within eyesight of this tent where I can reach her, I care not. I'll not have Graistan shut its gates on her while you bleed your last, dog."

"By God, Lindhurst," Rannulf roared, "I have had enough of you and your arrogance. Still your insulting tongue or I swear by all that is holy I will tear it from your mouth."

"Brother, I will do it for you," Temric offered, his voice taut with simmering rage.

Lindhurst glared at them all. "You may keep her in the bailey." He whirled and stormed into the tent.

Temric watched, his heart aching, as Lindhurst dragged his wife's unconscious form out of the canvas shelter. How was such uncaring cruelty possible? Dear God, but he wanted no more than to take Philippa into the safety of his own arms, and bear her as far from her husband as possible. Yet to move or speak against the nobleman was to reveal what lurked within his soul.

"Here she is," Roger said coldly, releasing his wife's arm. He took two steps away, his lady lying in a torn and muddy hollow of ground.

"You are overmatched," his mother sneered at the new knight. "Best you confess your sins this night, for it will be your last." She stepped inside the tent. Her son followed and closed the flap after him.

Margaret's voice rose from within, wafting through the thin material. "What is the matter with you? I will not waste my coin on some convent—" Her words were interrupted by the sound of a hard slap; after that, there was only silence.

"Jesus God," Lord Graistan said, his voice reflecting the same disgust toward Lindhurst's cruelty that Temric harbored. "You two, pick that poor woman up so she does not smother in the mud. Watt," he continued as the men he designated cradled Philippa in their arms, "run to my wife and tell her to send the one best skilled in healing to see to Lady Lindhurst. Tell Lady Graistan that by my command she remains within doors for she will wish to come." As Watt ran to do as bid, he said, "Odo, see to it my tent is set at the bailey's far end so they have a place to put her."

Only then did Rannulf turn to his exalted guest. "William, your help is most thankfully appreciated."

"Most happily offered," the bishop replied with a brief nod. "Now, I suggest we all repair to the hall. I think our dinner must be on the table with none but the dogs to enjoy it. What a waste that would be. That cook of yours is a marvel, Rannulf."

Temric watched his brother stiffen slightly. The prelate was not so subtly hinting at what compensation would best repay his assistance in this matter.

Rannulf managed a quick laugh. "I have suggested your interest to him. He says he would gladly leave Graistan for Hereford if he might take his woman with him when he goes."

William grinned broadly, immensely pleased. "But of course he should bring his family. They will be most welcome, most welcome, indeed. Come, let us eat."

"I would speak a moment with my brother. Let my folk begin service without me." The prelate nodded and walked away.

At Lord Graistan's command, all the others dispersed as well. Once they were alone, Rannulf took

Temric's elbow and forced him to move away from Lindhurst's tent. The loosely fastened belt at his hips opened and their father's sword dropped to the ground between them.

Temric reached for it, then caught himself. "How could you put this weapon on me?" he asked, his voice deep with pain.

"It is yours by right. You are the elder." Rannulf's eyes were hard with determination.

"The bastard," Temric shot back.

"My brother. Richard—"

"Do not call me by that name. Better the one my mother made for me, for it is neither Norman nor English, just as I am." The bitterness burned within him, an open wound that never healed.

"Fool!" Rannulf shook him slightly, then picked up the sword. A few more steps and they stood at the river's edge, far from any listening ears. "What made you do this insane thing? You must have known I'd have no choice but to knight you to save your neck."

Temric jerked from his grasp. "Would that you hadn't. If he'd stilled my heart I'd not have to imagine my future. Either I die on the morrow and she lives in torment with him or I take the day and I live in torment without her. Dear God, she nearly committed suicide in there and did it happily to give you what you do not need—more properties."

When Rannulf grimaced, Temric cried out, "Forgive me, my heart is in tatters and I know not what I say."

"You truly love her," his brother replied in consternation. "How can this be? You have always held so tightly to your affections."

"If I have held them it was for good reason," Temric shot back, his voice filled with his years of loneliness. "On whom was I to bestow my love? If I loved a common woman, I was loving beneath me. If I yearned for a noblewoman, she was out of reach." He stopped with a sigh. "Nay, the similarity of our births was only the lure that drew me to her. I love her because she is herself and will make you no excuses for my emotions." The pain of seeing Philippa broken and battered once again tore at him. In thoughtless reaction, harsh words poured from him. "Or are we who are baseborn not allowed to love foolishly, as others do?"

"Sweet Jesu, Richard," Rannulf spat out in impatience, "I tire of you forever wearing your birth like some badge of honor."

"I am what my father made me," Temric retorted, clenching his fists. "If he had wanted me to be more than his unrecognized by-blow, he would have done as he vowed and remembered me in his will."

Rannulf's eyes narrowed and his jaw stiffened. "So, now I have given you what you once craved and said Papa forgot. Because it was me and not our sire who did the deed, have you been suddenly changed? Are you no longer the man you were an hour ago? Do your promises to Alwyna now mean nothing?"

"You mock me," Temric growled.

"I do and rightly so. You have always held yourself above the rest of us in your suffering, but yours is no greater than mine. We all endure our tribulations until we can make our peace with them. It is time for you to do just that. Too long have I indulged you in this hatred you bear for the man who gave you life."

Temric covered his face with his hands. "I do not hate him," he cried out. "I loved him and he betrayed my love by forgetting me."

"Richard, he did not," Rannulf's voice gentled, "he only died too soon. If you must, hate Ermina for she took his soul with her when she died. He forgot us all. Was Papa's death without a will not our youngest brother's betrayal as well as yours? Gilliam is a legitimate son, left without lands or honors. What of me? Our father's death robbed me of my youth, giving me responsibility for all this"—his raised hand indicated Graistan's keep—"and the raising of Gilliam and Geoffrey as well, when I was but eighteen."

Now Rannulf gripped Temric by both arms and stared into his eyes. "No longer will I allow you to say he forgot you. He did not. You were no less his son than was I or Gilliam or Geoffrey. Tomorrow, take back your life. When you have done it, I will demand along with your oath that you acknowledge your father's love for you." He shoved their sire's sword into his brother's hands and strode away.

Temric stared after him, his fingers opening and closing over the sheathed weapon. He turned to stare into the roiling, gray water at his feet. The familiar bend in the river teased from him an ancient memory. He saw himself as a wee child, leaning far over the bank's edge to watch the water flow. The dirt beneath his hands and knees had given way. Down he'd tumbled, to sink beneath the murky surface. He could still remember his choking terror. Then his father had reached him. The child in Temric still reveled in the safety of his sire's arms around him.

"Papa," he muttered to himself, his eyes shut against the pain, "why did you forget me?"

Chapter Twelve

Philippa was surrounded by darkness. She cowered against it, lost and alone. Far, far in the distance shone a pale brightness. The light grew, warming her, driving away fear and loneliness. Here would she be safe and free from all pain. Aye, it was death she craved. Within herself she sighed in relief and reached out for it.

A figure, a dark silhouette against the glow, stood between her and the light. Philippa gasped without sound. Was this God? He extended his hand and she put hers into his. When his fingers closed over hers, she felt the heavy ring he wore.

His voice, deep and soothing, filled her from the inside out. This must be God, how else could she hear words with her heart and not her ears?

You cannot go. You must stay and wait for Richard. He needs you. . . .

Philippa hesitated in confusion. Who was Richard and why should she stay here for someone she didn't know? In the time it took to think the words, darkness overtook her again, its embrace warm and safe.

Moments? Hours? Days? Later, she turned, almost grasping wakefulness. Consciousness slipped in and out of her reach. She would almost feel it, only to be driven back into nothingness by the throbbing pain in her head.

A cool hand brushed her cheek. She jerked in reaction when it touched the broken skin across her temple. Around her voices eddied, rising and falling. She opened her eyes. The ceiling above her was not the familiar reedy roof of Lindhurst. Her heart leapt in fear. Where was she? Jesus Lord, but her head hurt. She turned her face to the side, searching for anything familiar. Her vision blurred and she gulped back her rising stomach.

She was on a cot in some place with cloth for walls, attended by two women and a boy. With swollen eyelids that would barely open, she watched them, sensing she should know them. The moments slipped away. There was nothing, no recall at all of who they might be. She was so tired. Her eyes closed as she listened.

"Look here," one woman was saying, "see? Silver pennies, eight of them. Think on what you could do with such wealth." Her ragged voice brought to Philippa's inner eye the image of a sour old woman. No name rose to accompany the face.

"I think you plan murder and I'll have naught to do with that for any price," the other female responded.

"Murder? Nay, not at all. I'd only make certain she comes home with us. 'Tis not right that a bishop seeks to separate man from wife."

"So, what is it you require of me?"

"The boy here will steal her away while my son battles the bastard. My folk will be waiting for her a furlong into the chase just beyond the fork in the north road. You must only confirm what I will say on the morrow. Oh, and I'll need to bruise you else they'll not be convinced."

"Eight pennies to be bruised and speak a few words? And he need only spirit her out of keep and town? There must be more to it than that."

"Nay, truly, that is all I require. Look, look upon this wealth."

"I will think of your offer."

"Nay, you decide now. If you do not want these"— the coins jangled and Philippa caught her breath in agony as the sound pierced her brain like a knife—"I will find someone else and you'll be the poorer."

"I'll do it, but you'll pay me all eight for it. If you want the boy's help as well, you'll pay him what he demands."

"Cheat!" The word was almost a curse in its harshness, although uttered no louder than a whisper.

"Hardly. You need us. Only by my word will your tale be believed. Is that not worth the cost?"

"Aye, so it is," came the bitter agreement.

Philippa could keep herself awake no longer. She sighed and drifted back down to a place where there was no sound or pain.

Temric stood atop the chapel stairway and stared out into the hall. Torches, cold and dead, hung over the hall piled deep with shadows. The fires spit and hissed in banked fury on their raised hearths, adding the scent of burning wood to the already stale air. Stretching out before him was a rough sea of humankind, rumbling and undulating beneath blankets and cloaks.

His troubled thoughts had left him sleepless and he'd come here from the garrison, meaning to seek out Rannulf. Now he hesitated. That his brother would rise from his bed to speak with him was beyond question. It was Temric who suddenly found himself feeling the intruder.

Once again, his new loneliness snapped at him. He was trapped between worlds, neither noble nor common, with no one left whom he could call fully "his." A touch on his arm made him start with surprise.

Father Edwin's homely, ancient visage was revealed by the rancid glow of his tallow lamp. The old man's eyes were yet heavy with sleep, as if he'd only just awakened.

"You should be abed," the priest chided gently, "seeking peace and strength for the morrow's battle."

"So I should," was Temric's soft reply. "How did you know I was here?"

Edwin gave a tiny shrug. "One I trusted told me of your need. Come, share a cup of my wine with me. This year's brew is better than my last vintage. We can talk, or have you forgotten that that is my purpose here?"

Temric managed a small smile. "Well, I know you are not our vintner."

The priest grinned up at him, slipping his twisted hand into the bend of Temric's arm. "I had expected you earlier. Were you not planning to confess and receive absolution prior to this contest? Aye, Richard, come, but do so in silence. Lady Benfield lies on the chapel floor, although I believe her prayers have become sleep."

Temric allowed himself to be led back down into the chapel. He peered at the altar and saw nothing save a candle's glow against deep midnight. Last night's odd vision had surely been the result of exhaustion. Then, within him, he caught the sense of presence where there should have been nothing at all.

He shuddered against his overactive imagination and forced all thought of such things from his mind.

"Here, Richard, take the lamp," Edwin said as he sat on the edge of his cot, "and find two more so I can see you clearly. Find yourself a stool as well, whilst I pour my brew."

While the old man busied himself with two wooden cups and a small cask, Temric gathered the lamps and retrieved the stool. Once all was done and he sat next to the cot, Edwin handed him his cup.

"Richard," the old priest said, then smiled. "Ah, but it is good to call you that once again. It is a name worthy of a true son of Graistan."

Temric only shook his head. "Rannulf should never have forced it back onto me."

"Forced it on you, did he now?" The lamplight accentuated the old man's amused expression by laying shadows in the deep creases of his face. "I'd bethought me you went chasing it when you faced Lindhurst."

"How so?" Temric asked.

"Boy, you cannot have it both ways. Behave as a lord and you are one, behave as a servant and so shall you be treated. Today, you shook off your mother's common heritage by demanding the rights of your noble father, even if you yet deny the name he had me give you."

Temric opened his mouth to protest, then sighed in realization. It was exactly what he had done. Lindhurst had not been his better when he'd attacked him. Nay, indeed, he'd thought the man his inferior. Too long had Rannulf shared Graistan's power with Temric.

"Now drink up." Edwin pointed at the cup he held. "After you've finished it, you can spill your sorrows."

Temric sipped the sweet concoction, content to sit

without words next to this man he'd known all his life. When the priest finally cocked his head to the side in invitation, he released his breath. "I have given my heart to Lady Lindhurst."

"I grieve for you. You must lose her."

"Aye." He stared down into the dregs at the bottom of his wooden cup.

"And so?" Edwin prodded.

"Mother of God," the words tore from him, "but when he accused me of adultery, I felt like a liar denying it. I have only kissed her, but in my dreams and thoughts I have done far worse." Staring into the man's ancient eyes, he pleaded, "Tell me I committed no sin."

"I cannot, but worry over your soul's health is not what hangs so heavily on you that you cannot sleep. 'Tis a deep emotion that troubles you. Look up, son, else I cannot hear what you say."

Temric forced himself to stare into Edwin's face. The man's expression was soft and gentle. "You already know what it is that troubles me."

"So I do. This pain of yours has gnawed your vitals for too many years. You'll not be free of it until you speak the words aloud. I rejoice that, however late, you're finally ready to do so."

Temric tensed. Years of holding so tight a rein on his emotions made it almost impossible to pass them from heart to mouth. "Lord God forgive me, but I have hated my father." Hearing himself say the words made him gasp in denial. "Nay, I do not hate him despite his betrayal. He swore love and promised an inheritance only to turn his back on me."

"Are you so certain?" There was a sadness in the old man's voice that made Temric shiver in response.

"Nay," he whispered. It took all his strength to continue looking at the old man so Edwin could "hear" him speak. "When you asked me the other day, I answered differently. This night I am distraught, wondering if I have clung to an untruth for some selfish reason I cannot fathom. But how can I be wrong when his will so clearly omitted my name?"

"Of all his sons you are the only one who reads the words while missing the meanings within their syllables." Edwin patted the younger man's hand. "The pity of it is not that you have misjudged your father, there's no man that doesn't do that from time to time. Rather it lies in how you have hurt yourself by seeking to prove Henry did what he had not done."

When Temric stared in confusion, Edwin spoke on. "Why does it matter whether some clerk scratched his pen across parchment at your father's behest or that Henry spoke words aloud for all to witness? Go, wake Lord Rannulf. Send messages to your other, noble brothers, Gilliam and Geoffrey, asking what Henry meant for you. Would they not all say that you are your father's acknowledged son on whom he intended to bestow both lands and home? Even Geoffrey will not deny you that."

Temric only shook his head slowly from side to side, hearing the truth for the first time.

Edwin stroked the younger man's hair. "Aye, laddie, there are times when your ears are more deaf than mine. But, then, you have always been a haunted child, convinced by your birth that you have no value. Do you remember when your mother left for Stanrudde? Nine, you were, and already living away from Graistan. I cannot forget the pain in the missive you sent your father. You saw her departure as proof she'd never truly wanted you.

"It was the same when your father died, his departure even more permanent than hers. At a time when you needed his reassurance and love, you discovered what seemed to be his ultimate rejection. It does not surprise me that you have spent your heart on the only woman who cannot reject you for your birth."

"My God, what have I done?" Temric cried out. "Papa, forgive me, it is I who have betrayed you." He bent beneath the weight of it.

Footsteps clattered against the chapel stairs. Temric spun around on his stool to see who came. Anne flew past Father Edwin's alcove on her way to the garrison door.

"Annette," Temric called out angrily. "Why have you left Lady Lindhurst?" He threw himself to his feet and met his cousin in the alcove's doorway.

Anne's eyes were wild as she spoke in rapid English. "You cannot countenance what has just happened. That old witch came, offering me eight pennies to spill a fanciful tale to the bishop on the morrow. She will have Peter take that poor chick into our forest to be killed!"

"What? Who offered you pennies? Peter will do what?"

"Lindhurst's dam did, offered the pennies, I mean. Eight of them. You see, Peter had come to spend time with me while I watched over Lady Philippa."

"What is that?" Edwin asked, having joined them with his lamp in hand. His gaze flew from mouth to mouth as he tried to interpret words spoken in a language he did not know.

Anne rushed on in explanation. "That old woman

would not admit that she wishes our Philippa dead, but why else would she come skulking and creeping with coins to offer? Hah! What she would give me is hardly more than the cost of a fat capon. Does she believe she can buy murder so cheaply?"

Within Temric rose a violent rush of hope. "Did you agree to it?" he demanded, still in his mother's tongue.

"Aye, so I did and urged Peter into doing likewise. I prayed that you could make some use of this to keep her safe from their plots and schemes. Tell me you can," she finished frantically.

"I cannot know that until you tell me what is to happen."

"What is it?" Edwin protested more loudly. "I cannot understand you."

Anne paid the priest no heed and continued in rapid-fire English. "Peter is to secretly take Lady Philippa from Lord Rannulf's tent, through the town and into the forest where Lindhurst's men await her. That old crone thinks I believe they will be there to take her safely back to Lindhurst so the Church cannot have her. Ha!

"For my part, I'm to run, bruised and torn, onto the field after your contest, to say that the lady awoke and fought free of us. That will ring true, for head wounds can cause such rages. When they search for her, I've no doubt they will find her body. It will seem as though she met her doom at the hands of some imagined fiends who surely must inhabit our chase. Do you not see? Her husband will be a widower, free to remarry for another dowry, and without blame on his hands."

Temric sucked in a deep breath for he saw more

than that. How could he prevent Philippa's death and still make it seem that she was truly dead? If he could do so, she would be free; she would be his. His mind ached for the answer.

"What is it?" Edwin demanded, his gentle voice no longer soft. It resounded against the stone arches and roof of the chapel, echoing throughout the room. "Someone best tell me what is afoot here."

Edith of Benfield rose from where the chapel's west wall met the floor. "Father, are you well?" she cried out in sleepy concern, rubbing her eyes into focus when she realized that the priest was not alone.

"Is no one going to tell me what progresses here?" Edwin asked irritably, not realizing he'd awakened Lady Benfield with his shout.

Temric put his arm around the old man. "It would be better if you did not know."

Edwin considered him for a long moment, then his gaze grew troubled. "So you plan and scheme, do you? Best you take heed, boy. Honesty always wins out. In subterfuge lurks the threat of one's own destruction."

"Seek your bed, old friend," Temric replied. "I will make my confession in the morning."

"I vow, Richard, you hear less than I do."

Temric grinned, no longer minding that name. If regaining his identity would send Philippa into his arms, he was glad of it. "You are probably right. I will see you in the morning." Edwin afforded him a last, narrow look, then turned and shuffled back to his alcove.

Lady Benfield rushed to join them, her skirts brushing softly on the wooden floor as she moved. "I came to pray and damn me, but I fell asleep. What is it?

Does my daughter yet live?" There was a terrible catch in her voice.

"Oh, my lady," Anne cried out, "they are plotting to murder her."

"Nay!" Edith cried out. "You must stop them!"

"Why should we?" Temric replied evenly. "Since it is obvious they would rather see her dead than convent bound, I think we should help them do it."

"Nay!" both women cried in shock.

"If the world *believes* her dead, can she not continue to live in safety elsewhere? We need only thwart their plans, while making it appear that they have succeeded."

Edith gasped in rising hope. "Aye, I see your meaning, but how can they be convinced without a body to prove her gone?"

"Temric, she is right," Anne cried out. "They will want her body." Outside the chapel windows, the night sighed with a damp, cool gust of wind. The candle's flame flickered wildly, then steadied.

"Aye," Edith continued, "else no one will truly believe her dead. Then, once she is free of them, where can she live that she will not be eventually recognized? The world is not such a big place that someone can disappear."

"Spoken as a true Norman in England," Temric retorted, his low voice ringing slightly off the stone columns. "What you say is true only as long as she retains title and nobility. I will take her to my mother's home at Stanrudde where she will take up life in a wool merchant's household. Even if she is seen, who would believe that a noblewoman would betray her class so?"

This time Edith gasped in outraged pride. "You would make her into a commoner?" Then she reached out as if to catch back the words. "Nay, pay me no heed. Take her where you will. I am content in giving her to you, having seen the evidence of your care for her. Do what I cannot, keep her safe from her husband. Make her life a happy one with my blessing."

"My lady, you have my solemn oath on that. I will be her protector for the rest of her days." Even as Temric spoke the words, he felt hope harden into determination. He would sacrifice it all, even his honor, to make Philippa his.

"Thank you," was Edith's simple response, her face beautiful in her relief. "Tell me how we can make this miracle happen."

Temric nodded. " 'Tis true Lindhurst might want a corpse, but not everyone else will need that proof. Think on it. Lindhurst's dam would say Philippa escaped Graistan while in mad delirium, but who besides Anne will stand witness to that? Neither the bishop nor Rannulf is so easily fooled. Lady Benfield"—he turned his gaze on Philippa's mother—"if servants and townspeople alike came forward to witness that they had not only seen but spoken with the madwoman, would that not prove she had done as Margaret claimed?"

"Aye, so it would," she breathed.

"When the searchers arrive at the sight of Philippa's destruction, they will find blood enough to satisfy them. Bits of hair and your daughter's torn and befouled gowns along with the testimony of the townsfolk will broadly suggest the outcome. If there is no body, is it not because those who attacked her bore it away for twisted reasons of their own?"

"Will not Lord Lindhurst cry for more searching when his own men have disappeared?" Anne asked.

"Will he dare to complain when the bishop names him widower? To speak even one word would reveal what he has plotted."

Edith threw her head back and laughed. The sound mingled amusement and hatred into a song of satisfaction. "Aye, I see it all now and how it fits with my own fate. It is right that I, who conceived her in secrecy, now make a pretense of her death. Anne, bring me her dresses. Let me mark my brow and stain my hair with pig's blood. On the morrow my daughter will walk from yon gates and there'll be none who doubts her death, this I vow."

"Annette," Temric said, "tell me again what is to happen and let us lay our traps."

By the hour's end, what Temric needed done was either planned or on its way to completion. Anne had returned to watch over Philippa, while Edith had sought out her pallet in the hall. Temric leaned against the altar, his mind once again working through the details. Content with what he'd plotted, he straightened and stretched, muscles protesting their stiffness.

While there was no guarantee of success, there was also nothing left to lose. He was forsaking all to steal another man's wife; vows were being shattered, sins committed. His heart would give him no other choice. He could not let her go.

What if Philippa did not accept him or his mother's life? Nay, it would not happen. Had not she, herself, said that she wished she could begin life again, choosing him as her mate? They were equals and she wanted him. Besides, even a commoner's life was better than no life at all. And what of him? Could he tolerate such a life? There would be no choice if the morrow's mummery worked to his benefit.

He stared blankly into the candle's guttering flame, his mind churning again over the details. A nagging worry bit at him. Something had been missed, but no matter how hard he thought, he could not identify what it was. Finally, he ran his fingers through his hair and yawned. It was but four hours before dawn and his body needed sleep.

"Richard."

The word sent a chill up his spine. He jerked upright, his heart pounding in his chest.

"Who is there?" Temric whispered, knowing full well there was no one save him within the confines of the chapel.

"Richard."

He knew. "Papa," he breathed. "This cannot be," he cried softly, keeping his eyes shut tight.

A moment later, just as he had seen his father's hand the night before, he recognized the feel of Henry's arms around him. He stiffened, but the sensation was so familiar, he could not retain his terror. It was his father.

Suddenly a storm of memories filled him, flashing through his mind, one after another. He watched the events of his life unfold, but through a different perspective. Through his father's eyes? There was his unexpected dunking in the river, learning to ride, his first sword and how he'd used it to drive holes through all the curtains in the hall. The recall of how he'd bested Rannulf at quintains the first time they'd ridden at them filled him. The pride he felt within him at this memory was not his own. Even in death, Henry gloried in his eldest son's triumph.

Without word or sign, his father spoke eloquently on. This time Temric knew a shaft of pain and saw Ermina on her deathbed, something he, himself, had not witnessed. The grief that flowed from his father was not for an adored wife's passing. Rather, Henry mourned his own failure to rise above the blow her death had dealt him. It was a father crying for his sons; he had quit life while they still needed him.

Especially one. The one who had most depended on him, needing more love, more assurance, and more attention than all the rest.

Temric's breath caught in a near sob. In his mind, Richard FitzHenry, son of Graistan, lay his head upon his father's broad shoulder and gave Henry the forgiveness he craved.

Chapter Thirteen

Temric awoke the next morning filled with a light-heartedness that belied the day's forthcoming events. He eagerly sought out the dusty trunks that held the treasure he thought never to claim. When he'd found the better suit of mail, the stuff created for his knighting then never used, he set the servants to cleaning it. After that, he bathed and visited Father Edwin.

It was a strained confession. There was no sense in admitting to sins that might never be committed if he lost his life at Lindhurst's hands. Humbly accepting his penance and absolution, he left the chapel to step outside the hall.

On the open porch atop the keep's exterior stairway, a chill breeze ruffled his hair. The morning mist settled softly against his shoulders. Above him, clouds scudded across the sky, dragging their ragged gray skirts behind them. Better grass slick with moisture than the dry heat of the past weeks. Too long at battle in such warmth brought on heat stroke and, sometimes, death.

When he retreated back behind the massive doors to break his fast, Graistan's folk offered him prayers and wishes on a successful challenge along with congratulations on his knighting. Their confidence was absolute; they were certain he'd have no trouble dispensing with Lindhurst. He returned their confidence with his own, trading jests and taking their advice with mock seriousness.

Returning to the garrison, he dressed in the heavily padded gambeson he wore beneath his armor. Before donning his newly cleaned mail hauberk and chausses, he checked the metal garments for chips and broken links. A necessary chore, considering how long they'd been stored away.

"Temric?" Peter stood in the garrison's doorway, his broad face marred with a frown. "Or should I call you Richard now?"

"You may use either name, for I am comfortable with both." Temric smiled when he realized he'd spoken the truth.

The boy glanced around, then squatted before him. When Peter spoke his voice was low and he carefully weighed each word. "I came to tell you that all is in readiness. Those you sent to go have gone, our cart is repacked, and the ponies harnessed. I've given Anne two pig stomachs, full up of blood, and she waits to speak with you at the gate." Now he eased even nearer. "What if you do not take the day?" Temric's youngest brother only breathed the question, his dark eyes soft and wide. "What am I to do then?"

Temric gave a snort of amusement. "You make it sound as if I face my execution. Do you think me so feeble or ill-trained? That arrogant little lordling will find it right difficult to land a blow. Should the worst happen, beg our mother in my name to care for Philippa as if she were your sister. Hey, lad, do not look so glum," he said, his voice rising to its normal tone.

"I will win. It will be a hard morning's work, but he'll not take me. Come help me arm so I can be off to the practice field to loosen my limbs."

With that, he smiled again. Aye, it would feel good to swing his sword at Lindhurst as equal against equal. His pride in this day's victory would ease the pain of the honor he would soon forsake. He lifted his mail hauberk. "You must hold the shirt like so while I crawl into it."

Peter pulled and tugged the piece into place over the padded shirt, then helped him don his metal stockings. With the coif laced up like a hood about his head, Temric reached for his surcoat. For the first time ever, he wore the garment that all Graistan's other knights wore.

Over this he buckled his father's sword belt and sword. He would wear it to honor his father as Rannulf had requested of him, discarding it only when the time came to meet Lindhurst on the field. For that encounter it was better to trust his own familiar blade. Bearing his helmet and his gauntlets, Temric walked with Peter from hall to courtyard. While his youngest brother went to the stable to claim their cart, he continued on to the inner gate. Anne was waiting for him in the shadows of the gatehouse.

"So how fares your patient this morn?" he asked quietly.

"She rests much easier now."

"And what of the trip to Stanrudde?" Temric awaited her answer in breathless hope.

"Aye, she'll endure the travel. Not so long ago she even spoke with me, although she does not remember who I am." Where Anne seemed pleased, Temric's heart plummeted.

"She's forgotten all?" Him, as well?

"Aye, but it is just temporary. When the head takes such a blow as she has had, it joggles all the things within it. Time will right her thoughts. Be at ease, you, and concentrate on your contest."

"Anne, do not forget that you must run into Graistan and hide the instant your performance is at an end. I pray I am wrong, but Lindhurst's men might well come looking for you to do more murder so there will be no witness." Temric lay a hand on his cousin's shoulder. "Promise me."

"I will. But if I must hide, it will not be for long. Otto told me that since the judgment is given, the bishop has no further excuse to linger. When he goes this afternoon, my husband and I leave with him." Anne smiled up at him. "Send word to me at Hereford. I will perish in worry until I hear from you. Also, tell your mother I dearly miss her."

"I will do so. Good fortune on your new life."

"And you, yours," she said as she slipped out of the shadows and hied back toward Rannulf's tent at the bailey's far end.

Temric strolled through the gate, forcing his helmet onto his head. As he walked toward the practice yard, he rolled his shoulders to release his back. Mist had become light rain, cool against his skin, the smell fresh and clean. Two knights already sparred on the grass, the steady beat of their swords jarring against the soft quiet of this gray day. He recognized Rannulf and watched his brother relentlessly drive one of Hereford's knights to the edge of the field. The man bowed in acceptance of his defeat. It appeared that Rannulf suggested a rematch, but the knight begged off and strode away.

Lord Graistan glanced briefly over his shoulder. "Arnult, come spar with me a moment. I need the exercise to spill my rage over what lies ahead."

"Arnult, is it now," Temric replied with a laugh. "Last night, my name was Richard. You will have to settle on one name and stay with it."

"Temric," Rannulf cried in surprise, not having recognized him dressed as he was.

"Well, make up your mind. Which one is it to be?" he asked in mock irritation.

Rannulf grinned. "Temric. I've called you that for so many years, I doubt Richard will come to my tongue anymore. Look at you," he breathed in amazement.

Temric glanced down at himself. He wore his own mail, the better stuff created years ago for the role he had refused. It gleamed like silver from beneath the pale blue surcoat that all Graistan's knights wore.

"You wear his sword." His brother's voice deepened with emotion.

"And why not? It is mine. Did not my father will it to me by his words?" Temric paused for a long beat, still surprised by the peace that had settled within him. "I was in the chapel last night. Did you know the dead can speak?"

"You jest." Rannulf looked horrified at the thought.

Temric shrugged, the experience so strange and private he was loath to discuss it in detail, even to Rannulf. "Aye, mayhap it was but my own thoughts and remembrances which spoke in me." He paused. Surely, that was the explanation for what had happened. It had been his own need to talk to his father that had conjured up his voice and image. "You are right, I did accuse him of what was not done. Our father loved me and loves me still. Come what may, I accept as my birthright this knighthood. You will understand if I cannot take the lands just now. I must first be quit of the vow I made my mother. To that end I will be leaving to join her as soon as I am finished with Lindhurst."

Rannulf opened his mouth, but Temric held up a hand to forestall his complaint. "I need time to come to an acceptance of this change you forced on me, so I pray you will not come chasing after me to take up those lands." Here he stopped, knowing his sudden pause would encourage Rannulf to make his own connections beyond the spoken words.

"Chase after you?" Rannulf's brows lifted in surprise as he acknowledged there was more in his brother's words than what had been said. A wondering dismay appeared to darken his pale eyes. "You would leave that poor broken bit of a girl behind you without another thought, would you?" However casually uttered, Rannulf was testing his newborn conclusions.

"What choice have I? She is another man's wife." To any ear save Rannulf's, Temric knew his voice would have sounded resigned and defeated.

Rannulf stiffened in reluctant understanding, then shrugged. "I will not ask you how you intend to accomplish what you plan."

"That would be best," Temric agreed.

"Harebrain," his brother breathed, then continued more loudly, "draw that blade and let us see what it sounds like after all these years of idling. I need the exercise. My back yet aches after my fall at Ashby and I cannot tolerate being sore."

"Is this your reason for braving the damp and bat-

tering William's man when you could be lying abed
with that wife of yours?"

His brother grinned. "Of course. What other reason
could there be?"

"What, indeed," Temric scoffed. With that he drew
his father's sword and they met, striking out in a pattern made familiar through long years of practice. He
enjoyed the rote stretch and reach of his muscles as
he matched his brother stroke for stroke. Then Rannulf shifted right with an odd sinuous motion. Caught
unawares, Temric automatically followed and found
Rannulf's sword tip touching his breast.

Rannulf laughed. "William's man, Ralph, has had
the pleasure of meeting Lindhurst during a melee. He
mentioned last night that Lindhurst has but a single
unusual move. I asked him to show it to me. Now,
come again and I will teach you what it is."

The crowd of townsfolk and servants exploded in a
roar of dismay as Temric fell. He lay prone on the
slick grass. A quick look to the side as he raised his
shield revealed his sword, just out of hand's reach.
Lindhurst brought his blade down on the shield's surface with a stroke so powerful it jarred Temric's teeth.

As Lindhurst drew back for another blow, Temric
rocked to one side. He caught his hilt in relief and
snatched the weapon close in time to brace both arms
beneath the shield for Lindhurst's next blow. The nobleman drew back again.

Using the dampness to his own advantage, Temric
levered himself around and swung with the flat of his
blade for Lindhurst's legs, catching his opponent mid-
calf. Lindhurst bellowed in pain as his feet went out
from beneath him. Temric felt the younger man's im-

pact as he hit the earth, then listened to the knight breathe in sobbing gasps against the fall.

Temric relaxed against the sod, his dignity sorely bruised. It would have been far better if Lindhurst had knocked him down, but to simply slip? What with the cup of wine he'd spilled the other day and now this fall, folk would begin to think him clumsy. Temric grinned at his thoughts, then caught it back against the ache in his injured cheek. Now, wasn't that just like a lad newly knighted? Stupid fool, he chided himself. He was no beardless boy who pretended skill where he did not own it.

Coming slowly to his feet, he paused to shake the stiffness from his legs. Lindhurst came scrabbling up after, his feet slipping and sliding in his haste. The nobleman instantly struck out in a halfhearted effort.

Temric caught the blow against his blade and shoved him back. A wayward glance over his shoulder revealed Walter. He let his shield take Lindhurst's next thrust as he focused his attention on the soldier, waiting for the arranged sign. Only when Walter had given a brief nod did Temric breathe again. Success! Philippa was his!

Braced with that knowledge, he turned with grim pleasure toward Lindhurst. No longer did he hoard his energy, he freely spent it in working to prolong their match. Stroke for stroke, no matter how Lindhurst came at him, Temric turned aside the blow. Each escape became a goad. As he expected, the nobleman's rage grew as his assaults were repulsed. Temric heard it in the man's gasping breath and saw it in the growing tenseness of Lindhurst's mouth. Minutes passed.

Once, twice, then a third time, the petty landholder

tried his ruse, feinting right, but Temric would not be lured. He smiled, knowing full well his confident expression would further enrage his opponent.

It did. Lindhurst growled and threw himself at Temric in an open frontal attack. He was easily beaten back. Then he bellowed in frustration and threw himself forward again. "Down, damn you," he screamed.

Temric feinted right, using his opponent's own move. To his astonishment, Lindhurst followed. Temric's blade shot in above the top of the man's shield and crashed into Lindhurst's mailed shoulder. He felt the iron links give way and knew his blow had drawn blood. When the man lurched to the left in instinctive reaction to the pain, his right arm lay unguarded. It was an easy matter to send the sword he held flying from his fingers. "Yield," Temric demanded.

"Nay," Lindhurst bellowed, "I will not." He leapt aside and grabbed up his sword.

"You must. Your shield arm is crippled."

"Do me no favors, commoner. I'll see you in hell before I yield."

Temric shrugged, then glanced at the bishop. The prelate nodded for them to continue, but it was no contest any longer. Pain made the younger man careless. When Temric landed a resounding blow against Lindhurst's shield, he fell to one knee, near crying.

The bishop raised his hand. "I declare this match at an end and Sir Richard, knight of Graistan, the victor. All honor has been satisfied. My lord Graistan, your brother's life is now his own and Lord Lindhurst will relinquish his wife to the Church as he has vowed."

"Roger," Margaret of Lindhurst screeched, dashing

across the field to her son's side. Her gown was torn and muddy and her wimple all askew.

"Leave me alone," her son sobbed. "I am no more than scratched."

The old woman gasped against his rejection, then whirled to face the bishop. "My lord bishop," she cried out, "my son's wife is gone!" Her pronouncement drew a shocked silence.

Temric pried off his helmet and watched with mild interest how the drama unfolded.

"How can this be?" The bishop sounded truly confused. "I thought she had yet to regain consciousness."

"But she has," the elder Lady Lindhurst said, "and so says the one who tended her as well as I. Come forward, you, and help me with this tale."

Anne stepped out of the crowd, her headcloth torn, two long scratches down her face. She made a show of respect before the bishop, then spilled the tale she'd been paid to tell. "My lords, I thought there was no chance of her waking, but she did. She was in such a state that she attacked me and, when Lady Lindhurst answered my calls for help, she did not recognize her mother-by-marriage. She threw us off when we would have held her, then ran through our gate and away." Anne's voice was filled with tearful consternation. "Would that I had seen some sign of this. I could have bound her to the cot against such an occurrence."

"I cannot believe it," Oswald scoffed. "The woman is so slight. It seems that the two of you could have easily held her."

"My lord, sometimes a sort of madness can take those suffering from this kind of injury. In that state, they are very strong." It was Anne's earnestness and her connection to Graistan that made her words worth weighing.

"Poor child," Lady Lindhurst moaned, wringing her hands. "For all the cruel things I have said, I truly did not wish to see her harmed. Will you not help us search for her?"

Rannulf sent a frowning glance toward Temric. He looked away to keep from smiling. Again, his brother was pondering over how he'd done it.

"Well, she surely could not have gone far in her condition," the bishop said. "Send men out to scour the town and fields below."

As Lord Lindhurst was helped away, the bishop went to fetch his own riding gear. Rannulf shouted orders, and as men scattered to do his bidding, he strode swiftly to meet Temric in the middle of the field. "Should you not be racing for your life?"

Temric took the cloth Rannulf offered and wiped his blade clean before sheathing it. "Why? What they find at the end of their search will satisfy them, both those who sought her death and those who seek to save her. No matter how it appears, know that murder has been prevented and those who were sent to do the deed have paid for their evil plans."

"How am I to explain this to her sister?" Rannulf sighed.

"How can you say anything to her when I have told you nothing?" Temric replied. "Whatever conclusions you have drawn are your own concoctions."

"You are leaving me an all too wide trail of hints to trace," Rannulf retorted.

"I'd not see you hurt should I be discovered." A sudden rush of sadness filled Temric. "You are right,

I should be leaving, but I could not go without speaking with you first."

"You are not coming back." Rannulf's words were filled with the same sadness.

"Who is to say for certain. It is time we make our own lives. Too long have we been like twins, the right and left hands on one body. You have your wife now. She will surely keep your loneliness at bay. You'll not notice I am missing." Temric grinned at him. Once again, his cheek set to aching; he scratched at the crusting blood to ease it.

Rannulf shrugged. "Aye, thoughts of her do tend to fill the hours that once lay heavy in my hands. It is good to see you smile so readily. I think I'd forgotten you knew how."

"Aye, so I had. Rannulf, the next time I place myself above you in my suffering, do not wait nigh on a score of years to tell me what I've done."

"You have my word on it."

Silence welled up between them. Neither wished to be the first to say farewell. Finally Temric asked, "And if I do return? Will I find you do not want me back?"

"This is your home, no matter what you've done." The words were warm with the love they shared. Rannulf continued briskly. "Now, begone with you. Jesus God, Temric, a wool merchant?" he finished in disgust.

"A fate worse than death, no doubt." Temric laughed and grabbed his brother in a close embrace.

Rannulf freed himself, then patted his brother on his injured cheek. "Now, that one will be an interesting scar."

Temric smiled and gave a jaunty salute, then strode

swiftly across the bailey to where a groom held his saddled gelding. Once mounted, he spurred the big steed toward the gate.

Across the bailey, Rannulf turned his back, unable to watch his brother ride out of this life they'd always shared.

Temric stared at the small clearing. The pale bark on the birches to the left were red with blood, the mossy ground torn and broken in a wide circle. Saplings and brush were uprooted. A stand of lilies had been crushed, the blossoms giving up their heavy perfume as they died.

"Jesu, Peter. It looks like a battle was fought here."

"There was," the boy replied, his face white in the sickness of first blooding. "Mary," he cried out and stumbled over a small rise to the stream beyond it. The sound of his empty retching echoed back to those who yet stood in the clearing.

"He took it well, in all," Graistan's chief forester, Hobb atte Lea, offered coolly. "Those two were none too eager to give up their lives, although they loosed their weapons the instant we came upon them and cried 'trespassers.'"

Temric breathed a sigh of relief. Lindhurst's men had challenged first, then lost. That was honorable enough.

Hobb was still speaking. "Good it is you were able to unearth this scheme of theirs. They had planned to murder Anne and Peter, along with the lady. Worse, one man had been paid to kill the other, then disappear." The huntsman made a face of disgust. "While my son dragged the first one away, the other blubbered the tale to me as he breathed his last. Food for worms they are now, deep inside the chase."

"That they plotted so does not surprise me," Temric replied as he dismounted. "My thanks for the help you and your kin have given. Bear the same to Walter and Guy when you are next at Graistan. Say to them that I wish I had more than my forgiveness for confining me in the tower to give them."

"Well, your forgiveness they would gladly accept, but no more. Nor would I or my son take anything save your kind regards, my lord."

It startled Temric to hear himself so called. All too quickly, it felt right. Too bad, for it would be the last time for him. To keep Philippa, he'd not hear the title again.

"Good journey, and bear my greetings to your mother." The huntsman slipped between the trees and was gone.

Temric went to join Lady Benfield at the wagon's side. Philippa was deep in sleep, the battered side of her face turned upward to spare further injury against the cart's bed. Anne had done a fine job of sewing the torn skin; there would be but a little scar visible once it had healed. Still, her cheek was swollen and already yellow-green, her eye deeply ringed with purple. He brushed his fingers against the curve of her jaw. Never again would she know such pain or abuse.

After a moment, he turned to Philippa's mother. "So, my lady, we part now. You must be on your way back to Graistan. Have you another gown in the wagon? This one must stay here."

The noblewoman was yet robed in Philippa's aqua and green gowns. Crusting blood stained them from shoulder to breast on one side. Their skirts were heavy

with mud and the sleeves soaked through by the continuing rain.

Edith turned to him, her expression filled with pleasure at Philippa's rescue. Animal blood had been
smeared on her face and hair. Her plait was torn loose
in supposed madness and pale hair hung softly against
her cheeks. Despite her disarray, in this moment she
rivaled either daughter in her beauty.

"Look," she said, then pulled open the blankets and
cloaks covering her daughter. "Look what he did to
her."

Temric stared at the woman he loved. It was not
the full curve of her breasts that trapped his gaze, but
the way light glistened off the myriad scars that traced
whimsically across her midsection. "Jesus God," he
breathed.

Emotions flew, one after the other, through him.
Horror gave way to pity for her pain only to disappear
beneath a deep and raging hate for the man who'd
done this to her. If he had seen these prior to their
combat, Roger of Lindhurst would have died, even if
the bishop had tried to stop him.

"He will pay for this," Temric managed in a ferocious whisper as he closed the blankets back around
her, "you have my word on it, my lady."

"Aye, he has earned that," Edith said quietly. "How
my arrogance and pride has hurt her." In the wagon's
bed she found a knife with a well-honed blade longer
than his hand. She moved gracefully to stand amid the
carnage in the copse. With the knife she sliced away
her belt, then severed the lacings at either side of her
overgown and nicked the gown's neckline. A single
pull and threads, weakened by years of storage, gave
way; the gown split down the front. She stepped from

it, still wearing the green undergown, then began to pick the tiny, precious stones from the aqua garment's trim.

Temric arched a brow at her in confusion. "What are you about?"

Edith laughed. "Are you so honest? If thieves were at fault for my daughter's death, it would hardly do for our searchers to find the gown, whole and folded, valuable gems yet in place, would it?"

When she had plucked it clean, she held out the handful of stones to him, the thin undergown whispering and flowing around her as she moved. "Here, take them," she insisted. "It must be right, else they'll not believe it. If you keep them, I can say I gave you a dowry for my daughter," she finished with a harsh laugh.

He let her pour the tiny bits of rock into his palm, then turned to his mount. From the pommel of his saddle hung a leather scrip. This he opened and dropped the gems within it. When he again faced Edith, she was watching him with an expression of worried sadness.

"Do you fear for your daughter, my lady?"

She gave her head a tiny shake. "Nay, I am pondering over what Graistan's priest has laid on me. I am to go on a pilgrimage to restore my soul through holy travel. So, too, has my younger daughter Rowena urged me. Do you know that when I knelt before Rowena and begged her forgiveness, she gave it?" Edith looked up, eyes filled with tears, as the words slipped from her in wonder. "Before I start on my journey, will you grant me a favor?"

At his nod, she continued. "Say to Philippa that I clung to a dream of what could never be and that I was wrong in giving her to Lindhurst. Now, I have entrusted her to you, but I have done it more carefully this time. I have asked of you at Graistan. All say you are a kind and caring man and that you value your common family as much as your noble kin. I have heard Rowena's tale of your love for your brother. All that needs doing is for you to swear to me that you will care for her."

"My lady, she shall be as my wife," Temric said, "and know only happiness with me."

"I am content. Tell her, then, that I gave her to you only after I was certain of your care." Edith's sigh was soft and sad. "What I forgot to do the first time, I have done the second."

"I will relate to her all you have said to me," he assured her. It pleased him that so much good was coming from this plan of his, but he was anxious to be gone.

Edith set her knife's tip to her undergown. The lethal blade slid from throat to midchest, whirring softly as it split the material. Dressed now only in a thin chemise, she tossed the gown to the opposite side of the copse.

"There," she said in satisfaction, "all is ready, save one last thing." With that she set the knife's point at the V of her ribs. "Will you push the blade home for me?"

Temric caught his breath in sudden understanding. "Edith," he said, his voice softening as he walked carefully toward her, "this is not necessary. Give me your knife and know you've done well in ruining the gowns. Give me your knife." He kept his tone calm and soothing.

"I cannot," she said with a sudden tremble in her voice. She jammed the blade upward into her chest.

"Nay!" Temric shouted in horror as he lunged for her.

Edith blanched against the pain. Blood throbbed from her, indicating a heart wound. "Oh, it hurts," she gasped quietly. Her hands clenched against the hilt, blood puddling between her fingers.

"What have you done?" he cried out in grief. "Philippa will be torn in pieces knowing you are damned to hell."

Edith dropped slowly to her knees, still staring against the pain. When she spoke, it was words with gasps between. "Can you not see how Roger will want her bones? Now, vow, whilst I can still hear you, to set me afire once I'm gone. There's oil in the cart for you. You see," she sighed, easing back to sit as her life flooded from her, "we're much alike, but there's no mistaking those marks."

"You cannot ask me to do that," Temric said as he knelt beside her, cradling her gently to make what was now unavoidable easier for her. " 'Tis not Christian."

"Do not fail me now," she begged, tears starting into her eyes, "else my sacrifice is wasted. I cannot be buried for what I've done. What difference does it make?" Her breath tore raggedly in her chest. "Do it, and pray after for forgiveness." A shadow clouded her eyes, then they dulled. Her breathing stilled.

"Jesus God, Temric, she's killed herself!" Peter stared at the third dead body he'd seen this day, his eyes unsteady in his still white face.

"Aye, damn her, and I've no choice but to do as she said." Sickness roiled within him at the thought. God would not soon forgive him, nor he, himself. He went to the cart to fetch her oil and saw the blood staining his mail sleeves and gauntlets. With the remains of the undergown, he wiped off what he could. It would not do to have someone see and send the searchers in his direction. "Gather up what dry wood you can find, boy."

Grief at what Edith had done made his voice harsh and rough, sending his brother leaping to his task. In moments she lay soaked in the flammable substance upon the best bed of branches they could make.

He stared down at her, thinking he should offer some prayer, if not for her, then for himself and what he did to her. No particular words came to mind. He set sparks to tinder, then glowing tinder to her final bower. Flames awoke, smoky and reeking. It would be worse 'ere too much longer.

"Get to the leads," he said to Peter. "I would be as far from here as quickly as we can get there." The boy led the ponies and cart out onto the roadbed. Temric mounted his gelding and wondered if he, too, shouldn't empty his stomach.

Chapter Fourteen

Philippa cried out, stiffening against the flash of pain that seared through her.

"Hush, little one," a man said. "Hold tight, we've not much farther to travel." His hand brushed her face, his skin warm against hers.

"My head aches," she managed through clenched teeth.

"To be sure. That was a mighty blow you endured."

His soft voice awoke a picture in her mind. Crooked nose, a neatly trimmed beard, dark hair and eyes that glowed golden when he looked at her. She sighed against the deep feeling that accompanied his image. Her brow creased as she fought to find his name, but nothing came to her. Philippa yelped as she was again jolted. This time the pain overwhelmed her and she dropped back into nothingness.

Temric grimly watched her exit from consciousness. The misty rain made her skin gleam where it was exposed beneath cloak and blanket. Thank God and His saints they were now within a stone's throw of their destination. He could only hope the inclement weather would not bring additional sickness onto her.

In habit borne from years of warring, he studied the gate towers that overhung Stanrudde's dry moat.

Thick and rectangular, their footings sloped outward to discourage sappers. Arrow slits appeared at regular intervals offering the defenders clear targets up and down the ditch. Massive wooden doors yet stood wide, revealing an iron portcullis at either end. Such a trap was usually indicative of murder holes or arrow loops set between either metal gate.

As they neared the gateway, Stanrudde's six churches all set their bells to ringing, warning the inhabitants that Compline was but a quarter hour away. They had arrived just in time, for the town gates closed at the onset of this, the last mass of the day.

It wasn't until they were on the tongue of wood spanning the ditch that the panic hit Temric; he would ride within these walls and be trapped forever, when his rightful lands went wanting their lord. Nothing in his life had ever felt as wrong as what he now contemplated. Then he glanced at Philippa. There were things more important than fiefs and keeps. By sheer willpower alone, he banished his worries. In time, he would grow accustomed to this life of his mother's.

He watched Peter, perched atop the lead pony, as the lad brought the little wagon to a halt. The boy's face had regained its color as shock faded, but he'd remained sober and quiet for the duration of their travel. Just as well. Temric doubted he could have tolerated idle conversation this day.

A man stepped forward, his scarlet capuchin brilliant against a dark cloak. "Your business?" he barked.

"Timothy, it is I, Peter, son of Peter the wool merchant. With me rides Richard FitzHenry of Graistan, my half brother and my mother's eldest son. We bring with us Richard's wife so she might dwell with my mother as she recovers from grave injury." The boy's voice was clear and strong.

How strange to hear Peter speak aloud what lay in Temric's heart. Despite his stringent control, Father Edwin's warnings against deceptions rang in his ears. His dying honor cried out for rescue. Nay, 'twas better to live in deceit, for life without Philippa would be impossible.

The gatekeeper gave Peter a broad grin and a wave of recognition. "Hey, laddie, I hardly recognized you. You stretch with each passing month. Tell Mistress Alwyna we have all prayed for Jehan's swift recovery."

His brother's nod was friendly in return. "I will surely do so and your prayers are gratefully accepted for our sake as well as Jehan's. He's driven us all mad with his screamings over life's unfairness."

"No doubt. Pass on."

They passed through the gate and entered Stan-rudde by the fuller's lane. This narrow street paralleled the river that cut the city in twain. The rushing water grew far tamer as they rode into the center of the city. Here, numerous canals diverted its flow, each meant to wash away offal and carry garbage beyond the walls, but the town council had been remiss about cleaning for the canals were dark and putrid, the water's movement sluggish.

"Peter," Temric finally called out, spurring his gelding forward to ride beside his brother for a bit, "what made you name Philippa my wife?"

The boy gave him an odd glance. "Who else would she be? You are incapable of hiding your affections for her. Nor do I think Mama would want to know she is another man's wife and your half sister by marriage."

Temric sighed. The complexity of what he attempted grew in successive stages, layer upon layer. He'd counted on Alwyna's support, not her condemnation. Peter was right, it was better if she did not know.

The lane abruptly narrowed, leaving just enough room for their cart providing the passersby squeezed up against the walls. Once these homes had borne bright paints and fanciful trims. Now, their walls were mold-stained and their paint peeled. Years of English dampness had bent their bones until they leaned far out over the lane, some actually touching their neighbors across the street.

From all around him came snippets of sound: a baby's cry, workmen calling out to one another, a girl's reedy voice raised in song. He caught the echo of a man and woman trapped in violent argument. The warm scent of boiling stew came wafting up from a cookshop, its front panels opened wide to attract customers.

Peter bore to the right, passing a second church and the wide grassy plain where the horse fair was held. Three monks, cowls drawn up against the mist, shuffled quickly by them, hurrying home for the night. At the city's southern end, nearer to the great abbey and the marketplace it claimed, stood the grander homes. Like their cousins at the city's center, they were built of wood with slate roofs, but these stretched to four stories in height. Here, the first floors were more likely to be storerooms filled with finished goods and backed by counting rooms with locked strongboxes rather than a tradesman's workroom.

Temric recognized his mother's home as Peter turned the lead pony's head onto the stone-paved entrance. They rode between house and stable and onto a cobbled square enclosed by those two buildings along with two warehouses. In the courtyard and protected by an awning of greased cloth, Alwyna's apprentices were scraping sheepskin in preparation for making parchments.

The boys waved to Peter, then one dashed into the house, chickens and a squealing piglet scattering before him. Temric had barely dismounted before Alwyna was on him. "Temric," she screamed in joy, "you've come. God be praised, you are here!"

He wrapped his arms around his mother in a warm embrace, then released her and stood back to look. "Mama, you're naught but bones." Her gowns hung loosely, and her face, usually round and full-cheeked, was gaunt, eyes deeply shadowed. Hair, once as dark as his own, was now heavily threaded with silver. "Are you ill?"

"Nay, I am but careworn and sad. Now that you are here, I will rest easier," she sighed, holding one of his hands tightly in her own while she lay her other one on the broken skin of his cheek. "What happened?"

"An old hag took a dislike to me," he said briefly, then leaned down to kiss his mother's cheek.

"Rannulf let her wound you?" she cried in sudden outrage. "I thought I raised him better than that."

"He had nothing to say in the matter," Temric replied with a laugh. Then he sighed, wishing he did not need to deceive his mother. He could only pray that she'd accept without question the tale he would tell her. "Mama, I've brought someone with me."

"Who?" she asked, yet clinging to his hand.

"Come and see." He led her to the wagon's side, then lifted out Philippa. Still trapped in her personal darkness, she curled instinctively into his embrace. He shifted her in his arms until her head was pillowed against his cloaked shoulder. By God, but it felt right to hold her close this way.

"Jesus, Mary, and Joseph," Alwyna breathed. "What has happened to her?" She reached up to brush her fingertips against the girl's bruised face. Philippa jerked slightly in his arms.

"I only just saved her from those who would have seen her dead," he said quietly.

Alwyna looked from Philippa to him, a shrewd expression in her eyes. "There is more to it than that. I can see it in your face. Well, come within and bring her with you. The more trouble the merrier, I always say, and we're laughing aplenty already." She could not still the catch in her voice.

Temric easily bore Philippa's slight weight as they crossed the courtyard and entered the tiny antechamber that fronted the counting room. Against the wall lay a steep flight of stairs. He followed Alwyna up these to the second story and the hall.

"Wait here a moment whilst I fetch Marta and Els. They'll care for that poor creature so you can take your ease and we can talk." Alwyna crossed the dimly lit room, her skirts brushing through the rushes on the floor, to the door in the wall dividing this room from the kitchen alongside it.

Little had changed here in the six years since his last visit. As always, parchment lined the three arched windows in the south wall and he thought the painted linen panels covering the walls might be different. The brick walls channeling smoke from the massive hearth outside the house were new. So, too, was the brightly painted cabinet standing next to the disassembled table, its shelves displaying the dining crockery. Four large wooden chairs sat near the fire, their backs to the doorway. From one of these chairs, Alwyna's middle son peered at him.

"Jehan," Temric said in cool greeting to his stare.

"So, the prodigal son returns," his half brother quipped, his snatch of laughter snide. "Come to gloat over my downfall, have you?"

"Do not start with me," Temric replied, keeping his voice emotionless. "I've had a trying enough day without enduring your rancor as well."

"I have reached my majority, Norman, and this is my house, not yours. I may do as I please."

"Jehan!" Alwyna snapped as she entered. At her heels were two girls, one bearing a bucket of steaming water, the other, toweling and a cloth for washing. "This house is mine until I give it to you."

"Pardon, Mama," Jehan retorted without a shred of sincerity, "but I wonder at you putting so much faith in him. He's no different than any other Norman, sneering at our life-style. Why, had you not sent Peter to fetch him, I doubt he would have come at all. He cares nothing for what plagues us."

Alwyna released a breath in irritation. "Pay him no heed, Temric. He snaps and snarls because of his injury which"—her tone grew steely as she stared directly at her middle son—"will not heal until his bile is settled."

Temric fought back his dislike for the man his brother had become. The moment Jehan had grown old enough to understand that Alwyna had been leman to a Norman lord, he had hated the result of that union. "He is entitled to his opinion, Mama," Temric replied.

"Do me no favors, Norman," Jehan retorted. "What is that you bring with you? A whore to warm your nights?"

Rage roared through Temric. "Shut your mouth, you insolent brat!"

Jehan smiled broadly. "Why, I believe I have finally stung you. I never imagined you capable of such passion."

Suddenly Temric's head throbbed and he closed his eyes. "Mama, forgive me. I have no right to behave so in your hall."

"Think no more on it," Alwyna said, turning him toward a second flight of stairs outside the hall. "Bear her upstairs to bed, then return. I'll have the boys fetch your chest in so you can disarm and eat in comfort. Marta and Els will see to your bit of trouble. Go." She motioned to the stairs.

As he started up, he heard Jehan say, "Not in the new bed! That is to be mine when Clarice and I wed."

"In my house I put her where I choose," Alwyna replied in barely concealed anger.

The third story was a single open room, occupying the length and width of the kitchen and solar directly beneath it. Linen curtains had been strung on a web of ropes to section it into private sleeping areas. The younger girl shoved aside one of these panels to reveal a simple bed.

Although the frame was plain, its draperies and clothes were not. Imported damask created a fabric ceiling and hung as curtains along all four sides. Wool blankets, rich and thick, lent their warmth to linen sheeting. Atop them lay a coverlet pieced together from squirrel pelts and bolsters filled with down. He settled Philippa onto the mattress. She moaned slightly and turned into the soft pillows.

"Go, Master Temric," said Marta. "We will care for her now. The mistress wishes some time with you." When he continued to hesitate, she smiled at him. "Be at ease. We will call you if she awakens."

He returned to Alwyna's hall and within the hour had disarmed, washed away the day's filth, and dressed in a clean shirt, plain brown robe, and soft shoes taken from his chest. He and Peter shared a meal of cold meat pies and cheeses with fresh ale to wash it down. All the while, Jehan stared sullenly into the flames on the hearth. After he'd given up his tray and cup, Temric eased back into his chair. There was no escaping what came next. Alwyna brought a stool to sit close beside him.

"So, what tale is it that follows that battered bit of a girl?"

"I have brought her here to protect her from those who would destroy her." He kept his voice low and soft.

"And why will no one come looking for her?" his mother asked.

"She is my wife. Who could come searching for her?"

Alwyna's brows rose as she struggled to accept what he said. "I think I will not question why I was not invited to the wedding."

"That would probably be best," he agreed.

"Wonderful," Jehan said, his voice heavy with sarcasm. "You beg him to help you and instead he comes to use us for his own purposes. I ask you, Mama, how much more can we tolerate? First, there was that damn ransom for our great and glorious king; we'll be paying our part of that for years. Then my father's death cost us lost trade and extra taxes. Now, I have fallen and rendered myself a cripple." His voice rose a notch in what was almost hysteria.

"Hold your tongue, Jehan," Alwyna snapped. "Aye, you've had a fall, but you're not helpless."

"Helpless!" he retorted. " 'Tis worse than that, I'm useless! I stand and my legs will not hold me. I am nothing! Gerard is right to reconsider my marriage to Clarice. Who wants their daughter tied to one such as I?" His voice rose to a high-pitched wail. "By all the saints, it sickens me to see you bow and scrape before him." He jabbed an angry finger toward Temric. "Do you believe he'll lower himself to our level or that his noble connections can help you? While you think to set him in my place, your precious bastard only uses you!" His final words rang into the silence of the room.

Alwyna leapt to her feet, whirling and striking out even before the echo of the last word died away. Her hand met Jehan's cheek with a loud crack of skin against skin. "How dare you," she hissed. "Rob, Tom," she shouted, "it is time to take Master Jehan to his bed."

"I am sorry, Mama," Jehan cried out, suddenly no more than a pitiful child. "I did not mean to hurt you, only him. We do not need him here. Let him and his woman return to his Norman kin where he belongs."

His mother turned her back on her middle son as the servants lifted him from his chair and carried him up the stairs. "How dare you speak so foully to me of my son—" she called out after him, but Temric interrupted her.

"Say no more, Mama. It will only goad him on in his hate for me."

The room dropped into a bitter quiet, disturbed only by the pop and hiss of the burning logs on the hearth. Peter stood and pretended a wide yawn. "I am done for. Good night, Mama." He kissed his mother's brow. "I will go keep Jehan company in his misery while you converse with Temric." He left the room to take the stairs, two at a time.

When he was gone, Alwyna turned on Temric, tears trembling on her lashes. "Do not heed Jehan, I beg you. If that woman needs sanctuary, I offer it willingly. I know you would not have brought her to me save in the gravest of need."

"My thanks, Mama," Temric said, reaching out from his chair to grasp her fingers. "Mayhap it is Jehan's injury which makes him act this way." Even as he said it, he did not believe it.

"Nay, you know that is not true, nor should you try and defend Jehan. I do enough of that for all of us. By God, it is not me who betrays him, but him me! After his father's death, I expected him to rise and take his father's place." Her voice broke and tears coursed down her cheeks.

"Oh, Peter," Alwyna mourned aloud to her departed husband, "I was not ready for you to go." She wrapped her arms around herself as she keened. Temric rose and embraced her so Alwyna could pour her heart into his shoulder. When she caught her breath in a final, jerky sob, she pushed away to wipe her eyes with a wide sleeve.

"Pardon me," she gasped out, "I am overly emotional and I miss your stepfather terribly. His absence has left a wrenching hole in my life as well as my heart. Now, because Jehan cannot or will not take Peter's place, we stand to lose everything his father and I worked so hard to gain. I should remarry as the guild would have me do, at least I'd have a partner with whom to share these burdens."

"Do you hesitate for your heart's sake?" Temric asked quietly, knowing how deeply his mother had adored her husband.

She shook her head as she reclaimed her stool beside his chair, then indicated he should sit again as well. "Nay, I need the help. 'Tis on Jehan's behalf I hold back. You heard him, even your assistance is intolerable. How would he hate me if I put a new master into the chair he thinks he owns? Ach, but he will not work to keep his place nor will he give it up, and I cannot bear his hate." Again, her eyes filled. "Damn me, if I could but cease these endless tears," she sighed.

Then she raised her eyes to him, their dark depths filled with pleading. "In January, when I originally asked you to come, it was but to have you at my side for a time to ease my heart. Now, I am begging help. I know it is an insult for a knight to lower himself into trade, but I need you to take Jehan's place, if just for a little while. Help me buy time enough for him to recover."

"An insult to help my mother when she needs it? Hardly," he said with a little smile. "Besides, I am no different than any other man, what skills I have were taught to me. If I learned once, I must not be such a dullard that I cannot learn something new. Tell me what you need."

"My thanks," she said, her relief evident. "You must travel on my behalf to those hamlets with whom we have buying agreements. The French grow increasingly more bold, no longer content to buy from us when they can go directly to the source. I fear if we do not appear upon our contracted date, our fleece will be sold out from beneath us."

Temric frowned. "Mama, I am an outsider who knows nothing of buying wool. Would I not be better here to manage your weavers and your warehouse? You should do the traveling."

She shook her head. "Nay, 'tis a man of respectable age and connection to my family that's required for dealing with the reeves and bailiffs. Tom will go with you; he was Peter's servant for years and most likely knows more than I about wool."

Temric looked at her for a long moment, then shrugged. "Are things so dire here that you must entrust me with such an undertaking?"

Alwyna's desperation revealed itself in the gaunt lines of her face. "If we lose even one fleece, I think we will not survive the blow. I was counting on the dowry of Jehan's bride to aid us, plus her hands to do what I cannot as I am now overburdened with the tasks Jehan and Peter once did. You must go for me on the morrow and do what I cannot."

"The morrow? What if Philippa has not yet awakened? I cannot leave her here without bidding her farewell."

His mother gave the shadow of a smile. "Oh, so her name is Philippa, is it? At least you've given me that much." Then all trace of amusement died. "Our need is that great. We're already overdue at three of the hamlets as of yesterday."

It was Temric's turn to sigh. If he was to guarantee Philippa's•life here, he had no choice but to do as Alwyna asked. "Well, then, the morrow will find me on the road once more. Send Tom with me and we will manage. Mayhap, by my return I'll be convinced the merchant life is equally as interesting as that of a soldier."

"Hold a moment," Alwyna said, her voice suddenly firming into harsh tones, "your help I crave, but the need is only temporary. Jehan will either improve and take his role, or I will remarry. You were bred for holding lands and I'll not take that from you. Is this more to do with your bitter feelings toward your father?" Her eyes narrowed.

"Nay, Mama," he said softly, "I no longer deny my father's affection for me. He did not forget me."

"Richard!" his mother cried, then grabbed Temric's face between her hands. As she studied him, her eyes slowly lit with pleasure. "You have accepted him! If you have found your peace, then how can you turn your back on what should be yours?"

He gave a little shrug, the corners of his mouth lifting just a bit.

" 'Tis that girl up there," she said harshly. "What have you done, my son? Stolen her from her family?"

He gave a start as her barb hit home. "Not precisely."

"You idiot," Alwyna breathed. "You've come here to hide with her. Have you fooled yourself into thinking you will like the way we live? Richard, you haven't the temperament for this life."

"I see no sense in arguing with you, when you have so great a need and I am available. There is no place safer for us than here." He rose to his feet and stretched. His muscles ached from the long ride and the battle of this morn. "Pardon, Mama, but it has been a day like as you would not believe. I am off to bed."

"Aye, hide your tale from me, just like you hide that girl from whoever seeks her," she said in irritation, "but you won't be able to hide from yourself. Traveling offers plenty of time to consider the error of your ways. I will bid you farewell on the morrow and when you return, you will do the same to me."

"Time will tell."

"You may stay until you are sick to death of us," she said, irritation suddenly easing into thankfulness. "And I will be glad for every moment you are here."

"If day to day is commitment enough for you, Mama, it is enough for me. Good night, Mama." He leaned down to kiss her cheek.

"Oh, Lord, where will I put you," Alwyna said, leaping to her feet. "That girl is in your bed."

"Mama," he said quietly, "I sleep with Philippa."

"Richard!" she cried out in protest. "You've all but told me she belongs to another man."

"Those words never crossed my lips, Mama. I told you she is my wife." He kept his voice toneless. "Go to bed, Mama," Temric said with a smile. "Say your prayers for my soul if you like, while I do your work for you." He left the room to join Philippa in their bed.

When he pushed aside the closed drape, the single tallow lamp on a stool cast an oily glow into the enclosed area. The younger maid had fallen asleep on her seat, her head upon the mattress. Temric smiled, then went to shake the girl awake. "Come, child, time to seek your own pallet," he said, his voice low.

The lass came awake with a yelp of fright. "Oh, master," she cried out, "I was dreaming."

Her cry startled Philippa into a low moan. Temric leaned across the bed to put his hand against her shoulder. "Hush, little one."

Philippa looked up at him, her eyes wide, clear. "Where am I?" she cried. Jerking away from his touch, she came straight up into a sitting position, then moaned as her swift movement caused her pain. Her hand flew to the side of her head. "It hurts," she sobbed.

Temric shooed the maid away and pulled the drapery shut before he sat beside Philippa on the bed. His heart ached when she eyed him in fear and flattened herself against the bed's wooden headboard. "This is not my home," she cried. "I do not know you. Please, I am frightened, let me go home. Help me," she begged, her eyelids drooping as she fought the sleep her brain demanded to heal its own injury.

"Hush, love, you are safe," he said gently.

"What has happened? Where am I?" she breathed, tears starting to her eyes. "My thoughts spin and whirl and I can keep nothing straight."

He leaned toward her, meaning to embrace her, and she caught her breath in a quiet gasp. "I know you." The words were uttered in such relief it made him smile. She reached out to trace the line of his nose, the curve of his cheek, then outlined his lips with a fingertip. When she smoothed her fingers against his beard, he had to close his eyes against the sudden desire her touch awoke within him.

"You are Temric." Her voice was filled with pleasure at her recognition of him.

"So I am," he replied. She had not forgotten him.

How mightily that pleased him. He gathered her into his arms and she immediately lay her head against his shoulder.

"You will keep me safe," she sighed. "I am so tired. Might I sleep again?" Even as she spoke he was easing her back down to lay upon the mattress. Her eyes were instantly closed and she was once again adrift within herself.

He began to pull the blankets back over her, then paused. With a fingertip, he touched one of the curling scars that crossed her midsection. It was fine and flat, made with a knife's tip some years ago. Again his stomach twisted in hate. A man like Lindhurst had no right to live.

Once he had seen these, he understood why in the glade she had looked at him in such fear. Then, her eyes had been wide with terror and her face devoid of color. With a sigh, he realized the possibility that what her husband had done might make her incapable of sharing her body with him.

Hope flared back to life. 'Twas she who initiated the kiss in the tower chamber. The passion she'd shown revealed she yet harbored a woman's desire. He smiled then in understanding. It had been his vow not to touch her that had freed her to approach him without fear of hurt. Aye, she would learn to trust him with her body if he was but gentle and patient.

He rose and pulled off his clothing, hanging them over the pole that forestalled mice and rats from making free with them. The linen bedclothes were comfortably soft when he slid beneath them, made so by her body's warmth. She had her back to him. He could not resist moving closer, fitting his legs against hers, curving his chest against her back.

Alwyna's maidservants had bathed her in water boiled with flowers. Her skin still bore their faint scent. He brushed his mouth against the smooth curve of her shoulder. She was his, now, his to hold and keep safe, to cherish and love. He relaxed against her. "Philippa of Stanrudde, you are heart of my heart and I will be yours when you are ready."

Chapter Fifteen

Philippa opened her eyes, blinking in surprise. She blinked again, thinking if she did so, the view might change. It did not. There was absolutely nothing familiar in what met her gaze. Not even the musty odor that filled her with every breath was known to her.

Soft pillows lay beneath her head and the coverlet beneath her fingers was silky fur. The mattress was covered in smooth linen sheets. Mayhap she only dreamed. She squeezed her eyes shut to force herself into wakefulness, then opened them again. Nothing changed.

Roger's image arose, his face twisted in rage. He had meant to kill her. Was she dead? If so, then heaven seemed an ordinary sort of place, save for the bed. It was draped in rich damask dyed a deep golden color. Sudden panic shot through her. What if she yet lived and it was Roger who held her here to further torture her?

As quickly as that thought came, she dismissed it. Not possible. If Roger held her, she would know no comfort. Nor would he ever grant her the use of a bed and certainly not one as rich as this.

Fearing an unknown watcher, Philippa remained si-

lent and motionless as she studied what lay beyond
the open bed curtains. A shaft of bright daylight sliced
through an otherwise murky dimness, its source a single arched window in the wall. Through that opening
also came the call of men and boys at work. Pack
animals brayed and a goose honked in outrage. Distant church bells added stern punctuation to it all.

There was another line of curtains, this plainer drapery reaching from beamed ceiling to a wooden floor
bare of any covering. A large chest, painted a bold
red with green trim carved like interconnecting leaves,
stood beneath the window. It was heavy; it had gouged
the floor when it had been pushed into its present
position.

Philippa frowned, probing her mind for some hint
of her location. Images swam before her inner vision.
Margaret with her stick held high. A kind woman with
dark hair and eyes. There'd been a reunion with her
mother and her sister. Pleasure washed over her. Her
joy at meeting them again still retained its potency.
Her family had reclaimed her as one of their own.

Someone else had claimed her as well. Her mouth
lifted at the recall. Temric. The very syllables of his
name evoked within her so many emotions, but of
them all it was her heart's ache for him that lingered.

From the deepest recesses of her mind awoke a
masculine figure, faceless and dark against a halo of
bright light. When he had spoken to her, his words
had echoed from the inside outward rather than
through her ears. But who was Richard? The only
men she knew by that name lived among Lindhurst's
peasantry and they were all referred to as either Dick
or Dickon, never Richard.

At last her swirling memories coalesced into something coherent. The bishop's gown had been threaded with gold. Graistan's priest had said he would beg the bishop to send her to a convent. She relaxed in hopeful comprehension. No doubt that was where she was.

Unwilling to risk the consequences were she wrong, Philippa rolled slowly onto her back, as if she yet slept. Cautiously, carefully, she turned her head toward the opposite side of the bed. A flash of movement drew her attention.

It was a man, pulling on a tunic over his shirt and chausses. A man? Then this could be no convent. Where, then? She watched as his head appeared through the neck opening.

"Temric," she gasped in shock, "what are you doing here? Where am I?" Philippa struggled into a sitting position despite the sharp stab of pain and instant nausea her swift movement caused. She groaned, her hands at her head to stop the intense throbbing and brace her against a whirling world.

Temric only smiled and came to sit on the bedside next to her. He studied her eyes, then said in the language of the commoners, "Good, you are centered in your thoughts again. Here, let me fix the bolsters so you can lean into them. The pain will ease for you if you do not try to sit upright." There was a wry note to his voice that indicated a personal experience with the same injury she suffered.

As he spoke, he reached around her to arrange her pillows. She lay a hand against his chest in an anxious need to prove to herself that this was no dream. He was solid beneath her fingers. By what miracle had she been freed from Roger and given to Temric?

Fear writhed back into life at the obvious answer. Temric had stolen her from her husband. "What have you done? He will come for me and seek my death in earnest. Jesu, Temric, but I cannot face him again!" Her voice lifted into a panicked yelp and she shuddered against the viciousness with which Roger had swung Margaret's stick.

"Quieter, little one," he said, then leaned down for something on the floor by the bed. It was a cup and he offered it to her. "We can speak freely just now as we are alone in this room, but that will not always be the case. Here, watered wine. I expect your mouth is dry as dust."

In truth, it was. She drank deeply, her worried gaze never leaving his face. Once the cup was empty and returned to the floor, he said, "This is my mother's home in Stanrudde. From this time on you must use your English when you speak. Nor should you reveal too much of your past. As for Roger, he will not look for you. Philippa of Lindhurst is dead."

She stared at him, horror atop her terror. Had she died? "Nay," she cried out and laid a hand on her breast. "My heart yet beats, how can I be dead? And you are solid to my touch."

Temric caressed the curve of her jaw with a finger. "Silly love, of course you live. 'Tis the rest of the world that believes your husband a widower."

"How?" she demanded.

"He meant to have you killed and I could not let you die. Trust me. He buries his wife and you are mine." The look he bent on her was so full of what lay in his heart, it took away her breath.

But if his love sent her spirits soaring, she knew his scheme was doomed to fail. "It will not work. Without certain proof that it is me he puts into the tomb,

Roger will never accept it." Her voice rang flat in her hopelessness.

"He has what he needs," Temric replied, his face suddenly taut and hard. "No one doubts your death."

"I do. Convince me," she pleaded softly. "Tell me why I need no longer fear my husband."

He hesitated, taking her hand in his and entwining their fingers. At last, he said, "Lindhurst had beaten you into unconsciousness by the time the bishop was moved to offer the Church's sanctuary. Your husband refused to free you, saying you were his to hold. I challenged him over this and we met sword to sword. He battled for the right to keep you and to take my life for daring the challenge. I fought for your right to enter a holy order."

"You fought for me?" she breathed. It was a great compliment he offered her.

"How could I do otherwise? You are heart of my heart." He raised her hand to his mouth and brushed his lips against her knuckles before continuing. "Lindhurst plotted to keep you from the Church, even if he lost, making it seem you'd run mad from Graistan and died at the hands of some unknown evildoers as portrayed by his own men. I was able to intervene, convincing him he had succeeded when he had not."

When he lapsed into silence, she asked, "And what proof remained that 'twas I who fell as he planned?" He said nothing and in that lengthening pause a horrible thought occurred to her. "Oh, Temric, say you did not do murder for me!"

"Nay, I did not," he replied, his voice now harsh in grief. "I tried to stop her, but I was too late." His grip tightened, his gaze strictly focused on their joined hands.

Philippa's heart broke in understanding. "Oh, Maman," she cried out, "not by her own hand!"

"Aye," he breathed.

A tear trickled its way down her face. When she reached for him, he drew her into his embrace, resting her uninjured cheek against his shoulder. "How could she," Philippa breathed into the soft fabric of his gown. "She left me all alone and damned herself for eternity on my behalf."

He gently rocked her in his arms. "Ah, love, do not mourn her too much. She sought to buy you life with the ending of her own. You are mine now. Your mother gave you to me that I should hold you as my own."

"She did that?" Philippa drew back in stark surprise. "She knew you were bastard born, yet gave me into your care?"

"Aye, she did," he said, running a soothing hand down her back. "She would have you know that she asked after me at Graistan, of my habits and character. She said what she did not do the first time, she did the second."

"Then my proud mother turned her back on all she cherished to grant me this new life," Philippa said softly. Grief paled in the light of so precious a gift.

"I hope you are not dissatisfied, for I've not much to offer you," he said in a rough voice. "A wool merchant's life is hardly grand and you must discard your nobility to accept it. From now on you will be only Philippa of Stanrudde, an orphan without knowledge of mother or father. If you agree, all who meet you will name you my wife."

The harsh lines of Temric's face dissolved into something else. His eyes darkened and she saw in them that he feared her rejection. He had sacrificed, too, to offer her what he could. If she must shed her identity, so did he.

Dear God, but it was a terrible risk. If their subterfuge was exposed, both of them would lose their lives, he for his adultery and she because her husband willed it. No one, not even his powerful brother or his influential cousin, could save them. But her heart's need was the stronger, overruling a fear of death.

"I want to live my life with you," she said in shy acceptance. "Oh, Lord, but I think I have just doomed myself to hell." A tiny laugh escaped her, ever so slightly colored with doubt. "At least when I arrive, I will find my mother awaiting me."

Temric's face relaxed into a wide smile and his eyes glowed golden in pleasure. "Philippa of Stanrudde, I vow you will not travel alone in this life or the next. Can you call me 'husband' knowing the deception we practice?" His tone pleaded for her to say she could.

Philippa smiled. It was wrong, wonderfully, gloriously wrong. "Aye, with the greatest of pleasure," then added in timid amendment, "but I cannot stand before God in His church and speak vows of marriage to you when I am already wed. Only then does the lie grow too great for my soul to bear." She peered up at him, praying he would not be angry at her refusal. There was only happiness in his face.

"I'll not ask that of you," he said, once again enclosing her in his embrace. "But will you trade a private vow with me? In some place beyond the reach of any church, I would offer you mine and hear you speak words that bind you to me."

"I would like that," she replied, her voice hushed against the violent rise of hope within her. He laughed. It was only the second time she'd heard him laugh and the sound of it was rich with his love for her. When he pressed his lips to the spot where her neck curved into her shoulder, she sighed in warm reaction. Aye, she would gladly cleave to him now and worry over her soul later.

Temric drew back to arm's length and studied her, his eyes sparkling with humor. "My, you are trusting. How do you know I will not someday sue you for bigamy?"

"Best you not attempt it else I will have to cry 'kidnapper,'" she retorted.

"I quake before your superior threat." He threw up his hands in mock fright.

Her laugh died into a gasp of pain. "Oh, Lord, but do not make me smile," she moaned half seriously. "How bad does it look?"

He eyed her dispassionately, as if critically weighing the merit of her bruising against others he had witnessed. "I think I have never seen an eye as blackened as yours. It is truly an awesome shade of purple."

Philippa grimaced slightly. "It feels it. Where does the coloring stop?"

With his fingertip, Temric traced the outline of the mark on her face down her cheek to below her chin, around to her ear, over her brow, and into her hair. When he took back his hand, he leaned forward to softly touch his lips to hers. "Hurry and heal. When I return I mean to kiss you far better than that," he murmured, then retreated to the bed's edge.

"Return?" she asked as he pulled on a boot.

He leaned down, wrapping his cross garters over that boot and then the next one as he spoke. "I must now ask your patience and understanding. This morn

I leave to do business on behalf of my mother, who is newly widowed and begs my aid. My half brother, who was to have taken his father's place in their trade, is now crippled by a fall. Without my assistance, we will lose this new life of ours."

All the pleasure within Philippa died away in shock. He was leaving her here, alone and unprotected! How was this any different than when her mother had given her to Roger. "You are deserting me," she cried in panic.

"You are not alone," he replied. "My mother will care—"

"As Margaret did?" All further protest was choked off as her throat closed in terror.

"Nay, love, never that," he said with a smile and a shake of his head. He lifted a leather hauberk from the bed's end and drew it on over his tunic. "My mother will love and honor you because I do."

"Do not go," she finally managed in a strangled voice, finding his words impossible to believe.

"I must and there's no help for it. Peter will bear you company. Do you remember him?"

The image of a lanky youth with fine hair sprang to mind. "Aye," she offered tentatively.

"It is only three, mayhap four weeks. Would that my mother had contracts with abbeys instead of a multitude of hamlets. Six stops makes for a far shorter trip than sixty. I will miss you." His eyes smiled at her even when his mouth did not.

If she were very careful and extremely compliant, she could endure so short a time. "Vow to me you will return. I will perish if you do not," Philippa said hopelessly.

"I do so swear," he replied.

"On what? There is nothing here on which to swear."

"I swear on the love I bear you." He leaned over and touched his lips to hers. "Fare you well, little one. Thrive despite my absence. When I return, we will make our vows." With that he rose, threw open the outer curtain, and strode away from her.

Philippa stared after him in despair, then sank down against the mattress. How could he leave her like this? She was without protector or family and even the location of the chamber pot was beyond her ken. In the wake of her terror came a bone-deep weariness. Against her determination to stay awake and guard herself, sleep overtook her. She drifted into troubled dreams, mourning her abandonment.

When she awoke, there was a girl of no more than thirteen sitting beside her bed. Philippa gave voice to a tiny whimper, the only hint of the fear that ate her vitals. The girl looked up from her needlework at the sound.

"Mistress, you are awake," she said in seeming pleasure. "Master Temric said before he left that you had regained your senses and now slept more normally. I can fetch you broth and bread, if you think you can tolerate it." Her voice was filled with cheerfulness, her mien harmless.

It was impossible for Philippa to maintain her fear against a child. She carefully eased herself into a sitting position, remembering that quick movement added to her pain and nausea. "I would rather the chamber pot," she replied shyly in English.

"How stupid of me." The girl laughed, moving the required item out from behind the curtains and closer to the bed. Once the little maid had closed the outer drapes, she held out her arms. "Here, let me help you rise." With great care and tiny steps, they managed the task between them.

"There," the girl said when she had tucked her charge back beneath the bedclothes, "I would bring you a bowl of broth and more to drink. It will only be a moment."

Still consumed by fear, Philippa watched as the girl ran off without closing either set of drapes behind her. Temric's assurances of love and care rang like footsteps on hollow stone. Why should anyone here accept her? Once again, she was the foreigner, the outsider, this time without even name or family on which to make an introduction. She stared hopelessly out into the chamber.

The light from the window had grown more diffuse, suggesting that the sun stood high above the house. She peered across the room. Another bed stood there, its curtains also open wide. Within it sat a man, his head resting on the headboard as if he studied the bed's ceiling.

It occurred to her Temric might not like another man to look on her, but she needed something to cover her nakedness if she was to rise and close the drapes. Philippa thrust her hand between the pillows. No chemise had been folded away there for her to find. Nor did any garment hang on the clothes pole behind the bed. Dear God, she was trapped here without even a rag to call her own. Fear drove into her, hard and sharp.

The man spoke without looking up. "So, Temric's woman finally awakens," he said, his tone derisive.

Philippa near squeaked in her alarm. "I sleep because I am hurt. I will be better on the morrow," she offered in timorous explanation of her laziness.

He made a rude sound of irritation and raised his head to stare at her. Dark-haired, his face was round, yet soft in lingering youth, unlike Temric's, which was all bold planes as befitted a man in the prime of his life. "What do I care?" he snapped.

Philippa frowned at this. Did he mean he did not care that she lingered in bed or he did not care for her excuses? It was safer to engage him in conversation, she decided, than to seem sullen as well as lazy. "I was told to remain here to await my breakfast."

That seemed to amuse him, for he freed a harsh laugh. "Aye, as do I, and they'd best be quick with it or I'll box someone's ears. I am hungry."

"Jehan, hold that nasty tongue of yours," came a voice from the doorway. A woman no larger than Philippa entered the room and started toward her bed. The serving girl trailed at her heels. "I would take a look at this bit of a girl my son has brought me."

Temric's mother! Philippa's fingers clenched into the bedclothes, her knuckles white, as she receded into the pillows. By the time the woman had reached her bedside, Philippa was crouched back into the bolsters, frozen in fear. Like Margaret, Temric's dam had hair grayed in age, but hers was smoothed into twin plaits. If her face was not so creased, it was too thin and hardened against life's many pains. Her garments were ill-fitting, belted as best they could be about her waist. There was not the slightest emotion in the dark eyes that considered her bedridden guest.

"I beg pardon for lingering so long in bed," Philippa dared in a quiet voice, then added "mistress." She prayed it was the right term. "I promise I will not do so on the morrow."

The woman's eyes flew wide in astonishment. "Of course you will stay in bed. One who's been injured as you have been must take time to let the brain find its place within your skull. You'll stay right where you are for at least a week."

Philippa was suffused in such relief, she sagged against the mattress. Tears spilled from her eyes. It would not be the same here. Shame followed that thought. How could she have doubted Temric?

"Sweet Mary, but they have used you hard," Temric's mother said, her words reflecting the kindness she'd taught her son. Then her face softened in understanding and she brushed stray hairs out of Philippa's face. "Have you been sitting here in terror of us all this time? Shame on me for not coming sooner. How it must have seemed to you, trapped here without knowledge of us or this house and not even a stitch of clothing in which to make your escape. You poor chick, your fear must have eaten you alive!"

The endearment was sweet to Philippa's ears. "Anne of Graistan says that," she murmured, incapable of any louder sound.

"I suppose she would, being my niece. My sister and I are both wont to overuse the phrase. I know you are Philippa, but do you know that I am Alwyna?" Alwyna offered a warm smile that softened her features.

"Temric's mother," Philippa acknowledged, more to convince herself that what was happening was real than in any need to confirm the woman's identity.

"Nay," Alwyna replied, her brown eyes gleaming in a sudden and lively amusement. "I bore no child named Temric. The lad I gave life to was christened Richard, Richard of Graistan. Temric is what comes of stuttering when I am in such a rage that I should not even attempt to speak." The laugh that followed her words was filled with irony. "Once I'd said it, he accepted it in stubborn pride and would not let it go."

"He is Richard?" Philippa breathed in shock. Temric was the Richard of her mysterious vision? Of course. It could be no one else. She swore her heart stilled in her chest, but a moment later she realized that it was the wonder within her that made it seem so.

She closed her eyes with a sigh. Her mother's sacrifice was not in vain. It must have been God who'd commanded her to stay in this life for Richard. She could call Temric husband without fear now, for their union was blessed. If God had given him to her, He would not take him from her.

She was free.

In her sudden release from the past, tiredness reached out to reclaim her once again. As she slipped back into slumber, she heard Alwyna say, "Poor chick, let her rest. She can try these clothes on in the morning."

Chapter Sixteen

When next she woke, Philippa's stomach growled loudly in complaint. Velvet darkness lay all about her save for a sliver of light. The wee beam shot through the meeting of the bed curtains, dividing the bed in twain. She lay still a moment. All she could hear was the rhythmic sounds of folk at rest.

Rolling onto her side, she tugged open the curtains. A small oil lamp stood atop a stool at the bedside. Its little flame burned in merry solitude, dancing and jigging as it consumed the lint. A cup stood there as well, and beside it a bowl and spoon. Philippa stuck a hopeful finger into the congealed liquid in the bowl, then tasted what clung to it.

Not just plain broth. It was meaty with chunks of lamb and had just the right intermingling of flavors. Her stomach growled again and hunger overwhelmed all else. She came swiftly upright and grabbed the bowl, eagerly spooning the thick mess into her mouth. Not until she'd finished it and drunk deeply of the watered wine did she realize that her movement had caused no discomfort. Indeed, her stomach gratefully accepted what she sent it and her eyes held their focus without a trace of dizziness. Aye, by the morrow she might well be steady on her feet.

She sat still for a moment, to mentally probe for healing. Within her now lay a strange calmness, seeping even deeper than skin and bone. All her hurts, whether of the body or the soul, grew easier to bear because of it. Her shoulders lifted. Somewhere in the last hours, her bonds of fear had fallen away. Temric had freed her from Roger's hold and the abuse of Lindhurst. Freedom was, indeed, a glorious thing.

Light flickered against a heap of something at the foot of the bed. She reached down and drew the pile toward her until the lamp could reveal what it was. It was the clothing Alwyna had mentioned, but 'twas more than a chemise and bedrobe. She turned those garments back to expose two plain undergowns and, beneath them, an overgown.

Philippa caught her breath in surprise as she tugged it from the bottom of the heap and held it in the light. It was a pale blue with a demure trim that was a braid of pink and green, the colors singing of springtime. Its simplicity of cut pleased her far more than the grand dress she'd worn at Graistan. She recognized the feel of linen; the weave was tight and even. Catching it to her, she pressed it along the contours of her body, stretching out an arm to gauge the sleeve's length. For a borrowed gown it would fit her well. She did not even flinch at the pain her smile caused her. Temric's mother had cared enough to borrow the right size gown for her.

In that instant Alwyna won her heart. Temric's mother would never regret her generosity toward the injured beggar her son had foisted upon her. Surely, there would be some sort of help Philippa could offer in repayment. Her spirits dimmed. Temric had also warned her to secrecy. Did Alwyna know the truth about her guest?

Philippa lay the overgown back down atop the pile, smoothing away the creases with her hands. Would Alwyna be so generous if she knew? She grimaced. On the morrow, she would listen and learn. For now, she retreated beneath the bedclothes and sought the healing embrace of sleep.

It was the chittering of small birds against the arrogant exclamations of Stanrudde's cocks that awakened her hours later. Philippa stretched in luxurious comfort, her blankets wrapped around her to hoard the warmth.

Dawn crept across the floor in front of her. Colors changed with each moment, from gray to pink to the sun's full golden brightness. Through the same window came the pungent scent of unwashed wool. A breeze danced in, kicking and playing in the outer draperies before it expired with a tiny, whirling sigh.

Finally an eagerness to try on the gown she'd so coveted in midnight's darkness made her toss aside the bedclothes. Kneeling on the mattress she grabbed up the chemise. Its wide neck made it easy to don without rising. Over that she pulled on the undergown. Both garments puddled softly around her knees. With the tight-fitted sleeves smoothed into place, although not tied as they should be, she reached for the overgown.

Its colors were richer in day's light than she'd thought they would be last night. Oh, even if it were only borrowed, it was a beautiful gown and she would wear it with pride. She pulled it on but could not reach the laces in the back. Sliding from the bed, she gained her feet, swayed an instant or two, then felt the world steady. It was with great pleasure that she smoothed her gown down into pretty, even folds, creasing then recreasing as she sought for perfection. So intent was she, she did not hear the footsteps and jerked in surprise when someone shoved aside the drapes.

"Well, now," Alwyna said with a smile. "I truly did not think you would regain your feet so quickly. Huh, I am a better judge of size than I thought. The hem is too long, but Els will quickly fix that. Sorry I am that I could only offer you a used gown from the old clothes seller, but the material is good, even if it is not my own, and the dye only a little faded. Once your bruising is gone, I will take you to the tailor. It'd not do to have the gossips say we mistreated you, eh? When you have something more suitable, we can discard this one."

"This gown is not borrowed?" Philippa stared in confusion at Temric's mother. "I do not have to give it back?"

"Nay, you do not," Alwyna replied, as if she did not quite understand what Philippa had asked. "I have bought it for you and it is yours, to keep or discard as you see fit."

"You bought it for me? This is mine?" Philippa replied in shock, sure she'd misunderstood.

Alwyna only gave her an odd look. "But of course. You came with nothing and I cannot imagine you would care to wander about undressed. Here, I've brought you stockings." She handed them to her along with two ribbon garters and a braid belt. "There are sabots under the bed for now, but the shoemaker comes to make a pattern for you later in the day. Turn around and I will do your laces."

Philippa ran a hand down the body of the gown in disbelief. Hers! When she did not turn, Alwyna went behind her and pulled the strings tight. Once it was knotted, she started on the sleeve openings of the undergown.

When Alwyna was done, Philippa caught her hand. She pressed a swift kiss to its back before releasing it. "Oh, mistress, thank you. It is a beautiful gown and I shall take especial care of it." She moved from foot to foot in delight, making the skirt swirl around her ankles. *Hers!*

"Silly twit." Alwyna laughed. "Some people are far too easily pleased. And best you call me Alwyna. I'll not have it said I make my son's wife a servant in his home."

Philippa caught her breath, both dismayed and restored by Alwyna's words. If one statement said Alwyna would never be like Margaret, the other proved that Temric had not told his mother her true identity. "As you wish, Alwyna," she said, then her exuberance overtook her once again. "Thank you, thank you, a hundredfold!"

Temric's mother laughed at her. "I give you equal welcomes. Do you feel fit enough to come below and eat or shall I have Els bring you something?"

A shout from outside the window overrode her question, a man's voice raised in angry tirade. Alwyna rolled her eyes and sighed, her shoulders slumping as she moved to the narrow opening. "Tom," she called, "bring Master Jehan back to his bed before he sours us all this morn."

Philippa sat on the bed to pull on stockings and shove her feet into the wood-soled shoes. Alwyna turned, her mouth now drooping sadly and the deep rings beneath her eyes darker still.

"I will beg pardon on Jehan's behalf before he arrives. He will insult you, but then he insults everyone." Her voice was dull and toneless. "Pay him no heed."

"Damn you, Mama," he was crying out even before they reached the doorway with him.

Philippa recognized the voice from yesterday's encounter with her roommate. Two serving men entered bearing between them this Jehan. At Alwyna's signal, they placed him in the bed across from hers, then beat a hasty retreat from the room. Jehan was gasping in what almost sounded like sobs.

Alwyna turned her back on him. "So, will you come below to break your fast?"

"I would like that very much," Philippa replied. "It is kind of you to invite this stranger to your table."

"Kind," Jehan snarled. "Hardly. Look at how she treats me. She cares for you because you belong to that bastard she adores, while she bears no affection for her true son."

Alwyna sighed, all trace of light leaving her eyes until they were but muddy brown. "A little peace, Jehan, that is all I ask. The day is barely begun and you have already exhausted me. Your shouting upsets us all and keeps us from our work."

"Aye, shove me up here where you do not need to look on me. Ignore me! Your heart is harder than a millstone." He slumped into his cushions as if he were destroyed.

Alwyna's face crumpled into hurt lines as tears started into her eyes. "Jehan, I do not mean to hurt you," she cried in protest. "I would give you mine own legs if there were but a way to do so."

Philippa's mouth compressed into a narrow line of understanding. She'd played this game of manipulation at Lindhurst and knew it well enough when she saw it. Alwyna's love for her son had become the weapon he used to hurt her. On the tail of the recognition came outrage too great to be stilled.

"Fie on you," she boldly scolded, shaking a finger at him. "Shame on the son who speaks so foully to his mother."

Jehan roared upright from his posture of self-pity. "I'll not be chided by a bastard's whore!" Philippa gave a laugh of disbelief at his paltry attempt to hurt her, but Alwyna cried out in shock.

"Jehan, do not speak so to Richard's wife. In my home you will treat her with the respect she's due." Again, Alwyna's words were double-edged.

Jehan readied himself to fling another attack at his mother. Philippa was the swifter. "Do not dare spew what sits on your lips, Master Jehan. What nags at you that makes you so disrespectful to your mother?"

"Listen how this little nothing speaks to me, Mama," Jehan cried in affront. "Are you going to let her treat me so?" Without thinking about what she did, Philippa took Alwyna by the arm and led her swiftly from the room, then shut the door behind her. Jehan's voice, raised in rage, was audible even through that thick panel. "I am the master in this house and am treated worse than a dog. Upstart! I can throw you into the street if I choose."

"If you had that power, you'd not have to shout about it," she called back, then pressed her hand against her head. "I should not shout at all. Oh, Alwyna, I beg pardon," she cried out, just now realizing what she'd done. "I had no right to interfere, but his choler is his own and I cannot bear that he spills it on you.''

Alwyna sighed, "Nay, 'tis I who should beg your forgiveness and give thanks for your care. You've done no wrong, while I am shamed by his behavior. He was once such a happy lad. What lies in that bed just now is someone I do not know. Forgive him for me, he is tortured by the loss of his father and his legs. If I did not also grieve and were not so exhausted, I could better endure him. In the way of all children, he seeks to share the burden of his pain with me, trusting my eternal love.''

In that moment Alwyna's visage revealed that she carried not only Jehan's pain, but all this family's cares and the burdens of both business and home. Along with her grief for her husband, it was almost more than she could bear. Alwyna's needs were indeed desperate. Philippa forgave Temric his abrupt departure, understanding now why he'd not refused.

"And here I am, yet another burden for you to shoulder,'' she said softly. "Rather that I were a help than a hindrance. With each day, I will grow stronger and more capable. Tell me what I can do for you,'' she pleaded, reaching out to take Alwyna's hand.

Alwyna leaned her head against Philippa's cheek and embraced her in a brief hug. "Daughter, that you should even offer is heaven. I think I will like you well, indeed, but you overestimate your strength. For now I would be content if you would bear me company whilst we break our fast.''

Philippa smiled. She followed Alwyna down the stairs, carefully placing her feet on each step against a sudden return of dizziness. Then, she glanced behind her at the bedchamber door. Determination hardened in her. Legs or not, Jehan had no right to behave so rudely toward his mother. She would find a way to make his abuse cease.

Six days later, Philippa sat on a stool before the kitchen hearth, her fingers flying as she braided onions into a long strand. When it was finished, it would hang alongside the garlic to dry in the fire's heat. She breathed deeply. The kitchen's air grew ever more spicy as summer offered up its bounty. Basil, rosemary, mint, marjoram, sage, dittany, and peppery thyme all hung drying from the great ceiling beams, loosing their fragrances into the atmosphere.

The festivities of Midsummer's Day were at an end; the house now lay in exhausted slumber after the raucous celebration. Still too bruised to feel comfortable meeting folk, Philippa had clung to her bedchamber with nothing to do. So much inactivity had left her sleepless and nervous.

Nay, that was a lie, just like the others she'd told these past days. Sweet Mary, but she could not even tell Alwyna who had beaten her. She was naught but an imposter living a borrowed life.

"Oh, Maman," she breathed to herself, "for this you gave your life? I shame your sacrifice by being nothing but a lie and a cheat." With her arms wrapped tightly around her against the ache in her heart, Philippa rocked back and forth as she grieved. A tune leapt to her lips. It was one her mother had sung to her when she was but a child.

She gave it soft voice. Bitterness at her loss mingled with the sweet memories the words evoked. At the song's end, she whispered a prayer for her mother's soul.

"Why are you not abed?"

Philippa gave a sharp cry of surprise, spilling onions from her lap as she whirled to look on Alwyna. A hand pressed against her chest to still her rapid heart, she said, "Why is it I never hear you come?"

"I am a sneaky sort," Alwyna said with a brief smile. "It comes of chasing after little lordlings always into mischief. Common folk are brighter than the nobles. They do not put swords into the hands of infants." Her bedrobe flowing about her too-thin frame, Alwyna came to kick another stool out from beneath the chopping block. Dragging it with a foot, she placed it beside Philippa's and sat without speaking, the flickering firelight revealing the deep rings that steadfastly clung beneath Alwyna's eyes.

"You should not concern yourself with me, when you get little enough sleep as it is," Philippa murmured softly as she leaned down to gather her onions back into her lap.

"Ah," Alwyna breathed quietly, "I bethought me as much. I, too, seek out mundane tasks when I am troubled. Only with my hands busy can I muddle through my problems."

Philippa glanced up at her with a wan smile. "It hasn't helped," she finally said, lifting the strand as evidence of her failure. "Too long. I will have to undo some of it."

Alwyna gave a quick laugh, then took one of Philippa's hands in her own. She studied it, turning it in her grasp from front to back. "Richard was wise to hide you here. Those who owned you before would not dream of looking for you in a commoner's household. How is it there is nothing about you that marks you as the noblewoman you are? Even your English is almost without accent."

Philippa's mind churned as she struggled to concoct some answer, but it was pointless. She was a hopeless liar. Her shoulders slumped in defeat. "I suppose it is because I have not lived a life as fine as that at Graistan."

"What, no protest against my error?" The merry glint in Alwyna's eyes was reminiscent of Anne. "Do you not even want to know how it is I solved this mystery? I would be perishing to know what had given me away. Peter did not tell," she said with a quick smile, "although I did try to pry the tale out of him. He refused to part with a single word. That boy will make a fine churchman one day, but do not dare to tell him I said so."

Philippa could only stare at her, hopeless and filled with regret. She liked Alwyna. It would hurt if Temric's mother came to despise her.

"Well, even if you do not ask, I will tell you." Alwyna shifted into Norman French. "I had only suspicions until I heard you singing a moment ago. The song is one Henry, Richard's father, taught me. His mother had sung it to him and it pleased Henry that I, as both Rannulf's nurse and Richard's mother, would teach it to his sons."

Tears prickled into being at the corners of Philippa's eyes. "Maman sang it to me," she replied in the same tongue. "The songs and stories she taught me are now all that remains of her." Her voice caught in a sob.

"Ah, *ma petite*," Alwyna said sadly, opening her arms in invitation. "Grieve with me for I know your pain."

The familiar endearment spoken in her own language tore away any hesitation. Philippa fell into Alwyna's embrace and let her tears flow. Temric's mother cradled her close until her sobs subsided.

Then, running a gentle hand down her back, Alwyna crooned softly, "Speak to me, *ma petite*. I have seen how what you hold within you has struggled against your control. Tell me and know peace."

Philippa cried out, her voice harsh. "I cannot bear that you might despise me when I am done."

"What could a sweet child like you have done that would cause my scorn? My son would not have made you the choice of his heart if you were not worthy of his affections."

Within her the need to speak the truth grew until she had no choice but to spill it all in as few words as possible. "I am married to another, but Temric and I will live here as man and wife. It is more than adultery we do, it is incest as well. My half sister is married to Lord Graistan."

Alwyna laughed, the sound short but rich with amusement. "That you were already wed I suspected," she said with neither condemnation nor shock in her tone. "But incest as well? Richard has done a right good job entangling himself, has he not? Is there more?" Alwyna's face was as bland as her words.

"Nay," Philippa said in confusion, then cried out, "Is that all you have to say?"

"I could add 'well come' to my home, Philippa of Stanrudde. I have no daughter of my own and am glad to share this house with another female. In all truth, I am overjoyed to learn there was one woman in the world capable of bestirring Richard's passion." Alwyna grinned widely. "He has ever been so, well, so righteous and controlled."

"He will treat me as his wife," Philippa murmured, still stunned by Alwyna's acceptance. "You do not mind that in reality I am nothing but his whore?" It was as if she wanted Alwyna's scorn, for her words were a blatant probe for response.

Alwyna leaned over and laid a cool hand against her cheek. "Sweetling, if I will not let Jehan call you that, neither will I let you abuse yourself with that title. Think on it a moment and see how you strike at me when you call yourself whore."

"My pardon," she gasped. "How stupid of me. The insult strikes at my own mother as well, for I, too, am bastard born."

Alwyna threw back her head and laughed. In that instant the tired old woman disappeared. Before Philippa sat a merry girl with sparkling eyes and an engaging smile. By the very sound of her laughter had Alwyna held her Norman nobleman.

"Ah, Richard, now I understand you and I am not surprised," she called to her absent son. "Philippa, daughter, come into my family and let me guard you from those bent on destroying you. You are more precious to my son than any woman on earth and, for that reason, more dear to me than I ever dreamed possible." She threw her arms around her.

Philippa sank into her embrace, accepting at last that this new life of hers was real. Nay, it was a miracle. She owned this happiness and no one would wrest it from her.

Chapter Seventeen

"Today is Dies Mala, bad luck," Marta offered in hopeful explanation for a stain that would not lift from the tablecloth. She squinted at her new mistress, only to sigh at the narrow-eyed look she received in return.

"It is not," Philippa retorted, fanning herself with a hand. Even this late in the day, August's breath remained hot and so thick with moisture it could not penetrate her gowns or wimple. "There are no Egyptian days after Lammas until month's end. More likely you sought to be done too soon. Put that tablecloth back in the trough to soak through the night. On the morrow truly use your arms to beat out the stain. If it lingers after that, we'll lay it in the sun and see if that does not bleach it."

"Aye, mistress," the woman replied in defeat.

Philippa turned away to start up the slope toward the house, a skip in her step. How it pleased her to be called that. Over the past four weeks she had assumed by tiny measures the role of housewife despite Alwyna's protest that she did too much too soon.

Where those first days had healed Philippa's soul, her body had swiftly followed. Margaret would be surprised to find Philippa using every lesson the old hag had so cruelly insisted she could not learn. Aye, they may have been Margaret's teachings, but only Alwyna's love could have coaxed Philippa into using them.

She wended her way around the warehouse corner, past two of the apprentices hard at their chores, then into the house by the rear door. Pausing in the antechamber until her eyes adjusted to the dimness, she heard Peter say, "Jehan, for Mama? It is easy, see? This line means twenty shillings." Peter's voice was soft to keep from agitating his brother into a rage.

"This is work for a clerk, not the master of the house," Jehan bit back. "She traps me here, but she cannot force me to do it."

"You are probably too dull to understand it, anyway," Philippa called to him in a voice dripping with honey. She peered into the room. "Shall I help? You must needs only remember there are twelve pence to a shilling and twenty shillings weigh a pound. Oh, and always check your pence that they are not poorly made or missing bits."

"Shut up," Jehan snarled at her. His chair was placed next to the counting table, but he'd turned his body until he portrayed naught but complete disinterest.

Peter leaned against the table, his stool cocked up on two legs and his finger yet indicating one of the lines on the tabletop. At his side stood Alwyna's strongbox, richly decorated and heavily banded in brass, ready to give up the amount he wanted Jehan to calculate.

"You should be kinder to him, Pippa," Peter said. "Now, go away or I will still be sitting here when the Compline bell rings."

"What care I for the words of one so insignificant

as she?" Jehan snapped. "She is no more than a flea
to a lion."

"Aye, despite my size the lion must lift his paw to
scratch, eh, Jehan? In answer to your chastisement,
Peter, Jehan has yet to earn my kindness." She offered
Jehan a sarcastic smile.

"Oh, look what she wears this day," Jehan sneered
in attack. " 'Tis that cloak pin the bastard sent her,
complete with maudlin sentiment."

Her hand lifted to touch the silver pin at her breast.
It had come from Temric by way of a merchant who
passed through Stanrudde during his summer travels.
Its face bore a French inscription that she had long
since memorized: *My heart is yours for my life's time.*

"Ha! If you want to hurt me you will have to try
harder," she said. "That bolt has missed the mark.
Remember, I am the one with simple tastes and who
is far too easily pleased, or so your mother would
have it."

He shrugged. "Such pins are commonplace, you
know. He'd have sent you something finer if he truly
valued you."

"You are shooting backward now!" Philippa
laughed, supremely confident in the value Temric
placed on her. Finished with her daily baiting of
Jehan, she turned to Peter. "Where is Alwyna?"

"She left to attend Vespers, then planned to visit
one of her weavers whose babe ails. If there was yet
time after that, she meant to see Alfred," Peter
replied.

Jehan groaned. "Not him! The way that man pants
after our business sickens me. He cares only that we
offer him a steady supply of cloth to full. Dear God,
he's nigh on fifteen years her junior. How one so

loathsome could have such a beautiful daughter is beyond all reckoning."

"I thought I saw you watching her at Lammas Day mass. Tut, tut. I will tell Clarice," Philippa said, laughing.

"Go ahead, we'll never be wed anyway. Her father twists and turns every time Mama mentions it to him."

Behind her the door flew open and young Will came dashing through it. "They come," he cried, "they are returned!"

"Temric—" Philippa caught her breath in excitement and whirled away to enter the courtyard.

Men and pack animals were steadily filling the small square. One of the palfreys was without its rider. Where was Temric? She clutched the breast of her tawny gown in growing worry.

The first man dismounted, his gaze darting across the familiar faces until he caught her eye. He offered her a nod of greeting. "Yours is the only face I do not know. Are you Mistress Philippa?"

"Where is Temric?" she demanded, her fear making her voice sharp.

The man handed his reins to a stable boy and came closer to pass a more private message. "He waits for you at the outer stable. He said if you choose not to go to him there, he will come here on the morrow, bearing in his heart no insult." He gave her a brief warm smile, then turned back to the animals to begin unloading their packs.

She stared after the man as she understood the message Temric had sent her. He meant to trade vows with her this very day. A fear she'd thought dead and gone twisted in her stomach. They would begin life as husband and wife.

Then her need to see Temric, to touch him again and confirm his reality, overwhelmed even that fear. As if there were wings on her feet, she sped from the courtyard. Dodging pedestrians and alehouse patrons, Philippa flew down streets now well known to her. She barely managed to raise her hand in greeting as she passed the baker she patronized. Down the cooper's street, through the shoemaker's alley and right, past the dyers toward Stanrudde's eastern gate, named Priory after the godly establishment that lay nearby. The gatekeeper waved at her as she flew by. His words floated after her on the breeze. Aye, sunset now came sooner than Compline, which meant she had less than an hour before the gates were locked. It wasn't until she was well onto the Bristol Road, passing the garden patches and orchards belonging to Stanrudde's folk, that she slowed her pace.

The nagging memory had returned, awaking a sudden worry. For all her heart claimed to know Temric, their acquaintance had been made over just a few days time. With a sigh she realized it was not her heart she doubted. That bit of her had been Temric's since that first day when he had called her "equal" and valued her because she was simply who she was. The source of her fear lay in the rest of her body.

After they had exchanged vows, he would want to lie with her, craving to release himself within the receptacle her body offered. Sweet Mary, but there was pain in that particular communion. It would linger for days, but this was Temric, her Temric. He would not mean to hurt her, it was just the natural outcome of what he desired.

Then she chided herself for a coward. He had fought for her, risked life and honor on her behalf. It was through him she had gained her happiness. What right had she to deny him his masculine pleasure? If she could but control her fear, the pain would be less. She turned onto the path and climbed the short rise, only to stop at the hill's crest. Below her, the fertile green meadow, fed by a sparkling stream and dotted with walnut trees, rolled peacefully into a distant copse. Temric's massive mount grazed in the field, a tall intruder amid the few sheep they kept.

She looked from pasture to stable, searching for the big steed's master. The chalky building was more barn than stable, and glowed brightly against the dark thatch of its roof. Behind it lay the garden, the maintenance of which was one of her new responsibilities. Then he appeared from around the stable's corner. "Temric!" she called, raising her hand in greeting.

He stopped and turned, then stood waiting for her. Dressed only in his chausses and boots, his bare skin gleamed against a recent drenching. Excitement buoyed her down the hill, then crashed into shyness when she stopped in front of him.

He was taller than she remembered. Without a shirt to cover him, the strong planes of his chest and hard curves of his shoulders and arms were intimidating. Her tongue tied in knots and she could only stare. He was watching her as well, his brown eyes alight with golden flecks beneath gently curving brows. "You came," he said softly. "I was not sure you would."

A month spent living in Alwyna's house revealed his resemblance to both Jehan and Peter, but Temric's face had a fineness that went lacking in theirs. Summer-bronzed skin exposed the outcome of Margaret's blow, a thin white stripe at his temple and jaw, wider across his cheekbone.

"Look at you," he was saying. "You're even more lovely now than when you wore Graistan's wealth. Those colors suit you well."

His commonplace words, words having nothing to do with what lay ahead of them, freed her from her reticence. She spread the skirts of her tawny overgown and yellow underdress and turned a circle for him. "They are mine and I have others as well," she replied, her voice filled with quiet pride. "Your mother paid for them, but she says I have earned them by my own effort."

The desire to say more filled her. She longed to tell him of her happiness at Stanrudde, of his mother's acceptance and the depth of her emotions toward him for having given her the life she now lived. Instead, insecurity held her tongue. How could she know him so well, yet know him not at all?

He took a step toward her. Inwardly, Philippa stiffened as her fear leapt out from her control. She hid her reaction beneath a sudden shift from foot to foot, but he did not grab her to him, only touched the pin she wore.

"This is meant to close a mantle," he said with a small laugh. "If I had known you wanted a pretty bit of stone and metal to wear atop a gown, I would have sent that instead."

His casual behavior relaxed her and she smiled. "It is jewel enough for me. The words upon it are more precious than gold."

"Are they?" he asked, his voice suddenly deep and warm. "If so, I will add them to my oath when I speak it to you."

He extended his hand to her in invitation, his fingers beautiful, long and tapered. The strength of his callused palm beckoned to her. Like the first time, she carefully set her hand in his. Her pulse leapt as his hand enclosed hers. When he drew her into his embrace, her breath caught within her chest, whether from nervousness or pleasure she could not say. Under his subtle guidance, she leaned her head against his shoulder. His hand stroked her back in a long, smooth motion.

"I would see your hair. Would you remove your wimple and loosen your braids for me?"

It was a request of great intimacy, for only a husband looked upon his wife's unbound hair. She reminded herself that he would not mean to hurt her. Steeled against fear, she stepped back and released the material that covered her head and throat. He took the linen and leather band from her to set it atop his own neatly stacked gear near the stable door.

She freed first one braid, then the other. Crimped into waves by the plaiting, her hair flowed down her back past her hips. He lifted a tress and rubbed it between his fingers. "It is like spun gold."

Then, with his forefinger, he touched the single line of scar that made its way from her brow into her hairline. "I am glad to see you healed so well. Anne did a fine job mending you. Philippa, you are so beautiful, it takes my breath away. Can you truly be willing to bestow yourself on a man like me?"

She studied him. It surprised her to learn that he, too, harbored fears. Yet, the evidence was in his eyes and not quite hidden beneath his careful expression. In that moment she recalled she'd seen his fear twice before. The first time had been in Graistan's tower when he'd dreaded she would reject his affections, the second on the day he left Stanrudde. That day he'd feared she would despise this life he offered her.

But Temric was a man bound by his belief in oaths and vows. Once he heard her swear to her love for him, he would be assured of her affections. How easy it was to assuage his doubts. Philippa smiled at him. "How can you even dream I might refuse you? I have been yours since that first day, when you said I should have belonged to you."

She took his hands in hers. "Richard FitzHenry of Graistan, I pledge to you my love, my heart and soul, in full knowledge of what it may cost me. Take from me the everlasting affection I bear for you and give to me yours."

Temric grinned broadly, his eyes amber-brown. This time he did grab her to him, lifting her from the ground to embrace her in his happiness. Although he did not kiss her, he held her where he could look directly into her eyes. "Ah, love, you cannot know how I have worried that you would hate me for what I'd done to you."

"You gave me freedom," she replied softly, surprised and relieved that she felt no fear in his arms. Mayhap, it would be different with him. She clung to that hope. "This life you and my mother bought for me is precious and dear."

The joy in his smile was dazzling and he laughed against it, the sound clear and free. "For that I give thanks to God," he breathed and touched his mouth to hers.

Philippa caught her breath at the light caress. It reminded her of the pleasure his other kisses had given her. Aye, it would be different, she would make it so. Then, he drew away and let her slide back down onto her toes. She was sorry to be released.

"I see someone has told you my name." He was yet smiling as he raised a hand to gently stroke her cheek, then comb his fingers through her hair.

"Aye and you would not believe me if I told you who," she replied, unable to speak of her vision to even him. "How came you to be called Temric? All Alwyna has said is that she made the name in anger."

Temric grinned wryly and took both her hands in his. "Sometimes young men are stubborn and foolish and can see no further than the ends of their noses. I took insult when my father's will did not include me as he had promised, and for spite refused the name he'd given me. Mama was incensed. In her rage she meant to ask if I had been only temporarily Richard. Instead, she stuttered so badly what she actually asked was if I were 'tem-ric.'" He laughed again. "You should have seen her spit and hiss when I made of her stutter a name."

"Have I offended you in using your true name?" Philippa asked, searching his face for sign of insult. His expression seemed peaceful enough with his tale.

"Nay, not at all," he replied, "you may call me by either name, or simply 'your love' if you prefer."

She answered without hesitation. "You will always be my love, but I have liked 'Temric' from the first moment I heard it. Richard is almost as common as William and there is nothing common about you." She smiled up at him, then bit at her lip in shyness. "I have given you my vow, will you share yours with me as well?"

His grip on her hands grew a little tighter. Philippa watched as he fought for words, then his expression softened and his mouth lifted at the corners. "I have thought much about what I would say, but could find nothing to match my heart's emotion. What I settled on now seems inadequate."

"Speak your words," she urged. "They will not be inadequate to me."

"Only at your command, love," he said with a smile that was almost nervous. "Philippa of Stanrudde, I would have you as my own love, to have and to hold from this day forward, keeping you in sickness and in health, in wealth and poverty, despising all others and cleaving alone to you. Keep you these words as my solemn vow."

"They are good words," she said in quiet joy. "I will treasure them."

"Just as I will treasure you." He released her to ease his fingers into the heavy fall of her hair at either side of her head.

Philippa trembled. He would kiss her again. A sudden giddiness raced through her. She laid both hands against the strong swell of his chest and raised her face in invitation. He gently rested his lips against hers. A tiny flare of pleasure awoke. She moved her mouth against his. He tasted of apples, shame on him but he'd been eating raw apples. The rasp of his beard against her jaw was so very welcome.

He moved to kiss her cheek, then the hollow where her jaw met her neck. She drew a quick, sharp breath against the jolt of sensation his lips teased from her. With a tilt of her head, she gave him the whole length of her neck. He accepted her invitation, his lips moving in slow caress down to her shoulder. She made a quiet sound of pleasure deep within her throat. His mouth returned to brush against her lips. The teasing glance of flesh against flesh made her gasp lightly in response. His fingers combed through her hair at the temples as his mouth moved on hers, pressing and releasing her sensitive lips.

She sighed, yielding to the pleasure as the lines of her body relaxed. His arm came around her. Slowly, gently, his embrace urged her closer, pressing her form more tightly to his. Her hands splayed against the contours of his chest, her palms burning from the heat of his bare skin beneath them. The pressure of his mouth on hers deepened. Again, she softened, now leaning fully against him. Oh, but it felt as if her bones were melting.

His heart beat a steady rhythm beneath her hands. Every inch of her felt as if it were afire. From a hidden place deep within her came a persistent throbbing. The searing heat that seemed to have replaced the blood in her veins left her dazed. She shifted against him and her whole body tingled.

At her movement, his mouth slanted across her lips, demanding in his need for her. His arms around her tightened, pulling her even closer to him. She was crushed to him, buried beneath his need for her.

Suddenly, fear exploded out of control. Old memories of tearing pain, lingering burning, and aching would not be denied. With a tiny, wild cry, she pushed at his chest. Instantly he released her. She stepped back several quick paces.

He made no attempt to grab her back to him, only extended his hand to her. "Philippa," he breathed, "come back." There was no anger in his face, only a gentle concern. Yet, beneath that kindness lingered the signs of his lust for her.

She stared at him, tears filling her eyes. Disappointment and shame choked her and she bowed her head. Why could she not give of herself to the one man who deserved it most? She prayed he would not hate her because she had spurned him.

"Why do you run?" he asked, his voice low and gentle.

"I am afraid," she whispered in humiliation.

Silence rose between them, punctuated by the soft drone of insects and the trill of a lark. The breeze played around them, lifting her hair and toying with the wide sleeves of her overgown. Lured by their stillness, a mouse darted toward Philippa's shoe, squeaked in alarm, and retreated.

"You fear me?" he finally asked, a harsh, hurt edge to his voice.

"Nay," she sobbed out. "I fear the pain of what must happen between us." She caught her breath at her unexpected honesty. "Oh, please do not be angry with me. If you will but try again, I swear I can force myself to endure it."

She chewed on her lower lip in worry as the silence again lengthened between them. At last, she dared to peer up at him. To her absolute shock he was grinning at her. Philippa breathed in relief, but felt the tiniest twinge of irritation that he had found her fear amusing.

He reached out and touched the tip of her nose with his finger. "Love, as long as you do not fear me, there is a cure for what ails you. We are private here. Come within and let me show you that what passes between us has nothing to do with pain or fear."

This time when he held out his hand, she shyly accepted. He led her into the stable, stopping only to find the blanket he had used as bedding during his travels. The building was empty of occupants just now and had been recently cleaned; the air within was fresh and blessedly cool. Through the tiny, square windows carved from the walls, sunlight sliced into the hazy shadows. Where its warmth reached the straw, it teased up spirals of dust motes into an airy dance. Back they went to the stable's farthest wall. He stopped in the final beam of light.

Without relinquishing his hold on her, he kicked together a thick pile of clean straw, then dropped his blanket atop it. When he turned toward her, he lifted her hand to his mouth to press a kiss against her fingers, then released her.

She watched him lean down to release his cross garters. When these had been tossed aside, he kicked off his soft boots. A moment later he had untied the string that held his chausses tight against his waist.

"Will you run?" he asked, his hands at the garment's waist.

"I do not know what you mean," she replied in confusion for she did not understand him at all.

"I am remembering our kiss in the glade after I'd taken you from Lindhurst. I saw then you feared my touch and were surprised when you found pleasure in it. Then, in the tower chamber at Graistan, 'twas you who kissed me. Did you do so fearing what would come of my touch?"

"Nay, I knew there would be pleasure and I craved it thinking I should never have another chance after that day," she said quietly.

He smiled. "Ah, then by experience you'd learned that my kisses do not hurt. Now, you must teach yourself that what we share between us will not cause you pain."

With that he stripped off the one-piece garment that served him as both stockings and underwear and dropped it to one side. It bared all of him for her to see.

Philippa drew a quick breath in surprise. In that brief instant she was aware of the naked length of him, of strong legs, of powerful arms and gentle hands. The sunlight caressed him, marking the strong swell and fall of his broad chest. Her gaze followed the faint line of hair that began near his belly. It led downward to widen and enclose the part of him that was most male of all.

Her startled gaze raced back to meet his. "What are you doing?" she cried out when what she meant to ask him was what he expected from her.

Temric only smiled. "Philippa," he said quietly, "teach yourself about me. Touch me, secure in the knowledge that I will not touch you in return until you give me leave to do so. When you are easy with my body, you will be able to lie with me without fear. If you find your fear too difficult to overcome, know that you may say 'nay' to me. I will honor your wishes and love you still."

Philippa only stared at him in shock.

"Come, love," he urged gently. "Come find there is pleasure for you in touching me."

Chapter Eighteen

Philippa's eyes flew even wider at his words. Dear God, he could not be serious. There could be no pleasure for her in lying with him. Everyone knew it was the price all Eve's descendants paid. Did not all priests preach that because of the first woman's grievous sin, all women who came after endured the pain of coupling and childbirth?

A silent moment passed, then another. Philippa tightly hugged herself, her hands clutching at her upper arms. She chewed her lip in consternation. Temric watched her, his brows now quirked up. She blinked. He truly expected her to touch him.

The memory of how she'd kissed him in the tower chamber lingered. Then, as now, he'd sworn not to touch her and he had not. She knew he would not grab or force, ignore or hurt her. Mayhap, he was right. If he were more familiar to her, she might better tolerate what had to be between them. He said he would love her even if she dared refuse him in his lust. It was her right to refuse him that finally freed her. Aye, she would try what he suggested, secure in his continuing affection.

Slowly, she extended a hand and lay a forefinger at the place where his neck met his shoulder. Temric closed his eyes, the corners of his mouth lifting ever so slightly. He made no other movement or sound.

With her fingertip she traced the powerful slope of his shoulder, then followed the heavy curve of his upper arm until it turned into the bend of his elbow. His skin was soft, belying the hard strength that lay beneath it.

She smoothed down the hair on his forearm, then let her touch descend until her finger outlined his thumb. When she drew a soft circle in the cup of his palm, Temric released his breath in a long, quiet sigh. A flash of heat seared through her. Her finger tingled. Touching him made her feel as if she had been touched as well.

Taking a step closer, she lay both hands on his shoulders. She drew her hands slowly down his chest. Her palms barely grazed across his flesh. It felt like fine silk against her skin. She shivered in the desire to feel more. That strange throbbing awoke again. It sent waves of heat through her until her cheeks burned with it. Her blood pulsed to the same beat.

"You are soft," she said quietly.

Temric's mouth lifted into a grin and his eyes opened. "What a thing to say to a man." He laughed, low and gentle.

"What should I have said?" she asked in innocent curiosity.

His eyes were alight with pleasure and humor. "You should ask after each of my scars so I might relate to you my many courageous deeds. You should say that my chest is like iron and my arms like steel. Soft is for little boys and old, fat men."

She stared at him for a brief instant, then smiled. "You are teasing me."

"Aye, so I am."

His eyes were warm and so golden, she sighed against the beauty of them. She touched a fingertip to his mouth. He pressed his lips to it. Rising to her toes she leaned against him to touch her mouth to his. She toyed with his lips, pressing hers to his this way, then that. Beneath her hands on his chest, she felt his flesh quiver in response to her little game. Then, of a sudden, it was play no longer.

From deep within her came a searing need. Her arms rose to encircle his neck and she pressed herself hard against him, her mouth slanting and moving across his to feed the aching emptiness within her. He made a deep sound, reached out as if to gather her to him, only to stop himself. She could feel his chest and shoulders tense with the effort. Still his lips took hers, his kiss deepening until she had to break away, her breath coming in shallow gasps.

Philippa leaned her head against the curve of his neck, her lips pressed to his shoulder. He tasted salty sweet. She buried one hand into his hair, while the other stroked his nape. Her fingers were alive with the feel of him.

How wondrous it would be to touch all of her skin to his. She stiffened against such a self-indulgent thought. It had naught to do with coming to know Temric better. Her selfishness drove her back from him.

As she struggled within herself, battling for control of her wanton nature, her gaze wandered over him. Then, without realizing where she looked, she found herself staring at his manhood. It had grown thicker and risen to stand as if it had a life of its own. Stunned that it could do such a thing without the aid Roger had demanded, she studied it in fascination.

"How does it do that?" she breathed, reaching out to lay a finger against its tip. It was already longer and harder than Roger's had ever managed.

"For the love of you," Temric replied, then groaned when she ran her fingertip down his shaft. "Love, I perish in wanting you. Do not touch me too much like that or I will not be able to give you the pleasure you deserve." His voice was low and gentle, but in its tones she heard how hard he worked to control his need for the release her body offered him.

"It is soft and hard, like the rest of you." She could not resist touching it again. In astonishment, she watched it quiver as if it had senses separate from its master. Trapped in wonder, she lay her palm against its tip, then slid her hand down its outer length. The skin below it was softer yet than any other place on him.

He tensed. She glanced up at him in concern that she'd hurt him. His face was taut, his eyes closed. She watched him as she slid her hand back up his shaft. He caught his breath in a quick gasp and she felt against her palm the heat of his pleasure.

"Please, love, I would—" His words fell away into a quiet moan as her hand enclosed his shaft. "Jesu, little one, you will make me spill my seed if you do not cease," he breathed. "Please, I would feel your skin against mine. Will you touch me with your body?"

His words shivered through her. She slammed the door on Margaret's many sermons. If Temric asked it of her, she would do it. Oh, to feel all her skin moving against him instead of just her hands. The very thought sent shock waves of pleasure through her.

She freed him to loosen the ties on her gowns and pull them off along with her chemise. Carefully draping her precious garments over the handle of a pitchfork, she removed her shoes, then rolled off her stockings. When she looked up, Temric was watching her, his eyes half-closed against his longing for her.

"By all that is holy, I swear you are the most beautiful woman I have ever seen," he breathed. His gaze caressed the fullness of her breasts, the slim line of her waist, then he sighed. "Tell me you do not think me capable of what he did to you."

Philippa glanced down at her midsection and the scars that crossed it. When she raised her head, it was with a confident smile. "Never," she said. "You would die before you hurt me apurpose, of that I am certain."

"I feared that you thought I would be like him," he said softly. "Come, touch me again, love."

Two steps brought her toe to toe with him. She raised her arms to encircle his neck and pulled herself up against him. They stood so, her breasts flattened against his chest, her thighs tight against his. Every inch of her burned in the sheer joy of feeling him. Against her stomach lay the hard warmth of his shaft. Even trapped between them as it was, the thing tried to move. Its futile attempts made her smile.

"I think it has a liking for me," she whispered against his throat.

"No less than the rest of me," he retorted quietly. "By God, I swear I will die if you do not kiss me."

"Where?" she replied, pressing her lips to his neck, then to the base of his throat. Her hands loosened as she kissed the broad sweep of his chest, her fingers seeking out the curve of his shoulders. He groaned.

Her mouth lowered as she eased to her knees. Her lips touched his ribs, the flat of his belly, her hands sliding down from his elbows to his forearms. Her woman's flesh grew heated and moist as she lowered her mouth farther to kiss the curve of his abdomen. That touching him could bring so much pleasure to her was a revelation. The more she touched him, the more she craved to touch him.

She traced circles in his palms with her fingertips. The heat within her grew to consume her. Her lips pressed against the base of his shaft. Their fingers intertwined.

She tasted its skin. Throbbing need flooded her. But pleasure was mingled with amusement at how she could make something so hard and stiff dance.

"Stop, I pray you," he pleaded, his voice gruff, "please God, cease. When I vowed not to touch you, I did not know you would be so quick to tease. Please, love, do not steal from me the chance to love you."

Philippa looked up at him. How he wanted her! She saw it in his eyes, in the curve of his mouth, along the now taut line of his jaw and corded sinews of his neck, but he would not take her until she gave him leave. He had made it her choice and the time had come to choose.

"Then you must do so," she breathed, wanting no more now than to have his mouth meet hers with all the passion she witnessed in him. As she came to her feet, she freed her hands from his. She buried her fingers in his hair and touched her mouth to his, her lips barely grazing across his as she whispered, "I free you from your vow."

With a groan, he caught her to him in a wild embrace. His mouth slashed across hers, his hands pressing her hard against him. There was no fear left within her, only a deep need that she knew his touch could fill.

He kissed her throat, then bent until he could take the tip of her breast in his mouth. She moaned as ripples of pleasure surged through her. Her fingers curled into his hair, holding him there when he would have moved away.

When he finally released her it was to kneel before her and press his mouth to the place where her nether lips folded closed. She cried out in shock at an echo from the past. She had been warned most strictly against this caress.

"Nay," she managed as the movement of his tongue against her most sensitive flesh made her tremble. "You should not," she cried when he did not stop.

He kissed the place where her leg curved into her hip. "Why?" he whispered against her skin. "Should I let you do this to me and not return the favor? Does it not please you?"

"Aye, it pleases me greatly, but is this not a sin?" she breathed, praying he would ignore her and not stop.

"How can love be sinful?" he replied with a laugh as he brushed his lips across the swell of her stomach.

"This is love?" she cried softly in surprise. Astonishment died away into sudden understanding. This touching was a way to show emotions that might otherwise stay trapped inside the heart.

"Aye," he said, taking her hand and tugging her down until she knelt across from him. He took her face in his hands and pressed a gentle kiss to her brow. "Now, let me show you how much I love you."

"Aye, show me," she begged softly.

He eased back onto the blanket, his mouth claiming hers. In a moment, she lay atop him, his legs between hers. When the tip of his shaft touched the center of her being, Philippa stiffened. Their position was so unfamiliar, she'd not expected him to attempt entry. She lay still, braced against what came next. An instant later and to her complete surprise, she held him fully within her without the slightest pain.

The incredible rightness of their joining tumbled through her, destroying all capacity for thought. Her mouth met his with a passion of her own. She felt the urge to move and followed it. A wave of pure joy flooded her.

It was wonderful, nay, spectacular. She moved again. He groaned, the sound rumbling in his chest. Again, pleasure soared within her. Then the need to move without stopping grew too great to deny. Flooded by the sensations she created within her body with each thrust against him, she clutched her arms around his neck, holding him as tightly as she could. Their mouths met in a heated kiss that only fed what expanded in her womb. Wave after wave of pleasure washed over her, each one driving her on to find the next.

His hands buried in her hair as he tore his mouth free, his breathing harsh and quick. He kissed her brow, her eyes, her ear. This fervent need of his only added to her enjoyment. He was murmuring something to her, his voice low and deep, but she was beyond comprehending.

Philippa cried out as what she experienced became

too much to contain, then shuddered as fullness exploded into something greater. She froze against it, incapable of even breathing. Temric stiffened beneath her, suddenly driving himself into her. In a blinding and instinctive knowing, she saw he sought to attain what she'd already experienced. Power beyond any she'd ever known filled her, for she could give him what he sought. Philippa rose above him, moving, seeking, finally finding the rhythm that made him cry out.

His hands held her at her waist, urging her down atop him, as if he would make her one with him. He arched beneath her and she felt his seed pour into her. His breath came in great sobbing gasps. With a final cry of her own, she collapsed atop him, beyond thought or motion.

He relaxed beneath her. She sighed in hazy awareness of her body pressed so intimately against him. His rapid heartbeat gradually slowed and his breathing calmed. To think she was capable of not only giving him pleasure, but of pleasing herself as well!

Philippa turned her face into the curve of his neck and pressed her lips to his throat. Temric shuddered and clutched her to him in a tight embrace. She felt neither trapped nor forced, only desired, needed, and, above all, loved. He was right, this was the bodily expression of their care for each other.

Margaret and Lindhurst's priest were exposed as either liars or fools. It was not natural for a woman to know pain with her husband. Nor could there be sin in lusting for the man she loved. To lie with a man for whom she had no care, or who meant to do her harm, as with Roger, that was sin indeed. No wonder it had hurt.

"Temric?" she whispered.

"Hmm?" he sighed and eased her to one side. She lay cradled in the bend of his arm, her head pillowed against his shoulder.

"There was no pain," she breathed, kissing his shoulder.

"So I gathered," he replied in a voice equally low and filled with deep contentment. He leaned his head against hers. She sighed and watched him drift into sleep. It was not long before she followed him.

Philippa awoke to a rustling near her ear. It was a mouse, wending its way through the thick straw beneath their blanket. Midnight's darkness was a heavy cloak made all the thicker for a moonless night. She waited until her eyes adjusted. Tiny squares filled with stars gradually appeared.

From above her came the faint mewling of newborn kittens and the haunting cry of a barn owl as it returned to its nest. A vixen's sharp bark echoed up from the dale. From just inside the door came the snuffling of a hedgehog and her little ones hunting up their supper.

How sweet the world was, especially because this man who was her heart slept beside her. To think that love could be so satisfying. How had she survived so many years without it? She stretched in her contentment, then grimaced in regret. Would Alwyna be worried for them when they did not return for the night? She hoped not. For now, there was nothing to do save lie here, next to Temric. Oh, Lord, but it was something she longed to do forever.

Philippa breathed deeply, enjoying the very scent of him. As she curled back into his embrace, the movement of her skin on his was a potent reminder of how much she had enjoyed him. Since her slight movements had not disturbed him, she carefully laid her arm across his chest in a light embrace. The skin of her inner arm tingled with his warmth.

Her hand moved just a little, the sensation of his skin against her palm intoxicating. The embers of her passion for him glowed with a new life. She forgot that he slept and stroked the line of his chest, down over his stomach, past his shaft to the curve of his thigh. Dear God, she had never known that simple touching could make her feel so alive. Philippa released a long sigh against the sudden heat that flared to life in her womb.

Lost in indolent sensation, she brushed her lips over his shoulder, then eased up onto her elbow to lay her mouth against the base of his neck. In tiny bites, she made her way up his neck to his ear. When she lay her mouth against his jaw, his short beard tickled her lips. With a sigh of pure pleasure, she pressed a light kiss to his mouth. His arms encircled her, pulling her back atop him, as his mouth claimed hers again. Her gasp of surprise gave way to a flood of desire and she readily responded to him with her own need.

It was Temric who broke away, gasping for breath. "So soon? You are a greedy wench," he chuckled.

" 'Twas you who said I must become familiar with you," she retorted quietly. 'I was only acquainting myself with your body as you suggested."

"And so you must," he replied seriously, but the meager starlight gleamed against his smile. "Come know me again," he urged. "I promise this time it will not go so quickly between us."

She melted against him at that thought. "I care only

that I please you," she whispered into his neck, suddenly shy with their banter. "Did I?"

Temric groaned. "Dear Lord, you nearly killed me with pleasure. Come, love, kill me again."

Philippa could not restrain her quick giggle. "To think I worried so over this."

He took her face between his hands, his thumbs gently stroking the hollows of her cheeks. "Does your worry linger?" he asked, suddenly solemn.

"Nay. It was only a silly misunderstanding," she replied with a derisive snort at herself, then sighed. "Oh, Temric, you are my own heart, just as you say I am yours. My heart," she pleaded, "show me again how much you love me and let me show you how much care I bear for you in my own heart."

She pressed her mouth against his. His hands slid into the thickness of her hair. Oh, to belong to this man for all the days of her life. It was a fate worthy of damnation.

Dawn came too soon. Temric eased his arm out from beneath Philippa. Nay, 'twas the rest of his life that came clamoring too quickly on his heels, not the newborn day. He rose carefully so as not to disturb her and stepped outside the barn to relieve himself.

Behind the stables lay the household garden. Somehow, it looked better kept than when he left. Apple and pear trees, now heavy with ripening fruit, stood along one side while a tangled hedge of currant and raspberry bordered the other. Bright blossoms for stewing, marigolds, violets, peonies, and roses grew among the orderly rows of leeks and beets. Herbs, both medicinal and for flavoring, waved their fronds in the cool breeze touched with just a hint of humidity.

In the distance cocks crowed and the woodland birds let fly their complex harmonies. That old fool of a horse tossed its head and lifted its tail like a colt as it came trotting toward the wall. Ground-nesting birds took flight at its passage. Unlike them, Temric had no avenue of escape. The trap closed around him with every day. Nay not trapped—he was here by choice. If the buying of wool had bored him, surely some other aspect of what Alwyna did would engage his interest. This routine was really no different than the one he'd known at Graistan.

Even there, each day had been filled with a continual sameness, save for the changing events of the seasons. And those days when he assembled and disassembled the siege engines stored at Graistan to check for rot. Or the days that he rode the perimeters on watch for signs of thieves. Or when he and Rannulf had hunted. Or when he broke new colts. Or . . .

Temric stopped himself with a sigh. Aye, so he'd loved the life at Graistan. If he gave himself enough time, he would find what appealed to him in this new world of his. After all, did he not now have Philippa? His happiness with her would surely substitute for the contentment he'd once found in his occupation.

His gelding whickered in invitation. Temric went first to pluck an apple from the nearest tree. This he offered as a way to beg forgiveness for his long absence. His old friend accepted it with all the dignity expected from one of its lineage. Then the twit made a sham of its great pride by leaning its head into Temric's shoulder as if to say it'd truly missed its master.

"Liar," Temric laughed, scratching at the proffered ear, "I can see by your belly you are liking it here well enough and have missed me not at all. I'll need to see to your exercise before you go soft on me." He gave the creature a last pat.

Aye, in time all would be right. He and Philippa would dwell here in happiness. Oh, Jesu, but what if she bore him children? It rankled that in their love they could only create bastards. He did not want his children to be trapped between worlds as he and Philippa were.

He went to the well and drew up the bucket. Once he'd splashed sleep from his face with the icy water, he hesitated. Aye, mayhap that would help to cool his regrets and shock himself into remembering why he was here. Raising the container over his head, he doused himself from head to toe. With a gasp against the cold water, he shook the droplets from his hair. When he'd wiped his dyes dry, he saw Philippa standing at the corner of the building, wearing only her hair.

Soft morning light gleamed off her skin, accentuating her feminine curves and hollows. "I dreamed you left me, then woke to find you were gone."

"I could sleep no more and came out here to keep from waking you." He rubbed the lingering moisture from his face and tossed back his hair. A breath of wind set his skin to prickling with the chill.

"What is it that disturbs you?" she asked in quiet concern.

"I was regretting that our children are doomed to be bastards, like ourselves."

"Now, why would such a thing give you even a moment's pause?" She cocked her head to the side in deep confusion. "I lacked no love because of my birth and knowing Alwyna as I now do, I cannot think you were deprived of affection, either. Would we not love our children just as much as our parents loved us? What difference does the name given their birth make against that?"

Temric straightened abruptly, then laughed at himself. "You are right and shame on me. I have been too long in the habit of hating my birth. Any child of ours would be cherished, indeed."

Philippa sighed and bowed her head as she did every time she disappointed herself. "You must not hope for children, Temric. I doubt I am capable of it. I've been twelve years married with nary a flicker of life within me."

He shrugged, almost relieved. Despite his words, he did not like it that the children of his seed must tolerate the stain of bastardy. "Then we will live content without children. Perhaps, it is just as well. I'm afeared I might produce a son much like Rannulf's Jordan. That wee lad is more trouble than the two of us were together." If his words were harsh, his tone reflected his fondness for his nephew and he shot her a broad grin.

"See, you love him well even though he is also a bastard." She would not be deterred from this point.

"Aye, so he is and I am rightfully chastised," he said with a smile. "Come, love, now you must hold me and ease the sting of your scolding."

"What, and let you use my hair for your towel? I think not. Oh, now, you—you stay away from me!" she cried out as he came toward her. When he did not stop, she turned and ran back into the barn. It was in pure delight that Temric laughed and chased after her. If the catching of her was fun, what followed was better still. He let himself lose his worries in her arms and the womanly warmth of her body.

Chapter Nineteen

The hour of Tierce had passed before Philippa made her way with Temric into Alwyna's courtyard. The stony square was strewn from one end to the other with the last of the merchandise Temric had been collecting. The wool clip was already being separated into grades, the best fleece going to feed the looms of Flanders, while Alwyna kept aside the coarser stuff as well as the wool that came from carcasses to busy her own weavers.

Peter and his mother stood at the courtyard's far end. Jehan had been set in a small, backless chair near the rear door of the house. Philippa glanced from one to the other. Alwyna's expression was harried, Peter's carefully blank, while Jehan's face looked like a thundercloud, promising a storm.

"Good morrow, Alwyna," Philippa called out, "I hope you did not worry over us last even. What a beautiful day it is, today." Any bit of nonsense just now would focus Jehan's attention onto her, thus protecting Alwyna.

"Worry! Why should I have? I knew where you were." The older woman forced a laugh, then her smile became more natural. Alwyna knew very well that Philippa intended to step between her and Jehan.

Crossing the courtyard, Temric's mother leaned up against her eldest son to kiss him on his scarred cheek. "A thousand thanks to you, Richard, for what you brought me."

"The wool?" Temric asked in surprise as his mother turned to slip her arm around Philippa in a brief hug before stepping to her side.

"Nay, you great fool," Alwyna retorted, "for this wondrous slip of a girl who makes life so good for me."

Philippa laughed. No dream could be this real. When she leaned against Temric, he wrapped his arms around her. She had earned this joy with her pain and sorrow and it was hers to hold for the rest of her life. She'd rather die than give it up.

"Well, well, Philippa," Jehan called from his seat, his tone harsh and snide. " 'Twould appear you've discovered a new talent. I think my mother's declaration of sainthood for you had best wait. By the look on the bastard's face, I'd say he's more than enjoyed his whore last even."

More swiftly than Philippa could have believed possible, Temric had released her and crossed the courtyard. His powerful backhanded blow sent the younger man sprawling onto the cobbles. Jehan moaned, then caught it back, blood trickling from the corner of his mouth.

Temric reached for him, his other hand readying for a second blow. Philippa gasped. In every taut line of his body she saw Jehan's death. Here was the warrior in Temric who had battled Roger and won. His gentleness toward her had made her forget that side of him.

Philippa flew to stand between them. Her hands caught Temric's upper arms as she tried to force him away from his brother. It was like pushing on a wall of stone.

"Alwyna," she cried, "come help me!"

To Temric, she said in a soothing tone, "Come, love, come away from him."

She glanced behind her. No one, not even the servants gathered at the courtyard's opposite end, had moved. "Peter, pick up your brother," she called to the boy.

Her voice was a lonely sound in the charged silence. Peter stood frozen and pale in shock, his hands locked as if in prayer. Terror reigned in Alwyna's expression; it was a mother's nightmare she faced.

Philippa's hands tightened in determination. She must needs do this by herself. Then, of a sudden, she understood that she was the only one who could. Jehan had enslaved this family with his behavior. He used them all, forcing even Temric to march to the pipe of his rages and tantrums.

Armed with what little power that knowledge gave her, she pressed herself to Temric. "Listen to me, love"—her voice was calm, but insistent—"you must not do this. If you loose your violence on him, you will hate yourself for it."

It was as if his face were carved stone. Even his eyes did not blink. Yet Philippa drew some encouragement. If he did not move back, neither did he set her aside to complete what he'd started.

"If you finish him, you will destroy your mother. As much as she hates what Jehan has become, he is still her son." Her hands pushed against Temric's arms. "You must assure her you will not kill him. Vow to her. Only when you are sworn can she breathe again."

Aye, and when he had sworn, she knew that he would be trapped by his own words. Once spoken, he'd not betray them. She waited for his response.

His gaze still fastened on Jehan, Temric narrowed his eyes in refusal. No sound, no other motion.

"Listen to me," she continued softly, speaking now in French, hoping to startle him into hearing. "I am not injured by his mean-spirited words. I know who I am, I am beloved to Richard of Graistan. It matters naught to me what filth he spews for his nastiness stains only him. I would not have you do murder on my behalf, it would hurt me."

The fatal rage eased from his face. Philippa released her breath in a slow sound of relief. Beneath her grip on his arms, his muscles relaxed. She leaned her head against his chest as her own terror for him ebbed. His heart yet pounded in anger.

"Speak to her," she whispered. "She is dying as she waits to see what you will do."

"Mama," Temric managed from between clenched teeth, "I will not tolerate his abuse of Philippa. He may say what he wants of me, but I vow to you I will beat him each time he speaks so to her. If you cannot bear that I punish him, best you convince him to hold his tongue for you will not stop me in this."

It was not what she'd requested, but it was better than the alternative. This time, when Philippa pushed against him in unspoken suggestion that he move back, he acceded. Those few steps set Jehan out of arm's reach.

Now that he thought himself safe, Jehan dared to speak. "How brave you are to strike a cripple," he snarled, raising himself into a sitting position. His lifeless limbs sprawled awkwardly across the smooth cobbles.

"Trust me, boy," Temric retorted, his muscles in his neck cording, "name her whore again and pay the price."

"Jehan, I have just saved your life," Philippa cried in outraged frustration. "Be still, you numbskull!"

"This is my home and I'll say what—" Jehan started in a nasty tone.

"Hold your tongue or I will cut it from your mouth with my dullest kitchen knife," Philippa interrupted. "Come, love," she urged Temric, "come within and let us break our fast. It is best if we leave him to his mother just now."

"What makes you think I want anything to do with that piece of filth?" Alwyna's steely voice was an arrow, shattering what Philippa had worked so to build. "I declare him changeling, for his manner makes him no son of mine. Richard, if he speaks foully to her again in your presence, you may thrash him until he learns to spew no more vicious words."

"Mama!" Jehan cried out, wiping the blood from his chin with a trembling hand. "How can you let him beat me?"

"Did I hear the wind whistling through here?" Alwyna asked icily to no one in particular. The old woman's eyes were narrowed and hard in her fury. "Or was it a coward who spoke? Why should you destroy others, then hide behind a mother's skirts to avoid the rightful outcome of your actions?"

Jehan blanched in horrified astonishment. So accustomed was he to being cosseted in his rages that he never considered his mother would turn her back on him. Then his expression hardened. "But, of course," he turned the simple words into a curse, "he is your most precious son, the one with noble connections to help you, and who you intend to set in my place. Why should I expect you to prevent him from abusing your helpless son?"

"Helpless," Alwyna snapped back, unable to let his words of attack die without response. "You are hardly that. Now, if you are beaten, know that you brought it upon yourself when you slandered his wife."

"Wife? She's no more married to him than Clarice is wed to me. You set her in my wife's place and seek to make him master in my home. By God, Mother, you even gave them our bed!"

"It is not your bed or your house!" she screamed. "Until you lift a finger to earn it, I will not give it to you!"

"Earn it?" There was a dangerous undercurrent in Jehan's voice now. "What do you know of earning, Mother? All you did was play whore to some fine nobleman and let his rich payment buy you my father and this trade."

Temric surged forward against Philippa's restraints. She wrapped her arms around him, making herself a weight to hold him in place. "Nay," she breathed. "This is not about you."

Alwyna gave a single wild gasp of pain, her face going white at her son's words. Peter rushed to his mother and threw his arms about her as if he could shield her from the insult with his body. "Nay, Mama, do not listen to him," the boy pleaded, his expression stricken. "He does not mean what he says."

"Do I not?" Jehan retorted. "Whoring was what she did before she wed our father. How do you think she got a bastard if she did not play bed games and make a harlot of herself?"

"Stop, Jehan," Peter cried in agony. "Do not say those things."

Alwyna, her dark eyes seeming all the darker for her bloodless face, very carefully and gently freed herself from her youngest's grasp. When she spoke, her voice was quiet and incredibly calm. "Nay, sweetling, do not stop him. 'Tis time he vented this hate of his." She turned to face her middle boy. "Is there more you wish to say?"

Jehan's callous facade cracked. "Tell me," he begged, "tell me he forced you, Mama, that it was rape and you cared nothing for him. By God, you were a rich man's toy! It tore away all my pride when I learned what you'd been." His voice was that of an aching child who had thought his parents perfect only to discover their humanity.

Alwyna drew herself up to the limit of her short height. "Peter, how do you feel about my past?" she asked of her youngest.

"Me?" Peter's newly deepened voice broke, his miserable expression revealing that he wished he were miles from this place. "It matters not a whit to me what you did before you married Papa. Temric is my brother, just as Jehan is, and you are my mother." He tried to smile, but failed utterly at it.

"My thanks for your kindness," Alwyna replied, her tone still deathly calm. "How sorry I am that you've had to witness your brother's hate, but I thought he'd grow tired of what he did and cease. Jehan has asked me questions, will it trouble you if I answer him?"

"Nay, Mama," Peter replied, catching her hand in his and pressing a kiss against her fingers.

Alwyna smiled and freed her hand to give his cheek

a pat, then called toward her eldest son, "Richard, and you?"

Philippa looked up to watch Temric's reaction and smiled at the love that was reflected in his eyes. When he drew her into his embrace, she leaned her head against his shoulder. "Why should I? I love and am loved by both my parents."

Alwyna crossed the distance between herself and Jehan to stand, back lance-straight, before him. "Listen well for I will say this but once. I cared deeply for Henry of Graistan and he for me. There was no rape or abuse, and if that makes me harlot, then I accept that title. In time, our caring for each other became only friendship. 'Twas then I met your father and how my heart sang for the wanting of him. Aye, I took what coins Richard's father offered me, but it was not payment for the time I spent in his bed. Lord Henry wanted to be certain I had what I needed to wed your father and insure my future happiness, so great was his care for me."

Jehan gasped. Written on his face was both denial and recognition of the wrong he'd done.

"Aye, my sorry, broken little man, the nobleman you so despise had greater love for me than does the son of my own womb." Her voice broke and the tears she'd worked so hard to avoid filled her eyes.

Philippa moved her lips to Temric's ear. "Take her away from here. Peter, too. Go anywhere, but be gone for the whole day's time."

"I'll not leave you with him." It was a harsh statement, with only a slight jerk of his head to indicate Jehan.

Philippa gave a swift laugh. "For all his supposed scorn, I think I am the only one he tolerates. Now, go."

Temric's brows lifted in concern, then he shrugged. "As you will, love." With a swift kiss, he went to his mother. "Come, Mama, it is time you showed me which properties you own. Aye, and introduce me to your tenants so they will give me their rents when I come collecting.

"Peter"—he motioned to his youngest brother— "come along with that purse of yours so you might buy us a bite to eat." When the lad would have resisted, Temric grabbed him by the arm and half carried him from the courtyard. His mother sagged in his other arm, her shoulders quaking with her sobs.

Philippa watched them go, then shook her head in dismay. Here, in this place where there should be only happiness, these folk had allowed one man's misery to poison them all. With a fortifying breath, she turned on the gaping apprentices and servants. "Will and Dickon, come and carry Jehan up into the hall for me before you take the animals out to the field." The two men picked the shocked and unprotesting young man off the cobbles and carried him into the house.

"Marta," Philippa called, "I need you to do my marketing for I'd serve duck brewet at the midday meal."

Marta's surprised look at the mention of Jehan's favorite dish devolved into subtle pleasure. "So, Master Jehan must sing for his supper, eh? If I hurry there's just enough time to have it finished for the meal." She turned and dashed inside to fetch the kitchen purse and a basket.

"Els and I will do what you must leave wanting," Philippa called after her and caught the sound of Marta's distant thanks. "The rest of you know that for this day you must not respond to any of Jehan's commands, only my own. Now, be on with your chores."

As they scattered, she made her way into the hall and found Jehan in his usual chair.

He stared stonily at the cold hearth. The set of his shoulders told her he had no intention of admitting his wrong. Now that she understood his bitterness had nothing to do with his legs, she realized that Alwyna had let his abuse of her become a habit when she should have long ago stopped it. He narrowed his eyes, his face becoming a mask of distaste. "Do not waste your breath on me. I'm in no mood to listen to a whore's sermon."

"Oh, ho, listen to the little dog yap. Useless and pointless, a dog without a bite, and this one has no teeth." She crossed her arms, taunting him with her cheery voice.

"Hold your tongue," he said, more loudly.

"Good advice from a man who's spilled his blood because he could not hold his own. Are you saying you have finally learned a lesson, Master Slow Wit?" she asked as she went to the hearth wall to fetch his unused crutches. She tossed the Y-shaped lengths of ash onto the floor before him.

Jehan's voice was gravelly and harsh. "I've told you before, I will not use them. Take them away."

"You will if you want to eat," she retorted, then added, "or piss. It's a long crawl to the privy, Jehan."

"You wouldn't," he yelped in surprise.

"I just did." Her smile was all sweetness and light. "Also, do not bother the servants with your commands. I've told them to pay you no heed. Now, I'll have at my work. If you need help bringing yourself to your feet on your crutches, scream for me as only you know how." She left the room to ascend to the bedchamber.

"Damn you!" he roared. "You will pay for this."

"More likely 'tis you who will pay," she sang back. "I walk, while you are trapped where you sit." Philippa hurried through her ablutions, counting to herself the chores she needed to finish before day's end. When she passed through the hall on her way to the kitchen, Jehan had not moved but now he made no sound. Marta had already returned.

By the second hour after midday, the meal was ready. When Philippa and Els came to set the table, they found Jehan asleep in his chair. Philippa stared in wonder at the young man's swollen cheek, already purpling from the blow Temric had struck. That Temric could harness his violent nature to show her such gentleness was remarkable and precious.

Where Els would have tread quietly, Philippa warned her against such coddling with a shake of her head. They set out the trestles, then lifted the table's top. Holding it just above its braces, Philippa raised her brows and grinned in mischief. Els giggled. Then, at the nod of her head, they released the heavy wooden oblong. It met the trestles with a thunderous retort.

Jehan started awake. Philippa only smiled at him. " 'Tis almost time to eat," she said cheerfully.

He crossed his arms and stared at them in stubborn silence as they laid the broadcloth over the wooden surface, then set out bowls, cups, spoons, and salt shaker from the cabinet. When the thickly sliced bread was at each place, the servants and apprentices washed their hands and found their seats. Philippa quietly asked them to leave room at the table for Jehan.

Once the prayer had been said, the others picked up their spoons and began to eat. Philippa toyed with the thick, rich broth before her, then loudly sighed. "Too bad for you, Jehan. 'Tis brewet of duck this day," she said. "Since you are not willing to share with me, I suppose I must eat your portion."

Jehan shrugged nonchalantly, secure that Alwyna would rescue him from this. "I'll eat when my mother returns. I do not share my meal with whores and servants."

Philippa only smiled. "You'll have a long wait. Alwyna will not be back until this even."

Jehan made no reply, only tensed his jaw and stared at her. She shrugged and began to eat. After a few moments she caught him hungrily eyeing the table. When he realized she watched him, he swiftly returned his gaze to his lap.

A few more moments passed. Finally, he straightened. "Rob, come fetch me to the table," he ordered none too politely of the serving man nearest him.

"Pardon, Master Jehan," the man replied. "Mistress Philippa says we must not." There was enough grim satisfaction in his voice to suggest he was glad for what was being done to his employer's son.

A cry of pure frustration escaped Jehan. "When my mother returns, I'll see you beaten for your refusal!"

Philippa rolled her eyes in irritation. "Jehan, you'll be fortunate if your mother does not set you outside yon gate. The morrow might find you with the other cripples begging for alms at the abbey's doorstep. Mayhap she should do so, at least then you'd earn a living."

A muted rumble of laughter went 'round the table.

"You presume much for a bastard's whore," he breathed in fury.

"I presume to make myself of use to someone by

whatever means I can," she retorted, "which is better than you do."

"Mistress," said Tom, the oldest of the servants, "I pray you do not judge this household by the young master's ways. If old Master Peter yet lived, he'd have hided his son for the outrage of this morn. I swear it."

"Shut your mouth, you old fool!" Jehan roared.

"Oh, my," Philippa said in a breathy voice worthy of the finest mummer, "there he is again, that toothless dog, yapping and barking."

"Damn you," he shouted. "You have no right to insult me so! I cannot help that I am crippled." The last words were almost a cry.

Philippa felt a brief stab of pity, then remembered his cruelty and selfishness and hardened her heart. "Aye, *that* you cannot help, and there's not man or woman here who bears you ill will for your injury. What have legs to do with your use in life? Find your purpose and your limbs will not matter."

When he tried to glare at her, Jehan's eyes were overly bright as if he fought back tears. "What use? I can do nothing without my legs," he said, on the verge of his usual tantrum.

"Jehan!" Philippa leapt angrily to her feet. "Are your brains in your legs? Use the crutches; *crawl*, if you must, but do something, give yourself purpose. Above all, stop complaining." With that she regained her seat on the bench.

A small smile fluttered at the corners of Els's mouth. From down the table's length some male servant whispered, "God be praised."

Hours later, long after the table had been cleared away and the day was drawing near to a close, Philippa returned to the hall. Jehan was staring morosely into the flames on the hearth. "Come to gloat?" he managed in a low voice.

"Nay, I've come to see if I can help you to the privy."

"Go away," he snarled, but his tone lacked its usual venom.

"If you'd rather, I'll bring you a pot. You need only walk a little ways, then. I know the crutches will be hard to use at first, but you can manage them. You must at least try, Jehan."

"Why?" There was contempt in his voice. "Mama will come home soon. She'll not let you do me so."

"Jehan, are you so blind?" she asked with a sigh. "Or is it just that you refuse to accept your manhood? I think 'tis this which causes Clarice's father to hold her from you, not your useless legs. Come now, take up your life and be a man."

"How can you say so to me? I am already a man of a score and five. Does a beard not cover my face, unlike Peter?" he retorted, but the anguish that filled his gaze made a lie of his protest.

"Poor man," she murmured. "The world has dropped heavily on your shoulders and you were not ready to take it up. It must be hard to follow your father. A kind man, the shopkeepers say of him. Gifted in trade, the guild says. His wife adored him, his children loved him. He was a pillar of the community. I think it would be easier being his good-for-nothing son than the one who must take up where Saint Peter the Wool Merchant left off."

"You understand," Jehan choked on his relief. "You see how it is for me." His words were soft, forgetting in that moment that he hated her. "It is better if you leave me as I am, for I cannot be him."

"Everyone knows that. It is enough for us that you be yourself." She leaned down and set his crutches up against the chair's arm.

He caught at her hand. "How can you force me on in this cruel fashion, when I can have no hope for success?"

Philippa extricated herself from his grasp. "Jehan, how can you know that until you have tried and failed? Here"—her hand touched the crutches—"here are the tools you need to free yourself from this awful trap of yours. Or would you rather depend on those around you for everything? Come, now, you can do it. I know you can." She started away from him.

"I'll see you pay for this," he snarled anxiously.

She heard one crutch, then its mate strike the wall. "How, when you are caught where you sit?" she called back over her shoulder and closed the door behind her.

It was well past Compline when Temric returned with his mother and brother. The tiny, first-floor entryway was pitch-dark save for the circle of light thrown by Philippa's lamp. In that little flame, the hollows beneath Alwyna's eyes seemed darker still.

"I am off for bed," Peter said immediately, seeing there were things to be said that he did not wish to hear.

Philippa waited until he was gone before explaining what she had done and what she expected from Alwyna. As she spoke, Temric came to stand behind her, encircling her in his arms. How it pleased her to lean against him after the tension of the long day.

"He needs to be forced into using his crutches and finding what is good within him, Alwyna," Philippa said. "He will beg for your help, but if you intervene, you will only make more of a cripple of him."

Alwyna sighed. "Are you sure what you do will help him?" There was a nervous tremor in her words.

"It cannot hurt him," Philippa said.

Alwyna's grin was lopsided. "If I weaken, might I cry for your aid?"

"Loudly and clearly," Philippa said with a laugh.

"Then I will honor what you have done. Now I am off to find my bed. The morning brings us another day, eh, Richard?"

"Aye, Mama," Temric replied, a faint bitterness in his voice.

Alwyna started up to the bedchamber, refusing the lamp. They remained where they stood, listening to her footsteps. Once she was securely within the bedchamber, Philippa turned in Temric's arms to search his face for some clue to his emotions. There was nothing for her to read.

"How was your day?" she asked in the hope of prodding him to speak of what bothered him.

"Incredibly long," he sighed. "I never realized simply looking at things could be so tiring." There was an unpleasant note to his voice.

"Poor love." She laughed lightly to hide the prickle of concern that woke within her. "Shall I take you to our bed and soothe you into sleep?"

His answering laugh was a mere rumble in his chest. "Aye, that would please me well. I missed you every moment we were apart."

She set her lamp upon a shelf so she could put her arms around his neck. "And I, you." Rising to her

toes, she touched her lips to his. Once again, that wondrous fiery sensation rushed through her. It was stun-
ning and glorious. Then, he was ending the caress,
drawing away from her. His sigh was somehow strange.
"What is it?" she asked.

"My mother has great plans for me, all of which
have us spending too much time apart. She'll soon
have me traveling with her to a Holyrood Day fair at
the far end of England."

"Nay, you'll bide here," Philippa said, raising her
mouth to touch the curve of his neck. He caught his
breath at her caress. "She won't be departing for some
weeks yet," Philippa continued. "When she goes,
she'll take Jehan with her. Mark my words." The last
of her statement was made between kisses.

He caught her to him in a tight embrace, lifting her
toes from the floor. "Lord, to be left here alone with
you, free from Jehan's hate and my mother's constant
teaching, that would be joy indeed. Aye, take me to
bed and soothe my poor aching head so I can face the
morrow with fresh eyes." After a swift kiss, he set her
feet back on the floor and took her hand.

Philippa willingly followed him up the stairs, but his
words troubled her. Were they not here because he
had discarded all desire for his knighthood to take this
life? His choice, not hers. Ah, well, if he found he
could not tolerate it here, they would leave. She would
miss Alwyna, but where Temric went, she would happily follow.

Then he was pulling aside the bed curtains. Within
moments, they were disrobed and beneath the bedclothes. When he gathered her into his arms and set
his mouth to hers, she forgot all else.

Chapter Twenty

Philippa hummed to herself a joyful tune, its lilting melody giving evidence to the completeness now within her. The brush in her hand flew as she cleaned the fur-lined garment stretched out in front of her. It was a winter cloak, just taken from storage and her last piece of work for the day. Els said this one belonged to Jehan.

The thought of that poor, tormented creature brought a wry grin to her lips. Alwyna had kept her promise, allowing Philippa to do as she pleased, and two months' time had accomplished much. He walked again, clumsily so with the aid of his crutches, but he was mobile, even managing the stairs. So, too, had he returned to supervising the men in their day-to-day chores. At first, only fear of Philippa's retribution had kept his tongue civil, but Jehan had swiftly become absorbed by his activities and forgot to be angry. He'd even come to the counting table, revealing that he'd already learned at his father's knee what Peter and Alwyna had thought to teach him.

Aye, slowly and steadily, and not always gently, Philippa had driven him where he could not drive himself. He'd even been stunned to discover that his crutches bothered no one in the marketplace or in the

guildhall. It had been the acceptance of those merchants he sought to emulate that had freed him to
attempt a horse for the journey to the Holyrood fair.

When Clarice's father, Gerard, had learned of their
journey, that auspicious merchant and Jehan's future
father-by-marriage had decided to go with them.
'Twas at Gerard's suggestion that they had scheduled
themselves to a second event after Holyrood. Although it seemed Philippa was the only one who saw
it, she believed Gerard went along to gauge Jehan's
progress. She fully expected that merchant to an-
nounce his daughter's marriage to Jehan once they
returned to Stanrudde on the morrow.

The reminder of Temric's family's homecoming
brought with it more disappointment than pleasure for
Philippa. These past weeks of privacy had been
heaven. For a short time, the house had been as if it
were hers and Temric's alone, she its mistress and he
its master. Would that they might someday have their
own home.

She leaned back from her work and made a wry
sound of irritation. If they did, it had best be some
farflung manor where Temric could be what he truly
was and not the merchant he pretended. Aye, no matter how he tried to hide it, he was the same powerful
knight who had so awed her when she'd first seen him.
Thank the Lord that Alwyna's absence had freed him
to join the town's guardsmen in their daily practice.
That familiar physical activity had eased his depression some.

Philippa sprinkled more cleaning compound onto
the fur, then sighed in sudden sadness, her previous
joy evaporating. Did Temric think she could not see
how heavily this life of Alwyna's weighed on him?

Within her grew the fear that if they stayed in Stanrudde much longer his dislike for this place might harden into hate for her. Why had he trapped himself here when it was obvious he still longed for a knight's life? Every time she tried to ask him this, he either diverted her attention with kisses or simply refused to speak.

Today he'd received a missive from Lord Graistan, although he'd not yet opened it. What if the words on that bit of parchment demanded his return to Lord Rannulf's service? She could not return to anyplace where she was known. Would he leave her? Her logic whispered that his unhappiness might drive him to it and her heart quaked in fear, even while refusing to believe he would.

Then, against all reason, her joy burst within her once again. She cradled new life within her, of that she was now certain. September's end brought Michaelmas, the tax collector's holiday. That day had signaled the passing of a second month without her woman's flow. "Poor wee babe," she crooned softly, placing her hand to her abdomen. "Will you be like me and never know your father?"

It was such a miracle. Philippa drew an ecstatic breath against the fullness of her womb and gave thanks for the child within her. Despite her uncertain future, she, who had believed herself barren, was carrying a child.

She smiled again, understanding now what she would never have known had she remained with Roger. Her husband was incapable; his mother's fondling had destroyed him. The strength of Temric's manhood made a mockery of Roger's fumbling attempts at coupling and futile, seedless thrusts.

Philippa closed her eyes at the surge of passion even the thought of Temric's touch woke in her. The enjoyment she received from his attentions never wavered. If anything it grew greater, matching her worry over him and making every moment they shared all the more precious.

Once again, she ceased brushing and sighed. What would Temric think if she told him she bore his child? In his present unhappiness, she could not bring herself to spill her secret, especially not now. Tonight was their last one alone before Alwyna and Jehan's return, to be spent only in pleasure and sweet words. She would hold her worries and her secret as her own for just a little longer. Content with what she'd decided, she set aside her chores and went to find Temric.

Temric eased from the bed, careful not to awaken Philippa. During their two months of living as man and wife, she had become all too astute at prying beneath his concealing layers to read his depression. He did not wish her to see how much what needed doing just now might upset him.

With the bed curtain pulled aside, the meager light of a waxing moon spilled into their small square of privacy. He donned his bedrobe and turned to study her. Philippa had slipped down from the bolsters to pillow her head against her arm as she curled into herself. Her hair flowed over her shoulder and pooled in front of her in a silken mass. Even now, after sating his passion for her earlier this night, he ached to touch her and feel her hands against him. If it was destroying him to stay here, it would be certain death to live without her.

He stared at the graceful curve of her back, at the

smooth length of her legs and her yet trim waist. 'Twas her second month without her flow and he no longer doubted that she'd proved herself fertile. He sighed. What sort of future could he offer his child? Retrieving the fold of parchment from beneath his bolsters, he left the room.

Shielded by the quiet of midnight's darkness, he crept down the stairs, through the hall to the kitchen. This room was warm and fragrant, the ever-burning flames on the hearth throwing bright flickers of light against the whitewashed walls. Temric pulled out a stool, then hesitated. It was the season for wine and a drop could not but ease his aching heart.

He set his parchment upon the hearth shelf, found the cask, and filled his cup. Once he'd drunk it to its thick dregs, he poured himself another and settled on the stool. The spice cabinet was locked. Too bad, this local brew would have tasted better heated, with a bit of clove and sweetened with honey.

He glanced around the room, now filled to overflowing with the abundance of the harvest. Stanrudde was a civilized place and merchant folk more often depended on what their coins could buy than on what they raised themselves. Yet, even in the city, the urgency of year's end drove them all. What could be stored against the coming season of barrenness was being put aside in bins, sacking, and crockery jars sealed with wax.

However, 'twas obvious Philippa had more rural roots. From their apple and pear trees, she had made cider and perry, stoppered into casks. Herbs and the other fruits and vegetables from Alwyna's garden had been dried or stored in the cool cellar. Beef and mutton were salted; the swine had met their fate, the resulting hams and bacons smoking in the chimney. She'd even pickled fish. Aye, that sweet woman of his was indeed the miracle worker his mother claimed, and not just in the kitchen.

As Philippa had predicted, Jehan left for the Holyrood Day fair with Alwyna. Temric cradled his cup in his hands, elbows braced on his knees. Where nothing else budged his half brother, that wee slip of a thing had brought him back into life's currents using only subtle goading and iron discipline. In doing so, Philippa had created a dilemma Temric had not foreseen.

He rubbed a weary hand on his brow. Jehan longed for a merchant's life with the same fervency that Temric now longed for his lands and the title "lord." It glowed in his brother's face when he haggled over a price for raw wool or handled finished material. One day, sooner or later, the boy would rightfully earn his place as master here. Then what would become of him and Philippa? As much as he hated Alwyna's life, it was all that was left to him if he was to provide for the woman he loved.

"Damn," he muttered, suddenly wishing it were in his nature to scream the way Jehan did. If he could, he'd crow a lungful against this trap he'd made for himself.

He finished his cup of wine and finally reached for the missive from Rannulf. Atop all his other worries, he hardly needed to see what brought his brother to set quill to parchment. But there was no choice, it needed opening. Breaking the wax seal, he unfolded it. Unlike his own tight and small hand, Rannulf's free-flowing script wandered gracefully down the page.

To my dearest brother, Richard, now the idiot wool merchant of Stanrudde,

Having heard no word from you, I must make assumptions as to your happiness and health. In my own case, I indeed find companionship with my dearest lady wife, greatly enjoying her company. If I have any complaint it is that I have been forced to take into my custody John of Ashby's now orphaned daughter, Nicola, an untamed and rude hoyden. She resides in a locked storeroom at this time to prevent yet another escape attempt. As I intend Gilliam to hold Ashby as his own, he must wed with this virago. Then again, such a fate is only rightful retribution for his youthful errors.

Temric could not forestall a wide grin. That Rannulf could lend such lightness to his words over Gilliam, their youngest brother, told him that Rannulf's bitter past was now truly buried. From what he remembered of this Nicola, Gilliam deserved her, if for no other reason than in payment for that boy's wicked wit. He read on:

With that said, I would tell you that the remains found in our glade now lie in our own burial vaults at Graistan's abbey. This was done at my wife's request even though she suspects that she must grieve for her mother as well as endure her sister's absence. No doubt time's passage will convince all others that Lady Edith found death in some forlorn spot whilst she traveled on her pilgrimage. In our hearts we are certain she set out on her travels seeking her life's end without anyone's foreknowledge of that event.

Temric leaned back on his stool as a wave of relief washed over him. He hadn't realized how deeply he'd worried over what had been discovered in that clearing and how what had happened would hurt others. Not only was Rannulf certain that Edith's death had been her own doing without Temric's foreknowledge or involvement, his brother had shared with his lady what little he knew of those events. At least in this, Temric's honor had remained intact. He lifted the parchment again.

Father Edwin slipped from life before Michaelmas was upon us. I was glad to have yet been at Graistan to witness his passage. He spoke of you at the last, bidding me tell you that your departure from Graistan left the chapel at peace for the first time in years. I make no sense of it, but mayhap you can.

This time Temric paused in complete astonishment. Edwin had known! Then again, why should a deaf man not also have heard the ghostly voice that had spoken so fluently? Uncertain whether to be comforted or disconcerted by these words, Temric took another sip of wine to settle his nerves before reading further.

In his great wisdom, our glorious king, Richard called Lion Heart, has commanded that tournaments be held in his realm. The cost for entrance is but ten marks for barons such as we. Gilliam's passion for the lance demands he go. The thought appeals to me as well, whilst even our cautious brother, Geoffrey, is now bent on a melee. Were you to join us, bringing together all the sons of Henry, Lord Graistan, we would greatly honor our father's memory.

This time Temric's sigh was bitter. The few hours a week he stole to practice with the town's guardsmen was barely enough to keep his skills sharp and only left him wanting more. Dear God, how he longed to sit a horse, lance fewtered against a worthy opponent. The thought of it was enough to send his blood to singing. Be damned, but he'd even be willing to let Geoffrey come at him with a mace, just for the joy of beating steel against a shield. He continued reading.

And lastly, but most importantly. As much as I despise to lay this decision upon you, I must. Word from Normandy has come announcing our uncle's passing. He retained his dislike for women until the end and has no heir, acknowledged or otherwise. Are you the new lord of these lands or do I install a castellan? If you do not care for Normandy, just as I do not care to have you so far from me, there are several fine properties in what my lady wife has just inherited. Again, I must needs know if 'tis to be you or a castellan. I am to soon swear my oath and cannot long wait upon your decision.

Signed at Upwood in all honor, respect, and love, this the fourth day after Michaelmas, year of Our Lord 1194, Rannulf FitzHenry, Lord of Graistan, now holder of more properties than I would rule on my own.

Beneath his signature and seal, Rannulf had added a postscript. *I thought I would not say it, but I cannot restrain myself. I need you. Your loyalty is as dear to me as anything I own.*

Temric's teeth clenched to hold back his shout of

rage and pain. He shoved the letter into the flames and watched the stinking mass writhe as if in agony as it was consumed. The price he was paying to keep Philippa was killing him.

He set aside the cup and yanked the belt of his robe tight about his waist. With his heart burning like a flame in his chest, he made his way out of the kitchen and back up the stairs to their bed.

Philippa felt Temric return to bed. She murmured, feigning sleep, as he wrapped his arms around her and drew her into his embrace. His tenseness told her the missive had brought him more trouble.

She sighed and eased closer, needing to feel more of him. Somehow, touching her skin to his reassured her of his continuing love. As always, the sensation was silky smooth. She shivered against the potency of the feeling. When she moved again, she knew full well she teased him.

He drew a quick breath and she smiled. Against her lower back she felt his response to her play. Then his hand came to trap the fullness of her breast and it was her turn to catch her breath.

A moment later she rolled onto her back. He raised himself to his elbow as if to peer down into the darkness at her face. If she could see nothing but the dim outline of him, neither could he see aught of her. Like one blinded, she reached out, tracing with her fingertips his cheekbones, his nose, then pressing her fingertips to his lips.

"Philippa," he breathed roughly, the sadness in him all too apparent. "I ache. Love me. Make me forget what hurts me so."

Now was not the time to ask questions. He needed

her. She put her arms around his neck and drew him
down until she could take his mouth with hers. Then,
by all he'd taught her of himself, she drove him into
exhaustion.

Afterward, she lay beside him, listening to him
sleep. On the morrow, Alwyna would arrive with
Jehan and life would return to the chaos it had been
over the last two months. What needed saying between them had best be uttered before then. Aye, it
was high time he opened his heart to her.

Chapter Twenty-one

"What do you mean you will not tell me!" Philippa's voice rose in agonized astonishment. "You frighten me near to death last night with your sadness, then disappear before dawn without a word as to where you go or when I should expect your return. Now, you have the gall to say that the pain I see in you is nothing and you will not talk to me of it? Oh, Temric!" Not knowing whether to cry or scream in anger, she settled for a halfhearted stomp of her foot, the hem of her best green gown jumping against her creamy undergown.

The hall had swiftly emptied at Temric's sudden appearance near the end of the midday meal. Peter flew to the safety of Brother Odo and the priory, while the menservants dashed for the warehouses. Marta and Els cowered behind the kitchen door, not daring to even clear the table.

Temric turned, showing her nothing but the back of his leather hauberk and dark gown. Philippa gave a huff of outrage as he tore off a chunk of bread and dipped it into the stew.

"How dare you turn your back on me. I have been worried to death this day. If nothing else, you owe me an explanation for your absence."

"Love, I will not discuss with you what does not concern you." His voice was grim. When he turned again, his expression was clean of all emotion, the lines of his features stony.

"That escape will not work for you this time," she snapped. "How adept you think yourself at concealing what you do not wish me to see. Fool! What was in that missive from your brother that has pierced you to the core?"

The briefest start of surprise danced across his face, then disappeared behind the enforced blandness of his expression. "I'll not have you call me fool."

"Then do not behave as one! What of the missive," she insisted.

"I do not recall that it was addressed to you," he retorted, anger now coloring his tone.

"Nay, but if I am expected to bear the brunt of whatever bad news lay upon that sheet, I'll have a reason for it. If you truly loved me, you would share your misfortunes with me."

"How can you question my affection?" he demanded more loudly, his anger deepening in his voice. "Do I not show you by all my words and deeds how much you mean to me?"

"Aye, now show me again by entrusting me with your pain," she demanded.

His jaw tensed and his eyes narrowed. "I am not Jehan to be pushed and prodded in whatever direction you would have me go. If I choose to tell you, I will. If I do not, you must accept that."

Finding one avenue blocked, Philippa tried another. "Aye, I know you yet love me," she cried, not completely feigning her anguish, "but for how long? Your unhappiness is already so great. Oh, Temric, how

much longer before your hatred of this place drives
away all your affection for me?"

She gasped and buried her face in her hands. The
very real fear within her lent her false cry just the
right degree of honesty. What her demands did not
win, feminine distress did. Temric's arms came around
her and he drew her close. "Ah, love, do not worry.
Did I not give you my vow? Pardon, but I am solitary
by nature and that part of me does not easily change.
You are right, this life of my mother's is burying me."

"Tell me something I do not know," she replied in
soft scorn, leaning back in his embrace to watch his
face as he spoke.

"Rannulf writes that my lands in Normandy lie
wanting their lord," he said, his voice touched with
longing. "He begs me to take my oath of him and
rule my rightful inheritance."

"Lands!" she cried, shoving herself free to stand a
few paces back and stare in shock at him. "How can
you have an inheritance and oaths to take when you
have refused your knighthood?"

He shrugged, the corners of his mouth lifting ever
so slightly. "When I intervened to save you from your
husband, I did so with my sword. My open attack
against one supposedly my better forced Rannulf into
knighting me. I was also required to give him my vow
as his vassal, just as my father had long intended."

Echoing up from the courtyard below them came
an explosion of sounds. Men shouted "well come" and
pack animals brayed. The travelers had returned.

"If you have lands, why do we stay here?" Philippa
cried, clutching for what was surely the answer to his
unhappiness. "Do you think I would wish to linger

here when such a place exists for us? Temric, I love you. Where you go, I follow."

"You cannot leave," he said dully. "As long as you remain at my side, only this life offers us the surety you will not be discovered. Think on it. Were I a lord and you my lady, news that Graistan's bastard was now enfeoffed and wed would surely spread, eventually even to Lindhurst. I can imagine that your husband will have some curiosity over who it was I took as a wife. He, or someone he sends, will come to see. Do you not think that at the slightest suspicion he would complain to the bishop? All he need do to prove it is you is to require you to reveal your midsections. Those marks of yours cannot be denied."

"Aye, that is true enough," she agreed, accepting the possibility of what he said. Roger, would, indeed, do just that, but she would have to be seen to be recognized. "Temric, why can I not be your exceeding shy wife, kept in seclusion in your own home? Until your arrival at Lindhurst, I had seen no strangers in all the twelve years I lived there."

Temric's brows lifted, his eyes suddenly brightening. " 'Struth? I did not know that. Such a thing never occurred to me."

"I am content to play such a role again," she insisted. Here was one decision that troubled her not the least. "Say that we might leave for your lands this very day!"

"Content you might be, but I cannot bear the risk," he said, his face dropping back into lines of resignation. "I would not be so careless with you, love."

"But, Temric, I can be recognized here as well as there, despite the disguise of your mother's life. We have no guarantee either way," Philippa protested.

"Rather that I enjoyed a single day, knowing you were happy, before being found out than to remain here in safety and watch you die of a broken heart."

Temric's eyes were yet lifeless. "Nay, not even for my own sake will I risk your life."

"You will not?" Philippa stared at him in shock. In his expression she saw finality. He would plod along in the same course simply because he had fixed his mind on this direction and could not turn from it. Her dismay swirled into rage. "What of me? By whose right do you make this decision without considering what sort of life I want?" she spat out.

"What?!" he replied in shock, his brows flying nearly into his hairline.

"If I choose to accept the risk, I will go." Philippa stubbornly folded her arms across her chest. " 'Tis my life that we discuss here. Stay if you wish, but I am off for Normandy."

Temric's eyes suddenly narrowed against her defiance. "Do you dare challenge me? Philippa, by your vow you gave me the right to be your protector. In that role, I decide what is best for you. Not even your bad behavior can goad me into dancing to your will."

"Why, you pompous, single-minded ass," she shot back, seeking the fluency of her native tongue in her anger. "How can you dream of trapping me here in another hell when we could have happiness elsewhere?"

"Pompous—?" he roared back automatically following her into French. "Do you insult me when I have traded all I value to give you this?"

Philippa's mouth narrowed. "Why not, when you give no consideration to what I want!"

"What you want could mean your death, you twit!"

"Better days of happiness than years of misery."

"Still your tongue, woman. It is my decision to make and I have made it."

"You have no control over me," she snapped. "I am neither your sister nor your wife." She arched a brow in confidence. "I go where I choose and I choose to leave."

Temric grabbed her to him, lifting her from the floor. "Do you think yourself so powerful? Defy me now, when your feet cannot reach the floor. Come, little one"—'twas he who goaded this time—"escape me by your will, for that is the only thing left to you now."

"Put me down," she cried, thrashing and arching against his hold. "I swear if you do not, I will never lie with you again!"

"An empty threat." There was a sudden lilt of laughter in his eyes and a smile played around the corners of his mouth.

"I will never, I swear it," she retorted. When he only laughed again, she snapped, "I will tell Alwyna I want no more to do with you."

Temric grinned broadly, his eyes alight with gold. "She will know you lie. You hunger for me."

"Nay," she breathed, recognizing the loss of her battle in his pleased expression. "I will not let you make this decision when I know what you've decided is wrong for us."

"I will not listen to you lie about your lust for me," he retorted softly, "or your love. You cannot go the day without my touch."

"Can I not?" she replied, stung by the truth that allowed such arrogance. "Do not count on it, Master Too Sure of Himself. By my will Jehan walks, and by my will I hold myself from you."

Temric watched her in amusement. "Now who is too sure?" He lowered his head and his lips melded to hers, demanding the response he knew he would find.

Philippa swore to herself she fought his caress, but somehow she could not deny him what he wanted. Her arms came around his neck, drawing herself tight against him. He freed his hold on her and she slid down onto the tips of her toes and pressed herself to him. This weapon of his cut two ways. She clung to his mouth, giving back what he gave until his hands moved against her back, molding her to him.

Temric freed his mouth from hers, his lips moving against hers as he spoke. "I will hear no more of you refusing me," he breathed.

"You try only to divert me from my course and I will not let you," she insisted. "I would go to your lands."

"I shall consider your suggestion," he said between small kisses.

"Consider? You'll do more than that," she said hotly, regaining her anger even in the face of her lust for him.

"It is still not your decision to make," he said, his tone entirely too condescending.

"Why you pompous—!"

"You have used that one already," he warned in amusement.

"You'll not mock me! I am right and you know it," Philippa retorted in frustration. She thrust herself out of his embrace and whirled on her heel to show him her back just as Alwyna sailed through the hall door.

"Peter will be here as soon as Tom fetches him from the church," the good dame was saying to whoever followed her. "Look," she cried to Philippa, "you will not believe the illustrious traveler we met along the road looking for our own Peter!"

From the stairwell came a mellow voice, "I assure you, mistress, your son's talent awed my lord."

"Christus," Temric sighed, all trace of amusement gone from his voice, " 'twas Peter's scribbling I forgot."

Oswald of Hereford strode self-importantly through the doorway, dressed in bright blue robes with a jaunty feather in his velvet cap. He froze midstep as he stared at Philippa. "Jesus God Almighty. Philippa of Lindhurst," he cried, "but you are dead!"

Philippa gave a shriek of righteous outrage. "I told you it could happen here as well as any other place. We should have been long gone across the channel!" she cried, whirling to point an accusing finger at Temric. "Now, see how your pigheadedness has cheated us!"

"Why, Philippa, our visitor seems to know you," Jehan said in glee as he hobbled in on his crutches, passing the churchman on his way to his chair. "How grand!"

His nasty words sent her rage spiraling past any hope of control. "Do you think I care, Jehan?" she spat out. "The churchman's presence here means naught to me save that I must endure another assault by some fool man who thinks he owns me. Go ahead," she demanded of the slight cleric, "see if you can ruin my life any more than has already happened. At least you are not capable of using my affections against me."

"Philippa," Temric snapped, "mind your tongue. Oswald, make no mistake, your discovery means the forfeit of my life. If you think to take her, it will only be upon my death."

"I do not remember naming you my champion," Philippa shot over her shoulder to him.

"By your vow you did. Now be still," Temric commanded.

"Be still! Whose life is this?" Philippa threw her arms wide in supreme frustration. "All my life I have been used as if I were but some puppet on a stick. You must sew a straight seam, Philippa. Wed here and submit to abuse, Philippa. I am taking you, Philippa. Live as a commoner, Philippa." She glared at them all. "No one ever asks me what is my will! Well, no longer, do you hear? From this moment on, I decide what is best for me. Make no mistake in this," she said, aiming a rigid finger at Oswald. "If you think that even the power of the Church can force me back to Lindhurst, best you think again. I *will not go*."

Oswald groaned at that. "Mother of God, I forgot me! Roger of Lindhurst is remarried!"

"Bigamist!" Philippa crowed in hard satisfaction. "At least, he'll no longer want me."

Jehan gave a sharp laugh. "How I have enjoyed these last moments. No point in my remaining to watch the bloodbath when what I've heard is enough for my revenge on you, Philippa." He struggled awkwardly back onto his crutches and clumped across the hall to its door, then, his laughter echoing from the stairway as he made his way down the stairs.

"Jehan!" Alwyna cried out after him.

Philippa paid neither of them any heed. Her eyes ablaze, she stared at Oswald. "So, little man, what is it to be?"

The young cleric was unnerved by the steel in her

voice. "You must give yourself over to my custody," he declared uncertainly. "Your sin here is very great."

"Ha! What do I look like?" She crossed her arms and narrowed her eyes at him. "A dog who comes at the snap of your fingers?"

"I will not let her go!" Temric said, his words fierce. "No matter how rude she is, or how ungrateful for this life I bought her at the risk of my own."

"Ungrateful!" Philippa shouted. "Well, beg my pardon, but you did not ask me what I wanted. A home of my own where my children need share their lives with only us—now that I know you have such a place, how can you deny it to me?"

"I do what is best for us!" he shouted back. "I'll not let you spurn what I give you."

"Stop this!" Oswald roared, finding his voice at last. "Do you think you can cow me into ignoring what goes ahead here by this ridiculous behavior? Nay, not this time! Temric, you are right, you forfeit your life to her husband for your adultery. Lady Philippa, you will come with me!" He bellowed the words and the walls shook with their power. Then he thrust his hand out as if he truly expected her to do as he bid.

Philippa gave a wild cry as true fright pierced her rage. Dashing to hide behind Temric, she wound her arms tightly about his chest. "Nay," she said from behind him, "I will not let you steal Temric from me. I will not go!"

Temric gave a huff of amusement. "Oswald, I believe you have your answer. Philippa will not leave me, even if she thinks me a pompous ass."

"I was angry," she muttered into the shoulder of his leather hauberk. In acceptance of her apology, he laid his hand atop the two of hers where they clutched together as if in prayer.

"You must come." Oswald's words held a note of disbelief as if he could not comprehend their refusal to bow to his authority. "Mistress," he whirled on Alwyna, "tell me you do not condone what they do here."

Alwyna gave a casual lift to her shoulders. "I am the wrong one to judge what they do, as I've once before been fined for adultery myself."

"Then I must call the guard and have you taken forcibly from here," Oswald threatened.

"Say something," Philippa pleaded of the man she loved.

"He has already heard what I have to say. I will give my life before I let you go," Temric replied mildly. "You may speak for yourself if you desire to do so."

Philippa glared at Oswald from over Temric's shoulder. "Then if Temric must die, so will I. Call your guards. By the time they arrive, I will be dead and this time not in pretense. It will not only be suicide, but murder as well, for I bear a child."

Oswald groaned. "Nay! Say you would not."

"Why not? Aye, it all rests on your soul, churchman. You intend to expose us as adulterers. This means the man I now call husband must lose his life. Were I to live after his death, you'd either force Roger to set aside his new wife and take me back or force me into a convent. Roger would swiftly see me dead as well as any child I bore. As for a nunnery, well, there is no room for a child in such a place. Either way, you will steal my love and my child. I would prefer suicide and murder."

"You will be damned to hell!" Oswald cried, horrified by what she threatened.

"To meet my mother there when I arrive." Philippa laughed harshly when Oswald jerked at her words. "Well, who did you think was buried in my place?"

"Oswald," Temric said, " 'twas by her own hand and no one else's urging that she died. I had no part in her private plot."

"Jesu, but she lies on hallowed ground in the abbey!"

"If God has not spit her out by now," Alwyna offered quietly, "He must not mind her resting where she is."

"You are all blasphemers and heretics!" Oswald roared, thoroughly scandalized.

That brought Philippa bolt upright, her grasp on Temric loosening. "Nay, not true! I love God with all my heart for it is by His direct intervention that I live and have Richard as my own. It is you who sin when you think to force me from the man that God commanded I keep." She gasped in surprise at what had flooded past her lips.

Oswald stiffened at the tone of her voice. "What?" he asked, his words suddenly hushed. "Explain yourself."

"I cannot say more," she said in distress, still too uncomfortable to speak about the strange vision she experienced during her unconscious time.

"Explain yourself this instant or I swear I will denounce you as heretic and see you burn in punishment!"

Philippa bowed her head, reluctance giving way to Oswald's threat. When she slipped out from behind Temric, he offered her his hand and she twined her fingers with his. As always, there was magic in his touch and she found the strength to reveal what she'd never meant to share outside herself.

"After Roger's blow, I felt death come for me and I welcomed it for it meant the end of my torment at Lindhurst. Then," she sighed, "I saw a figure, light streaming from around him. I thought he must be God. When I would have gone beyond him for that other life that lay just out of my reach, he refused to let me pass. He would only say, his words filling me from the inside out, not by way of my ears, that I must stay for Richard."

She turned to Temric. His expression had softened; his gaze was calm and considering. "I knew you only as Temric, not Richard. I did not understand this command to me until your mother told me your true name after I had come back to the living."

"Glad I am you were held here," he said with a small smile.

"Nay," Oswald protested. "This tale of yours is only a falsehood meant to make me ignore the sin I have found here."

Philippa shook her head, her gaze unwavering as she met Oswald's. "I, too, have struggled to accept the experience, but no matter what question I ask of myself the truth remains the same. I knew of no Richard, save a few peasants at Lindhurst more commonly called Dickon, until Alwyna spoke my Temric's true name. I will swear on any relic, endure any ordeal you set before me, for I do not lie. Test me at your will."

Oswald's dark brows pulled down as he clutched at the breast of his rich gown in confusion. "I do not know what to do."

"Then do nothing," Temric said, his voice hard. "Can you not see how concealing Philippa's continued existence benefits you? What would become of you were you to reveal her to your bishop? 'Twas your lord who declared her dead. He'll not much care to learn that your cousin has made a fool of him. Who was it that granted Lindhurst the right to remarry? Who allowed Lady Edith to be buried in the abbey? Your lord, the fool twice more. When we appear, having conceived a child in adultery and incest, we have besmirched the family name of his favorite cleric. Nay, Bishop William will not look so fondly on you when you expose all this for him to see."

The churchman gasped as if his career had slipped suddenly from his grip. 'Twas obvious Oswald knew his master very well, indeed.

"What if God has intervened with us?" Philippa asked gently. "Our love is very great. I wonder if it is not a test of your faith that this judgment has been laid before you. You were the one sent to fetch Peter," she pointed out, "not some other who would not have known me."

Oswald bent under the weight of her words. "I am so confused. I must think. Aye, a night of prayer will make all things clear to me."

He turned on Alwyna once again. "Mistress, I must decline your invitation to bide here. I make my residence this night at the priory. Send young Peter to me and I will speak to him without prejudice from these events. Temric," he turned on his cousin, his mouth open to say more, but Temric interrupted.

"Do not ask me to vow anything, for I will not give you any word at all."

"I need no more than the knowledge that you are a sworn knight. That, alone, will keep you here until I call for you on the morrow." With a final grim look at both of them, Oswald turned on his boot heel and strode from the hall.

Alwyna stared at them for a long moment, then cried out in desperate fear, "Run, go, hide as quickly as you can!"

"Mama," Temric said with a shake of his head. "I will not run. Now that she is revealed, there is nowhere left to hide."

Alwyna's voice rose again. "Do you tell me that for honor's sake you'll stay here to lose your life whilst I must look helplessly on? Nay, I will not!"

"Love?" Temric asked of Philippa. In that one word he instilled their whole future together.

"You are right. Where will we run to that they cannot find us? Hiding is no sort of life at all." She wound her arms around him and held him close. "In these short months I have had more happiness than I ever dreamed to own. I cannot regret one minute, even if the morrow brings the end of it."

"I am sorry, Mama," Temric said, "but it is better to die than be hunted down in fear and dishonor. A life of lies and running is hardly the sort you'd want for your grandchild, is it?"

" 'Tis better than no life," Alwyna begged.

"Nay, I think that is not true," Philippa sighed, then touched Temric on his scarred cheek. "My pardon, love, I should have told you of our child before I announced it so openly."

"I knew." His comment was so succinct that she stared up at him in stark surprise and he smiled. "You, too, were keeping secrets you could not hide. No women save those too young, too old, or breeding miss their courses two months in a row. You have not been unavailable." His voice deepened in remembered passion and he laid his arm about her shoulders.

"Oh, to lose not only my firstborn son, but the daughter of my heart and my grandchild as well," Alwyna said, her voice rising. "Oh, Richard, you turned the world on its ear to have this woman you adore, how can you now let a churchman steal her from you?"

Suddenly Alwyna pulled herself together and stood up to her tallest. "Nay, I will fight them!" she swore, tears filling her eyes. "My husband's name still has influence. I will bring witnesses to swear you are not the Lady Philippa, but Pippa of Stanrudde. I will have a marriage document made, all signed and sealed, proving you were wed to my Temric before midsummer!"

Philippa went to take the woman in her embrace, soothing her with a a gentle hand on Alwyna's back. "Do not. My life has always been a tangle of other people's lies and I will live that way no longer. On the morrow, I fear we will fall in the truth."

"Aye, so it seems," Alwyna sighed, wiping away her tears with the back of her hand. "I would rather that I lost you to my son's other life and your nobility. At least then I might see you from time to time."

"You will soon have Clarice to take my place," Philippa offered with a tremulous smile. "You will like her as well as me."

Alwyna shook her head, struggling to regain her control. "Not as well, but well enough. Aye, Gerard intends to come on the morrow to speak with me about it. I've not told Jehan as I am not completely certain of Gerard's intentions. Here's another of my sons who's trapped himself when he need not be caught. I would have been just as pleased with children of less complexity, God," she called up toward the heavens. "Now that You've given them to me, might You consider lending them a hand in their present difficulties?"

"Philippa," Temric said, catching her hand in his, "let us spend our next hours alone."

"Aye, go," Alwyna insisted, "but swear you will do nothing until the churchman has given you his decision. There might yet be hope."

"I swear to that," Philippa said, struggling to still her tears as she spoke. She followed Temric up the stairs to gather what they needed. In the hall below she heard Alwyna shout, "Marta! Els! Why does food yet stand on the table? Have you gone slovenly on me in my absence? Hie, hie!" The pretended anger barely covered the older woman's pain.

Moments later Temric had belted on his sword and taken as a second weapon a dagger with a long blade, while Philippa had donned her mantle, then found Temric's cloak. She fingered the pin he'd given her as they strode from the courtyard to walk along the streets of Stanrudde.

Even though she was now accustomed to the rush and push of the city's many folk, the noise grated on her. Temric pulled her beneath an overhanging second story as an upper window opened and filthy water spewed from it. Nay, it was intolerable today. What lay before them demanded the peace and quiet waiting outside Stanrudde's walls.

"Temric," she begged, "might we go to the stables? I need the sight of trees and the feel of grass beneath my feet." *One more time,* but she could not bring herself to say the words aloud.

They stopped to purchase a bit of food and drink to

take with them, then went to Priory Gate. Evidently, Oswald had put his full trust in Temric's honor, for there was no challenge when they exited.

Philippa sighed in relief as the walls receded behind them. "No matter how much I love your mother, those streets are so close they press down on me until I feel I cannot breathe."

Temric laughed, the sound clear despite the severity of their situation. "You, too? I cannot bear them around me, although I think it has more to do with being trapped into my mother's life than the walls themselves."

They walked on in silence past fields, scythed down to ankle-deep stubble, and orchards, now plucked clean. Meadowlands had become a rolling sea of drying grasses, while copse and thicket were colored in tawny browns, oranges, and deep gold. She breathed deeply. The myriad stinks created by the folk within Stanrudde's walls were gone. Here, the air was spicy fresh and cool, despite a warm sun behind misty clouds. Above her soared an uncertain "V" of swans, their calls raucous as they vied for leadership in their flight. Save for the distant cawing of a crow, the woodlands seemed overly quiet after summer's many melodies.

Finally, the little building was at hand. A few late fruits yet clung to the trees in the garden. As they rounded the stable's corner, Temric's massive steed came to greet them at the fence. Temric went first to pluck an apple, then offered it to his horse.

"What is his name?" Philippa asked, her voice subdued in sadness from her seat on the well enclosure as she watched Temric rub the big gelding's ears.

"Horse," he said bluntly, then laughed. "I am afraid

there's no romance in my soul. I'll leave Rannulf and Gilliam to name their steeds after great heroes. You also answer to 'idiot' and 'pigheaded fool,' do you not?" The big brown steed nodded in amiable agreement, then snorted as if it, too, enjoyed the jest. Temric gave the beast a final pat, then came to stand in front of his avowed wife.

"I would apologize to you for my rage," Philippa said meekly. "In all honesty, I have never before behaved so—so, well, so like Rowena."

Temric frowned. "Aye, and fie on you for doing so. How shocked I am to discover my gentle dove has fangs."

Philippa started to hang her head in shame, then caught herself. "Oh, you are only teasing me."

"So I am."

She caught her breath, remembering when they had last spoken those same words. It had been here, in this building. The memory of her hands sliding over his bare chest filled her, warming every crevice within her. She could not imagine life without him at her side. Aye, 'twas better to face death with him than to exist in a world of barren emptiness without him.

"Temric," she breathed, "I fear this will be our last night together. How would you spend it with me?"

"Silly woman," he said with quiet reproach. "I thought that was why we came here."

When he extended his hand in invitation, she accepted. As always, the gentle enclosing of her palm in his sent a thrill through her. He drew her to her feet, then touched his mouth to hers in a sweet caress. Tears seeped from her eyes, but when he would have pulled away, she wrapped her arms around his neck to keep him close. There was not enough time left for pain, only love.

Chapter Twenty-two

D awn shot rosy fingers of light through the tiny stable windows, the air brisk. From high above the roof Temric heard the sounds of geese and ducks on the wing, departing for their wintering grounds. There, too, was the gentle bleat of sheep, the crow of a cock. A stag bellowed his lonely call. Aye, life gathered around him in all its fullness.

Philippa was cradled at his side, sharing her warmth beneath the blanket of her mantle. Her hair spilled over him in a silky fall, her heart beating in time with his own. And within her grew his child, created by their love.

That others would name his offspring "bastard" no longer mattered. Would that they lived long enough to worry over such a mundane matter. A sudden sadness filled him. His child would never know how great his father's love for him had been.

He sighed. So had Temric's own father felt about him when Alwyna carried him beneath her heart. How had he dared to refuse that love in a quibble over what had been left off a scrap of sheep's skin?

Within him grew a list of regrets, things he'd wished he'd done, things he'd done and wished he hadn't. For the first time in years, life was unbearably precious. It would not be easy to give it up. Still, he had spoken the truth. Like Philippa, he'd had enough of lies and deception.

Philippa breathed deeply and stretched against him. Her skin slid deliciously along his as she moved, teasing him just as she no doubt meant to do. Temric smiled. His fear that he might never gain enough of her trust to love her as a man loved his wife had proved wondrously groundless.

"Not again," he groaned, pretending weakness. It was a doomed attempt for his shaft betrayed him.

"If you have not the strength," she said quietly, her words dying away when she could not still the quiver in her voice.

"We agreed there would be no more tears," he said, hiding his own sadness.

"The morning is now upon us and I find I am suddenly jealous for my life. I am afraid! Temric, you must love me until I cannot think," she pleaded.

"As you will," he said softly. He touched his mouth to hers in gentle caress as he slid his hand down the length of her side to the roundness of her hip. She placed her hand on his chest, running her palm downward to his belly. "Nay," he said, catching her hand in his. "Do you know, I've never repaid you for that first time?"

"Repaid?" she asked in surprise.

"For the way you touched me," he said with a smile. Heat grew within him, taunting him with images of his hands on her, tracing and teasing. "Let me touch you," he breathed, kissing her chin, then down her throat.

Philippa caught her breath, her senses filling with him as he kissed along her collarbone. She closed her eyes as the need to feel the love and care that was reflected in his touch won over all other concerns. Coming to her feet, she tossed her hair over her shoulders. "I would like that," she said.

When he stood, it was to lay his hands on her shoulders. She felt his palms, hard with calluses, sliding gently and slowly down the length of her arms. Her skin seemed to come to life at his touch, warming and tingling at the same time. When he reached her hands, he raised one to his mouth and kissed her palm.

Philippa caught her breath as the sensation jolted up her arm. Her fingers curled so she could touch his cheek as he pressed his lips to the base of her fingers. Then he kissed her wrist. Her eyes closed as she sighed. His tongue found the curve of her elbow and she shuddered against her body's growing heat.

When he brushed his lips across her shoulder, she tilted her head to the side in invitation. Instead of kissing her mouth, his hands came to catch the fullness of her breasts and she gloried in the feeling. He knelt before her, to use his mouth as well as his fingers. With each caress, each time he teased her nipples with his lips and teeth and tongue a fiery need within her grew. She combed his hair with her fingers, stroked his nape and the width of his shoulders while she prayed he would never cease.

Then he was leaning away. "Why is it," he murmured, "that no matter how well you satisfy me, I forever want more of you?"

She sighed, already languid in her passion for him. "Because there is so much love in our hearts, we must keep showing it to each other, else our emotions might eat us alive," she replied softly, then knelt before him.

"I cannot bear not having your arms around me any longer. Hold me and let me feel you within me. It makes me complete in a way I cannot explain."

He caught her into his embrace and took her mouth with all the passion that the future might deny them. She let his need surge over her. His shaft, hot and hard, lay against her belly. Easing back onto their makeshift bed, she stretched beneath him and opened herself to him, begging by her motion that he might fill her emptiness. He entered her, holding himself above her and exquisitely still within her.

As always, the fullness was shattering, bringing with it waves of pleasure. She shifted against the pressure and watched him quiver in response. His eyes closed and he eased down atop her. Moving softly beneath him, she could not help her smile as he caught his breath in enjoyment. Philippa joined her hands behind his neck, lifting herself a little to press her breasts against his chest. "Take me," she breathed.

He gasped and moved, knowing that as he pleased himself, so did he please her. With each simple motion her enjoyment grew. She caught his mouth with hers, their need for each other almost bruising in its intensity. Clasping him to her, she locked her legs around his. The heat of him inside her was scorching, forcing her rhythm to quicken. Then he tore his mouth from hers to whisper to her of his love, of how everything she did pleased him, of his desire to spill his seed within her.

She cried out, driven by his words beyond pleasure. As she arched beneath him, he groaned, holding her tightly against him while he poured himself into her. And, in that instant, they were one.

*   *   *

It was not long after that Alwyna sent a messenger to the stable, saying that Oswald awaited them at the priory. If there was no hesitation in their step as they made their way back into the city and to the priory door, neither did they rush headlong into their fate.

While the monk who acted as porter held the wooden door wide, Philippa hung back, her reluctance too great to overcome. "Temric," she cried softly.

He stared down at her, his heartache written clearly in his gaze. Then he stroked her jaw with a gentle finger. "There is no need for you to do this. Find peace in a convent, if you will."

"Nay," she replied instantly, winding her arms around him to hold him.

"Have these last months been worth the price?" he breathed.

"Aye," she answered, "the happiest I've known. But I am jealous and want more. If that cannot be, rather that I left life with you at my side for I could not bear the loneliness without you."

Temric drew her close, his arms about her warm and secure. "I thank you for that, love." He took her hand in his and, together, they followed the monk into the cloister.

Up a tiled walkway, shielded from the elements by a roof supported on great arches of stone, they walked. The morning sun slanted across the path. She looked out into a pretty garden square where two monks collected rose hips from thorny branches. At the walk's far end sat a group of boys, gathered to learn their lessons as Peter had been taught. Two days ago, all these scenes would have been unworthy of her notice. Now, she valued each instant and event.

The monk opened a dark wooden door, its metal

hinges rotating with subtle groans. They entered together, then the door was closed behind them. Oswald already sat in the prior's ornately carved chair. To one side of him stood a scribe's raised desk, the stub of a candle the only thing on its bare surface. Save for him and the statue of a saint, the tiny office was empty.

Philippa leaned heavily against Temric, wondering at his calm when her own heart felt like a lead weight in her chest. His arm tightened around her. She stared at the man who held their fate in his hands; Oswald's face was forbidding in its harsh angles and angry planes. "So," he said after dragging the moment's silence out to an unendurable length, "Lady Philippa, are you still set on suicide and murder if I attempt to remove you from Temric's custody?"

"Aye," she said quietly, turning her eyes down to stare at the floor. Bits of dew-moistened grass clung to the tips of her soft shoes and the morning's dampness had darkened the hem of her green gown, staining her pale undergown.

Temric drew her closer, into the protection of his body. She felt his motion as he lifted aside his mantle to display his sword and dagger belted at his side. "Nor did we come unprepared for this meeting, Oswald," he said softly. "If you call the guard, we will die here."

"All this you do to avoid the responsibility of your sin?" Oswald asked harshly of Philippa.

"Nay, Oswald, I freely admit to both adultery and incest," she said with a sigh, raising her gaze to meet his. "When the time comes that I can confess, I will gladly accept my penance and perform it as I am instructed. I cannot leave Temric, nor let you wrest me from him, for I truly believe God has willed me to stay. If Temric's life must end on my account, then mine must, as well."

"And you, Richard?"

Temric gave the smallest of shrugs, his hand moving slightly against her waist in a soothing motion. "She is mine and I will keep her, honoring her as my wife for all my days. If she says God has given her to me, I can but believe her claim of divine intervention. It explains how I so easily stole her away from Lindhurst's plot to kill her."

This startled the young churchman, sending his black brows arching up into sharp points. "Plot?" he repeated in surprise. "What plot?"

"Come now," Temric retorted, his voice touched with sarcasm, "you cannot have believed that ruse his mother played out after I defeated Lindhurst on the field. They had plotted to spirit Philippa out of Graistan while her son and I battled. Two of Lindhurst's men awaited inside our hunting grounds with instructions to do murder. Afterward, one was to have killed the other, then run to avoid revelation."

"I believed my husband would seek my death if I lost the inheritance and so I told Father Edwin," Philippa cried softly. "How did you come to discover it?"

Temric glanced down at her with a swift smile. "I forgot that you have not yet heard this tale. 'Twas Anne who tended you after your husband beat you. Margaret did not know Anne was my cousin when she came offering her pennies."

"Eight pennies," Philippa murmured as Margaret's words came rushing from her fractured memory with sudden and startling clarity. Two stewing hens, that was all her death had been worth to Margaret. "How can you steal me from one who loves me to send me back to those who seek my death?" she demanded of Oswald in disbelief.

"How do I know he speaks the truth?" Oswald challenged.

"If you need corroboration, ask of my half brother, Peter," Temric said. "He was present to hear Lindhurst's dam present her bribes. So, too, was he present when the hired killers died and heard what they spewed of the plot. Upon your return to Hereford ask for Anne of Graistan, who stood beside Margaret and made the old woman's tale ring true. Say to her that Temric bid her do so, and she, too, will spill a tale of coins exchanged to assure Philippa's death."

At that, Oswald frowned. "I must accept that you speak the truth, for I doubted that tale from the first," he finally said and sighed as if in defeat. "Lindhurst's dam made it very clear she did not want to pay the cost of giving her son's wife to the Church when they had just lost a substantial fortune. Lord Lindhurst's new wife is well dowered, I have seen the contract. I think the girl is not so fresh, for her parents were in great haste to see her wed," he added soberly, then fell silent as if in consideration.

Philippa shifted nervously from foot to foot as they waited. Temric took her hand in his, his fingers tight and hard against hers. Again, the quiet became unbearable. "Oswald," she said when she could tolerate it no longer, "what is your plan for us?"

"Plan?" the churchman snapped in impatience. "What options do you leave me? I am trapped here between what I've been taught is right and what I believe is best. I cannot do anything. I'd not have your suicide and the murder of your child on my soul. As for Richard's cruel attempt at manipulation by suggesting my lord's disfavor, he is all too correct. The events of the past months would reflect badly on me should they come to light. The only hope for me in all this is that my faith listens eagerly to your tale of a holy encounter. I take solace in this possibility. At this time, my only aim is to seek some way of assuring that your true identity remains hidden and pray that God will not damn me for what I do."

Temric stiffened in shock, his grip tightening to almost an unbearable pressure on her fingers. "You will do nothing?"

"Nothing, save protect myself. Now, go away. I will bide here a day or two longer while I search for a way to achieve what must be done. I want no hint to remain that I have been here and seen what I have seen."

Philippa tore away from Temric to turn and stare up at him, her hands pressed to her face in shock and joy. He was reaching for her, the smile on his face beautiful to behold. Her knees weakened and she sank toward the floor, but he caught her in his arms, lifting her into his embrace, holding her tightly as if she were not close enough.

"We live," she breathed. He cradled her in his arms as she pillowed her head against his cloaked shoulder. "We live."

"Oswald," he said quietly, "your gift this day will not be forgotten."

"Speak no more to me, cousin," Oswald said coldly. "I do not appreciate how you have used me. Do not think I have forgiven you."

"I humbly accept your scorn as part of my penance. If you ever have need of me, know that I will come bearing only goodwill in my heart."

"I pray I never sink so low as to need to call upon you." Oswald's words were bitter.

"So be it," Temric said quietly, then turned and carried her back into life.

Although Philippa pleaded for him to put her down, saying that she weighed too much for him to bear, that the shopkeepers would think them besotted fools, he refused to do so until they reached Alwyna's courtyard.

There, her voice rose in insistence. "Temric, you must put me down or Alwyna will fear the worst."

Temric was grinning like a fool and he knew it. "Nay, that she sees us at all will tell her to rejoice. I keep thinking that it came too easily, too cheaply, despite the fact that I have made of Oswald an implacable enemy."

"Oh, love, leave the future where it belongs," she cried in laughter as he set her feet upon the cobbles, keeping an arm around her because he could not bear to break his contact with her yet. "I will enjoy this life of mine, moment by moment, without questioning what comes next. Now, tell me you will write to Lord Rannulf and take your oath of him so we might live on your lands instead of here."

Jehan hobbled over on his crutches, a gleam of a smile on his lips. "Good morrow, brother, Philippa. I have been hard at work these past hours, while you two lazed the morning away. In all truth, I thought you were long gone, escaping that prancing churchman."

Temric only grinned at him, incapable of responding to Jehan's spite after the miracle he'd been given. Then, his brother was staring over his shoulder in surprise. Temric turned to watch Gerard of Stanrudde stride into their courtyard.

The portly man, bald to a fringe around the back of his head, came confidently toward them. There was no mistaking the merchant's opinion of himself. His rich red gown, vibrant green chausses, and fine leather boots shouted status from beneath a dark mantle lined with otter. In case anyone still doubted, Gerard had adorned his thick fingers with heavy rings, while a massive gold chain lay atop mantle and tunic.

"Why, Master Gerard, good morrow to you. What brings you here?" Jehan asked, obviously startled that this important townsman had chose to visit.

"Good morrow, Master Jehan," Gerard said, offering the younger man a subtle compliment in his use of that title. "Glad I am to have found you here. Clarice has been nagging at me to set a date for your wedding day and I have decided the time was come to do so. Is Alwyna about so we might have at this thorny problem?"

"Master Gerard," Alwyna called from the back door of the house, "how good of you to stop by. Why, Richard and Philippa, are you so soon returned from the priory?" Her voice lifted and cracked slightly as she asked the question, but there was no other hint of her concern for them.

"That we are," Temric called back, "and an extremely successful visit it was."

Alwyna's eyes closed and she leaned against the open door for the briefest of seconds, then straightened. "And what brings you calling this morn, Gerard? Would you care to come inside for a drop of wine?"

"Wine and plans, Mistress Alwyna," came the merchant's cheerful reply. "I think me it is time to join our two houses."

"Well, then 'tis indeed time to plan," she retorted pleasantly. "Come in and let the young ones do our labors whilst we take our ease."

When Gerard grinned broadly and started away, Jehan caught at his arm. "Wait! Why?"

"Why what, lad?" The older man arched a brow at him in surprise. "This betrothal has dragged on for too long. Clarice says she will be too old to bear children if we wait any longer."

"Three months ago, I was certain you meant to annul our betrothal."

Gerard gave a casual shake of his head. "Three months ago you were not the man you are today. I cannot tell you how your rapid improvements have startled the whole guild. There were those among us who believed you'd never rise above the blows of your father's death and the loss of your legs. Master Jehan, you have proved us all wrongheaded fools. Not only have you worked hard, but I think me you've the same gift for our trade that your father had. Aye, you're a bit rough yet, but you're young. You'll grow into it. We look forward to your taking of full membership with us."

Temric watched as Jehan turned confused eyes on Philippa. "Nay," Jehan cried softly, then he stuttered, "I mean, thank you, Master Gerard. Your compliments turn my head. I do not know what to think."

"I think you should say your thanks to your brother's wife." Gerard offered Philippa a swift wink. "Who hasn't seen her at your side offering her encouragements, eh? A close and loving family makes for strong trade and good business, that's what I always say."

With that, Gerard strode to the door to join Alwyna in toasting the celebrations.

Jehan stared at Philippa, his face now devoid of color. "Nay," he breathed in shock. "I never thought to have this. I mean, my legs—" His voice trailed away.

"Are your brains in your legs, Jehan?" Philippa asked softly. "Clarice cares only for you and Gerard cares for naught but your intelligence and skill. Crutches and a packhorse supply all the mobility you need."

"I'd have none of this but for you," Jehan breathed in dismay. "Nay!" he cried, wrenching himself about on his crutches to hobble into the warehouse.

"Jehan!" Temric called after him in sudden concern. Jehan had done something, the guilt was written on his face.

"Now what has bitten him?" Philippa mused. "He should be happy over what he's achieved. I thought he loved Clarice."

Shouting broke out within the little storehouse. Suddenly, Tom was launched through the doorway, to slide along the cobbles on his belly. Temric was already loping to the building as Rob came screaming out its door, "Help, help, Master Jehan has gone mad!"

Past stacks of parchment quires, hemp bales, and bundles of cloth Temric ran. Jehan had fallen to lie on the hard-packed earthen floor, his crutches splayed against the opposite wall, one splintered by the force of his throw. Bright silks were piled softly about him as he tore at another bundle.

"Cease, Jehan," Temric commanded in the voice that brought instant compliance from all his men.

Jehan dropped the cloth, then sagged into the materials.

When Temric knelt beside him, his brother turned, grabbing him by the front of his leather vest. He was sobbing as if his heart had been torn from him. "Temric," he cried, "run."

"Jehan," Philippa cried out as she came to kneel in front of the young man, "what is it?"

"Run! I paid for the fastest messenger I could buy. Get as far from here as you can," he begged her, then groaned in agony as he turned his attention back to his brother. "Temric, I have been a fool. I knew it was her doing it all the time. I hated myself for being so afraid to fail. How could I ever be as good as Papa? She made me so angry, I hated her for what she forced on me."

Temric knew a stab of fear, remembering Jehan's parting words as he left the hall yesterday. "Be clear, boy, what have you done?"

"Oh, God," Jehan choked on his tears, "I sent word to Philippa's husband that she was here and to hurry because you would run. When I heard the churchman name him, I thought only of my own need to avenge myself for all the abuse I thought she'd heaped on me. Oh, God, I have betrayed you both, when you've done me nothing but good!"

Alwyna and Gerard came dashing into the warehouse. "What is it?" Jehan's mother cried as she knelt beside her son. "What has happened?"

"We were almost free," Philippa said softly. Her face had whitened to a ghostly pallor, her expression was deathly still.

Temric roared in agony. "If I cannot stop him, he will kill her. Have you not seen the marks he laid on her? How can you hate so deeply?" He drew back a hand to strike his brother.

"Nay," Jehan shouted, grabbing his brother's arm. Two months of supporting himself on crutches had given the boy new power and Jehan held him off. With a hiss of rage, Temric wrenched his arm free of his brother's hold.

"Temric," Jehan said, "I swear I shall willingly submit to your beating after you have saved her from him. He will come here looking for me, and I must be conscious to lead him on a false trail. Leave now, before it is too late," he pleaded. "Go!"

"What is it that goes on here?" Gerard asked, his deep voice booming about the small room. He stood, his feet planted wide apart, his hands braced on his hips as he narrowly eyed the younger man sprawled at his feet.

Jehan turned his frantic gaze on his future father-by-marriage. "We played a foolish game of wills, Philippa and I, but I have unthinkingly gone one step too far. She is not yet free of one who once owned her. I knew that she had barely escaped this one with her life intact and know as well that if her former owner finds her, he will surely kill her. Idiot that I am, I let my ire over something I'd imagined she'd done rule my sense and sent word to this man as to where she was. If what I've done causes you to retract your offer for Clarice's hand in marriage, then it is no more than I deserve for my cruelty and stupidity."

"It has not yet been a year and a day for her?" Gerard asked, as he glanced from face to face. Somehow, Jehan's oblique explanation had made him believe Philippa a serf come to hide from her noble owner. Only the expiration of that legal time period could terminate her slavery. He wrenched a ring from one of his fingers and shoved it into Temric's hand. "Take her to Bristol and ask for the wine merchant, John, son of Walter. Tell him to hide her as I hid him. Be gone with you." He waved them on their way.

Temric leapt up, grabbing Philippa by the hand, and pulled her to her feet. He forced her along behind him as he strode from the warehouse. At the middle of the courtyard, she wrenched her hand from his and stopped.

"We are not going to have this life, are we?" she asked sharply, still trapped in her fear of her husband. "I am not going to have my child or my love. This has all been nothing but a dream and now it is ending."

"Nay," Temric swore, "I will not let him have you."

"He will come here and force them to say where I have gone. Sweet Mary, but there is no place left to hide now that he knows I exist! He will search and search."

"Nay," Temric said, "we are not hiding. We ride to Bristol and from there we sail to Normandy. Once I have you safe within my own walls, let him try to take you from me. His marriage becomes our shield, for to reveal your existence makes him a bigamist and cheats him of his new wife's dowry." He turned and strode out of the courtyard, praying she would follow. There was no time to spend convincing her. "Come, love, we must saddle our mounts and ride for our future."

"What if he finds us on the road," Philippa cried out as she ran to come abreast him.

"Then, we fight," he said with a grimace. As much as he craved the protection of his armor, to don it and ride from Stanrudde with a single woman at his side would be like carrying a red pennant calling Lindhurst to them. "Come faster, little one."

"He will have men with him," she pleaded.

"He might," he said, then lifted his brows in scorn. "Nay, I know better. 'Twill be the same now as when he was bent on murdering you in secret. He dares not let even a hint of what he plans for you exist. He'll come with only one or two, intending to kill those men himself to prevent any chance of revelation."

"Aye, and I will die," she said in a terrified whisper, "and you, as well. Oh, Lord, but the knowledge that another man has loved me will drive him to great cruelty. He will need to hurt us both, as much as he can, to soothe his injured pride."

"Mayhap, but what choice have we save to reach for the future? If the worst happens and he finds us on the road, then you must pray that this life of my mother's has not made me too soft to do what needs doing. . . . Oh, my love, but consider the possibilities if we survive!" With that, he grabbed her by the hand and forced her to keep pace with his swift lope.

Chapter Twenty-three

Philippa sat astride one of Alwyna's palfreys, her skirts hiked up above her knees. Never had she been so cold; her fingers were frozen on the reins, despite the warmth of the midday sun. Her cheeks ached as if frostbitten while a spicy autumn breeze tangled in her braids. They trotted steadily along the Bristol road, her little beast hard-pressed to keep pace with the big gelding's longer legs.

Summer's end had brought the finish of the merchant's high season. Most stored their carts and put their beasts out to pasture until the next spring, leaving the roads far emptier now. Philippa glanced nervously behind her. Stanrudde's walls were long out of sight and the track in that direction was empty, neither horse nor footman to be seen. She would have turned backward in her saddle, if Temric would let her, so desperate was she to make certain Roger did not ride up from behind them.

Instead, she forced herself to focus on what lay around her. At the verge on either side of the road stood thick stands of elm and beech. Folk had already been into the woodland, pruning what they could by hook or crook to feed their winter fires. Several stacks of dead, dry wood yet lay along the roadbed for collecting, as did many piles of withered elm leaves meant for fodder.

"Mayhap, he will ignore Jehan's message," she said, trying to fool herself into calm, but she knew better. Her husband would come.

"Love, do not lie to yourself." Temric's voice was gentle. "He will come looking for both of us. We are a thorn that festers in him, threatening to drive him mad with the pain. If you must hope for something, hope that Jehan is able to send him looking in the wrong direction just long enough for us to gain a decent lead."

Philippa stared wide-eyed at him. "You sound as if you do not believe Jehan will succeed."

"I do not. Just now, I pray only that Lindhurst does not do too much damage to either Jehan or my other kin when he finds you have escaped him once again. Think on it. If he wants no witnesses to your continued life, then would not Jehan have to die as well? He was the great fool who sent the message with his right name attached to it." His words were impatient with Jehan, but not angry or even displeased.

"Then we should go back. We cannot leave your mother unprotected!" she cried.

"Love, they will call the guard. What can Lindhurst say when the town's soldiery appear? That he seeks his dead wife?" Again, the calm reason in his answer seemed so very wrong to their dire circumstances. When he shot her a look, he was surprisingly relaxed, even amused.

"Well, then, are we not safer in Stanrudde? We, too, can call the guard and say he was assaulting us," Philippa offered hopefully.

"Nay, if he challenges us, it will force Oswald into

revealing what he knows, no matter his reluctance. If we must meet your husband at all, 'tis far better that we meet him here upon this empty road with only the rabbits as witnesses."

"You are not only looking forward to his coming," she cried in sudden understanding, "you are hoping for it!"

"Aye, and he will die this time. The pain those scars cost you guarantees him that," he stated harshly. "When he is dead, we will be free to marry."

"Not true! No churchman will join us. We remain related by the marriage of our siblings. Ach!" She wrenched on the reins and brought her mount to a halt. "I am just as mad as you, for I love you even though your reasoning is twisted and confused."

"Come, love, set all this from your mind and put your heels to that stubborn creature, else he'll think he can stop for the day." Again, Temric seemed disconcertingly pleased with himself.

Philippa's stomach twisted with the depth of her fear. "Might we stop for just a moment?" she breathed, using every bit of her control to keep from retching onto her best gowns. "I need to seek the privacy of the woods right now."

"As you will, love." He laughed then. "Aye, battling your husband will purge the stink of trade from me and make a man of me again."

Philippa turned on her saddle to glare at him, the strength of her irritation steadying her stomach. "I am sick with fright and you laugh," she said coldly.

Temric's eyes gleamed golden. " 'Tis better to die with my sword in my hand than old and sick as my stepfather did."

"I am insane to love you!" she cried in frustration,

then dismounted and shoved her skirts back down around her legs. "I am going to run screaming into yon woods and let you ride on to Bristol, playing tag with my husband. Mayhap, some kindly passerby will take pity on me in my madness for you."

At her rising hysteria, he dismounted and came to hold her close. "Your fear makes him seem more dangerous than he is. Remember, he has nearly fallen once before beneath my blade. Trust me and trust that holy dream of yours. We are opposite halves of one whole and this life of ours has been given to us to keep."

"Oh, leave me be," she said irritably, pushing her way out of his embrace to stride for the nearest thicket. "This is a hundredfold worse than facing Oswald."

"Not for me," he retorted. "Here is something over which I have a particle of control."

"And I do not!" She stomped into the thickness of the brush and rusty fern. A sudden vivid memory of Roger, his handsome features twisted in vicious rage as he swung at her, made her heart quake in fear. From the roadbed came Temric's call. He wanted her to come back this moment. Well, she was not ready yet. It was fine for him to go dashing off, full of battle lust and courage. But what of her?

Yesterday, she had owned a rage great enough to let her face a churchman bent on destroying her. Her heart bolstered with that; she turned and made her way back between branch and thorn to the wood's edge, then caught her breath in terror.

Temric's great steed lifted, its massive forehooves tearing at air. From the direction of Stanrudde came two mounted men, racing toward Temric. Neither wore metal armor of any kind, but she could not mistake Roger, wild with rage, bared sword in hand. The second man slowed his steed to reload his crossbow, letting the nobleman precede him.

"Stay where you are," Temric shouted to her, ripping off his cloak and taking a position in the center of the road, dagger in one hand, sword in the other. Philippa could only stare as he faced on foot the man who had nearly finished her.

"Die, commoner," Lindhurst screamed, his blade already descending in a great sweeping arc.

If Temric stayed where he stood, Roger's blow would take him. Fear for him overwhelmed all else. She leapt from her concealment shouting "Roger!" to catch her husband's attention.

It was enough of a distraction to make Roger choke on his down stroke. Temric's blade opened the belly of Roger's mount as the creature rode past. The massive horse whirled in agony, rising onto its hindquarters, striking out in deadly blows against its own pain.

Overbalanced by the impetus of the attack, Temric fell. Hooves flashed above him, striking a glancing blow as the animal collapsed. Philippa screamed, but Temric rolled away from the dying steed as Roger threw himself from his saddle. Her husband came to his feet while Temric was yet on one knee, an arm wrapped around his chest as he struggled to rise.

The second man rode toward her wounded love. "Hold him here," Roger yelled to his soldier. "Keep him from intervening, but do not kill him. His life is mine to finish." Then her husband turned on her, his fine features hard, his eyes icy blue in rage. He juggled his sword in his hand as he walked, as if testing its readiness to take her life. When he spoke, his words were calm and clear. "Bitch, you do not know when to die, do you? I keep killing you and killing you, and now you've made a bigamist of me. This time I will watch you until I am certain your life is spent."

Philippa made no sound as Roger struck at her, only lurched back. She tripped over a clutch of branches. the fall saved her, for Roger missed his target.

She leapt to her feet and raced for the protection of the woods. Cursing loudly at his arrogant mistake, Roger stormed after her. From the roadbed, she heard the clash of swords as the soldier engaged Temric. He could not help her now.

As she ran, she glanced behind her to see how close her husband was, but Roger had not followed. Instead, he whirled and started toward Temric. Nay! it would be the two of them against her one man and him already injured.

Rage, blinding in its intensity, seared through her. Nay! She turned so swiftly, she fell, her feet sliding from beneath her. Her hands scraped against rough bark, burning at the injury she did to herself. Philippa threw herself to her feet, every bit of her focused on Roger's back.

"Nay," she breathed in fiery hate, "not you. Above all, you will not be the one to steal him from me!"

She roared from the woods faster than she'd dreamed possible. Without thought she reached for a hefty branch atop the nearest pile. She drew it back for a blow.

Roger readied himself to swing his sword into Temric's middle back.

Philippa's makeshift weapon whistled through the air as she wielded it. "Nay!" she screamed.

The power of her blow carried Roger forward,

sending his blade spinning from his hands. He dropped to his knees. She drew back to strike again. Roger lurched to one side, grasping for his sword as he moved. Her blow found only empty air and the momentum made her stumble away, helpless to stop.

Her torn hands burned in agony as she clutched at the ragged branch. Roger leapt to his feet, grimacing in pain. He lifted his blade. She'd have no further opportunity to use her meager force against him.

Her makeshift club dropped from her fingers and she stepped backward, glancing from side to side in search of an escape. When she looked back to Roger to gauge his nearness, her eyes saw him as if for the first time. Against all sense and reason, the picture made her laugh.

Roger's pretty features were twisted into an obscene expression. His leather vest was old and tattered, his gown patched, his stockings darned. There were worn spots in his shoes. His shoulders were narrow, his arms thin, his legs like those of a chicken. Aye, a chicken, that was what he most resembled. Philippa laughed.

"By God, you are pathetic," she cried to him. Her heart lifted in hope. Here was a weapon for which Roger had no shield. Aye, if it meant her death, so be it, but she would make him pay for killing her; his pride would be his forfeit.

"Pathetic little lordling," she taunted, "go home and tell your mother you want new clothing. Look at me, dressed better on a merchant's coin than you are. What sort of lord are you, anyway?"

Roger's mouth twisted. "Die, bitch," he managed

between clenched teeth. He stormed toward her, but she danced lightly away.

"You'll need to catch me to kill me, for I'll not easily let you do it. Ha! You are not worthy of taking my life, being only half a man. How my stomach turned at your touch."

She saw the harsh creases at either side of his mouth whiten against her insult. "What?" she teased. "Are you yet having trouble catching me? Try harder, lordling. What sort of knight are you? Your mother has turned you into naught but a revolting mockery of a man."

This time she only barely managed to dart from beneath his blow. Her heart rose into her throat as she heard his harsh breathing from so close behind her. As she scrambled past another pile of branches, she pushed them behind her. There was great satisfaction in hearing the dead wood strike his feet and legs.

She glanced at Temric in the hopes that he was finished with the other man. Nay, the soldier yet held him at bay. She would have to save herself. With that thought, she grabbed up her skirts and raced up the verge.

"Run, bitch, but I will take your lover's life," Roger threw after her. "As he lies bleeding his last, I will lay you next to him so he must watch me take you. When I am done, I will choke the life from you. Jesu, but it will please me when you squirm and fight beneath me."

Philippa turned on him, her eyes narrowed. "Take me! How? Your shaft is an empty instrument incapable of doing what a man's should do!"

"Barren bitch," he screamed. "My new wife is with child."

"If she is, it is not yours," she shouted back, fear now all but forgotten. "Aye, I have heard she was not so fresh when you took her to wife. Was there blood on the sheets, Roger? Or were you so drunk that you cannot remember what happened that night?"

He blanched as her barb hit the mark. "Ha! I thought as much. You see, Roger," she paused to gain his full attention, "I am with child."

His sword tip dipped toward the ground, then jerked up again. "Liar," he hissed.

"Nay, no lie," she retorted. "In these few months Temric has sown what you could not. He has set a child in my womb."

"Liar," he cried again, but with less conviction.

"Poor petted Roger, how your mother has ruined you. Tell me," she purred in malicious hatred, "for I have always wondered, does she stroke your chest? Do her ancient claws tangle in your hair, mocking love play? What is it she wrings from you behind those closed curtains?"

Roger made a retching sound against her words, his arms quivering as he bent against her revelation of what he hid from himself. His hands loosened on his sword's hilt, the blade tilting in his grip. Then he straightened.

When he turned his eyes back on her, his gaze was fully mad. She'd driven him too far. Philippa caught back a scream and turned to run, her skirts in her hands. His legs were longer, and unencumbered.

Her breath seared her lungs, burning, tearing with each gasp. Her legs screamed in agony as she raced along the roadbed. He was gaining on her.

Then she was falling. She hit the ground and blackness ringed around her. A whimper of defeat was her only sound, as she rolled desperately to one side in an attempt to rise. Roger, panting in hate and exertion, kicked her onto her back. He jammed his foot at her stomach, but she curled up and turned so that the boot glanced off her hip. Blood lust colored his face. He drew back his blade.

Suddenly he arched awkwardly, his blade dropping behind him. She saw the bolt that pierced him. Blood spattered down on her.

She shoved desperately with her heels to move herself out from beneath him as he reached for his sword. When he straightened, he was grinning like death. "Not good enough," he choked out.

Blackness closed in on her even as she clawed toward her new life with all her desire to keep it. She kicked weakly at him, felt her heartbeat pound through her. Nay, she would not die.

"I'll take you with me," he was gasping as unconsciousness washed over her.

Temric clutched at his chest as he released the crossbow's catch. Jesus God, he'd forgotten how much a broken rib hurt.

Lindhurst arched at the bolt's impact and lowered his blade.

Damn, but the man did not fall.

Gasping, Temric grabbed the soldier's mount and threw himself into the saddle. Lurching against the sickening pain, he resettled his sword into the cup of palm and viciously struck his boot heels into the creature's sides. His teeth gritted as each hoofbeat tore through him.

One hand holding the saddle to brace himself, he drew his blade back for a sweeping blow. He let the horse carry him forward as he swung, lifting Lindhurst with his weapon's edge. He heard bones snap but did not know if they were his or Lindhurst's. Pain washed over him in black waves. Then he was falling. Damn, but what if it were not enough?

Chapter Twenty-four

Philippa choked and coughed, the taste of dirt and fear yet clinging to her mouth. She fought her way onto her side, curled against the ache in her hip. Oh, God, but where was Roger?

The urge to rise and run was great, but she could only lie still and listen. The sound of her own continuing heartbeat thudded powerfully within her. A horse snorted and breathed heavily, not too far distant. Squirrels chattered in the nearby trees. The sharp scent of blood filled her with every breath, but there was no sound of battle, no man's harsh voice raised in attack, not even a shuffling footstep of one wounded and falling. She sat up.

Roger lay an arm's length away. His head was twisted to an impossible angle. She glanced down and gulped back what her stomach would have spewed. Jesus God, but he was nearly torn in two. Oh, Lord, if Roger was dead, where was Temric?

"Temric!" she cried feebly, coming to her feet. There was no reply. Her legs wobbled horribly as she hurried back to where he and the soldier had fought. Roger's man lay in a pool of his own blood. No sign of Temric. "Temric!" she called again, walking slowly up the desolate road, looking to either side for him.

When she had to walk past Roger, she averted her eyes, only to cry out at what met her gaze.

Temric lay, half-buried in a pile of leaves, still as death. Blood stained his sleeve and arm. She flew to his side, her hand trembling as she laid it against the vein in his neck. Why could she find no pulse? In her desperation, she pressed harder against his throat and he made a tiny sound. Philippa bent in relief. He lived.

Fingers shaking, she tore at the laces of his leather vest, all the while her lips moving in a murmured prayer of thanks. She yanked the garment open and he groaned more loudly, instinctively clutching at what gave him pain. With gentle fingers, she carefully felt through his tunic and shirt along his side.

Something moved that should not; he'd broken a rib. She leaned close to listen to his breathing. Although labored and shallow, there was no bubbling rasp to suggest he'd torn a lung. Again, she gave thanks, for such a thing would have meant his death. A simple break could heal given time.

Only when she was assured of Temric's safety did she acknowledge what had happened. They lived while Roger had perished. Philippa leaned back on her knees to stare skyward in disbelief, her eyes threatening to overflow against the joy of existing past this encounter.

Temric groaned again, then instantly caught it back. "By Christ's holy cock," he managed between gasps as he came into full awareness of his pain. His eyes opened and he panted out, "You live. Prayed not too late." His breathing steadied as he sought and found the depth he could tolerate. "Why'd you call out? You made him jerk the beast into me."

"Well I beg your pardon, but I thought I was saving

your life," she retorted, too pleased that he was conscious and speaking to put any sting in her words.

"Woman, meddle not where you know not," he grunted, but his words also lacked any chiding edge. "Thank God you live," he sighed. "Are you injured?"

"Nay." She leaned forward and set her lips to his. His response was sweet, but short, as he tore his mouth from hers to breathe again. Her hands moved over him, prodding and probing as she spoke. " 'Twas a near thing and I shall have a pretty bruise on my hip from his foot. Beyond that, I am unharmed. Damn me, Temric, I can find no source for this blood!"

"Not mine," he managed as he struggled and worked to sit up. "We leave. Now." He gave a choked cry as he thrust himself to his feet. Philippa put her arms around him to steady him, but Temric held her off with a hand. "Nay, do not touch me, I cannot bear it."

He reached for the reins of the horse standing beside him, then leaned against the shivering animal. "Run, fetch me my cloak so I might cover these bloodstains, then mount as well. We must be away from here as swiftly as possible."

"What of your own steed?" she cried.

"Leave him. I'll send someone from Stanrudde to fetch him later. To bring him back wounded will tie us to what has happened here. We dare no explanations, for what we have done damns us." He set his foot in the stirrup and groaned at what it cost him. "Lord, but if I cannot lift myself, we will have to walk."

Philippa smiled at him, untouched by the urgency that drove him. Roger was dead, the day was beautiful, the sun warm, and Temric would heal. She cared for no more than that.

Hoofbeats echoed from the direction of Stanrudde. Four members of the town's guard raced toward them in their steel-sewn leather vests, metal caps upon their heads.

"Too late," Temric cried in dismay.

"Master Richard," one man called out as he sharply reined in his mount, "you are wounded!"

"Aye, his rib is broken," Philippa swiftly replied, searching for the right tone of distress to color her words. "Help us, these men came attacking us, bent on murder!" Temric glanced at her in surprise, but the look she sent him in return kept him silent.

"So we know. They went first to your house to do other violence," the man replied, dismounting and signaling for the others to do so as well, "only to escape before we arrived in answer to the call. When we learned they'd asked at all Stanrudde's gates to find the one by which you had departed, we came racing after in the hopes of catching them."

"And my mother?" Temric asked harshly.

" 'Twas no one at home save Master Jehan when they came, but Master Gerard happened by during the attack and called for us," the guardsman said. "By all that is holy, Master Richard," he said as he peered down at what remained of Roger, "you've done our job for us, I think me. Here's two brigands who'll trouble our folk no longer."

"Aye," Philippa replied, "we believe they saw only a merchant and his wife out for a day's pleasure and, therefore, easy pickings. They could not know my husband had spent long years soldiering before he came to Stanrudde and took up a gentler life." She paused to paste a frown of confusion on her face. "Now, here you come saying that they were seeking us, not just any victim. That befuddles me. Why should they do so, when we know them not at all?" When the time came to do her penance, she would add this little lie to her already lengthy list of sins.

"Master Jehan says that this summer your house bought several notes of promise from another merchant who was dearly strapped for coins. He recently sent messages to all the debtors, warning of this change of ownership and saying that Master Richard, here, would soon come collecting what was due you. 'Tis Master Gerard's belief that this one"—he toed Roger's unmoving foot—"decided to delay repayment, if not completely free himself from debt, by destroying the new note holders. Since you had never met him, you would have been off your guard when he came knocking at your door planning your demise."

"Ah, that would explain it," Philippa said, then gave a sharp cry. "You say Master Jehan was alone when these men came? Have they hurt him?" Suddenly, what Jehan had done was no longer horrible. By bringing Roger here to be destroyed, he'd given them the key which would free them. She could not bear that Jehan might have paid with his life so she and Temric could live theirs together.

"Aye, mistress, he has taken a cruel battering." The man glanced at Temric when he made an odd choked sound. "Not to worry, Master Richard, he will survive it. You men, stay here and gather up the dead. I'll escort these good folk back to Stanrudde. Do you think that Mistress Alwyna would mind sending word to her debtors once again? If Masters Jehan and Gerard are correct, mayhap one family will come and collect these men for burial."

"I am sure she will not mind at all," Temric managed between gasps. "Can your men bring with them my steed? The beast is injured, but he's calmer than most of his breed and should be approachable."

"Aye, surely," the guardsman said with a nod, then shot Temric a commiserating glance as he came alongside him to help him mount. "I think 'twill be a painful ride for you."

"True," Philippa said softly, coming to Temric's other side, "but at least we still live to feel our pain. It was a near thing for us and I thank you for rushing to our aid. Come, husband, let him help you into the saddle, so we may share the joy of our survival with those who must now wait in fear over what has become of us."

Where yesterday Stanrudde's walls had been suffocating, this day they were warm and enclosing. Philippa rode gratefully into Alwyna's courtyard behind Temric. Tom appeared from the warehouse, none the worse for wear from his encounter with Jehan this morn.

"Help me down," Temric said. When his feet were on the ground, both she and Tom reached out as if to brace him. He stiffened. "Nay, do not touch me, only catch me if I fall." By little steps, he made his way into the house, then slowly rose up the stairway. "I hate these stairs," he muttered in the middle of the first set.

Philippa laughed aloud, unable to feel anything but grateful shock and happy disbelief for what this day had brought her. Temric would soon heal and they would own their lives. How incredible that she'd awakened this morn thinking her time was at its end. Instead, she had once again eluded death and gained freedom from her past.

"Philippa?" came Alwyna's high-pitched question.

"We are yet whole and gladly returned," she called back.

"God be praised," Temric's mother shouted, flying down the stairs to greet them. "I cannot believe this," she cried in simple joy, her arms around Philippa. "You live!"

"Barely," Temric managed, his face now grim with his effort. "I would lie down, Mama. Get out of my path."

"Nay, do not try to help him," Philippa said swiftly, turning a worried Alwyna around and urging her back up to the bedchamber. "He has broken a rib and needs a few weeks to heal, then he will be himself again."

"And what of the one who sought you?" Alwyna's eyes opened wide in hope, mingled with fear.

"He is no more," Philippa said in a low voice. "What is this tale of notes and debts that the guard spun to us?"

"In truth, 'twas Jehan's idea. He was in a frenzy of worry over what he had done and how to correct it. He and Gerard concocted the tale before your husband had even arrived. Mind you, if you should speak to Gerard of this, he yet thinks you a serf, escaping your noble owner as he did as a lad. Come, Jehan wishes to speak with you."

Alwyna led her to Jehan's bedside. Philippa caught her breath as she looked at him. Both eyes were blackened and blood crusted along his chin from where his lip had been split. His head was wrapped in white material, now stained red with seepage from the torn flesh on his scalp. One arm was splinted.

"You live," Jehan breathed, staring up at her.

"Better than that," she said with a smile, "I am free, all because of you."

"You forgive me?" The words whistled through his swollen lips in an agony of disbelief.

"What is there to forgive? You have helped to end my torment. The one who wished me dead has been killed in my stead. Now can Temric and I take up the lives we wish to own."

" 'Tis fair then, for you have given me what I would never have achieved without your aid. Gerard says this beating is payment enough for my foolishness and trusts I will not repeat my error. The wedding yet goes forth." He reached out with his whole hand to grasp hers. "Thank you for your kindness and your care, sister."

Philippa wrinkled her nose at him as she squeezed his hand, then released it. "Now, do not go maudlin on me. I am too accustomed to your barbs and insults to tolerate such niceness from you. Neither should you think that you'll spend weeks in lazy recovery. I'll see to it that you are soon up and at your duties once again for we all know idleness makes you mean." Jehan gave a hiccough of a laugh and closed his eyes with a sigh at her words.

Behind her, Temric entered the bedchamber, leaning against the wall with a quiet groan. When Alwyna would have led him to their bed, he resisted. "I would see him, first." White-faced from exertion, he made his way to Jehan's bedside. After staring down at his half brother for a long moment, he gave a quiet huff of amusement. "No need for that beating from me, I think."

To Philippa's shock, Jehan smiled in return. "Nay, I suppose not. Is what I've done enough to keep your wife safe?"

"Aye, brother, it is. My thanks," he sighed. "Now tell me why he did not kill you."

Jehan made a motion that passed for a shrug. "He said he did not want to foul any blade with the blood of a cripple. Instead, he bid his man beat me to death. It is the first time I've been glad to submit to fists," the young man added with a quiet breath, "since I knew Gerard would be along within moments."

Temric nodded in consideration. "It seems we shall share the room in recovering."

"Jesus God, I will not survive it," Jehan said harshly, yet his mouth remained twisted in a grin.

Temric caught back his laugh with a moan, then let Philippa take him to their bed. While Alwyna went to find linen to use in wrapping his ribs, she eased his hauberk from him, then split the seam of his tunic with a knife rather than force him to raise his arm. His shirt went next, revealing a great purpling mark on his side.

"I am tired unto death. Bind it tightly, then let me sleep," he said.

"I knew that," she retorted. Within moments she and Alwyna had bandaged his ribs, binding his arm into immobility to prevent further damage.

When he leaned back into the bolsters, it was with a tiny breath of relief. He reached out for her with his free hand, running his fingers across the fine planes of her face, down the curve of her throat to rest on the swell of her breasts. "I know you are but a recent widow, but will you have me to husband?" he said quietly.

"I think not," she replied with a soft smile. "You are very stubborn and self-contained, constantly deciding what is good for me without listening to what I have to say."

He closed his eyes with a soft laugh. "I will take that as an agreement to my proposal."

"So you would," she said with a touch of scorn, then sighed against the impossibility of it. "Temric, no churchman will marry us. We are related."

He replied softly without opening his eyes, "We have not come this far to be stopped by something a cleric scribbles on parchment over your family."

Philippa's heart ached to be his true wife, but it simply could not be. She leaned forward to lay her mouth against his. His lips moved softly on hers, communicating the depth of his relief and love in a way his words could not. Her own heart's emotion swept over her, filling her with such joy she could not forestall her tears. She leaned back to scrub them away. "If there were any way to wed you, I would gladly do so," she sighed.

"Well, we haven't long to find the way. I fear Lindhurst's dam may come searching and I'd not risk you being here for her to find." He paused to catch his breath, then opened one eye to look up at his mother. "Mama?"

Alwyna leaned forward. "Yes, my son?"

"Send to Upwood, to Rannulf. Tell him I am ready to return and have decided already on a wife to bring with me. As my overlord, he should come immediately to help me arrange this marriage."

"Nay! Temric, I am dowerless!" Philippa protested,

her heart numbing in shock. "Your brother cannot help us. Just as Oswald sees how I sin, Lord Graistan must see my impoverished state. Even if he could forgive us for the trick we've played on him, he'd be a fool to wed one of his vassals to a beggar."

Temric raised a brow as his eyes shut. "You are not dowerless. I took a handful of stones from your mother for you. Say no more. Rannulf must come for he can do what I cannot."

"Nay," she whispered. Once again, what she most wanted had been almost in her grasp, only to be snatched from her. "Why must we wed?" she cried out. "I am content to live with you, keeping only the words we've already spoken to bind us. You can adopt our children as your own if you do not wish them to be bastards." Philippa stared in disbelief at the stubborn expression that crept across his features. He was not hearing her. Once again, he had decided and he would go forward without consideration of what she wanted. "Listen to me," she pleaded bitterly.

"We wed, for I will bring no bastard into this world." He opened his eyes briefly, then reached out to wipe her cheek. "Your face is dirty, and your tears are making mud of it. Best go wash it. Now leave me to sleep."

Philippa caught her breath in a near sob, her heart aching. She could see he would not be moved, but what he wanted would be the end of them. Marriages were made between properties, not people. Lord Graistan would surely refuse Temric's request to wed her. After that, he would find Temric an heiress with an estate. Depression drained what remained of her energy. She was so tired of fighting.

Alwyna wrapped an arm around her and led her

from the room. "Now that he is tended to, I would see to your injuries."

"Me?' Philippa said her voice weary. "There is nothing wrong with me save a broken heart. Alwyna, what he wants, no one will grant him. Do not send that message to Lord Graistan," she pleaded as they reached the landing.

"If you are not injured, then whose blood is this?" Alwyna asked with a finger aimed at the breast of Philippa's pretty green gown.

"Blood?" she cried out, then remembered Roger standing over her, bow-shot and bleeding. She held her gown away from her and stared down in horror at the crusting red stains that crossed it. "Oh, Alwyna, it is my favorite and now it's ruined!" Her eyes filled again. Suddenly it was all too much to be endured. Her mouth trembled and fresh tears streaked down her face.

Alwyna hugged her close. "Come, I think I'll have Marta set our tub in the kitchen. You need a long, quiet soak and a big cup of wine to steady your nerves." She led the weeping Philippa down the stairs to the kitchen.

By the hour's end, Philippa could cry no more. If depression yet clung to her, at least she was clean. Alwyna sat, listening patiently as she stuttered out the whole tale, from their encounter with Oswald to the town guardsmen's arrival. Philippa handed Els the toweling when she was dried and the little maid helped her to don her bedrobe.

"All this exertion worries me," Alwyna said. "How is it with the child?"

Philippa drew a deep breath and probed within her for any sign that something was amiss. "I feel nothing different." At that reminder of her predicament, tears again sprang into her now burning eyes. "Alwyna, for the sake of your grandchild," she pleaded sadly, "do not send the message to Lord Graistan. I would that this babe knows its father, unlike I who have not even a name to put to my sire."

"What makes you think your child will not?" Alwyna asked softly.

"You heard what Temric wants. It will not happen. Lord Graistan will come and discover that I live when I should be dead. He will separate us."

Alwyna laughed. "You fear where you have no need to fear. I've known Rannulf from the day of his birth, and raised my Richard beside him. They are closer than most siblings. I'd wager Rannulf already knows you are here, alive and well."

"I cannot believe it," Philippa despaired.

Alwyna's smile was lilting. "If I am right and that child is a girl, you name her for me."

"Aye, and if you are wrong, I pay a most terrible price. Why must it be that every man around me has more power over my own fate than I?" Philippa said in frustration.

"Where is that firebrand who screamed at the poor churchman yesterday?" Alwyna asked with a smile.

"I'm tired," Philippa snapped. "Tired of being a pawn to be used and moved as everyone else wishes."

"Go to bed, then, daughter of my heart. Rest in the knowledge that Rannulf will not deny Richard the woman he desires for any reason. I raised him better than that." She rose and stretched. "Well, now, I best be getting that message off for the sooner this is sent, the sooner you'll be wed."

Chapter Twenty-five

The rest of that day and the night after passed in an agony of worry for Philippa. Temric awoke twice, but refused to discuss the matter with her at all and she alternated between wishing she could rage or weep forever. When the next morning dawned, dark and gloomy, she rose to be swept into the press of her daily chores. Beneath her usual routine, her concerns lost their aching edge.

Once the household had broken its fast, she left to do the shopping, her list long and her purse heavy. Alwyna wished to prepare a rich meal. It seemed that Upwood lay near to Stanrudde and there was a chance Lord Graistan might arrive early enough to dine with them.

The cool mist settled against Philippa's shoulders as she strode down the lane, while ragged bits of cloud swirled around her ankles. In the fog all colors dimmed to somber shades of gray and the world became a peaceful place trapped in a thick silence. Yet, in its embrace she could be only Pippa, housewife of Stanrudde with no greater decision hanging on her than which goose was plumpest or whether to serve a ripe or new cheese. For that short time she forgot that her life might yet be torn asunder by day's end.

When she was climbing the stairs into the hall, Alwyna's laugh echoed down the well to her. Temric's mother sounded extremely pleased, her voice rising and falling animatedly as she spoke. Philippa wondered if Gerard had returned for more wedding plans. She entered the room, meaning to slip through it to the kitchen without disturbing anyone, only to come to an abrupt halt.

Lord Graistan stood near the hearth, cup in hand. He was dressed in mail, his sodden cloak yet swirling around mud-stained boots. Alwyna clung to his arm chatting brightly up at the tall man about Jehan's coming marriage. Her sister's husband caught sight of Philippa from the corner of his eye. She swallowed back her tears, her mouth trembling as she awaited his disapproval.

He turned toward her with a smile. "Well now, fancy meeting a ghost in so common a place as this. 'Tis good to see you looking so well, Lady Philippa, when so recently we feared for your life." He was not the slightest bit surprised to see her.

Her baskets dropped to the floor as she stared at him. "You knew," she said quietly.

"Did I not tell you?" Alwyna asked with a gay laugh.

"I knew nothing at all," Lord Rannulf protested, running a hand through his dark hair, his harsh face softening as he fought a grin. "Temric was very careful with what he told me, fearing I might be hurt if his harebrained plot were uncovered."

"Harebrained!" Temric retorted from a chair, then struggled to his feet to smile at her. A bedrobe was draped over his shoulders, revealing he wore only chausses and shoes. "Hardly so, for see how I now hold all I sought to achieve? Come, love, greet my brother."

"I come bearing greetings from your sister as well," Lord Rannulf said.

"Rowena knows? And approves?" Philippa found this too farfetched to be believed. Her sister's shocked reaction in the tower chamber, when she'd witnessed their affection, still stung.

"Let us say she struggles mightily with what goes forth here," Lord Rannulf amended quietly, "but believes 'tis better to look forward to seeing you again than to grieve for you. Mostly, she is troubled by your tomb, knowing full well that the one within it has no right to lie there."

"If God has not spit her out of her tomb by now," Alwyna began pragmatically.

"Odd," Lord Rannulf interrupted with a quick laugh, "that was what I said to her. You have infected me with your cynicism, Alwyna."

"Nay, I cannot believe this," Philippa cried, unable to comprehend what was happening around her. "Lord Rannulf, you cannot tell me you will allow Temric to marry me. Not only are we related, but I am now a penniless widow without connection." Her voice caught with despair. "What gain is there for you in our wedding? I do not even have a dowry to recommend me. The three hides of land I brought to Lindhurst reverted to Rowena upon my 'death.' "

"Temric says he took a handful of stones from your mother as dowry," Lord Rannulf said blandly.

"You accept that!" Her voice rose in disbelief.

Her sister's powerful husband only laughed. "Philippa, you are the answer to my brother's prayers, and, therefore, to my own. I understand you are already with child, so I think we must find a way to marry the two of you as quickly as possible. There are bastards enough in this family, as it is. Or would you rather your child had no name?"

"Nay, of course not, but—" Her voice faded away in silence as she stared at him in surprise, then looked to Temric.

He only smiled at her. "Did you think I was not certain of this when I called him to come?" Temric said softly. "Believe me, love, he is standing there chortling in glee because he thinks he has trapped me where he has always wanted me."

"Aye," Rannulf replied swiftly, "if he is to have you, he must also take from me his lands while giving me his oath in return. You cannot know how long I have waited for this." He glanced at his brother. "But now that I've experienced your absence, Normandy is too far. I will keep you closer than that."

"I have missed you, as well, brother." Temric laughed. "Know that I have learned the extent of my foolishness and be grateful to this place." He lifted a hand to indicate his mother's house. "It, more than anything else, has driven me back to you."

"My son has not the temperament for trade," Alwyna scoffed. "I told him so the day he arrived, but he was too stubborn to admit such a thing might be possible."

"Mama, you were right. I am and always have been naught but a stiff-necked knight," Temric said, laughing. "I run from Stanrudde with relief."

Philippa shook her head, stunned but unconvinced. "Lord Rannulf, I accept that you wish to see us wed, but even you have not the power to bend the Church to your will. We remain related," she warned.

Lord Rannulf smiled at her. "For that I have Oswald, but this discussion can wait. I've been riding since first light, such as it was this morn. I would disarm," he said, turning to Alwyna. "There is clothing in my saddlepack. Also, I would appreciate a bite to eat, old woman."

"Old!" Alwyna squealed in insult. "Watch your tongue, brat. I box ears as well as I ever have," she warned.

He threw up a hand in mock fear. "A thousand pardons," he retorted, "but if I do not quake before your threat it is because you cannot reach my ears without a stool."

"Is your hope restored?" Temric asked, coming to stand beside Philippa.

"Nay," she said, even as she let him take her into his embrace. She leaned her head against his bare shoulder, his skin soft against her cheek. "I see only that your brother is as mad as you. Have you told him that Oswald hates us just now?"

Temric shook his head. "When Oswald sees that Rannulf supports me, what has been done will not matter so much to him. Go now into the kitchen and work your magic. Oswald comes to dine with us and like his master, the bishop, he loves his food. A grand meal replete with fine wines cannot hurt our cause."

"I think I do not understand any of this at all," Philippa sighed. Still, she retrieved her baskets and went to see to the meal's preparation. If she sent Els back out with the week's allowance to buy fine wines, fruits, and wafers, 'twas because the hope within her refused to listen to her common sense. She was as mad as they.

*   *   *

"Rannulf!" Oswald cried in protest, having claimed the best chair after the meal's end. "What you want is not possible. Aye, so she is now widowed, it does not change the fact that she is sister to your wife." He leaned forward, his elbows braced on his brightly robed knees, a cup of Stanrudde's finest wine between his beringed hands. His gaze flickered toward Philippa, who sat on a stool beside Temric's chair. She shrugged, hoping he read in her motion that she, too, had said as much.

"Oswald," Lord Rannulf said smoothly, standing at the hearth dressed in a gown of dark velvet, golden embroidery trimming its neckline, "I have lands aching for their lord and Temric will not take them without Philippa as his wife. Come, now, the poor lass is with child. There must be a way."

"They are related!" the churchman retorted.

Temric reached out and took her hand in his, intertwining their fingers, the empty sleeves of his bedrobe falling back as he moved forward. "Oswald," he said, "Philippa of Lindhurst is dead. We know this is true because her name is inscribed on a tomb in Graistan's abbey. Before you now sits an orphan, born in Stanrudde, who knows nothing of her heritage. I would marry this poor orphan."

"I think you ask too much of him," Philippa said quietly, incapable of believing the angry churchman would aid them. "He has done enough in saying he will keep our secret for us."

"Look, a woman understands where you two do not!" Oswald cried in relief. "You cannot ask me to do the impossible."

"You may have to content yourself with the private

vows we spoke between us," Philippa said to Temric. "I am."

"While I am not," Temric said stubbornly. "I will wed you."

Rannulf laughed. "Oswald, I think you have not foreseen what can come of this wedding. For their life's span, they'll be buying masses and making donations to appease God's wrath. Lord, but an abbey could be founded on what their sin will cost them." His tone said he was completely unwilling to accept his cousin's declaration of refusal. "I need Temric to be installed on his properties. Now, tell me how we can wed them so I might have him back."

"I cannot," Oswald said firmly.

Alwyna lifted haughty brows. "I know I promised to say nothing," she said, warning all that she would not be stopped, "but with coins and the right seal, anything is possible. Tomorrow, twenty good men, honest and true, will swear she is Pippa of Stanrudde, an orphan raised in such and such a house. Bring your scribe, for her entire genealogy, tracing her ancestry back to King Alfred, will be laid before you. You will find in it not one instance of relationship to my son."

"Why not?" Rannulf asked with a shrug. "If a man can forge a family tree to prove himself related to a wife he no longer wants, why not concoct for her an identity that makes legitimate children from bastards?"

"Such a thing will make a lie of me," Philippa whispered to Temric. "Will it not stain our joining?"

Temric touched his lips to her brow. "Here is one lie that serves a good purpose, love. I refuse to be kept from you by what Oswald would set between us. Let us supply them the meat to satisfy their requirements, then dance to the tune of their empty rituals. I place my trust in that holy dream of yours."

"Aye, then so must I," Philippa sighed. "But say it will be the final falsehood between us."

"So it will be and, through this, do we give our children a complete family and the greater choice in mates," Temric reminded her.

Oswald turned his cup in his hands for a long moment, his hesitancy to reply suggesting that he considered what Alwyna offered. "Nay, it will not work," he finally said. "The identity will do fine for those who have no knowledge of her, but she can yet be named by others who have seen her."

"Love," Temric said quietly, "the assurance Oswald seeks you have already offered me. Will you offer it to me again?"

Philippa came straighter on her stool as she understood what he said. Then she grabbed for her future with both hands. "Oswald, you are right, but to be recognized I must be seen," she said in a determined voice. "I am content to be Temric's exceedingly shy wife who cannot bear strangers and prefers to remain at home when he is called to his lord's court. In time's passage, the first Philippa will be forgotten for she was hardly known at all save between Lindhurst and Benfield."

Rannulf shook his head in denial. " 'Tis good of you to say so, my lady, but such a role would be a great burden."

"Mayhap for one accustomed to the freedom given to a man," she replied. "I have not had your luxury. For all my life, I have been held close. In the first twelve years it was to suit my mother's selfish dreams for me, the second twelve sated my husband's twisted whims. Having known no different life, I am comfortable in isolation. Besides, those who know and accept what we do will come to see me."

"What of you, brother?" Lord Graistan asked of Temric. "Can you bear that your wife will not be included in our family?"

Temric laughed. "Rannulf, your love for me ofttimes blinds you. I've excluded myself from the majority of the family we share as they disapprove of your affection for me."

"Not true," Oswald said. "Well, perhaps not completely true. I have never minded you."

"Until recently,'" Temric reminded gently.

Oswald waved his words away with an unconcerned hand. "Things have changed since yesterday," he said blithely.

Temric sent Philippa a laughing glance. She smiled in return. He knew his family well indeed. "So, my love, I will ask you again. Will you wed me and let me hold you close behind my own boundaries?"

"Happily, for all my life," she replied. Then, despite the fact that everyone watched, she needed to feel her mouth against his. Philippa leaned forward and pressed a kiss to his lips, then sighed as he answered her caress with his own, his arm coming around her to draw her nearer still.

Oswald groaned. "I am sick of you two. I swear the only reason I am doing this is so that I need never see you kiss again! Bring your witnesses, Mistress Alwyna. Their observations and memories will be duly noted and Pippa of Stanrudde created."

Philippa laughed, the joy within her too great to be borne and tore away from Temric's hold to settle back onto her stool. "Alwyna, on this new heritage of mine?" She smiled at the older woman.

Alwyna grinned broadly. "Aye, daughter of my heart?"

"Best give me a goodly dollop of Norman blood, or no one will wish to wed their child to ours. I do not mind being a bastard once again." Philippa met Temric's startled look with a wry laugh. " 'Tis true, love, I have never minded it."

Alwyna's laugh rang against the rafters, merry and pleased at what she'd said.

Epilogue

"Lord Meynell!"

Temric turned atop his steed, his leather hauberk groaning beneath his rain-soaked cloak. From behind him came a palfrey and rider picking their way through the thick woods. It was one of the brothers who worked in Meynell's stables, but he couldn't remember the lad's name.

"My lord," the man cried out, "your lady delivers. The midwife says you must come."

"Damn," he snapped, "the woman swore the babe would wait another two weeks." He wrenched his steed around, and without a thought to the foresters he left behind him, he set spurs into the big gelding's side.

Seven months had done much to restore the poor creature, but it could not pick its way fast enough through the thick growth of birch, alder, yew, and fir. Against all his efforts to block it, Temric remembered how Rannulf had lost his first two wives to childbirth. Damn him, why had he agreed to become warden of the bishop's chase? Now he was ten miles away from Meynell.

When he finally broke free of the woodlands, Temric sent his steed tearing across the green, rain-swept plain that lifted gradually into a chalky hill. Atop it, the thick walls of his new home seemed to melt into the low-hanging clouds. The big horse pounded along the narrow pathways through rich field and fertile lea. As they traversed the village to enter his walls, chickens and geese scattered hastily out of their way.

The soughing wind tore around the squat keep tower, whisking away the smoke from the roof of the wooden hall. A single stable boy appeared, his mantle clutched shut against this day's bitter weather. Temric threw himself out of the saddle, his need to run tempered by the fear of what news awaited him.

He strode up the short stairway and through the big door. There, he stopped in surprise for the hall was empty save for the dogs. At the room's end lay the wooden partition he'd raised to create a private sleeping area. His footsteps echoed hollowly in this unusual silence, as he strode swiftly to the new door and stepped into his bedchamber.

Here, too, quiet reigned, the only sound that of the fire crackling and hissing on the hearth. Its wavering light made dark shadows in the rich folds of material curtaining his bed. He stared at the closed draperies. There were no maids in the room, no sign of the midwife, and, worse, no sound at all from the bed.

Unable to bear not knowing, he crossed the room and pushed back a curtain. Philippa, her eyes closed, lay in utter stillness amid the twisted bedclothes. Hair, once neatly confined to a sober plait, now lay in wild disarray around her exhausted face.

Temric's heart stopped. The babe had killed her. He sat on the mattress and ripped off a glove to lay a hand on her neck. She started at his cold touch, then stirred slightly. His sigh was deep with gratitude as he stood to remove his sodden cloak, then sat once again.

Philippa's eyes slowly opened. "Temric," she breathed almost sadly, " 'tis but a girl child I've given you."

He raised her up beside him, bracing her against his chest. She rested her head against his shoulder, her face turned into the curve of his neck. Beneath his enclosing arm, he felt the strong, steady beat of her heart.

"You live," he said gently, "I care for nothing more than that." His arm around her tightened as he once again realized how precious she was to him. "So, where is this child of ours? I would look upon the creature who's so rudely stolen my wife from me this past month," he teased her.

"I was delivered so swiftly and we knew not when you would return. The midwife said she should be baptized," Philippa murmured, her words warm against his chilled skin. "Oh, Temric, why couldn't I have held back until the next week when my sister comes? Little Alwyna should have had noble godparents as befits Meynell's heir."

He felt her hot tears and lifted her face to touch his mouth to hers. Her lips trembled at first. Then, what began as a gentle caress, steadily deepened into a fiery kiss, which had nothing to do with comfort. He pulled her closer, no longer hampered by the babe's bulk. Finally, he tore his mouth free. "By God, but it is good to be able to put my arms around you once again," he whispered in her ear.

Suddenly the door burst open to admit a troop of women, his wife's maids, the midwife, and female villagers as well. It was the miller's wife who bore her lord's heir. The heavyset woman swept across the short room toward the cradle standing beside the bed, but Temric indicated she should bring the squalling babe to him. A moment later, and he held his swaddled daughter in his arms. Her christening cap had been pushed so low upon her tiny forehead, he could not see her face.

Philippa leaned across him to adjust the head covering. "Look," she said, a new strength in her voice as she teased wispy strands of hair out from beneath the cap. At her mother's touch, their child's cries quieted to a soft whimper. "She has dark hair like yours, but I think that's all of you I see in her."

"Thank God," Temric retorted with a quick laugh.

"Aye, she's a beauty, my lord," Agnes the midwife proudly offered. "She had no caul upon her and no disfigurements at all to mar her."

Temric stared down at this wee bit of humanity that he'd made and saw nothing beautiful at all. Yet, she was so small and helpless, so needful of his protection, it pained his heart to think on it. So had his father felt about him and thus did a father love his child, without heeding reason or logic.

Philippa stooped to press a kiss against their babe's soft cheek. Temric watched his daughter turn her face toward Philippa. Temric breathed deeply at the sweetness of it.

"My lord, give the child to me," the midwife commanded.

"Nay, I will keep her a little longer," he replied, not wanting anyone else to touch his daughter. Lord, but it would be only a mere dozen or so years before he would have to give her up to another man. Too soon! He lay a fingertip against his daughter's face and smiled when she also turned toward his touch. "Leave us for a time."

Graciously ignoring the muttered comments of the women, Temric waited until they were gone before he looked at his wife. Philippa was watching him, the expression on her face so soft and filled with love that it made him sigh.

"You are not disappointed that she is but a lass?" she asked a moment later.

"Disappointed?" he replied, strictly containing his smile while cocking a brow. "Aye, horribly. How you have failed me, wife. Because of you I am forced to endure the travails of vassalage to my brother, title, lands, home, and, now, family."

Philippa laughed. "Oh, you. You are teasing me again."

"So I am," he retorted, no longer able to restrain his grin, then he sobered. "And what of you, love? Are you content with this life of ours?"

"Aye," she said, smiling. "But I am sorely aggrieved at you, sweetling," she said, lifting their daughter from his arms. "Too long have you kept me from my husband's bed."

"Aye," he said to the babe, " 'tis a dangerous thing to stand between your mother and her lust."

"Temric! Do not say such things before this sweet innocent," Philippa protested, then sighed in pleasure as she relaxed back into his embrace. "Besides, 'tis not lust," she said softly, "only my heart's ache to feel you once again showing me how much you love me."

"Now, who is teasing?" he replied, touching his lips to Philippa's cheek as he watched his daughter clasp her tiny mouth to her mother's breast. "Wee one, keep your eyes shut. I have much to show your mother just now."